Praise f

"Sparkles with laugh-out-loud humor, a rare sensitivity to postwar trauma, touching emotion, thrilling historical detail, and exquisitely drawn characters . . . Run, don't walk, to your local bookstore, and don't miss out on this stunning new talent!" —*Affaire de Coeur*

"Wonderfully written! This is an impressive debut from a bright new author. Readers will devour it."
—Cathy Maxwell

"What a wonderful read. *A Rogue's Pleasure* [has] all the makings of a great novel: vivid historical detail, vibrant characters, and a fast-paced adventure—everything I look for in a historical romance." —Victoria Lynne

"Hope Tarr's first novel is an overall winner. Fast-paced, intriguing, and loaded with sexual tension, *A Rogue's Pleasure* is a real page-turner. With one book, this author has already gone onto my 'must buy' list." —*The Romance Reader*

"Ms. Tarr's debut is a smashing success. Here is a new and fresh voice for the historical romance genre. . . . A must-read for those who like sexy heroes, strong-willed heroines, and fast-moving plots. This one goes on my keeper shelf and Ms. Tarr becomes an automatic buy for me."
—*Sime-Gen Romance Reviews*

"An impressive debut . . . I enjoyed *A Rogue's Pleasure* very much and plan on reading more of Hope Tarr. She can create very good characters and knows how to pace a story."
—*All About Romance*

Also by Hope Tarr

A ROGUE’S PLEASURE

Hope Tarr

JOVE BOOKS, NEW YORK

MY LORD JACK

A Jove Book / published by arrangement with the author

PRINTING HISTORY
Jove edition / May 2002

For information address: The Berkley Publishing Group, a division of Penguin Putnam Inc.,
375 Hudson Street, New York, New York 10014.

Visit our website at
www.penguinputnam.com

ISBN: 0-515-13339-6

A JOVE BOOK®
Jove Books are published by The Berkley Publishing Group, a division of Penguin Putnam Inc.,
375 Hudson Street, New York, New York 10014.
JOVE and the "J" design are trademarks belonging to Penguin Putnam Inc.

PRINTED IN THE UNITED STATES OF AMERICA

10 9 8 7 6 5 4 3 2 1

To Kathy Huntsman, D.V.M., veterinarian extraordinaire and a true guardian of "all creatures great and small."

Acknowledgments

To my husband, Earl Pence, who serves on the frontlines as manuscript reader and reviewer and behind the lines as my life partner and touchstone.

To my editor, Cindy Hwang, and my agent, Jenny Bent—I feel doubly blessed to have you both as partners and guideposts to steer me through this madcap and wonderful venture called publishing.

To my friend, critique partner, and conference roomie, Carole Bellacera, for being such a great source of personal and professional support. Carole, the chicken scene—consider it dedicated to you!

To the following friends who so generously shared their expertise, resources, and, in many cases, *time* as fact-finders: Julie Kendrick, Palmer Christian Bassich, Robyn Allen, Karen Irvine Lewis, and Dominique Otterson. Special thanks to Julie, my aficionado of Scottish history, who served as my research assistant in searching the Net. Any errors that may have found their way into the final manuscript are, of course, entirely my own.

To June Remy Allen, Gloria Chestnut, and the other "wenches" of the Rising Sun Tavern in Fredericksburg, Virginia, for opening up to me not only the museum but also their truly amazing storehouse of collective knowledge on eighteenth-century manners and tavern life.

And last but never least, to my mother, Nancy Louise Tarr, for her unflagging support, and encouragement of my writing.

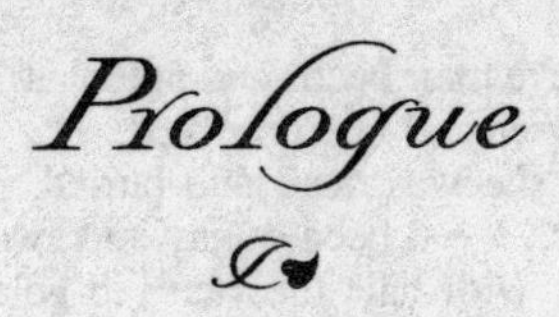

The life of man is but a span,
It's like a morning flower;
We're here today, tomorrow we are gone,
We are dead within one hour.

—"The Moon Shines Bright," a Warwickshire ballad,
author unknown

A Village near Selkirk, in the Scottish Border Country
September 1773

It was a fine day for a hanging.

The rolling green hillside was shot purple with heather and golden with gorse and the tart breeze of early autumn carried the peaty pungency of recently tilled crofts. That eve there would be a grand *cèilidh* with whiskey, food, and fiddling. Who knew, but if no English patrols were sighted perhaps a dirge or two on the outlawed pipes might be risked.

For sweet Margaret "Maggie" Campbell lay in the kirkyard beneath a makeshift wooden marker that likely wouldna last out the winter. Ten years before she'd done the unthinkable, spread her legs for a Sassenach dragoon. 'Twas only her swollen belly that had saved her from being tarred and feathered and set on display in the stocks. As matters stood, she was to count herself fortunate that Tam McBride, the blacksmith, had come forward to take her to wife even if he was old enough to be her da and had a taste for the whiskey. And if in the years that followed, her fair face was more often than not marred by bruises and her honey-brown eyes dulled with weeping, there were those to shake their heads and note that 'twas no better nor worse than the wretched lass deserved.

But now that she was dead and buried, it was easy to remember that once she'd been bonny and sweet, a fine full figure of a woman with hair the rich red-gold of a shiny new copper and a smile to warm a man in all the right places. Scant shame there seemed now in tipping back a dram in honor of her memory or swiping at an errant tear.

Or in turning out to give her murderer a proper Scottish sendoff.

Maggie had been slain by a thief on her way home from market and, according to those who'd found her puir battered body on the roadside, he'd enjoyed her aplenty before striking the fatal blow. That her eldest boy, Jack, the child of her sinning, had escaped the blackguard's notice by cowering in the mound of straw at the back of the dray was either a minor miracle or proof positive that the Devil did indeed mind his own. Unnatural creature, the wean had yet to give up a tear or utter so much as a word on his murdered maither's behalf, though a sennight had passed since the tragedy.

The "unnatural creature" stood still as a statue beside his stepfather, staring up at the scaffold with amber-brown eyes the exact color and shape of his mother's. His half brother, five-year-old Callum, hunkered down in the dirt by his da's feet, too busy poking his stick into the mouth of the green glass jar containing the butterfly he'd captured that morning to take much note of the proceedings.

But Jack saw, smelled, heard—felt—everything. The tension of anticipation thickened the crisp fall air, stirring feet to shuffle and cutting tempers short. Even the earth beneath his own bare feet seemed to pulse with an eerie watchfulness, keeping time with the staccato pounding of his own heavy heart and the drumbeats guiding the grim processional from gaol to scaffold.

Da dum, da dum.

The crowd's whispers quieted to a dull murmur as the prisoner, white-faced and quaking, approached the planked platform steps. Hands bound in front of him, he hesitated, starting up only after receiving the warder's shove. Looking on, Jack swiped his own sweaty hands down the front of his breeks but kept his gaze fixed on the gallows where the functionaries were assembling.

Stepping onto the platform were the priest, Father Angus, the village apothecary whose job it would be to confirm death, and finally Seumas, the hangman. Once the sight of Seumas in black cape and hood would have sent Jack tearing off in the opposite direction. A week older and a lifetime wiser, he kent that it wasna spooks and goblins a boy need fear but the savagery of flesh-and-blood men. He now saw the hangman not as a bogeyman but as a dark prince, an avenging angel charged with upholding all that was good and pure and just.

Mam had been those things and more—sweet and kind and sad. Most of all, she'd loved Jack with all her heart, as he had her. Now, like the kitten his little brother had snatched from his arms and tossed down the well, she was lost to him. Never again would she come to his room to hear his prayers at night, scold him for not scrubbing behind his ears, or croon words of comfort to take the sting from the taunts the other children cast along with their stones. *Sassenach spawn, Devil's changeling, bastard.*

Da dum, da dum.

Black cloak catching the wind like a sail, the hangman strode to the platform's center. Amidst the priest's droning of Latin prayers, he bowed to the crowd, then turned back to tend his prisoner. From where he stood, Jack saw that the latter's legs quivered like jelly; positioning him beneath the beam, toes to the chalk line, couldn't have been simple, but the hangman made it seem so. Taking hold of the rope, he slipped the loop over the prisoner's head with almost loving care, murmuring words of encouragement even as he cinched it about the scrawny throat, making small adjustments until the metal eye was situated just so over the bobbing Adam's apple.

Da dum, da dum.

Jack felt the prick of gooseflesh on his upper arms as the white cloth was dropped over the condemned man's face, blocking out his last earthly view. Then the executioner stepped back to take his place by the pulley. The crowd, and Jack with it, held its collective breath, waiting for the single, swift stroke that would launch the killer of Maggie Campbell McBride into eternity.

A sudden heave of the rope hoisted the culprit heavenward, feet dancing on air, scarecrow's body swiveling on the four winds like a weather vane. Later Jack would learn that nigh on forty minutes passed before the horn was sounded and the black flag raised. But for the small, unblinking boy, time froze into a single moment, with neither beginning nor end. Like an insect caught in the sticky resin that would harden into amber, the terrible, raw beauty of the struggle would be preserved in his memory for all time.

And though he'd years yet before he'd begin to fill out his long limbs and big clumsy hands and feet, though it had never once occurred to him to harm a living soul, from that day forward Jack knew what he would be when he was a man grown.

Jack Campbell was going to be a hangman.

Ah! Ça ira, ça ira, ça ira
Les aristocrates à la lanterne.
Ah! Ça ira, ça ira, ça ira
Les aristocrates, on les pendra.

Ah! It's coming, it's coming, it's coming
Aristocrats from the lamppost.
Ah! It's coming, it's coming, it's coming
Aristocrats, we will hang them.

—Popular song of the French Revolution

Twenty Years Later, October 1793

"*Imbécile! Voleur! Brigand!*"

Shivering as much from outrage as from the pelting rain, her sodden cloak weighing down her aching shoulders like an anchor, Claudia seized on the sole reliable remedy for warding off the tears that threatened. She hauled back her foot and dealt the coach's mired and broken rear wheel a sound kick. Unfortunately temper and the thin leather of her worn half boot proved to be scant shields against solid metal. Silver-tailed stars flashed amidst the sheeting of rain.

Blinking hard against the smarting of a stubbed but hopefully unbroken big toe, she lifted watery eyes to the mail coachman and shouted, "You take my money. You . . . you promise I will arrive in Edinburgh by nightfall, in Linlithgow by the morning next, and now you tell me that we must spend the night here. *Here!*"

Here was a squat, thatch-roofed structure that served as both coaching inn and local public house. That she, Claudia Valemont, should be forced to lodge in such a hovel was ample cause for humiliation. That she no longer possessed the funds to pay for bed and board was beyond humiliation. Beyond bearing.

The back of the driver's broad, hatless head reappeared from the bowels of the coach boot. He twisted about to look back at her, a pained expression hanging on his ruddy, weather-beaten features. "Wheesht, there's nay cause tae get yerself in a swivet o'er what canna be helped. 'Tis a mercy we made it 'ere afore that axle went."

Whatever it was that passed for mercy in this barbarous country of Scotland, Claudia had experienced precious little of it since crossing the border the day before. If England was a nation of shopkeepers, surely Scotland was a land of savages. Shaggy brutes all, their manners were as coarse as their unappetizing peasant food, their thoughts as unfathomable as their vulgar, discordant dialect. Had she known when she landed in Dover that Linlithgow, not London, was to be her destination; that the bumpy Channel crossing was to be the forerunner to an even bumpier, more punishing journey north by coach; she might have sailed back to Paris and let the mob have her.

But now there would be no turning back. Determined to be heard above the wind's howling and the battering of the rain, she yelled, "I tell you I will not stay in this despicable place." No lie, that, for she'd surrendered the last of her Scotch pounds for coach fare to fund the final leg of her journey.

From the hollow of the boot, the muffled reply echoed, "We're tae bide 'ere and there's no a blessed thing ye can do aboot it, so ye may as well go on inside wi' t'others."

In true British fashion, her five fellow passengers had collected their bags and filed across the muddy inn yard like so many sheep. No doubt they were even now ensconced before a roaring fire, quaffing their coarse ale and tearing into their beefsteak suppers. Claudia felt a pang of envy take root in the pit of her belly, the first thing to fill it since the single, miserable oatcake she had supped on the evening before. *Petite bourgeoisie* and peasants though her travel companions were, their unfashionable clothes looked sturdy and snug and their flesh well fed.

Chafing against her helplessness, she clenched the handle of the leather traveling bag. Small as it was, it contained the sum of her worldly riches: the mother-of-pearl comb; the precious vial of rose perfume, from which she doled out one daily dab behind each ear; and the sole proof of her paternity, the tartan brooch that once had belonged to her father.

Her father, Gearald Drummond, the earl of Aberdaire. In London she'd presented herself on the marble steps of his Berkeley Square town house only to discover that several weeks prior, His Lordship had decamped to his grouse moor near Linlithgow, five leagues or so west of Edinburgh. What he would say when his bastard daughter turned up at his door in Scotland was anyone's guess, but the small, fragile part of her still capable of hope insisted that once he recovered from the shock he would be pleased and willing to keep her with him.

Peering around the edge of her cloak hood, she lifted her gaze heavenward. *Père, please let him want me, for what will I do, where will I go, if he sends me away?*

The boot hatch slammed closed, startling Claudia back to her immediate problem. The driver started down, a burlap sack slung over one shoulder. "Look, miss, I dinna ken how it is folk travel where ye come from, but ye're in Scotland now. Even if the roads was dry as bone, we'd no get verra far wi' only three workin' wheels."

Claudia's command of Scots vernacular was imperfect at best, but sarcasm was easy enough to recognize in any language. Throat raw from raising her voice, she waited until his big feet met the spongy ground with a squishy thud before snapping back, "There is a *forgeron,* a blacksmith, in this *misérable* village, is there not? But of course there must be. You have only to call for him to repair the wheel and we can be on our way."

"Ask Tam McBride tae come out in this weather!" He tossed back his great, grizzled head and guffawed, nearly unseating his burdens. "Like as no the auld sot's inside, drunk as David's sow and toastin' his toes by the fire." The flinty gaze tucked beneath the jutting brow lost its mirth as he added, "Where I've a mind tae be if ye'll cease yer haverin' and kindly step out o' my way."

But Claudia had only begun to "haver." Hoisting her chin, she fixed him the stare that once had cowed a Parisian street mob bent on bloodletting. Transferring her luggage to her left hand, she held out her right palm up. "*Alors,* since you refuse to honor your word, I must insist you return my fare."

Once the rain lightened, she would hire a hack from the stables and be on her way. Traveling alone would render her an easy mark for bandits or worse but she had a small knife tucked into her right boot; in Paris she had proven to herself that she could draw it if the need arose. Even so, images of her last weeks there, the remembered feel of rough hands dragging her toward the swinging noose amidst shouts of "*À la lanterne!*" drew a shudder that owed nothing to the biting wind.

"No a chance, unless . . ." He hesitated, running his tongue over wind-cracked lips, and Claudia's heart leapt with hope. "Unless, that is, ye're minded tae earn it. Let's 'ave a look at ye." He reached for her, knocking back her hood.

"*Non!*" The sudden dump of rainwater on her bared head was a shock, but a small one compared to the terror of seeing that large, thickly gloved paw coming toward her. With no conscious thought beyond her body's instinct to preserve itself, she hauled back her curled hand and struck.

The blow clipped him below the chin. He blinked, surprise and the weight on his back sending him staggering backwards.

Steadying himself, he shook a fist in her face. "Bloody Frog scut! Stay out 'ere all the bloody night if ye've a mind, only see ye steer clear o' me." With that, he turned and plodded across the inn yard.

Shaking with reaction, Claudia fixed her senses on the heavy *slap, slap* of his retreating footfalls and drew several calming breaths. Chaos gradually ebbed, leaving her aware of throbbing knuckles and the rivulets of icy rainwater streaking down her back.

Yanking the hood over her wet head, she vowed, "I will walk to Linlithgow if I must. *Oui,* if I must, then that is what I will do."

But first she would have a word with the blacksmith. The one thing she had learned about this miserable island since her arrival was the fickleness of its weather. The skies could change from brilliant blue to deepest black and back again within a few short minutes. Despite the gray skies overhead, it was still light and the accursed coach was equipped with lanterns, after all. If she could find this Tam McBride and convince him to repair the wheel, then surely her fellow passengers, now fortified with food and drink, would join her in demanding their driver carry on? While he might ignore one *havering* woman, five disgruntled passengers, two of them men, would be considerably more difficult to dismiss.

Contemplating the coachman's face when he realized that she'd raised his entire human cargo to mutiny, Claudia felt a small smile, her first in weeks, curve her lips. She took firm hold of her bag and started forward. Unfortunately her feet failed to follow. Falling headfirst, she let out a shriek, her free hand flailing for purchase on the nearest solid object, the coach door. Saved, she stared down. *Merde.* Only the very tops of her boots were visible, the laces encased in a sticky paste of mud and grass, the heels and soles sucked below the bog. Muttering one of the more elaborate curses that her former protector, Phillippe, had shouted when he was vexed at her, she yanked one foot free then the other, hiked her waterlogged skirts to midcalf, and slogged across the yard to the inn.

Life, the inn's taproom teemed with it. His day's business discharged, Jack settled the clay pipe between his back teeth, stretched his long legs out in front of him, and sent his senses on a slow, lazy expedition about the low-ceilinged room. Peadair and Pol, both veterans of the Battle of Prestonpans and weathered as ancient stones, squinting over a draughts board and trading tales of bygone glory days. A table of young rowdies, cheeks ruddy with drink and voices raised, making a muckle mess of the tavern puzzle known as Satan's Stirrup. A party of Sassenach travelers holed up in a corner booth chattering like monkeys. Picking up a thread of their conversation, he gathered that the mail coach they'd arrived on was mired in the inn yard with a broken wheel.

Hating the thought of venturing out into the rain again, he nonetheless started up, thinking to find the driver and offer what help he might. Then young Rabbie Campbell, a cousin thrice removed on Jack's mother's side, unglued his snub nose from the window overlooking the inn yard and twisted about to shout, "'Tis him. 'E's coomin'."

The boy's exclamation acted on the sleepy late afternoon assembly like a battle cry. Men and even the few women present abandoned their benches and rushed to the rear of the tavern.

The door to the outside was yanked open, sending a current of damp chill knifing through the oily warmth. A man of middling years wearing a coachman's caped greatcoat and with a burlap mail sack slung over one crooked shoulder stepped inside. Greeters clinging to him like fleas on a dog, he made his way to the bar.

Knowing there would be no letter for him, Jack settled back into his seat. As he listened with half an ear to the commotion of correspondence being claimed by those who could afford the cost of postage, he was aware of a rare prickle of envy. Loneliness had been a feature of his existence for as long as he could remember; accepting the mantle of lord high executioner after Seumas's retirement had widened the gulf between himself and his fellows, but not appreciably so. As a bastard and half English, he'd been born to the lot of outcast much as he'd been born to red hair and the physicality of a broad, six-foot-four-inch frame. Growing up, wherever he'd gone, whatever he'd done, the whispers and dagger looks had dogged him. By the time he reached manhood, he'd acquired the knack of closing off not only his eyes and ears but his heart as well. If half the village kent him to be a clot-head and the other half a bloodthirsty Sassenach devil, then so be it. At nine and twenty years of age, he'd just as soon shrug and be on his way than argue the point.

The present pull to sleep, however, was not so easily shrugged aside, for it had been more than twenty-four hours since his head had met with a pillow. But then he never slept the night before an execution. Not because he was troubled by guilt, he wasna, but because he liked to mull over each and every detail of the proceedings in his mind. No matter how heinous the crime the condemned had committed, a long drop, a quick clean snapping of the vertebrae was ever Jack's aim. He'd only missed his mark once and through no fault of his. A coiner from Dundee who'd slit his crony's throat had been teary-eyed as a wean and twitchy as a cat. At the critical moment, the wee fool lost his nerve and backed away from the chalk line, with the unfortunate result that he'd gotten caught up in the rope, twisting to and fro like a tattered sail. When Jack had stepped forward to cut him down, the sheriff had ordered him to hold his place on pain of death. For the first time in his life, Jack had wanted to strangle someone for the pure pleasure of it, and it hadn't been the condemned.

That morning's business, however, had gone off without a hitch. Warm, dry, and with a tankard of the inn's finest ale filling his belly, he could feel relaxation begin to unknot his muscles and loosen his taut limbs. His eyelids felt as heavy as the weights he'd used to test the trap, his eyes as scratchy as the sand with which he'd filled the bags.

Slipping the pipe into his pocket, he glanced down at his wolfhound, Elf, sprawled beneath his chair. Smothering a yawn with the back of one hand, he addressed the dog, "I've a mind to wait out the rain and have a wee nap myself before we head for home."

Elf lifted her gaze to his face but kept her big head glued to the hearth rug, confirmation that she didn't mind their tarrying in the least.

Accordingly, he folded his arms across his chest, closed his eyes, and prepared to cast off into the sea of nonvisual sensation. Floating on the edge of sleep, he was dimly aware of the solid feel of the wooden chair beneath his bum; the collective hum of competing conversations; the rich pungency of burning peat, damp wool, and the sweat of honest labor. He heard the main door screech open once more, felt the chilly rush of rain-soaked air prick the back of his neck just before it closed again, this time with a definite slam. Inhaling the fragrance of flowers, he let his heavy head fall forward.

Flowers? Eyes closed, Jack lifted his chin from his chest and took a good whiff. Hyacinth, or perhaps lavender, with a strong undercurrent of roses. Aye, roses to be sure. Hereabouts, the only plants village folk cultivated were for eating, and this late in the season the frost had taken care of most vegetation, decorative or otherwise.

Perfume? A highwayman from Liverpool he'd turned off a few years back had slathered himself with the stuff on the morning of his execution. The sickly sweetness was so potent that arranging the noose about the man's neck had sent Jack into a fit of sneezing. But few Scots, certainly none of the crofters he knew, had coin to spare for fripperies like bottled scent. And yet both the fragrance and the ticklishness teasing his nostrils seemed to grow stronger with each breath drawn.

Deciding that his curiosity could wait but sleep couldn't, he ignored the sounds of Elf stirring beneath him and tucked his arms across his chest. He was halfway to bliss when something cold and wet struck the bridge of his nose. Making a mental note to tell Alistair, the innkeeper, about the hole in the thatching, he unfolded his arms and rubbed the edge of his thumb over the spot.

A second drop fell, catching him on the cheek. He cracked open an eye.

"*Monsieur, réveillez.* Wake up." Bent over him and dripping like a faucet, the wee woman seized his right shoulder in a pinching grip and attempted to shake it.

Both eyes now open, he looked up at the fine-boned face hovering bare inches from his own. Dark hair, possibly black, plastered pale high-boned cheeks, emphasizing the determined set of mouth and jaw.

Beneath his chair, Elf emitted a low warning growl. Jack reached down and laid a calming hand on the hound's neck. "Wheesht, the lass means us no harm."

"*Certainement,* I . . ." Her voice dropped off and she swallowed hard, sending a nervous ripple down the long ivory column of her throat. Holding one blue eye on Elf, she very slowly withdrew her hand from Jack's arm and straightened. "I only thought . . . you are the blacksmith, are you not?"

French, he decided, scarcely registering her question. Though he hadn't any of the language himself, her accented speech sounded much like what he recalled from the handful of French émigrés he'd encountered on his forays into England. And something about the shape of her nose, long and straight and just a wee bit arrogant, struck him at once as utterly Gallic and delectably feminine.

French or no, she hadn't a clue as to who he was or how he earned his living. Anonymity was a pleasant novelty and one he found he wasn't eager to relinquish.

Shamelessly prolonging the interlude, he asked, "And what need have ye for a blacksmith at this hour, milady? Your horse, it dinna throw a shoe, did it? Or is it the coach that brought ye?"

The fabric of his sleeve bunched beneath the tension in her slender fingers. "Oh, *oui,* yes, the coach." An enthusiastic bobbing of her head sent fresh rainwater spraying his shirtfront and wool jerkin. "The wheel, it is broken, and stuck . . . in the *mud,*" she added as if that last bit of information were essential to his understanding. "You will come with me to fix it, yes?"

She took back her hand, but her eyes, the rich, deep blue of cobalt, still held his. "Please, *monsieur,* you will come?"

He hesitated. Whoever she was, she was desperate. Travelers were common enough in the summer and early fall, but only the heartiest undertook the trek north this late in the season—and the lass looked anything but hearty. Jack had seen too many prisoners on execution eve to miss the bruised crescents carved beneath those lovely eyes or the haunted look reflected in their violet-blue depths.

Squinting through the haze of smoke to the room beyond, he honed his gaze on the coachman. The man had shed his greatcoat and was taking his ease at one of the long, planked tables lining the room. A glass of whiskey in hand and several empties already lined up before him, he didn't look disposed to budge anytime soon. Even if he were amenable, Jack wouldn't trust him to navigate a coach and four through foul weather and washed-out roads.

He looked back to the girl and shook his head. "I dinna ken who it was told ye I was the blacksmith, but—"

"*Personne* . . . No one told me. I . . ." Her gaze fell on the breadth of beefy shoulder she'd just released.

So that was the way of it. Jack felt his pleasure in the moment burn off with the swiftness of a Highland mist. Deliberately exaggerating his Scots burr, he said, "A big, rough brute such as I maun be the blacksmith, aye? Och, woman, d'ye no ken that a strong arm can be put t' uses besides striking hammer t' anvil?"

Her eyes went blank, high forehead bunching into a frown. Watching her, Jack knew the exact moment when she strung together a sufficient number of words to ken his meaning.

Her perfectly shaped black brows arched, then snapped together. "Are you or are you not Monsieur Tam McBride? A simple yes or *non, s'il vous plait.*"

As always, the mention of his stepfather's name caused the stiffness to settle into the back of his neck. Unable to keep the edge from his voice, he answered, "Seeing as ye put it that way, so simple and clear like, I'll have to say nay, I'm no him."

"Oh." Directing her disappointed gaze on the room beyond him, she rose up on her toes. "In that case, you will be so good as to point him out to me?" She reached up with both hands, presumably to shield her eyes against the sting of burning tallow and smoke.

It was common knowledge that Tam was abed with the ague. Jack opened his mouth to say as much when the front of her cloak fell open and he found himself on eye level with a firm and delectably full bosom. He sucked in his breath. For all she was small, with a wee waist he could span with his two hands, she wasna small everywhere. The bodice of her sprigged muslin frock, pale yellow and rendered to transparency by the rainwater, molded to her like wallpaper. Nipples that looked to be a shade somewhere between coral and pale rose pressed against the thin fabric, leaving no doubt that aye, the lass was cold.

Jack, however, felt very warm indeed.

The sudden, swift image of how easy it would be to lean forward and bury his face in that sweet, soft pillow flared without warning. It had been a considerable while, years in fact, since he'd found himself this close to a woman, at least one who was comely and younger than sixty odd. He'd come to regard the physical urges that reared from time to time as a manageable nuisance, no match for an ironclad will bent on upholding a twenty-year vow. But now sparks of desire fired through his lower belly and groin, making his balls ache and his heart yearn.

She yanked the ends of her cloak together. "Close your mouth, *monsieur.* Were it summer, you would be in danger of admitting the flies." Her regard raked over his face, telling him she kent just where he'd been looking.

Jack clamped closed the mouth he only now realized he'd left hanging open. *Clot-head! Gomeral!* Ears hot and certain to be rimmed in red, it was all he could do to croak out the words, "Tam, he's no in the—"

She cut him off with an irritated huff. "I will find him myself."

Dropping her gaze, she glared at his big, booted feet, apparently blocking her preferred path. Before he could draw them back, she stepped over, her muddy skirts mopping the legs of his breeches.

Light-headed as if he'd drunk a keg of ale instead of a single pint, he watched her trot off into the crowd, lovely nose pointed north and back held ramrod straight.

Remembering himself, he staggered to his feet, narrowly avoiding treading on the dog in his haste. Cupping his hands about his mouth to amplify the sound, he called after her, "Hold, mistress! Tam, he's no here. He's . . ."

It was no use. Tiny as a faerie and every bit as nimble, she'd already moved beyond earshot. Or perhaps, given that he'd been gaping at her bubbies like a bloody slack-jawed idiot, she was choosing to ignore him. Either way, she didn't so much as look back his way.

Fresh humiliation heating his cheeks, he reached into his sporran, plunked several coins beside his empty tankard, and signaled to Elf to rise. "Ah, well, she'll find out for herself soon enough, aye, lass? 'Tis home for us, and it's a bonny fire I'll lay once we're there."

The dog cut him a sour look but dutifully rose, lingering only to stretch before coming to attention by his side.

His bill of fare settled, there was no cause to dally, but the nervous twitch in his gut bade him turn back for one last glimpse. Standing head and shoulders above the other patrons gave him the advantage, and he soon sighted his mystery woman working her way toward the front of the room. Ducking beneath raised arms and squeezing through tiny alleys of exposed space, she seemed not to see the male heads turning in her direction nor the appreciative glances that followed long after she swept past.

But Jack saw them and more. Lolling along the benches of one of the planked tables set nearest the bar, the party of drunken young men numbered a half dozen. Between quaffing ale and shouting abuses to all and sundry, they'd found time to pull down several of the tavern puzzles hanging from pegs on the wall behind them. Too bleary-eyed to piece them back together, they'd been using the disjointed pieces to torment those unfortunate enough to come within arm's length of their table. Alistair had been over once to urge them to hold their peace, but to no avail. Now it seemed that the French lass would succeed where the innkeeper had failed. As she stepped out into the open, a collective hush swept down their line. Six heads swiveled in her direction, eyes popping like wine corks.

Jack swallowed hard, forcing himself to hold back. The wee lass might be foreign but she was no fool, he'd give her that.

Seeing what she'd walked into, she cut a sharp left, veering off toward a stack of brandy casks.

The ringleader, a tousled mop of brown hair hanging low over one eye, turned to address the table at large. Jack was too far away to overhear his remarks but, whatever their nature was, they drew a chorus of ribald laughter from his cronies.

Jack, however, was not amused.

The brown-haired one rose from the bench. Weaving slightly, he started after the French girl. She cut a quick backward glance and quickened her steps, now directed toward the main door. He caught up with her before she could reach it. Grabbing her by the elbow, he yanked her roughly to him.

Holy Mother of God. Jack had seen more than enough. He plunged into the thick of the crowd, narrowly avoiding colliding with his friend Milread, the barmaid, and her tray of ale. Calling out an apology, he pushed onward, using his mass to carve a path across the room.

He was halfway to his goal when a female voice rang out, "*Cochon!* Pig! Take your filthy hands from me."

"Wheesht, lass, be still. I'm only wantin' tae see if ye're other pap be as soft as this one."

The brown-haired one had caged her into a corner, a hand braced on the stones on either side of her slender shoulders. Suddenly he jerked backwards. "She cut me! The shewolf cut me!" He hauled back his hand and struck.

The slapping sound of flesh striking flesh sliced through the fragile ribbon of Jack's self-control. He launched forward, the raw rage inside him exploding in a deep, guttural growl. In one fluid motion, he wrapped his arm about his quarry's neck, tore him from the girl, and sent him hurtling into the onlookers. The latter obliged by parting to either side like the Red Sea, consigning the unfortunate to crashing into the far wall. With a ragged groan, he slipped down the stones and landed in a heap on the earthen floor. The hanging tavern puzzles, jarred free from their pegs, rained down on his head in a jangle of metal, drawing small but audible moans.

Sweat rolling down his sides, Jack swung around to the girl. Pale and shivering though she was, she was still on her feet, which was more than could be said for her attacker.

Claudia caught her breath as her rescuer closed the distance between them. At first glance she had thought him handsome albeit in a rough, peasant sort of way; now the raw, savage beauty of him striding toward her stole her breath. The top of his red-gold head nearly reached the timbered ceiling, his broad shoulders tested the fabric of his homespun shirt to the point of renting, and his snug-fitting breeches hugged his tree trunk–size thighs and muscular calves like a second skin.

Drawing up in front of her, he reached out one large hand to touch the side of her face where she'd been struck. From habit she flinched away, but his blunt fingers were gentle as he stroked them from her cheekbone to jaw. So gentle that she found herself staring with open longing at his other hand, still held at his side, the broad back of which was dusted with red-gold hairs that looked like they must feel very soft, a sensual contrast to the faint roughness edging his fingertips. Phillippe's hands, she recalled, had been soft as a woman's and bald as an egg, yet his touch had been impersonal at best, hurtful at worst.

The Scotsman drew his hand away and Claudia felt the absence of its warmth like the loss of a cherished friend. "Are ye hurt, lass?"

He was tall, so tall she had to tilt her head against the stones to meet his concerned, brown-eyed gaze. She shook her head, as much to answer him as to confirm to herself that it still rested on her shoulders. "I do not think so."

His lean face registered relief. A tiny trickle of perspiration wended its way down the side of his face, from temple to the high, flat plane of his Viking cheekbone to his square jaw. Trailing its progress, she had the absurd thought that, under more promising circumstances, she might like to catch the bead of moisture on the tip of her tongue.

He dropped his regard. "In that case, ye'll no be needin' that wee dagger."

She followed his downward gaze to the knife she held in a tight-fisted grip at her side. Seeing the dull sheen of crimson tipping the blade, she choked on a gasp. "*Mon Dieu,* I have killed him!" Her fingers went as weak as her knees and it was only the Scotsman's quick action in extricating the knife from her limp grasp that saved it from clattering to the floor.

"Dinna fash." He tucked the weapon inside the leather belt cinched about his tapered waist. Broad of shoulder yet lean about the middle and hips, he put Claudia in mind of the statue of Atlas she once had glimpsed in the gardens of Versailles.

"He'll be havin' the devil of a headache on the morrow and the wee cut on his shoulder willna feel verra pleasant either but otherwise he'll no be the worse for wear, which is more than I can say for you." A small smile tugged one corner of his mouth higher than the other, revealing a fleeting glimpse of teeth that looked to be both strong and white.

Something about that smile seemed to drain the last of the resistance from Claudia's body. Boneless as an eel, she sagged forward, reaching for him to ground herself as she had the coach door earlier. Cheek pressed against the rock-hard casing of breastbone and ribs, she felt the wave of shock ripple through him, the muscles of torso and arms tautening with tension.

For a moment, she thought he would cast her aside, then his big arms enfolded her, closing off her view of the curiosity seekers gathering about them like hungry crows. "Och, lass, you're all but dead on your feet. We've to get you to bed and soon."

The words dragged her from the fog into the present. As much as she would like to go to bed, either alone or with him, she could not.

Linlithgow. Father. She lifted her head from his chest and looked up. "I cannot. I must . . ." She started, a dog's sudden growl alerting her to the flicker of movement from behind.

Peering around the broad slope of the Scotsman's shoulder, she saw her attacker rise to a half-crouch, one hand clutching the scarlet blossom on the shoulder of his shirtsleeve.

And the other fisted about the hilt of a small but lethal-looking knife.

She opened her mouth, and a woman's voice, her voice, rang out, "*Attention!* Look out!"

The room seesawed and Claudia with it. Black, spidery shapes crawled about the edges of her vision, reducing her savior's stunned face to a jumble of colors and shapes. Like a snuffed candle, a single poof extinguished the last of the light, leaving fathomless blackness.

Claudia fainted.

chapter 2

Love, love when you take hold,
We can say farewell to caution.

—Jean De La Fontaine

F*ortunately for Jack, the prickly stiffening of the soft hairs* at the back of his neck never *ever* lied. His guardian angel blowing its breath upon him to get his attention, or so his mother had been wont to say. For certain there had been but two times in his nearly thirty years of earthly existence when he'd failed to heed the warning, both in his ninth year. The first had been the day his little brother, Callum, had asked, all innocence, might he not hold Jack's tabby kitten, Clare, for just the moment. Jack had hesitated, stomach knotted, considering. Just a moment's wavering, a second's slackening of his hold on the precious bundle nestled against his chest, but it was enough. If he lived to be as old as Peadair and Pol, Jack would never forget the ugly triumph twisting Callum's cherub face just before he snatched the cat and dashed off, a shrieking Clare pinioned under one pudgy arm. Nor how his own heart had leapt to lodge in his throat when he'd realized they were heading for the well. Breathing hard, Callum had stood at the side, taunting Jack to "coom and get 'er," even as he hoisted the howling cat high and then let go. There was that horrible moment, suspended in time, when wee Clare had seemed to hover in midair, white paws splayed and clawing at the emptiness, and then she'd dropped like a stone. A faint *plop, plop* and then a final, fatal gurgling had confirmed that he was too late.

And then there'd been the day Mam died.

Both times he'd failed to heed the warning wrenching belly

and bowels and both times a loved one had been lost forever. The lesson, bitterly learned, was deeply ingrained.

And so even before the woman's warning scream, Jack's sixth sense alerted him to his sibling's impending attack. The slight scuffling behind him, the movement of limbs cutting through currents of still air, the sudden sharp breath that Callum gathered to gird himself just before he lunged—all cued Jack to prepare himself, to make ready.

But there was the woman to consider. The scream seemed to have siphoned the very last of her strength and nerve. Black pupils bulged, nearly obliterating the violet-blue iris. A half-second later those same eyes rolled back and her faerie form slackened.

Jesus, Joseph, and Mary.

Jack threw out his arm, catching her before she could hit the floor. Cursing beneath his breath, he pinned her to his left side and whipped about, barely in time to dodge a clumsy if lethal thrust to his right. The blade of the *sgian dhu* missed him by a hairbreadth, snagging on the loose fabric of his jerkin before the momentum of the thrust sent the slighter man sailing forward.

Callum caught himself, landed in a half-crouch, and then spun about. Eyes blazing with bloodlust, the whites shot with pink, he spat, "Ye always was one for hidin' behind a woman's skirts. Old habits die hard, aye, Jacko?"

Jack thought of the woman's knife tucked into his belt and hoped he would not be called upon to draw it. "I dinna care to hurt ye, *mo bràthair,* but I will if ye'll no see sense and go home."

"D'ye dare tell *me* where I may go, ye bloody Sassenach bastard?" Callum's red-rimmed gaze fell on the woman filling Jack's left arm and his mouth twisted in a sneer. "Forbye, it seems ye've your hands full."

He circled, weapon at the ready, and Jack knew then that he had no choice. Slight as the French lass was, dead weight was dead weight, and bone and muscle seemed to gain a good stone as he worked to hold her upright with his left arm while keeping his right free to fend off attack. Keeping one eye trained on his opponent, he whistled for his dog. Elf rushed to his side and, satisfied that the girl would have a steadfast guardian, he hunkered down and laid her limp form on the floor.

The vulnerable posture provided his opponent the opening for which he'd been waiting, but then Jack had anticipated that. With a whoop, Callum sprang, knife raised. Jack counted to three and then shot up, arcing his right fist in a powerful undercut, knuckles plowing into the hollow of his brother's midriff in a blow calculated to drive stomach into lungs.

"Ahhhh!" A raw groan ripped forth from Callum's slack mouth, sending saliva spewing. Doubled over, he dropped to his knees, his arm wound about his belly like a bandage and the knife falling from his unfurled fingers to the floor. "D-damn ye, J-Jacko. Ye'll be s-sorry, I t-tell ye." He stretched his free hand toward the knife, black-rimmed fingernails raking the floorboards in his struggle to reel it in.

Milread, who'd pushed her way to the forefront of the fight, hurried forward and clamped the heel of her clog onto the flat of the blade. "Now, now, my fine laddie. There's been blood enough spilled on my clean boards this day wi'out adding the more. I'll just borrow this wee dagger and see it safe." She snatched up the *sgian dhu* and tucked it inside the bone lining of her bodice.

The excitement over, the crowd began to disperse. The few stragglers went back to nursing their pints and Alistair to keeping the bar. Callum's mates, sobered by the sight of their ringleader brought to his knees, closed in to help him to his feet.

Watching them bear him toward the door, Jack could only shake his head. His half-brother's hatred of him ran deep and though Jack had never kent the cause, he'd long ago learned not to fash over what wasna in his power to change. But then there were those things he could do something about.

The French lass lay on the sticky floor where he'd been forced to deposit her, Elf dutifully flanking her side. "Good, lass," he said to the dog and went down on his knees beside the woman's prone form. He slipped an arm beneath the sharp shoulder blades and gently lifted her against him. "Mistress?" He cupped her cheek, registering its satin smoothness even as he gave it a gentle pat. "Mistress, can ye hear me?"

That was when it struck him that he didn't even ken her name. Nor she his. Their acquaintance such as it was had been brief, to be sure, but definitely memorable. Odd that it should end with them as strangers. Odder still that the prospect should prompt him to feel such a sharp stab of mingled disappointment and regret.

"Ah well, a rose by any other name, aye, lass?" Steeling himself to ignore the swell of what promised to be a truly bonny bottom, he slid a second arm beneath her and rose to his feet. Of Milread, he asked, "Has Alistair a room to let, preferably one where she can be private until the coach leaves on the morrow?"

The barmaid straightened from the table she'd been clearing and twisted about to glance at the girl. "I dinna ken if we're full up or no but the lass can share mine if the need be."

Jack shook his head. "I dinna like to ask it of ye. We dinna ken anything about her, no so much as her name."

Milread rolled her hazel eyes. "Oh aye, and a verra dangerous character she looks tae be, too."

Jack ventured a downward glance to the dark head trustingly tucked into the curve of his shoulder. Long-lidded eyes closed in sleep and lips sweetly parted, the lass looked more celestial than earthly, the very picture of divine innocence, a dark angel fallen to ground or, more properly, into his very arms.

Mindful of how appearances so often deceived, of how very un-angel-like the lass had behaved before she'd dropped off, Jack tore his gaze away and turned it up to Milread. "All the same, I've coin to spend and I suppose Alistair's pockets will do as well as any other's."

The wretch he'd escorted into eternity that morning had had more steel in his spine than most, though not a great deal of trust. Once positioned beneath the beam, he'd pressed the purse he held between his hobbled hands into Jack's gloved palm and urged, "Take it, man, for pity's sake. I dinna wish tae be gaggin' at the end o' the rope like my da did."

Twice Jack had refused. On the third plea, he'd relented and accepted but only to give the puir bastard peace of mind so he'd hold steady and still. *Blood money,* he'd thought to himself, and vowed to drop it in the parish poor box before the week's end. But now it occurred to him that both charity and necessity might be better served if he used it to pay the French lassie's bed and board.

He carried his burden over to the bar, Elf trailing. Ignoring the gawking men fanned about the rail, he addressed himself to the innkeeper. "Have ye a room to let? A private one?"

From inside the bar, Alistair looked up from the oily cloth he'd been using to mop the spillage. "A need to be *private,* have we now?" Mouth twitching, he slid his gaze over the unconscious female in Jack's arms. " 'Tis glad I am tae see ye finally take an interest, laddie, but ye should ken there's a livelier time tae be had when they're awake."

A burst of laughter fired about the bar, followed by a bevy of bawdy comments that brought the heat sizzling into Jack's neck and cheeks. Ignoring the poke of an elbow in his side, he held his gaze level and his temper in check as he waited for the rumpus to die down. Eventually it did, and he asked, "Have you a room or no?"

Alistair raked a stubby hand through the nonexistent hair that twenty-odd years ago had grown thick and brown as a chestnut atop his now shiny pate. "Oh aye, I do, but only the one, and it'll cost ye dear."

In neither mood nor position to haggle, Jack set his jaw. "How much?"

Alistair hesitated, his mouth working in silent calculation, and then announced, "Three pounds six."

"Done."

From halfway across the taproom, Milread slammed her tray of emptied tankards down atop the nearest table. "Why ye clarty son of a gypsy," she spat, marching up to the bar. "Ye're nay better than a highwayman t'ask such a sum." She swung about to Jack, pinched his arm. "Dinna pay him. The lass can share my bed."

Jack opened his mouth to answer that he could well mind his own affairs, but before he could, Alistair threw up the pass-through, tore off his apron, and stomped to the front of the bar. "Oh she can, can she?" Hands fisted on his beefy hips, he added, "It so happens, my fine lassie, that *yer* bed, as ye care tae call it, lies within *my* inn, and so long as it does I'll no thole yer lettin' it out tae prospective *payin'* customers."

"Oh ye'll no, will ye?" Milread shot back, eyes blazing, and Jack could see she was working herself up to a fine rant on his behalf. "Well, let me just . . ."

Jack closed his eyes and called inwardly for patience. Until that day he and Callum had not so much as spoken a word to each other in nigh on ten years, and their recent explosive encounter had left him drained. His eyes burned from going too long without the salve of sleep and the tension knotting the muscles of his neck and shoulders made him long for his bed, lonely and empty though it was. But before he laid his head on his own pillow, he would see the wee woman in his arms safely settled. And if that meant paying an arm and a leg to tuck her up in a private room, removed from Callum's or anyone else's reach until her coach left the day next, then so be it.

Patience at an end, he raised his voice a good notch so that he might be heard above the shouting. "Enough! Close your clappers, the both of ye." He swung about to Alistair, nearly clipping him with the Frenchwoman's wee feet. "I'll take it." Spearing the innkeeper with a hard look, he added, "But mind ye're no stingy with the peat or the washing water. A full bath with *hot* water, ye ken, and a proper supper to go with it."

Poking her flaxen head between the two men, Milread piped up, "Oh, he'll no hold back, I'll see tae it. The lass shall have all her due—and more."

Alistair muttered something about serving wenches getting above themselves but in the end he nodded his assent.

"Verra well," Jack said, already starting for the set of side stairs that led to the guest chambers above. "Point the way."

"The French," *Milread announced not five minutes later,* with a knowing nod to the unconscious woman in the center of the worn counterpane, "have verra hard heads."

Standing by the bedside, Elf's breath fanning the side of his leg, Jack tried to draw comfort from those words. Tried and failed. Hard though the lassie's head might be, her pale flesh was satin-soft, the bones beneath as fragile as those of a wee bird.

Swallowing a sigh, he dipped the cloth into the stoneware washbasin Milread had filled with cool water, wrung it out, and then gently laid it over the bright bruise, Callum's mark, swelling the girl's sharply boned cheek. He looked across the bed to Milread, bent to settle a coverlet over the girl's stocking feet, several delicate toes protruding through the holes. "I dinna suppose ye've any smelling salts?"

"Oh aye," she replied, rolling her eyes. "I always keep a barrel or two of the stuff on hand just in case some French lassie takes it into her head tae faint on my floorboards."

Shoulders tensing, he said, "I wish I had my wee box with me. Helichrysum would help considerable to cut the pain."

That drew Milread's chortle. "She doesna seem tae me tae be feelin' any pain." He shot her a sharp look and, contrite, she quickly added, "Och, lad, dinna fash yerself. She'll be on her feet in nay time. Like as no she's more in need o' good, nourishing food than your herbs, skilled though ye are. I'll fetch some broth from the kitchen the verra moment she comes awake, and if she keeps that down there'll be solid fare tae follow."

A muffled moan rose from the bed, drawing his gaze downward. The lassie shifted onto her side, kicking free of the coverlet and knocking off the folded cloth. Like a parched man suddenly handed a glass of cool ale, Jack drank in the purity of her profiled features: the feathered arc of jet brow and the long lid of the closed eye beneath. The delicate bones that gave subtle shape to nose and cheek and jaw. The full, softly parted mouth, its top lip a pale pink ribbon, the bottom a deeper hue of rose and so full and generous and ripe that just staring at it prompted a sharp tug in the vicinity of his groin.

So this was lust.

Until now sexual need had been a solitary affair, a basic physical call little different from hunger or thirst and detached from anything or anyone outside the sphere of his own body. But this, this *feeling* blossoming inside him was a different beast entirely. The girl, stranger and foreigner though she was . . . he wanted *her.* That he couldn't have her, even if she'd been well and willing, suddenly seemed a minor point. He wanted her and in the wanting, the lusting, lay his downfall. No simple lust, this, for lurking beneath its surface was the drive to shelter and defend, to comfort and heal. And it was those soft sentiments, more so than the lusting, that scared the hell out of him.

The sound of a throat being cleared brought him back into the awareness that he was not alone. He turned away from the vision on the bed, straightened his features, and said, "I'll be going then. You'll send word when she's gone?"

"Och, ye dinna mean tae stay 'til she wakes?" A wicked grin stretched Milread's wide mouth wider still and she added, "Ye could feed her like ye do that wee birdie o' yers."

"Lady is a hawk and no so wee and like the other beasties will be cross at havin' to wait so long for her supper." He cast his gaze to the narrow window where a feeble shaft of late afternoon sunlight gilded the last droplets of clinging rain. "Forbye, the rain's let up. Best Elf and I set out before it starts again."

As excuses went it was plausible enough, if lacking in inventiveness. And far more face-saving than the bald truth—he was *scared* to stay.

Accordingly, he forced his footsteps toward the door. On the threshold, he whistled for Elf to follow but for once the hound balked. A soulful look in her yellow eyes, she kept to her post by the bed until Jack had no choice but to retrace his steps, take firm hold of her collar, and half drag her toward the door.

On the threshold, he weakened, turning back for one last look. A glossy strand of still damp hair clung to the Frenchwoman's pale cheek, and her long, slender fingers plucked at the coverlet as if seeking something or someone who existed only in the shadow world of dreams.

Hard-pressed to hold in a sigh, he shifted his gaze to Milread, who'd followed him to the door. "Ye're certain ye can manage, then? Alistair—"

"Will fash and threaten, but in the end I'll have my way." Winking, she added, " 'Tis true my bed lies within his inn, but I've still some say as tae who I let in it—and who I turn away."

His mate from childhood, Milread once had invited Jack to share her bed. Though he'd appreciated the offer, he'd declined—vow aside, she was like a sister to him—and to her credit she'd only shrugged and told him he dinna ken what he was missing.

Now he reached out and, in brotherly fashion, bestowed a light pinch on her freckled cheek. "Ye're a braw lass and a good friend."

"Humph, am I now." Glancing over her shoulder, she said, "But no so bonny as that one, more's the pity."

It was Jack's turn to wink. "But ye've a heart the size of Edinburgh Castle and a fine, fat arse to go with it."

She broke into a gap-toothed grin, taking in good humor what a lesser woman would have taken in offense. "That I do, Jack Campbell, that I do, though more's the trouble it brings me. Now off wi' ye before I take it into my head tae coax ye tae come back tae *my* room and stop wastin' what the good Lord intended should be used." She darted out a hand and gave his crotch a good squeeze.

Taken unawares, he jerked back. "Christ, woman, mind your

claws. I may have promised no to use it, but that doesna mean I'm looking to be gelded." A protective hand cupped over the sensitive area in question, he backed into the hallway, face warm and sure to be glowing.

Wiggling sandy eyebrows, she took a menacing step forward. "Nay worries on that score, laddie. I'll lay odds it'd *rise* to the occasion." Chuckling, she made a show of shooing him away. "But off wi' ye, then, and mind ye take your great mangy beastie wi' ye afore she pisses all o'er my floor."

Jack looked down at the dog, still staring fixedly back inside the room. "Come along, Elf. We ken when we're no wanted."

When she dug in her doggie heels, he sighed and reached down to once more take hold of her collar. Wondering at his boon companion's uncharacteristic stubbornness, he turned to go but found he couldn't resist firing one last, parting shot. "Though, come to think of it, a bit of piss might just see it clean."

"Gomeral!" Milread swatted at him but her heart wasn't in it and forbye he'd already moved beyond reach. Always beyond her reach, was Jack.

Listening to his footfalls drumming back down the hallway, echoed in the softer clicking of his dog's paws, she vented the lifetime's longing that built in her breast on those rare occasions when she let herself dream of what would never be.

Around a heavy sigh, she whispered, "What a waste. What a terrible waste."

The price of souls: even hell, with thee to boot,
Is made worth Heaven.

—Ben Jonson, *Volpone,* act 1, scene 1

Claudia's first impressions upon waking were of the crunch of the straw-stuffed mattress beneath her, a female's off-key humming, and the strong, clean scent of evergreen; the latter seemed to sheathe her person like a protective mantle. For some reason yet to be recalled, her muzzy mind associated that aroma with a particular person, only she couldn't remember whom. Male—no mistaking that—and large. Add to that her vague recollection of hair the color of a sunset, arms like steel bands, and the deep timbre of a softly burred voice—a *Scots* burr.

Clues to a yet-to-be-solved riddle, snippets of recollected impressions stole out from their hiding place to form a sensory sequence: the past week's journey north into Scotland, the broken-down coach, the tavern room so densely packed that it brought to mind a barrel of cured fish. Standing head and shoulders above the crowd had been the tall, red-haired Scotsman with the big, strong body and the soft, sad eyes. Someone had struck her, she recalled that now, and he'd come to her aid. Afterwards, he'd touched her face with roughly gentle fingers, pried the knife from her clammy grasp, and then taken her against the warmth of his hard chest. For those lovely few seconds she'd turned her face into the coarse crispness of his homespun shirt, redolent with the fresh clean fragrance of evergreen, and had known what it was to feel cherished and safe. And then she'd chanced to look up, to look beyond him, and had glimpsed the telling flash of light striking upon steel. A knife, only this time not hers, and aimed for her rescuer's broad back.

Claudia bolted upright in the bed, belatedly coming into an awareness of myriad fists pummeling her cheek. "Ouf!" she let out and clamped one hand to the source of the pain, a frighteningly large bulge that felt as though it must encompass half her face.

The humming abruptly quit. "So ye're awake," stated the homey voice from the far end of the room, rather unnecessarily, Claudia thought, and far, far too loudly for good manners, but then this *was* Scotland. "I said ye'd come about in your own good time, but he wouldna listen."

Squinting through the haze of pounding pain, Claudia espied the source of the voice, a wide-hipped female kneeling before the hearth, working the bellows to rouse what looked—and smelled—to be an already decent-sized peat fire.

Addressing the broad backside, she asked, "The man who fought for me, he is . . . ?" And then, as the horrible, chilling possibility leapt to mind, freezing out all other thoughts save one, she blurted out, "*Merci aux saints,* he is not dead, is he?"

A loud chortle greeted the latter and nearly resulted in the bellows being dropped into the fire. "Jack dead from a wee tangle wi' that codless coof, Callum—no hardly. Why who d'ye ken it was who bore ye upstairs?"

Jack, so that was her rescuer's name. Claudia sagged back against the headboard and covered her hands over her face as she fought to think her way through the throbbing. The episode in the taproom and the altercation with the coachman before it had brought home just how perilous travel could be for a woman on her own. As much as she needed transport, she needed a protector—a man strong and trustworthy to navigate her safely to her destination.

If the impressive display of pugilism she'd witnessed prior to passing out was any indication, Monsieur Jack of surname unknown more than met her first requirement. As for trustworthiness, he hadn't taken advantage of her after she'd fainted—at least she didn't think he had. That he also happened to possess the chiseled features and sculpted muscles associated with statues of Greek gods was a minor consideration as well as a happy circumstance. Going to bed with him—and surely he would expect some reward for his pains—should prove to be no hardship.

And yet the prospect of offering herself in trade once again, even if this time safe passage and not jewels and silks and servants was the commodity to be bartered, tore at her. Freedom had cost her dearly but she had paid its price and, despite her wretched state, she cherished her newfound liberty as once she'd cherished diamonds and pearls. Submission, even as a temporary state, would not come easily. It just possibly might not come at all.

Cross that bridge when you come to it, gel, she told herself, but in her head it was the voice of Miss Chitterly, her former English governess, that she heard.

Returned to the practicality by the memory of those very clipped, very *British* tones, she drew her hands away from her face and asked, "Jack, he will return soon?"

Apparently the maid finally found satisfaction with the fire, the delicious warmth of which Claudia could feel thawing her toes, for she put down the bellows, rose, and turned about to reveal a pie-faced countenance liberally sprinkled with freckles. "Nay, I shouldna think so." Swiping sooty hands down her apron, she started over to the bed. "He left a wee while ago, just before ye awoke."

"Left!" Forgetting to heed the pain in her head, Claudia tossed off the coverlet and swung her legs over the side of the bed.

The room canted as her stocking-clad feet met the floorboards, putting her in mind of her landing at Dover when she'd disembarked only to find that solid ground seemed to pitch and roll just as the ship had. But she'd soon regained her "land legs," as the English sailors had promised, and she was even more determined to do so now, for they were her only means of transportation.

But, she hoped, not for long.

"*Mon Dieu,* this is terrible, *un désastre.* Why did you not wake me?" Sighting her mud-caked half boots set before the fire to dry, she pressed a steadying hand to the plaster wall and started toward them.

The maid seemed to find the question amusing. "Why not, indeed?" she repeated, the corners of her wide mouth twitching as her hazel eyes followed Claudia to the hearth. "But nay worries, both your bed and board are paid in full, Jack saw tae that, and I've told him I'd stay on tae see ye settled for the night."

In the midst of shoving her right foot into the shrunken leather,

Claudia stalled. Up until now she'd been too focused on her goal to bother with wondering how it was that she, a penniless refugee, had come to occupy an inn room all to herself.

Wondering if she might have misunderstood, she asked, "He . . . he did all that for me? But I am but a stranger to him."

The Scotswoman lifted her broad shoulders in a shrug but her gaze was thoughtful as she answered, "Stranger or no, everyone's somebody tae Jack. It's just his way. Now," she added, abruptly switching to the lilting tone one used to cajole very young, very spoiled children, "there's some lovely broth on its way up and, if ye manage tae keep it down, there'll be haggis and bannocks and a pudding tae follow."

Now that she'd stirred, Claudia was aware that her stomach was empty to the point of aching. Whatever *haggis* was (and with Scottish fare, she'd learned it was often better not to know), the name alone suddenly sounded delicious.

But even as her gastronomy voiced its plea for nourishment in the form of an embarrassing gurgle, she reached for her other boot and forced her foot inside. "First I must speak with, er, Jacques."

The maid narrowed her gaze, all traces of humor vanishing as she asked, "And, stranger that ye be, what further business might ye have wi' *Jack*?"

"My own," she answered, then turned away to gather up the rest of her belongings.

Her cloak, or more properly her maid Evette's cloak, had been draped over the back of the warming chair so that it might dry in the fire's heat. She knew a moment's guilt as it occurred to her that the woman she'd just insulted likely had been the one to hang it there. Then guilt drowned in the sudden surge of panic.

"*Mon sac!* My bag!" Her dizziness forgotten, she whirled on the maid. "What have you done with it?"

A snort sounded from the far end of the room. "Well, I've no nicked it if that's what yer worrit for. 'Tis right before ye, plain as the nose on your face," she added, tapping the bridge of her own rather bulbous beak.

Claudia swung back around and whisked the cloak from the slatted chair back. Sure enough, tucked between the wooden chair legs was her portmanteau. It didn't looked to have been rifled but . . . Heart hammering and mouth dry, she dragged it out into plain view, dropped to her knees, and yanked it open.

Only when she found the brooch tucked into an inside compartment, carefully wrapped in its handkerchief just as she'd left it, did she dare to breathe. Feeling relieved and very, very foolish, she started up. "*Mademoiselle, excusez-moi.* It is only that I—"

A large foot clamping down on the bag's leather handle brought a halt to her apology. "The name's Milread, no whatever gibberish ye just called me. And ye're no tae budge from this room until the mail coach leaves on the morrow. I promised Jack."

With no choice but to let go, Claudia stumbled to her feet. Straightening to her full height of five feet two inches, she lifted her chin to stare up into the maid's steely eyes. "You cannot keep me here against my will. Now release my valise or I shall . . ." She hesitated, scouring her brain for whatever schoolroom facts remained regarding British common law. "Or I shall have you—and Jacques—before the magistrate for . . . for abduction."

Milread's reaction was predictable and deeply, *deeply* gratifying. Her eyes widened and her square jaw dropped. "Have Jack before the law, will ye?"

But before Claudia could bask in the satisfaction of having cowed the formidable Milread, a gale of laughter broke forth, sending the maid staggering back. "Ye . . . take *him* . . . Och, but that's rich. If ye only kent . . ."

Above all things, Claudia detested being laughed at and yet the unseemly cackling did have one highly desirable outcome: Milread had backed off the bag.

Seizing her opportunity, Claudia swooped. Slight she might be and the nearest thing to starved, but desperation seemed to steady her head even as it lent wings to her feet. Bag in hand, cloak draped over one arm, she yanked open the door and sped down the hallway.

The inn was a small and relatively simple structure, the upper floor ending in a set of crooked wooden stairs that, judging by the muffled conversations drifting up, led below to the taproom. The doors to the other chambers were closed save for one. The sound of heavy footfalls closing in prompted her to take her chances and dart inside. She found herself in a storeroom of sorts. Heart skipping beats, she squeezed between a spinning wheel and a linen press just as Milread poked her capped head inside. Burrowed into her hiding place, Claudia held her breath, waiting. After a moment's hesitation, Milread faced about and bounded down the corridor toward the stairs.

Claudia held back, counted to three, and then rose up. Cobwebs and dust motes fell like snowflakes from the folds of her cloak as she dashed out into the hallway and down the stairs, skidding to a halt at the bottom landing.

The taproom she stepped off into was a far tamer place than that which she'd left, the earlier crowd having dwindled to a handful who hovered about the bar, nursing their pints. Barring the coachman, whose gaze she avoided, the company looked harmless enough, ancient even. Certainly a tall, virile, flame-haired young Scotsman would be hard-pressed to hide out among them. Which must mean he had left.

Merde. Hoping he might still be in the vicinity, Claudia made a beeline for the bar, where she threw herself, luggage and all, on the polished wood. Addressing herself to the pudgy, bald man standing behind it, she opened her mouth . . . and promptly forgot every English word she'd ever known. *"Où est Jacques?"* Where is Jack?

Frustrated when her question was met with blank stares and a caustic comment from the coachman on the subject of "bleedin' furreners," she used her hands to sketch what, if failing to do full justice to that magnificent physique, might at least convey a general sense of height and proportion.

"And he has red hair," she added, in English this time, then looked about and saw that so did several of them, at least what hair they had left.

"She maun mean Jack," the innkeeper announced, vaulting his voice to address the gawkers gathering about her. Gesturing to the main door leading to the yard outside, he added, "Ye're out o' luck, lassie, for he left no five minutes past."

"He is gone." Whispering the words, Claudia felt a leaden weight lay anchor in her chest. Until now she hadn't realized just how very much she'd been counting on having the handsome Scotsman accompany her.

Grinning from ear to ear, the innkeeper answered, "Aye, he's gone and 'tis glad o' it ye should be. 'Tis a dangerous thing tae tangle wi' Jack Ketch, lassie, for ye're like as no tae find your pretty toes tappin' the wind."

Toes tapping the wind? Claudia opened her mouth to unravel this latest bit of foolishness when, from behind her, the coachman bellowed, "Maun have finished his *business* and meant tae be on his way."

"Oh aye," chimed in the old man standing to Claudia's left, his leathery face splitting into a broad smile of few teeth and generous gums. "He maun be a quick worker, our Jack, but no verra thorough if the wench is comin' abeggin' a'ready."

Anger spiking and head swimming, Claudia didn't notice the coachman creeping up behind her until she felt his sour breath scoring her cheek. One large paw groping her buttocks, he pulled her hard against him. "Only come wi' me on the morrow, sweeting, and I'll show ye just how *thorough* a shaggin' age and experience can give."

"You are . . . disgusting," she sputtered, drawing fresh guffaws from the group as she tried in vain to pull away. "Let me go."

There was no mistaking the threat behind the boast just as there was no mistaking the sharp bulge knifing into her backside. Panicked, she tried again to shove him away but pinned between her tormentor and the bar and hemmed in on all sides by the men gathered about, it was no use.

In the throes of her flailing, a woman's voice called out, "Leave her be, clot-head."

Twisting her head about, Claudia saw Milread, red-faced and huffing, entering through the small door at the back of the room. Arms and hips working, she shoved her way toward the bar. Reaching it, she used her elbow to deal the coachman a sharp poke in the ribs. He fell back a step and Claudia lost no time in slipping free.

"Merci," Claudia murmured, turning about on shaking legs and then filling her compressed lungs with a deep steadying breath.

Milread responded with a small nod and reached down to retrieve Claudia's cloak, which had fallen to the floor along with her traveling bag.

"Ye heard 'em, Jack's gone so ye maun as well come back upstairs. I'll bring your supper up and then the bath." Her brow furrowed and she added, "If ye're still sure ye'll want tae risk lung fever, that is?"

A meal, a bed, and, Sacred Virgin, a bath—all could be Claudia's for one blissful, restful night. After what had just transpired, she was even more in need of respite than she'd been before. In the midst of battling temptation, she felt a hard, angry gaze raking over her. She shifted her regard from the maid to the far end of the bar where the coachman hunched, glaring at her from over the rim of his raised tankard. Meeting that unrepentant stare, she acknowledged that her possibilities for safe transport to Linlithgow had just dwindled to one: she must find Jack Ketch and convince him to take her the rest of the way.

Turning back to Milread, she accepted her damp cloak and then reached out to take her traveling bag. "My apologies, *mademoiselle,* but first I must find your *Monsieur* Ketch."

Handing over the bag, the maid's mouth dropped open. She started to speak but mindful of the precious minutes ticking away, Claudia hurried past her toward the door.

"But keep them warm for me, *s'il vous plait.* The bath especially. It may be that after I find him, we will return."

Armed with her rescuer's full name, Claudia darted out the inn's main door to the yard outside. Miracle of miracles, the rain had ceased and though it was cold enough to congeal the edges of the puddles that lingered, there was the specter of a sun in the gray-washed sky above.

One of its wan rays struck the black hulk of the coach, springs keening as it canted back and forth in the gusting wind. Eager to put it and her recent encounter with its driver behind her, Claudia veered off the main path—and in doing so caught sight of her quarry leading his horse out from the stable, his enormous dog trotting a yard or so ahead.

Walking Beelzebub onto the path toward the road, Jack was oblivious to the excitement his appearance had stirred at the opposite end of the yard. He would have been on his way ere now but, exhausted though he was, he hadn't been able to resist stopping to examine the broken coach wheel. He might not be a proper blacksmith, but he'd put in his share of hours at the forge, having apprenticed with his stepfather Tam until Callum had taken a sudden interest in the smithy, effectively ousting him from his place. Not that Jack had minded. The release from his obligation had been the answer to a prayer, for though he'd labored long and hard his heart had never been in the work.

Since the age of nine, he'd meant to be a hangman.

There was skill in it as there was in most trades, but beyond that there was science and a certain innate knack. The touch, his mentor, Seumas, had called the latter, something you were either born with or no. Jack had the touch and he kent the science and though the honing of the technique was a never-ended thing, he prided himself that he was well on his way to one day standing at the forefront of his profession.

And yet earlier in the taproom, looking up into the Frenchwoman's canny violet-blue eyes, he'd felt ashamed to own who he was and what he did.

Daft to let a stranger shame him, he who'd shrugged off the insults and curses of those whom he'd kent all his days. He didn't even have her name and likely never would, and yet in that brief interlude before she'd fainted she'd managed to muddle his thoughts, set his body on fire, and turn his very world on its ear.

And so at first when he heard the husky silk of her voice calling to him from across the path, he told himself it must be a trick of the creaking carriage. Or rather his own foolish fancy, for hadn't he perhaps stayed on to tinker with that wee wheel in the hope of just such a "chance" encounter?

His heart skipping beats, he halted and raised a hesitant hand in greeting. "Hallo."

The Frenchwoman returned his greeting, all but dancing on the toes of her tiny booted feet. "Jack Ketch. Monsieur Ketch!" Waving wildly, she started toward him.

His heart dipped even as his temper spiked. Ketch, the common moniker for executioner, and a foul insult it was too, for the real Jack Ketch had been a ham-handed blunderer, a drunkard who'd been known to mount the scaffold soused as David's sow.

Skill, science, knack—Jack had them all and in abundance. He'd not let the French lassie, nor whomever it was who'd put her on to this mischief, make him bow his head in shame again. He fisted his hand on the leather strap and turned his horse toward the road.

"M*onsieur Ketch!" Willing her spinning head to settle,* Claudia used what breath remained to call out again, "Monsieur Jacques Ketch!"

Although Monsieur Ketch appeared unhurried, one of his

long strides was the equal of several of Claudia's. Was it her imagination or did those broad shoulders of his stiffen? Either way, he kept on. Despite his size, he moved with a silent swiftness that brought to mind the gazelles that once had populated the park of Château du Marmac. At this rate, he would reach the road in no time at all.

But Claudia was determined. She hoisted her skirts and cut across the field, sloshing through mud and knee-high wet grass to reach him. Persistence at last paid off, and she caught up with him at the signpost marking the entrance to the main road. Rounding his horse's wide rump, she fell into running step beside him.

Over his dog's frenzied barking, she shouted, "*Monsieur, arrêtez!* Halt!" With her free hand she reached out and caught hold of his forearm, so that he must either stop or drag her along with him.

He swung about then, with such force that Claudia felt her feet leave the paving stones. "Dinna touch me!"

Holding on for dear life, she could feel his strength, his tension, pulsing beneath the pads of her fingers. For all that he was a peasant with no better occupation than to loll away his afternoon in a tavern, the man was tightly wound as a clock, his big body held rigid as a suit of armor.

"I'll no stand to be mocked." Facing her down with fierce, smoldering eyes, he shook her off. "And you can bloody well go back inside and tell Alistair, or whomever it was sent you, that I said to go to the Devil." Not even his Scots burr could blunt the steel edging each and every word.

Flummoxed, Claudia dropped her hand and backed up beneath his glowering gaze, sorting through the recent chaos for what she might have said or done to offend. Other than that unfortunate quip about open mouths admitting flies, which had seemed harmless enough at the time, she could think of nothing. Nonetheless, the past seven years as Phillippe du Marmac's mistress had taught her to heed a man's anger *before* the storm broke forth.

Accordingly, edging her gaze up to that lean, strong-boned face, she made sure to paint on the small, sultry half-smile that had charmed Phillippe from his temper a time or two. "Mocked? *Mais non, monsieur,* why do you say such a thing? And no one sent me. I only wish to thank you for your gallantry, first in rescuing me from that man most horrible and then in securing me a room. Why, *monsieur,* you are kindness itself."

"And you are?"

A bloodred beam from the dying sun struck his crown, and Claudia saw that what passed for red hair in the dimly lit taproom was in fact copper threaded with rich, brilliant gold. In the midst of her plotting, she found herself imagining what it would be like to feather her fingers through those soft, sunkissed strands.

Reminded that he awaited her answer, she held out her hand. "Claudia Valemont. Mademoiselle Claudia Valemont. *Miss* as you say in English."

He showed no sign of taking either her offered hand or the broad hint but instead stared down to her other hand, weighted with the portmanteau. "What more do ye want with me, Mistress Valemont? Is the room no to your liking?" Sensing it was too soon, she withdrew her hand and opened her mouth to demur, but he silenced her with a look that seared through pretense to her soul's truth. "Oh aye, ye want something, dinna trouble yourself to deny it, for I'm no such a wee fool as to believe ye left behind food and fire only to thank me."

She shook her head, biting back a wince as pain sang through her temples. "It is true that I wish to thank you but also I come to beg of you a *bienfait* . . . a boon. I must find my way to Linlithgow. It lies just west of—"

"I ken it. What I dinna ken is why you canna wait upon the mail coach. Is it no good enough for ye?"

Sharp though his words were, his gaze had softened. Claudia saw then that his eyes were amber, not brown, and rimmed in long, thick lashes that any woman would envy. Tipped in dusky gold, they brushed the strong, high planes of his Viking cheeks, a startling contrast to the rawboned masculinity of his features.

Distracted as she was, it took her a full moment to formulate the lie. "A position, *monsieur,* in a dressmaker's shop. I was expected a week ago. If I do not arrive soon, I fear it will be given to another." Unnerved by his steely stare, her shoulders and neck already aching with the effort of looking up to him, she asked, "If not to Linlithgow, will you escort me so far as Edinburgh?"

He looked her up and down, a slow, steady perusal that made her painfully aware of the dusty footprint fronting her shabby cloak and the too tight gown bodice beneath it. Though she hadn't blushed since the age of twelve, when she'd walked in upon her mother and Maman's latest lover *en flagrante delicto* on the satin sheets, Claudia felt shame's heat sparking her cheeks. *It is the burn of the wind,* she told herself, but deep inside she knew the cause to be the Scotsman. Accustomed though she was to male attention, to poets lauding the sweetness of her angel face and the perfection of her rose-tipped breasts, Monsieur Ketch's steely stare made her limbs tremble and her breath catch.

The pity of it was that, unlike her, he did not seem to greatly care for what he saw. Even her breasts, which earlier she'd caught him ogling in the taproom, now merited little more than a cool glance.

At length he asked, "And why should I do that, mistress?"

It was, she had to admit if only to herself, a perfectly reasonable question. Cheeks burning, she fixed her shamefaced gaze on his chest, or rather on the vee of golden hair peaking out from the neck of his collarless shirt, and admitted, "I have no money to pay, but I am willing . . . if you should want . . . my body, *monsieur,* until we reach the end of our journey, you may use me as you wish."

Monsieur Ketch heaved a heavy breath and then slowly blew it out, stretching the fabric of his linen shirt to its limit as it fought to cover a rippling sea of muscle from pectorals to abdomen. "Nay, I willna."

Thin and disheveled though she was, it had never occurred to her that he might refuse. Closer to outrage than to shame, she shot her gaze back to his face. "*Non!* But why . . . why not?"

He gave a sharp shake of his head. "I've no taste for further travel and no liking for your terms." Hatless as he was, he touched his forelock in the briefest of salutes. "I bid you good eve, mistress." He tugged the horse's reins and whistled for his dog, who'd dallied from the path to chase after a squirrel.

Panic plowed into Claudia's empty stomach with the force of a man's fist. She'd thought in relinquishing the contents of her jewelry chest to the smuggler who'd borne her away from France that she'd shed the last of her pride, but she'd been wrong, so very wrong.

Hating the desperate, craven creature she'd become, she

nonetheless caught at his arm. "I beg of you, monsieur, do not leave me alone in this desolate place."

His high brow folded into a frown but the eyes beneath were shot with pain. "My name's Campbell, no Ketch. Jack Campbell." Above his open shirt collar, his Adam's apple rose and fell as he pulled a hard swallow, bringing into prominence the cording of muscle that bridged neck and shoulder. "And mark me when I say that I'll no be taking you to Linlithgow or Edinburgh . . . or anywhere else."

For once stunned beyond words, Claudia slackened her grip on Monsieur Campbell's sleeve, and then her hand fell away altogether. There was a charged moment when time seemed to grind to a standstill and they stared at each other as if one or both of them meant to say more but was at a loss as to what "more" might be. And then the invisible clock resumed its ticking, and Monsieur Campbell yanked on his horse's reins and turned abruptly about. Watching him lead the bay onto the rutted road, wolf dog trotting in tow, Claudia could only wonder if she hadn't imagined that he'd ever hesitated at all.

For some reason that prospect depressed her almost as much as his leaving and for the first time since setting foot on foreign soil, she surrendered to the hot press of tears. Drop by drop, the warm saline splashed her face as earlier the rain had done, drowning her vision of both man and beasts in one large, fathomless pool.

Standing weeping by the roadside suddenly struck her as too pathetic to be borne and so she hiked up her skirts and started walking. Somehow she found herself on the path branching back to the stable. It seemed as good or as poor a course as any; hungry and tired though she was, she couldn't bear going back inside the inn just yet, not with the evidence of her distress marking her cheeks and swelling her eyes. Coming up on the stable, she sagged against its stone façade. Her back against the damp stones, she turned teary eyes heavenward to watch the setting of the sun, already reduced to a demilune on the horizon. A moment more and then the last sliver of amber orb fell into the murky bank of encroaching night. For some morose reason, that golden yellow brought to mind Monsieur Campbell's eyes. Like the sun, he had disappeared beyond her reach but unlike that guidepost, he'd not be returning to greet her on the morrow.

She shivered at the thought and pulled her still damp cloak more tightly about her. The wind had kicked up since she'd left the shelter of the inn. Perhaps she really ought to go back inside, brave the passage through the taproom one last time and have a hot supper and then an even hotter bath. Afterwards she could tuck herself in between the warming pan–treated sheets and, for the night at least, indulge in the luxury of forgetting all her woes.

She was on the verge of doing so, of admitting defeat, when the beautiful simplicity of it struck her—the structure at her back was a *stable.* And not just any stable but one belonging to a coaching inn. As such, it housed not only the guests' horses but also those that would serve as fresh teams for the sundry coaches that passed through. And how glad Claudia would have been to bide here for the night and then, rested and refreshed, set out on the next northbound passenger coach, for to continue on with the mail coach had become unthinkable.

But though thanks to Jack Campbell she had a night's food and lodging paid for and waiting, she still hadn't a copper to her name. On the morrow, she would find herself stranded and alone. Unless . . .

The broad-backed bay she'd seen Monsieur Ketch—Campbell—lead away a few moments before had looked sturdy and surefooted. Surely more such able-bodied creatures were to be found within? Resolve renewed, she sniffed back the last of her tears, shoved away from the wall, and marched up to the planked stable door.

Yes, she was still prepared to walk to Linlithgow if she must . . . but she'd really much rather ride.

We often meet our destiny when taking steps to avoid it.

—Jean De La Fontaine

Idjut. Gomeral. Clot-head.

Too fidgety to sit in the saddle, too busy berating himself to mind the wetness splashing up from the rutted bog of a road onto his legs, Jack walked his horse the two miles or so home, Elf keeping pace beside him. Bachelor though he was and always would be, the cottage he'd built with his own two hands was more than a place to hang his hat or lay his head. Bordered by a small copse on one side and a trickle of a stream on the other, with a backdrop of softly rolling hills just beyond, it was his haven from the world's madness. Most days all it took was one glimpse of the thatched roof and beloved whitewashed walls, of the cobblestone path that wound through the boxwood-bordered front yard to the welcoming arch of scrubbed oak door, for him to feel his soul ease and his demons fade into oblivion.

But not this night, he allowed, opening the gate and leading Beelzebub across the wet grass to the small, sloped-roof byre backing the house. Once inside, not even giving the horse a thorough rubdown, his failsafe for settling an unquiet mind, could salve his conscience's stinging censure nor put to bed the tormenting inner voice that proclaimed in no uncertain terms: Ye've done wrong.

French and only just arrived from the bloody tumult of a toppled monarchy, the lass, Mistress Valemont, would have had no notion that calling him "Ketch" amounted to lobbing the foulest of insults. To her the moniker must have sounded as good a

Scots surname as Campbell or any other. Surely she'd no be so foolish as to purposely insult him and then ask him to take her to Linlithgow.

My body, monsieur, *until we reach the end of our journey, you may use me as you wish.*

Puir wee lassie, whatever it was that drew her to Linlithgow—and he wasna convinced that a position in a dressmaker's shop was the whole of it—she must be desperate indeed to offer up her lovely self in order to get there. That for the span of a heartbeat he'd actually been tempted—sorely tempted—to take her up on it was certain to be a sin but hardly the most grievous wrong he'd done her. Far worse, he felt sure, was giving in to his hurt pride and abandoning her at the inn gate. Defenseless, alone, and fair near to fainting, she would be an easy mark for the likes of Callum or anyone else who meant to use her ill. He could only hope—pray—that she'd seen sense and gone back inside before any harm could befall her.

As for himself, surely the Lord Jesus and Mother Mary and the whole heavenly host of angels and archangels, martyrs, and saints, must be frowning down upon him even now, shaking their haloed heads in celestial contempt at not only his sinning thoughts but also his unforgivable lack of gallantry. But nothing they could say or do could begin to compete with the very real loathing he felt for himself.

Resting his forehead against Beelzebub's smooth side, which even now put him in mind of the sleek ebony of the Frenchwoman's hair, he closed his eyes and prayed. For forgiveness at having come closer than he'd ever thought to come to taking carnal advantage of a woman's fear and weakness. For the willpower to put from his thoughts the Frenchwoman's flashing eyes, saucy smile, and comely body, the image of which even now crowded his thoughts and caused his wretched flesh to harden and heat.

But mostly he prayed for Claudia Valemont and for the chance, should their paths cross again, to make amends to her. For whatever her real reason in setting out on her own for Linlithgow, she was in need of help, God's help, indeed.

C*laudia had learned to ride for the same reason she'd done* many things—because Phillippe had wished it. Even so, the rebel within her had balked against the enforced lessons and she'd retained little beyond the rudiments of keeping her seat. Certainly she'd never before saddled her own horse, mounted without the assistance of a groom, or ridden astride. And yet standing on the threshold of the stable, she acknowledged she was about to do all three.

But then she'd never before stolen her mount, either.

Fumbling in the darkness, she followed the smells of leather and saddle oil to the tack room. It was dark but someone had thought to leave a lantern alight. Standing on tiptoe, she took it down from its peg along with one of the saddles. Shouldering the latter, she started back down the aisle between stalls, stopping at the one nearest the stable door where she'd set down her valise.

The stall gate opened on shrieking hinges. Teeth clenched, she pushed her way inside. The beast, a swaybacked draft horse, lifted its head as she approached, nipping at her hair and slathering the side of her face. Armed with neither carrot nor sugar cone, she pushed the burrowing muzzle to the side and reached up to lead the horse out toward the mounting block. To her horror, the action set off a jingle that, to her sensitized ears, sounded like the pealing from the bell tower of Notre Dame. Feeling her way in the semidarkness, she found still more bells woven into the braided mane.

Zut, alors! Just her luck, she must have happened upon a tinker's horse.

As if picking up on her tension, the beast balked. Nearly dropping the lantern, Claudia leapt clear of a kicking hoof. Blowing the loose hair out of her eyes, she edged forward to try again.

A loud creaking had her whipping about but too late. The door to the stable was thrown open, admitting a beacon of light and the sudden shout of, "Halt, thief!"

Heart flying to her throat, she raised up a hand to shield her eyes from the sudden rush of blinding light.

"As ye value yer life, step away from that horse."

Squinting, she counted five men, six if she were to include a sleepy-eyed ostler, standing just outside the stall door. At least one among them, the innkeeper, was armed. Hearing the telltale click of a pistol hammer being cocked brought to mind the bloody, battered bodies of the pigeons and morning doves

Phillippe had loved to "hunt." The image of her body equally bloodied and battered and lying limp on the straw-sprinkled boards threatened to send her legs folding beneath her.

"Please, *messieurs,* there is some mistake." Futile though it was, she backed up, lifting her free hand to ward them off. "I have done nothing wrong. I am no thief."

But it was a lie, and their eyes, hard as stones as they advanced on her, told her they meant to show no mercy.

And worse even than their hands taking bruising hold of her arms, of having to stand by and watch as they rifled her things, was that in her heart of hearts Claudia knew it, too.

D*espite being seized and then tossed into a prison cell to* pass the night on a flea-ridden pallet unfit for a dog, Claudia somehow managed to keep up the illusion that the events of the past four-and-twenty hours were all part of an intricate and truly awful dream. At any time she would awaken to the bucking of the mail coach, to Madame Smith's snoring and Monsieur Brumble's hand insinuating itself on her knee.

Not paradise, by any stretch of the imagination, but not a gaol cell in the Selkirk tollbooth, either.

It wasn't until the following morning when her gaoler arrived to lead her from her cell that reality struck in the heavy shudder of shackles being clapped about her wrists. Staring down at the thick bands of solid iron encasing her wrists, Claudia felt a frozen, fixed horror start to overtake her. She'd seen first her lover and then her mother bound thus and led away and in both cases they'd been dead within the week. And so in Claudia's mind shackled hands were inextricably linked to the guillotine, to the mob's pitiless roar, to blood and pain and death. Even though she doubted they meant to go so far as to cut off her head, she couldn't seem to leave off shaking—or to take that first seemingly huge step over the cell threshold.

"Come on wi' ye, I've no got all the day."

Her gaoler, a whiskey-breathed, hairy skeleton of a man known as Wallis, jerked her outside. The sharp reek of urine and despair hit her in the face like a wave as they cut across the semicircular courtyard; the din of prisoners' spoons clanking against metal bars and hoarse shouts of "Let me out" followed her to the narrow flight of curved stairs. Single file they started up, the gaoler poking her along, cursing at her when she hesitated. The slimy stones seemed to close in with each halting step; halfway up, both her teeth and knees had taken to knocking together like balls on a billiard table.

At the top, a second guard materialized to throw home the bolt, and the iron-studded door leading to the great world beyond the prison walls miraculously opened. They emerged into the muddy patch of prison yard, and Claudia gulped down the blessed sweetness of the rain-soaked air and blinked against the almost blinding haze of sun breaking through the cloud-soaked sky. A nettle shrub grazed the back of her hand as they came up on a lych-gate, and she fixed her mind on the slight sting to keep the fearful numbness at bay.

She'd been expecting the pillory at best, the scaffold at worst, so when she emerged on the other side to see a square wattle-and-daub structure instead, she relaxed a fraction. From the outside it looked benign, charming even, with a clutch of ivy running along its façade, and the whole bordered by hedge, the cheerful orange-red berries of which still clung to life. It wasn't until they drew up to the front steps that the rumble of raised voices from within caused Claudia's heart to quail and her feet to falter.

The gaoler's ham-handed shove at her back sent her stumbling through the square doorway. Pausing to regain her balance, she looked up into sudden, dead silence. Ahead of her was a gallery filled with rough-hewn benches, a narrow aisle cutting through the center to the platform fronting the room.

"Ga' on wi' ye, then," came the impatient voice at her back. "Them be waitin'."

Heart quaking, she started down the aisle, the focal point for row upon row of scowling, stiff-backed Scots, their hard stares boring into her and their communal silence drumming her ears as if it were the most deafening of dins. Sprawled at the end of one bench was her attacker from the tavern. He turned his bruised face up to hers and a gloating smile twisted his thin lips.

Mon Dieu, je regrette . . .

Her armpits damp with sweat, she reached the front of the chamber. Two short steps led up to the platform where a lean-faced man of middling years and garbed in sober black, presumably the judge, presided over a polished oak writing desk. A large leather tome lay on the desk before him along with a wooden gavel resting to his right. On the step below him stood a wizened old man, knobby knees and shrunken shanks visible beneath the folds of his faded kilt. One of the two draughts players from the tavern, she thought, but before she could decide he came forward to reclaim her from the gaoler, who then faded into the background. Laying a palsied hand upon her arm, he steered her over to a raised wooden box, a set of three wooden steps leading inside. Set at an angle, it faced the judge and afforded the prisoner standing within a peripheral view of the gallery. The prisoner's dock, she thought it was called in English, and her stomach gave a treacherous heave.

"Mind yer step," he counseled in a rusted voice and then released her to open the gated door.

Holding it for her, he mumbled some incoherent phrase, which she took as an invitation to enter. She did and then turned to face the front of the room, flinching as the gate whined closed behind her. *Boxed in on all sides,* she thought, and felt the bile blaze a trail from stomach to throat. She gripped the bar with both hobbled hands, the wood worn smooth and slipping beneath her clammy palms, and turned her gaze on the judge. A smart crack of his gavel called the assembly to order. Over the buzzing filling her ears, she strained to hear as the crime for which she stood accused was read aloud.

Returning to his post, the old man unfurled a scrolled writ and, with obvious self-importance, began to read aloud, "She who stands afore us is one Claudia Valemont, late o' Paris, France, and accused o' the crime o' horse thievery, Your Worship."

On the word "thievery," panic plowed into her abdomen like a fist. Not only did she stand accused as a thief but, *Mon Dieu,* she really was one! She had stolen that horse or at least had given her best effort to doing so. Under English law, was one still considered to be a thief even if the object of theft was never quite . . . thieved?

Mon Dieu, je regrette . . .

Prayer fell off in favor of ticking off the possible punishments. Dunking and trial by fire were reserved for accused witches, the pillory for lesser crimes, such as lying and scandal mongering. Branding, yes, that was the usual punishment for thieves, in France at least. Most often on the upper arm but sometimes the mark of shame was burned into the center of the forehead instead. Shaking, Claudia reached up and touched her fingertips to the smooth expanse of clammy brow.

Mon Dieu, je regrette . . .

Based on what little she recalled of her governess' lessons on English common law, she didn't think the accused was permitted to speak on his or her own behalf. Just as well, really, for even if the English words were to miraculously find their way to her tongue, she wouldn't know what to say, how to frame her problem. On the one hand, revealing her noble parentage was her trump card, her best and perhaps only chance of avoiding whatever punishment they meant to mete out to her. Bastard though she was, noble blood—the Aberdaire blood—ran in her veins just as surely as if she'd been born of a union blessed by the Holy Church. And yet illegitimate and half French, her welcome in her father's house was tenuous at best, her place by no means assured. To arrive as a convicted felon, a common horse thief no less, all but guaranteed that His Lordship would send her packing.

And then what will become of me?

The future loomed too large a concept to even get her muddled mind around; better to focus on the present and whatever it was that the bailiff's rusted voice was proclaiming.

"Thievery of a man's horse, indeed of any property judged tae be o' greater worth than five shillings, is tae be hangit by the neck 'til dead."

The room exploded into a cacophany of gibberish; bright, curious gazes fixed themselves upon the spectacle of Claudia's sweating face. Death by hanging! Could it be she'd outwitted a bloodthirsty Parisian mob, survived a perilous sea crossing in a smuggler's sloop, and crossed league after league of British soil only to come to this?

Digging her nails into the smooth wood, she allowed she now had no choice but to surrender her future in order to save her life. "You cannot hang me," she cried out, pushing the words over the dry lump in her throat. "My father is a very great man, a nobleman. An *earl,* as you say in English. And Scottish," she added on afterthought, hoping that alone might weigh the odds in her favor.

She'd expected stunned silence but instead ribald laughter exploded from the gallery. "Och, but dinna be sae modest, dearie. Faith but ye maun be the daughter o' King Geordie himself come tae Scotland for a wee goodwill visit," shrilled one squat matron.

Applause and more mocking laughter greeted this statement, encouraging yet another to shout, "Aye, a royal princess indeed, though wi' all the taxes the Sassenaches levy us, ye'd think she'd maun be able t'afford a decent dress."

Claudia started to reply, to explain, but the gavel drowned out her rasping and called the room to order. "Silence! Silence I say." Addressing himself to Claudia, the judge inquired in an almost gentle tone, "Have ye any people in Scotland who might be summoned to stand witness for your character? If ye've a father, earl or no, 'twould behoove ye to give up his name."

A bead of sweat struck her rib and streaked down her side like a tear. It was hopeless; it was over. They thought she was a madwoman. Nothing she said now would make any difference. Better to accept her fate and die with honor as her mother had, as had so many of her countrymen, than to beg and plead and grovel only to meet the same wretched end.

Head bowed, she said, "I cannot claim the protection of a name that has never been mine to own."

The judge heaved an audible sigh. Shaking his head, he asked of the gallery, "Is there no one to bear witness for this puir wretched woman?"

There was a pregnant pause and then he struck the gavel once, twice . . .

"Hold! I will speak for her."

Heads whipped about and necks craned for a glimpse of the owner of the deeply timbered masculine voice. Claudia joined them, stretching her neck to peer back over her left shoulder.

She caught her breath, for it was none other than Jack Ketch—Campbell—breaking free of the latecomers crowding the back of the chamber to stride forward. Muffled murmurs marked his progress from aisle to platform steps. Passing by the prisoner's dock, his gaze brushed over Claudia, and she felt the warmth of those amber eyes holding hers like a consoling caress.

The judge hefted his gavel again and cracked it once, then twice, calling the assembly to order. On the third strike, the roar dropped to a low buzz. "Jack Campbell has the floor." To Jack, he asked, "What have ye to say, Jack Campbell, that might be brought to bear on this puir wretched woman's behalf?"

Looking Mistress Valemont's way, albeit briefly, had been a mistake, Jack allowed. He'd meant to offer solace, some unspoken reassurance that all would be well, yet the sight of her, pale-faced, hollow-eyed, and visibly trembling had threatened to undo him, tearing at his heart to the point of physical pain. Gone was the braw lassie who had so boldly made her way through the taproom but the day before. In her eyes he saw that she was counting on him to save her—clearly this was his God-given chance to make amends—and yet in his heart he knew that she'd meant to steal that horse. What could he possibly say?

Feeling the assembly's gazes boring into his back, hearing the shuffling feet and prodding coughs, he filled his lungs with a deep breath. Exhaling slowly, he willed his image of the crowd to dissolve until only three people remained in the room: the magistrate, Duncan MacGregor; himself; and Claudia Valemont.

Calmer now, inexorably more grounded, he began, "No an hour before the *alleged* theft, Mistress Valemont was set upon by one of our lads drinking at the tavern." Aware of Callum watching from the back of the room, he continued, "'Tis certain he meant no real harm, but bein' foreign and no used to our rough country ways, the lass dropped to the floor like a stone and cracked her head."

Duncan would, of course, have heard of the brawl in the tavern. "Ye mean to say she maun have addled her pate?" He cast a long, assessing look in Claudia's direction.

Not daring to risk a second glance, at least not until she was out of danger, Jack kept his gaze fixed on Duncan's stern countenance and nodded. "Aye, Your Worship, I ken it to be a distinct possibility. Ye've but to mark the great bruise on her face to see how hard hit she was."

Frowning, Duncan looked beyond Jack to address the floor. "There are witnesses who can substantiate this claim?"

Jack didn't hesitate. "Aye, there are. Milread the tavern wench for one."

Milread popped up from her hastily taken seat on one of the benches at back. "Aye, 'tis true. She was out cold for nigh on a half hour."

Jack turned partway around and shot her a grateful smile, not only for speaking up but for earlier having left the tavern to come and fetch him. If it hadn't been for her, news of Mistress Valemont's plight might not have reached him until she was well and truly beyond his help.

His gaze picked out the innkeeper and his smile fell. "Alistair can bear witness as well."

Beneath his powdered peruke, Duncan's lifted brow creased like a washboard. "Alistair, this is true?"

The innkeeper had been keeping his silence but now he rose to stand. Fiddling with his drooping stock, he admitted, "Aye, it is," although he looked none too pleased about it. A raucous lot Callum and his cronies might be, they were also his best customers, spending nigh on every coin they earned in the taproom. "I, er, dinna see as it had any bearing on the case, Yer Worship."

"Did ye no?" Shifting his hawklike gaze back to Jack, Duncan said, "As lord high executioner for the Crown, ye maun come into contact with all manner of rogues and scalawags, is this not so?"

From the prisoner's dock, a gasp sounded and though he fought the urge to turn about, Jack felt the sharpness of it like a knife in his heart. *Well, at least she knows now I'm no the blacksmith,* he thought, then turned his attention to answering the question. "Aye, milord, 'tis true enough. Before they can set out to meet their Maker, they must by necessity keep company with me."

A salvo of raucous laughter fired about the hall. Jack felt the vibration like a wave breaking over his back, but he held his shoulders straight and his gaze on the judge.

Order restored, Duncan continued, "And is it your opinion then, your *professional* opinion, that Mistress Valemont is one among their ranks?"

"Nay, milord, I dinna ken her to be such as they. As to whether she meant to 'borrow' the tinker's wee horse or no, I canna say, but I can say for certain that she wasna in her right mind at the time. I had occasion to meet up with her again just before she went inside the stable, and she struck me as being verra"—he turned halfway about to spear Claudia with a warning look—"confused."

"Dinna heed him, he's lyin'." Amidst the crowd's shocked murmurs, Callum stormed his way to the front of the room.

Scowling, Duncan cracked his gavel. "Silence, Callum

McBride. Ye'll have your say in a bit if ye must, but for now ye'll hold your peace or hold up in the tollbooth, as ye will."

Scalp prickling, Jack turned to face his brother, who stood a few paces behind him. Hazel collided with amber as the brothers locked gazes in a silent contest of wills. From birth they'd been as different as night and day, as moon and sun, and yet always, always there'd been this . . . connection.

Calling on it now, Jack said, *Dinna make me do it.*

A second later, Callum's hazel gaze flashed the angry retort, *Ye wouldna dare.*

Jack hesitated and then shot back with, *Will ye test me, then?* A second's pause and then, turning away from his half-brother to Duncan, he opened his mouth to give voice to the words that would signal the end of a decade's truce.

"I dinna ken how Callum can speak for the lass's state of mind, as he and the lads took their leave long before either myself or the lady. And Callum in particular was no feeling verra well at the time . . ." He halted to let the impact of his words sink in.

Snickers sounded about the gallery, for Callum, like his da, was well known to have a taste for the drink.

"Silence!" Duncan cracked his gavel and the din petered. He shifted his fierce gaze to Callum, whose face had flushed a deep scarlet to rival that of the berries outside. "What say ye to that, Callum McBride?"

"Aye, I'd left but I heard tell—"

"'Tis what ye saw or didna see that concerns us here, no hearsay, and so that will be all." Addressing the room at large, he said, "In light of the evidence and that Mistress Valemont is a stranger to both our land and our ways, she shall be set free."

But while the judge and crowd were content to let the matter lie, Callum was not. Face contorted, he cried out, "Ye canna mean tae let her go! No only did she steal the horse but she tried tae kill me. Cut me wi' her wee dagger just here." He tore at the front of his shirt, sending a button flying off onto the floor, and twisted his shoulder to display the thin line of freshly scabbed wound.

From the prisoner's docket, a French-accented voice called out, "He lies! He seized me, tried to force me to leave with him. I asked him to release me but he would not, and so—"

"Silence!" Duncan called out. "Under English law, a prisoner may speak only through his representative."

Looking well pleased, Callum pulled his shirt back in place. "I dinna ken ye'd call it askin'. Cursed a blue streak is more like it and then drew her wee knife and had at me."

Gaze narrowed, Duncan regarded him with obvious disdain. "But ye admit to laying hands on her wi'out her permission? And you were in your cups, were ye no?"

Callum shrugged his thin shoulders. "Och, the lads and I maybe had a few rounds but no so many that I was drunk, mind. 'Twas her that approached me, bold as brass, arse switchin' and bubbies bared for anyone who cared to look. I'm in the right, I am. And I'll take my case tae the assizes if ye'll no try it here."

And then she will surely hang, Jack thought, and a shudder shot through him.

Duncan looked at Callum with cold dislike. "In light of this new 'evidence' I canna verra well set the lass free. But," he added, tamping down Callum's gloating smile with a crafty one of his own, "given that it may be she's weak in the mind, I canna in good conscience condemn her to be hangit, either. Instead I remand her to the custody of Jack Campbell for six months' indenture."

Stunned, Jack stood stock-still as Pol unfurled a sheepskin scroll and read out the terms of Claudia's indenture. Mistress Valemont was to labor for the common good, undertaking "cheerfully and wi' a willing heart," those tasks set forth by her keeper. As such, it fell to Jack to administer "physical correction" once each week. A leather tawse was acceptable provided the strap was sufficiently lightweight and broad so as not to incur unintended injury. A rod made of birch and stripped clean might do as well. Either way, the instrument of punishment was to be applied to the prisoner's backside and not to exceed twenty strokes, barring the truly grievous offense in which case a half dozen more might be administered for good measure.

Jack felt physically ill. In nearly thirty years of living he'd yet to raise his hand to a woman, and he'd no intention of taking up the practice now. And yet if he owned as much, Mistress Valemont would be placed in the hands—literally—of one who would not scruple to do so.

Pol finally paused for breath, and Duncan slanted his gaze to

Jack. "Jack Campbell, will ye accept this office and with it the conditions as stated before this court?"

Jack swallowed hard, willing his rising stomach to settle even as he steeled himself to lie—again. "Aye, Your Worship, I will."

" 'Tis settled then." Another bang of the gavel drove the point home and brought the room to order. "Let the rolls show that the prisoner, one Claudia Valemont, late o' Paris, France, is heretofore remanded to the custody of Master Jack Campbell, occupant of the office of Lord High Executioner to His Majesty, King George the Third, for a term of six months to begin this day and end the first Friday of April in the year of Our Lord 1794, when she shall be released once more into her own keeping." He looked up from the tome and addressed himself to Claudia. "Mark me well, mistress, for I'll say this but the once. Should ye run off at any time o'er the next six months and should ye be so unlucky as to be captured and brought back before me, the original punishment shall stand—ye shall be hangit from the neck until dead. D'ye ken me?"

"Y-yes, my lord."

For the first time during the proceedings, the judge's angular face relaxed into a smile. "Good, because ye've a verra pretty neck and 'twould be a rare pity to make me call upon Jack to stretch it."

The room exploded into raucous laughter punctuated with a hand or two of applause. Only three people stood without cracking a smile: the prisoner, her reluctant gaoler—and Callum McBride.

Callum rounded on Jack as the crowd dispersed. "Well, well, it seems we've another bastard in our midst, aye, Jacko? I ken now why the two of ye got on so verra well, but then ye ken the auld saying about birds of a feather, aye?"

In no mood, Jack made to shoulder past him. "It's over, Callum, now stand aside."

"Wheesht, I'll stand aside a'right . . . for now. But mind ye, I'll be watchin'—and waitin.' One false step and your ladybird will find 'erself dancin' on the wind."

Clenching his jaw to keep from retorting in kind, Jack turned his back on his brother and made his way to the prisoner's dock. Standing just outside it, Mistress Valemont held out her manacled wrists, staring down at them in a fixed, frozen sort of way while Pol, palsied and more than half blind, struggled to fit the key into the lock.

She looked up as Jack approached and her blank stare slipped into a scowl. "I suppose I should thank you for saving my life, *monsieur.*"

"Aye, I suppose you should." He turned to Pol and held out his hand for the ring of keys. "I'll have at it if ye dinna mind."

The old man turned the ring of keys over with a grudging air. "'Tis the wee silver one, third on the left," he said, then stumped away to greet his mate, Peadair, who'd risen from the benches.

Key in hand, Jack stepped forward. "If ye'll allow me, mistress . . ."

She hesitated, then raised her manacled wrists, a wry smile playing about her mouth. "It seems, *Monsieur le Borreau,* that I have no choice."

T*hat night, as he lay abed and tried to sleep, Duncan Mac*Gregor was treated to a round earful.

"For shame, Duncan MacGregor," his wife, Dorcas, said for what must have been the tenth time. "What was it ye were thinkin' tae grant Jack leave tae beat the puir lass and she but a wee slip of a thing and *saft* in the head, too."

Seeing that he would get no rest until his wife was satisfied, Duncan pulled himself up to sit against the banked pillows. "Wheesht, woman, have ye no kent Jack Campbell since he was a bairn? And," he continued, turning to clamp a hand over her mouth when she showed signs of opening it, "in all these years, have you ever kent him tae raise his hand tae strike a living soul that dinna provoke him first?" She shook her head and, satisfied, he let his hand slide to his side. "Calm yourself, my love, for Mistress Valemont will no come tae harm through Jack. Though," he added on afterthought, the beginnings of a chuckle tickling the back of his throat, "hiking up the lassie's skirts and giving her a good poke might just do the lad a world o' good."

Dorcas paused from plumping her pillow to scowl over at him. "Dinna say ye mean tae make a match between Jack and the foreign lassie and him sworn to celibacy and the lass a convicted horse thief and would-be murderess—and *French* into the bargain!" She contrived to look shocked but after twenty-odd years of marriage Duncan knew her face far too well to be fooled. Even in semidarkness, neither the glint in her eyes nor the slight twitching at the corners of her mouth was lost on him.

"What I mean is tae let nature take its course, speakin' o' which . . ." He slid a hand beneath the covers and cupped her soft breast.

"Oooh." She squealed and shoved against his chest but not so hard that she might budge him. "Ye're the very Devil, Duncan MacGregor, and ye've no a dram of shame in ye."

"Aye, that I am, wife." He planted a hearty kiss on her startled mouth. "Though, devil that I am, I'm minded tae pay a visit tae heaven before night's end."

The MacGregors were far from the only folk too fixed on that day's trial for sleep. The taproom of the inn was abuzz with talk of little else, or so it seemed to Callum as he reached for his glass of whiskey, his sixth in half as many hours.

He was on his way to being drunk but had yet to reach that state of grace where hurts were numbed and cares erased if only for the moment. If anything, the whiskey had fueled the outrage that had mounted steadily ever since Jack had taken it upon himself to stand witness for the accused.

Jack. As always his half-brother was at the core of Callum's misery. Even as bairns, Jack's presence had cast a pall over what Callum was convinced would have otherwise been an idyllic life. But then, the Sassenach bastard had ever been their mother's favorite. Like a coach horse, she'd worn blinders where her eldest was concerned, as unseeing of Jack's many faults and failures as she was of her youngest son's worth. Even after all these years, Callum could still recall the way her amber eyes, *Jack's* eyes, had lit up whenever the gangling bastard had walked into a room, how she'd take him onto her lap and croon endearments into his ear, heedless of Callum standing watch at her knee.

Jack, always Jack.

How many nights had Callum lain awake, too terrified to close his eyes, listening to his parents argue in the other room? Da, his voice slurred but steeled with hate, swearing he'd send the "unnatural creature" away. Mam, just as adamant, swearing that Jack would stay or the both of them would be on their way.

Jack, always Jack.

Lying on the cot across from Callum's, Jack must have heard them, too, must have known his leaving was the answer. And yet he'd stayed on, the selfish bastard. Stayed, as had Callum, to hear the raised voices mount toward crescendo, the crash of some treasured possession hurled to the floor, and the sharp bruising smack of a fist plowing into tender flesh. Mam's flesh. And finally the soft, almost peaceful keening of Mam weeping, sometimes Da with her. The following morning always brought to mind the aftermath of a storm, only instead of felled trees and broken fences the wreckage would like as no be a bloodied nose, a split lip, or a mottled cheek. A week of calm, perhaps two, and then the tension would mount anew and the cycle repeat.

Jack's fault, all Jack's fault.

Heretofore his half-brother's self-imposed semi-exile from village life had allowed Callum to let sleeping dogs lie. But the coming of the Frenchwoman had changed all that. Jack's setting himself against Callum for her sake, the evening before in the tavern and then earlier that day in the hall, had unbarred the door on a lifetime of pent-up hate.

Callum drained his glass and shouted to Milread to fetch him another, a smile—his first that day—lifting the corners of his cracked lips. He might not be as tall as Jack or as bonnie a fighter or as clever with the books, but he had gifts of his own and chief among them was the knack for searching out a person's weak spot. And so even in the throes of his anger that day, he'd made it a point to watch and to listen. He'd seen the softness sweep over his half-brother's chiseled features whenever he'd gazed upon the Frog bitch, had heard the warmth in his tone when he'd turned to her, keys in hand, and said, "If ye'll allow me . . ."

For a man whose heart heretofore had been given only to the miserable, flea-ridden menagerie he herded about him, these were signs, powerful signs. Change was in the air, Callum could feel it like a strong wind at his back, and the Frenchwoman—and whatever secret she kept—was at the heart of it. For where there was love, pain and loss were quick to follow. Jack might not love Claudia Valemont, not yet, but the seeds of that sentiment were planted firm and deep. All Callum need do was bide his time and let nature take its course. Sooner or later those seeds would spring forth, bear fruit, and then, like a farmer wielding a scythe at harvest time, Callum would strike. Hard and heavy, again and again until not a stalk was left standing.

Claudia Valemont would fall and Brother Jack with her. Callum would crush the bastard beneath his heel and then, only then, would he know peace.

He could hardly wait to begin.

Nothing is so burdensome as a secret.

—French proverb

"*Mind your head." Monsieur Campbell held open the* door to his cottage and stepped back for Claudia to enter.

Less mannered was his dog, Elf. The wolfhound bolted inside, treading on Claudia's foot in her haste to reach home and hearth.

Far from eager herself, Claudia hesitated, gulping down her dread, and then crossed the threshold, the crown of her head clearing the lintel with inches to spare.

Coming up behind her, Monsieur Campbell murmured, "Aye, I forget how small ye are." He ducked inside and pulled the door closed.

Nerves strung on tenterhooks, Claudia started at the sound. *"Eh bien,"* she said around a nervous laugh, "you know what the English say about good things and small packages, yes?"

Judging from his blank look he didn't, which was likely to be for the best. "I'll see to building a wee fire and then to our supper." He set her valise down inside the door and then moved to take the cloak from her shoulders.

"Non, merci," she said with a shake of her head and then backed up to the wall.

No point in surrendering her cloak or her foothold by the door until she'd determined whether or not what lay inside would behoove her to turn about and run.

Back pressed against the cold stones, she followed him with her eyes as he crossed to the hearth, shrugged out of his broadcloth coat, and, after hanging it neatly over the back of the chair, turned to the cold hearth. Only when he'd faced away, squatting to rout through a wooden box filled with bricks of scraggly sod, did she venture to leave the shelter of the wall to look about.

What she saw allayed the very worst of her fears, for the cottage in no way resembled the chamber of horrors she'd spent the short journey from the tollbooth dreading. The few possessions in sight were all common, workaday things—no ropes or thumbscrews or severed heads, at least none in plain view. Suspended from a beam above the fireplace grate was an assortment of earthenware cooking vessels and a great gleaming copper kettle. Herbs tied into neat bundles hung drying from the rafter nearest the hearth, perfuming the air with rosemary, lavender, and peppermint. A small reading table and a stuffed armchair—the latter with a black-and-white cat curled upon the seat—took pride of place before the hearth. A few paces to the left sat a scrubbed pine table, a bench on either side. Spartan to be sure, but nothing sinister, and all so spotless and tidy as to belie Monsieur Campbell's bachelor status. The only obvious anomaly was the richly grained walnut and mahogany mantelpiece. Elaborately carved with a profusion of lions and other fanciful forest creatures, it seemed more in keeping with the grandeur of a palace than with the present humble surroundings, as did the library of leather-bound books ranged along the scrolled shelf.

The books!

"You can read, *monsieur?"*

Forgetting her fear, Claudia rounded on the hearth and went down the line to read the titles on the tooled leather spines. Culpeper's *The English Physitian or an Astrologo-Physical Discourse of the Vulgar Herbs of This Nation,* Sir Thomas More's *Utopia,* a small berry-colored leather compendium of Shakespeare's sonnets. *The Chimney-piece Maker's Daily Assistant*—might that explain the extraordinary mantel? *The State of Prisons* by John Howard and *Commentaries on the Laws of England* by Sir William Blackstone—well, at least those two made some sense. And finally there was Voltaire's *Candide* and Rousseau's *Emile,* both translated into the English but impressive nonetheless.

Kneeling outside the circle of flattened stones, he fed another piece of peat to the fledgling flame. "That surprises ye, does it?" She couldn't see his face but she thought she heard disappointment straining his tone.

Would she never learn to think before she spoke? *"Oui,"* she admitted, dropping her gaze to admire the strong, capable hands stacking the peat into a neat pyramid.

When he'd touched her cheek in the tavern the other day, his big, blunt fingers had traced the edges of the bruise in the lightest of touches as though she were made of fine porcelain instead of mere flesh and bone. The only other man's touch she'd known was Phillippe's and *certainement* his had never conveyed such gentleness. Nor did she imagine for a moment that he would have shown much, indeed *any,* interest in the books on literature and philosophy queued above her head, for his passions had run more to hunting and gaming, dancing and drinking.

By way of offering an olive branch, she added, "But it is a most pleasant surprise. Perhaps in the evenings we will read aloud together?"

He dusted off his hands and reached for the bellows. "My evening hours are my own, mistress, but you may do with yours as ye wish."

Seeing that he meant to ignore her, Claudia fell to roaming the room. As fear dissipated, curiosity returned and soon her restless footsteps bore her toward the shadowed alcove that, until now, she'd avoided. Sans headboard, the simple rope bed was crudely constructed and yet the mattress looked to be sturdy and more than able to accommodate two, with a quaint quilt serving as a counterpane. Wondering if she would be expected to share her gaoler's bed as a condition of her parole, she stole a glance at the Scotsman's broad back. She still feared him, yes, but he intrigued her, too. Would his red-gold hair feel as silky as it looked? Could his arms and chest possibly be half as hard, as beautifully sculpted as the outline beneath his shirt promised?

Phillippe had been accounted to be a fine figure of a man; certainly Maman had never tired of telling her how fortunate she was to have such a young and handsome protector. Yet the sight of his slender, wiry form had never stirred Claudia. As for Monsieur Campbell, she wasn't entirely sure she even liked the man, certainly she abhorred his "profession." And yet, consummmate liar that she was becoming, she still hadn't the trick of lying to herself. Monsieur Jack Campbell moved her.

She dealt herself a brisk mental shake. The man was a *bourreau* and thus a brother to Monsieur Sanson, who operated the guillotine in France with such lethal skill. Vowing not to forget that all-important fact again, she turned her attention to the bed.

"I thought ye might have need of this."

She whirled to find Monsieur Campbell standing just behind her, her valise dangling from one hand. Caught up in her thoughts, she hadn't heard him come up behind her. On eye level with the triangle of his dun-colored waistcoat she could see the shadow of crisp chest hair beneath the well-worn cloth of his white shirt and felt a strange fluttering low in her belly.

"*Merci.* Thank you." All too aware of the bed at her back, of the fact that they were well and truly alone together, she swallowed hard and backed up a step.

"I suppose ye'll be wantin' a moment to yourself and forbye supper will no cook itself." He set the valise atop the blanket chest at the foot of the bed and turned to go.

Glancing at his broad, retreating back, she blurted out the question that had been preying upon her mind since they'd left the hall. "Do you mean to sleep with me *monsieur?"*

The clumsy question seemed to stun both of them, freezing Monsieur Campbell in midstep. Heart pounding, she watched him slowly turn back to face her.

Scarlet limned his Viking cheekbones and his eyes were fierce as he stared her down. "Duncan granted me leave to beat you, no to bed ye."

Claudia had all but forgotten that particular condition of her punishment. Faced with the threat, and her gaoler's obvious ability to act on it, she curled her hands into fists at her sides.

Her chin shot up. "Do not think to lay so much as a hand on me, for if you do I will scratch out your eyes!"

It was false bravado, and they both knew it. If he so wished, he could overpower her in a second, draw up her skirts, and turn her over his knee or the kitchen table, as he pleased.

Even so, she fancied there was a grudging respect in his voice and a growing softness to his amber eyes when he said, "Dinna fash, lass. I've yet to raise a hand to a woman, so I dinna suppose I'll start with you." Holding her gaze, he added, "Nor need ye be worrit that I'll come to ye in the night for I swear to you that I willna." In answer to her unspoken question, he added, "My plaid and the floor shall suit me well enough, and after we've eaten I'll hang a blanket or some such so that you may be private."

"Thank you." Fidgeting under the intensity of his gaze, Claudia looked away. "I did not mean to insult your honor, *monsieur,* I only thought—"

"That I spared ye from being hangit only because I'd reconsidered your er, *offer*?" he asked, gaze narrowing, daring her to deny what they both knew to be the truth.

Thinking on how she'd humbled herself before him, offering herself up as though she were a common harlot and a desperate one at that, had the heat of embarrassment blistering her own cheeks. Reminding herself that she was *une femme du monde,* a woman of the world, she tried for a shrug. "We are strangers, *monsieur.* If not to take me to your bed, then why put yourself to the trouble of speaking for me today?"

"You mean why would I *lie* for you?"

She hesitated, then nodded. "*Oui.* Yes, why did you?"

He pulled a hard swallow, and Claudia watched the long ripple travel down his throat, saw the big chest rise, then fall, heard the slight rasp in his voice as at last he admitted, "I canna say as I know, mistress. Truly I canna say."

Supper, likewise, proved to be a strained and embarrassing affair. The ordeal commenced with Monsieur Campbell dumping several musty-smelling lumps—some sort of an edible root, she supposed—from a burlap bag onto the table, plunking a wickedly sharp knife beside the pile, and instructing Claudia to "Have at it." Without further instruction, he picked up an empty wooden pail and headed out the door. When he returned minutes later with a full bucket of water in hand, she was contemplating the largest of the round lumps, which she gingerly held pinched between her thumb and forefinger.

Wordless, he poured the water from the bucket into the largest of the earthenware pots and heaved the vessel onto the grate above the flames. Without turning around, he said, "Dinna tell me, only let me guess. Ye've ne'er peeled potatoes before?"

Les pommes de terre. Potatoes. So this was what they looked like in their natural state. Having tasted them in casseroles and the occasional ragout, Claudia found it almost impossible to reconcile those small, pearlescent, *civilized* cubes with the bulbous, dirt-covered lumps set before her.

Straightening, he rose and turned to her, a look of profound disgust marring the clean lines of mouth and jaw. "But of course ye hav'na. Ye're *French.* And I dinna suppose that an *earl's* daughter has much use for potato peeling, aye?"

The latter was so heavily laced with sarcasm as to assure her that he must have arrived at the hall that afternoon in time to witness the public reception to her desperate and ill-conceived confession of nobility. That he seemed to view both her claim and herself as something of a jest worked in her favor, of course—for him or anyone else to one day connect Mademoiselle Claudia Valemont to *Lady* Claudia Drummond would be a disaster—but it also rankled.

Equally insupportable, though, was that he had joined the rest of the village in judging her as *une folle,* a madwoman. Absurd as it was for her to care what this savage Scotsman, this bloodthirsty *borreau,* might think of *her,* the unhappy truth was that for some strange, unknown reason she did.

And so she shifted her shoulders in a shrug and said, "I only said so because I did not wish to be hung. Can you blame me, *monsieur?"*

"It's no my place to judge," he said, dropping onto the bench across the table from her.

"And yet you kill those whom others have judged?"

"Execute," he corrected and took one of the roots in one hand and the knife in the other. "Now, shall we have a wee lesson in potato peelin' before you begin? First ye've to get a good grip on it like so."

"B-but it is . . . *dirty."*

He glanced upwards to the rafters as though calling upon the Divine for patience. Apparently finding it, he lowered his gaze to her and continued. "That would be what the water's for, aye?" He held out his hand and after a moment's hesitation, Claudia surrendered her potato. "Here, mind how it's done. It's verra simple really."

He demonstrated, neatly shaving off a broad swathe of brown skin without so much as a nick to the flesh. A few more swipes bared the rest of the root which, barring a spot or two, gleamed the gray-white of a pearl. A half dozen quick chops with the knife reduced the whole to a neat pile of cubes.

Facing her, he announced, "Your turn."

Gingerly, she took hold of the knife and another potato, then dug in with the tip of the blade.

Milky white water squirted her face. "Ouf," she let out, then swiped her sleeve over the wetness.

"Ye're to peel it, no butcher it." Shaking his head at her, he made a scoffing—and utterly *Scottish*—sound low in his throat. "They'll no be anything left to cook if ye cut deep like that."

Angling the blade in imitation of what he had done, she drew it back, the shaving of skin curling to bare a narrow, snaking strip.

"No bad," he conceded, offering a smile of encouragement that set her head adrift and her heart aflutter.

It is hunger, she told herself, and forced her attention from that firm, beautifully shaped mouth to the mountain of yet-to-be peeled potatoes.

The prospect of the latter quickly brought her feet back down to earth, and she heaved a heavy sigh. "But I fear I do not possess your . . . er, talent, *monsieur.* I will be peeling potatoes all night."

Now that she'd mastered this peasant task, it lost all appeal. And she was hungry, starved really. At the prison, they'd given her a single oatcake for supper and another for breakfast. Her stomach, if indeed she still possessed one, must be shrunken to the size of a peach pit. And she was sleepy, her shoulders stiff from the previous night passed on her cell pallet.

But if Monsieur Campbell was moved to pity, he hid it well. Shrugging, he said, "Then it's maybe a good idea if ye learn the trick of it and fast, aye?"

"You, *Monsieur le Borreau,* are not a nice man." Annoyed when he only chuckled and picked up a leek to start chopping, she stabbed the knife in the potato and yanked it straight back. The blade slipped, finding purchase deep in the flesh of her thumb.

"Ouf!"

Monsieur Campbell's red-gold head shot up. Expression pained, he said, "Och, but you've cut yourself, hav'na ye?"

Feeling unspeakably foolish, she shoved her hand beneath the table. Swaddling her bleeding thumb in her skirts, she said, "A small prick, it is nothing."

"I'll be the judge of that." He stood and came around to her side of the table. "Let me see."

Muttering curses in French, she brought up her hand from its hiding place. A scarlet arc spurted, putting her in mind of the fountain of burgundy wine from which she'd once drunk.

He went down on bended knee beside her. "Jesus, Joseph, and Mary!" Beneath the ruddy glow of his tan, the edges of his face had gone the pearlescent white of a peeled potato. "Christ, woman, if this is what ye call a 'prick,' Callum should count himself fortunate ye dinna take his whole arm."

Staring at the sight, Claudia felt herself growing woozy. She started to lower her arm.

He snatched her elbow and hoisted her arm above her head. "Nay, hold it up. *High.*"

Head bowed, he made an examination of the wound. Staring down upon his russet crown, feeling the warmth of his breath falling on her damaged hand and wrist, it occurred to her that the only time they'd been closer was the day before, in the tavern, when she'd cast herself into his arms. Thinking of that episode, of her own foolishness then and since, was all it took to bring whatever blood she had left shooting into her cheeks.

He looked up and said, "Ye'll maybe live but it wants for tendin'."

As the implication of his words sank in, she tried to pull away. "But you . . . you are not a physician."

"Nay worries. My maither's maither's people were MacLays and like them I ken something of the healing. Ye've no cut into bone nor muscle and if ye hold still and let me tend it proper you'll maybe no lose the hand."

She gasped. "Lose my hand! But—" She stopped when she saw one corner of his mouth lift in the beginning of a lopsided smile. "Beast! You wish only to frighten me."

He didn't deny it. "Frighten some sense into ye maybe, and to coax ye to hold still." Gently, very gently, he transferred the wounded hand back into her keeping and then rose. He tugged the loosely knotted neck cloth free from his throat and handed it to her. "Here, wrap this tight about it whilst I go to fetch my wee chest."

She hesitated, then reached out with her good hand to take it. The starch-stiffened linen smelled of the strong mint-scented soap he used and held the warmth of his skin. As embarrassed as though she held his unmentionables rather than a mere cravat, she nonetheless managed a quick nod and did as she was bid. By the time he returned from rifling the kitchen cupboard, a small rosewood chest held between his broad palms, the cloth was crimson and the temporary numbness had subsided, leaving the wound to throb with the regularity of a beating heart.

Humming as if he did this every day—but then she supposed indifference to the sight of blood must be part of his job requirements—he flipped open the box lid and began taking out vials and setting them on the table. An "Ah-hah!" apparently signaled that his search was met with success. He produced a small glass jar, removed the lid, and sunk two broad fingers into the green gunk.

Claudia wrinkled her nose as the foul fumes rose. "What is it?"

He reached for her hand. "Oh, a bit o' this and that. Helichrysum, or 'everlasting' if you prefer, to stem the bleeding and tea tree and chamomile to keep the wound from turning putrid. As to the secret ingredient, trust me, ye dinna want to know." Despite its strong odor and dubious color, the salve felt pleasantly cool on her skin. She was starting to relax when suddenly he said, "You've verra queer hands for a seamstress."

Wondering what he might mean, she held out her other hand and regarded it. She'd always been more than a little vain about her hands. Unlike her mother's, her fingers were long and tapered and tipped with strong, even nails.

"Dinna look so put out," he cautioned her, reaching inside the chest for a strip of clean white cloth to wrap about the wound. "'Tis only that hands tell a lot about a person. Most women who ply their needle with fair frequency have a wee callus on the thumb that wears the thimble. And the tips of their fingers tend to be rough on account of them pricking themselves, no smooth as yours are."

Zut, alors! Thinking, and thinking fast, Claudia settled on an explanation that cobbled together the best of fact with fiction. "Ah well, *monsieur,* you have found me out," she said around a little sigh. "Caught me in the 'little white lie,' as you say in English, for I am not a seamstress by trade. Oh yes," she quickly added, in response to the sudden lift to his roan-colored brows, "I know when we first met I told you I was on my way to work in a modiste's shop—and I was, *monsieur,* truly I was."

For the sake of effect, she allowed her shoulders to slump forward just the tiniest bit, before continuing, "But *hélas,* I was not entirely honest with my future employer, either, for my hope was that she might take pity on me and permit me to stay on to learn."

"Then what is your *trade?*"

Claudia did not care for the way he accented that last word or for the speculative gleam in his amber gaze, which brought to mind that she had, after all, offered up her body as payment for his safe escort. Thinking on that humiliating episode, including his oh so humiliating refusal, she felt the heat of shame creeping into her cheeks even as she turned her attention to explaining how someone from the working class might have hands that were soft and unblemished and not rough and callused.

"I was a lady's maid, *monsieur.*"

"Aye?"

She nodded vigorously.

"Exactly what does a lady's maid do, mistress?" At her frown, he added mildly, "I've always wondered, but as it happens you're the verra first I've ever met to ask."

Merde! What *had* her maid Evette's duties been? "Well, I, er, dressed my mistress's hair and helped her to bathe."

He frowned up at her. "Was she an invalid, then, that she couldna wash herself?"

"She was a *lady,*" she shot back, well and truly annoyed on behalf of her fictional mistress as well as herself, for Evette had indeed undertaken that office for her, preparing delightful baths of milk and rosewater. "It was my responsibility to see to the keeping of her clothes—only light mending, though," she added quickly, before he could question her. "She had a seamstress for the rest." Warming to her tale, a more or less fact-based account of her life before the revolution, she went on, "And then there were the flowers from her many admirers—such roses, *monsieur,* you have yet to see, for they were known to be her favorite. When they came, she . . . er, *I* would arrange them about her boudoir. And then there were the calling cards and the invitations and the . . . Ah, well," she said around a genuine sigh of regret for that gay, lost life, "It was a long time ago."

"It all sounds verra grand," he remarked and finished tying

the ends of the bandage into a neat knot. "But 'twould serve you better now had you labored in the kitchen instead."

He wished she'd been what, a scullery maid? Shuddering at the thought, she asked, "Why?"

"Well, because it occurs to me that while you're with us you might make yourself most useful by helping out in the tavern."

"You expect me to work in a *taverne!*"

"'Tis gainful employment, to be sure, and ye'd be servin' a need, as Jenny—that's Milread's cousin and the other barmaid—broke her arm this sennight past. The apothecary set the bone as best he could but until it heals, *if* it heals, she canna use it and so puir Milread's been left to fend for herself."

"Milread?"

"Aye, *Milread,*" he said again as though that name should mean something to her, and she didn't much care for the censure she saw in his narrowing eyes. "Surely you must mind the woman who spoke for you in the hall today and, before that, helped me care for you when you'd fainted?"

And the very woman whom I caused to chase after me, she added mentally as the memory came streaking back to her. Slinking back to the bench, she ventured, "Surely there is some other occupation to which I am better suited, *monsieur.* Some better use for my talents?"

He shook his head. "'Tis the Border Country of Scotland we're in, no Paris, France. All of us here ken how to comb our own hair and wash our own arses. As for flowers, most died upon the frost this fortnight past, but I've a vegetable garden out back and you're welcome to help me harvest what's left o' the turnips and peas when ye're no at Alistair's."

It was not often that Claudia was struck speechless but *certainement* the present moment stood to be one of those rare times. To fetch tankards and pints for the loudmouthed louts she'd seen in the taproom the day before like a common slattern. To grope in the dirt for roots like the lowliest peasant. It was too horrible, certainly too patently unfair, to even put into words, English or French.

Seemingly satisfied, he rose to put the box away and then promptly removed all sharp objects from her reach with the admonition that "maybe might she keep from killin' herself until after they'd supped."

Coming out of her stupor, Claudia perched on the bench

while he made short work of the rest of the potatoes, and then an assortment of vegetables and herbs, his movements marked by a brisk efficiency, a grace that she couldn't help but admire. At some point, the black-and-white cat jumped down from its perch on the armchair and strolled over to sniff her feet. She must have passed muster for the beast began slinking about her ankles. Claudia hesitated, then reached down to stroke the soft fur, then to scratch that spot of chin where she recalled cats adored being scratched. Once she'd had a cat, a fluffy gray kitten with large, luminous jade-green eyes, but that had been a long time ago and, owing to Phillippe's contempt for all creatures furry and four-footed, had ended so badly that she'd sworn never to take in another.

Eventually the one-eyed cat moved on and Claudia's tedium mounted until finally, desperate for the sound of a human voice, she remarked, "Your accent, *monsieur,* your Scots 'burr,' it is not as strong as that of the others in the village. You speak almost as a gentleman."

Closing the cupboard, from which he'd just taken down a round of cheese and a loaf of brown bread, he turned to regard her. "Oh, *my* accent, is it?" He made a sound low in his throat, which emerged somewhere between a snort and a *mmphm.*

Still smarting over the potato-peeling debacle, nerves frayed to a thread from brooding on just what manner of "reception" she could expect when she presented herself at the inn, she lifted her chin and snapped, "You do not like me, *monsieur.* I wish to know why."

He set the cheese board down on the table and glanced over at her. "'Tis no a matter of liking or no liking. Mostly I'm just no used to havin' a wee foreign female underfoot and such a talkative one at that."

Ignoring her smarting thumb, she gestured with her hands to encompass the room's four walls. "And where in this . . . this *palace* to which you have brought me shall I take myself so that I am not under your feets?"

"Underfoot," he repeated mildly, returning to stir the stew, "and though you're fine as you are, you might set the table as supper's a'most ready." With his elbow, he pointed to a pine cupboard built into one corner.

Yet more manual labor! If she were to stay and serve out the six months, she'd be worn to a nub. With a huff she rose and stomped over to the cupboard, pulling out stoneware bowls and cups and slamming them down upon the table.

True to his word, a short while later he announced that supper was indeed ready. "Best eat it whilst it's hot," he advised, handing her a brimming bowl from which a cloud of steam rose.

Accepting it and then taking her seat, she stared down into the murky depths of roan-colored mush and asked, "What is it?"

He vented a put-upon sigh. "We call it hotchpotch."

"Hotchpotch?" Having tested the word on her tongue, she decided the dish sounded no more appetizing than it looked. "What is in it . . . other than potatoes, I mean?"

Back to her, he lifted his amazing shoulders in a shrug. "A bit o' this and that."

She stirred her spoon about, excavating a bit of carrot here, a stray pea there. Coming up empty, she glanced across the table to the man who would serve as the sole source of her body's sustenance for the following six months—at least until she found the means to escape—and asked, "No meat?"

The sudden scowl beetling his high brow made him look fierce indeed but, Claudia reasoned, as he hadn't struck her thus far, he wasn't likely to interrupt his supper to do so now. "Betimes I'll put in a bit o' salmon, but I've no exactly had the time to fish these few days past, now have I?"

More by way of conversation than complaint, she asked, "What of the chickens I saw in the yard? And *certainement* there must be rabbits and deer in those woods?"

It was an innocent question, she hadn't meant to offend, but the tightening of his jaw told her she'd done that and more.

Color rising, he gave an adamant shake of his head. "The chickens I keep for their eggs and their company. As to the other, 'twould be akin to supping on the flesh of a friend."

What manner of man kept company with chickens? Wondering if he might not be a bit mad himself, she cleared her throat to ask, "If you do not eat meat, how is it then that you live?"

Ladling broth into a second bowl, he answered with a question of his own. "Do I look to be wastin' away, then?"

Unprepared for the question, Claudia drew a deep if shaky breath. Broad of shoulder, with powerful arms and thighs the circumference of small tree trunks, Jack Campbell appeared to be both hearty and hale. Indeed he was the biggest man she'd ever seen, yet there wasn't a jot of fat on him. Even his forearms, dusted with golden hair and exposed by his rolled-up shirtsleeves, were knotted with muscle and pulsating with power.

Finding her voice, husky though it was, she admitted, "No, *monsieur,* you appear to be quite, er, robust."

"Well, then," he said, taking his seat across from her. "There's your answer." Spoon in hand, he delved in, proving that he did indeed possess a hearty appetite.

Wisps of steam still rose from her soup bowl, carrying the aroma of spices and herbs upward to tickle not only her nose but her taste buds as well. She slid her spoon into the broth, blew gently on the filled reservoir, and then slowly slid it between her parted lips.

"Hmm," she murmured in pure appreciation, running her tongue along her slightly scored bottom lip to cool the burn.

Opening her eyes, which she'd closed to better savor the surprisingly delicate flavor, she caught Monsieur Campbell's stark gaze riveted on her face and his spoon clenched in midair.

Recalling her former high-strung chef, she hastened to reassure him. "*C'est magnifique.* It is magnificent. I think," she teased, "the reason you will not tell me the ingredients is that you fear I will steal your receipt."

His face relaxed, he lowered his spoon and, miracle of miracles, his mouth lifted in a for once unguarded smile. Setting down the spoon in favor of cutting bread and cheese for two, he said, "You'd be safe if ye did, for I doubt it's worth so much as five shillings."

Oh, he was sharp, she'd give him that. To show she hadn't missed his meaning, she shot back, "You would know, would you not, *Monsieur le Borreau.*"

Instantly she regretted having spoken so, for his smile dissolved into a look of wary puzzlement. "What is it that you call me?"

She cast her gaze down to her food. "*Borreau.* It is the French word for executioner." They ate in awkward silence for a while until, weary of the tension, she struck up the courage to ask, "Do you . . ." How to put it? "Do you *enjoy* your work?"

He looked up from cutting a wedge of cheese in two to hold her gaze for a long, unnerving moment. Shrugging, he answered, "It's a living. And," he added, amber eyes glinting, "most times no so messy as peelin' potatoes with a French lassie who doesna ken a turnip from a potato."

Claudia had to resist the urge to poke out her tongue. "*Touché.* But you are an educated man, *monsieur, un homme des lettres. Non,* do not trouble yourself to deny it," she said when he showed signs of shaking his head. "For I have seen the books upon your shelf. *Certainement* you need not resort to murder to earn your living."

Amber eyes narrowed, glowing lethal bright. "I've never *murdered* anyone. Those I meet upon the scaffold have been tried in a court of law where learned men have found them to be guilty. Guilty of terrible crimes that, for all your worldly-wise ways, would shock even you."

The memory of that morning, of how very close she'd come to the gibbet herself for what amounted to a moment's mistake, throbbed raw and fresh as the cut on her thumb. Forgetting fear, abandoning caution, she hoisted her chin and spat out, "To steal something that is said to be worth more than . . . but what was this princely sum? Ah, yes, five shillings. A crime most shocking indeed."

A muscle ticking in his square jaw, he reached over and stabbed the blade of the cheese knife into the table boards. Caught unaware, Claudia jerked back, the breath catching in her throat.

From the opposite side of the quivering blade, he glowered at her. "I've yet to meet the thief who could claim to have plied his trade without takin' at least one life along the way."

Pulling her tattered dignity about her, determined not to be afraid, she hoisted her chin and said, "Perhaps you are dining with one now."

Something in his gaze, the sudden stark pain that lay just behind his eyes, made her regret having started down this path. Feeling as though holes were being burned into her flesh, she broke eye contact at last. Stirring her spoon about, all too aware of his fixed gaze trained on her, she waited for the unnerving tension to ease.

When after a time it showed no signs of doing so, she demanded, "Why do you stare, *monsieur?*"

"From here on, if you want an answer from me, you'll call me Jack."

Message delivered, he turned his attention back to his supper, leaving Claudia with little choice but to do the same. Between spoonfuls of soup and bites of bread and cheese, she waited once more for him to end their silence.

But despite calling out to his dog and twice ordering the cat away from the table, he didn't address her for the remainder of the night.

Fair tresses man's imperial race insnare, [sic]
And beauty draws us with a single hair.

—Alexander Pope, *The Rape of the Lock*

C*laudia had never understood that odd species of individual* known among the English as a "morning person." In the days before bloody revolution had driven her to flee home and country, she'd rarely if ever risen before noon. Indeed, "rising" had constituted little more than sitting propped against a bank of snowy pillows, sipping her cup of *chocolat* and nibbling at her croissant, which Evette would have carried in on the silver breakfast tray along with the morning post.

And yet the big hand descending on her shoulder felt nothing like Evette's tentative touch, the palm broad and warm, the long blunt fingers holding fast to her flesh.

Clinging to the memory of better days nonetheless, Claudia turned her face into the pillow and murmured in French, "Evette, I did not ring for you. It is early yet. Away, away." She flexed her shoulder, seeking to dislodge the hand holding her back from bliss.

It wouldn't budge.

Still muzzy with sleep, she became aware of the strong, clean scent of evergreen hovering over her like a cloud. Mingled with the mint associated with a man's shaving soap, it marked the identity of her morning "caller" as indelibly as did his red hair and towering height.

And, lest there be any residual doubt, there was the deep, rich timbre of his voice as he said, "I dinna ken any Evettes, but what I do ken is ye're getting your arse out of this bed and *now.*"

Hoping she might be dreaming still, that the past forty-eight hours would prove to be a fiction of her fraught mind, Claudia rolled onto her back and cracked open a cautious eye.

Candle in hand, Monsieur Campbell—Jack—scowled down at her, his strong Nordic jaw locked in the clear determination to have his way. The flickering light cast the clean, strong planes of his freshly shaved face into sharp relief, at the same time softening the grim set of his wide and rather pleasantly shaped mouth. The marks of a comb's teeth showed in the thick mass of red hair, still damp at the temples, that he'd gathered back into a tidy, leather-bound club. The latter cued Claudia to the terrible truth: it must be morning.

Not yet prepared to face reality, let alone a fanatically early-rising Scotsman, she snapped both eyes closed, yanked the coverlet to chin level, and rolled back onto her side. "Go away."

"Come now," he said, a hint of coaxing tempering the steel in his tone. " 'Tis your verra first day. Ye'll no want to be late," he added reasonably, then treated both her and the mattress to a gentle jiggling.

But Claudia was in no mood to be coaxed, reasoned with, or jiggled. Her body, coming into consciousness despite her best efforts, was beginning to register the ill effects of the previous forty-eight hours, including the night spent on the cold and very hard stones of the prison cell floor. She'd yet to do more than shift position and already she ached in places for which she hadn't names.

"I do not care."

Another nudge, firmed with purpose, as was the voice that replied, "Be that as it may, *I* care. And I canna wait about all mornin' while you take your beauty rest."

By now well and truly awake, Claudia grabbed hold of the covers with both hands and bolted upright, fixing him with an openly hostile gaze. "But of course, you will have an eventful day, *monsieur.* No, do not tell me but allow me to make the guess. Places to go, people to murder? That is it, yes? *Eh bien,* do not let me keep you from these labors most worthy. *Au revoir* or better yet, *adieu.*"

He slammed the candle atop the bedside table, sending wax splashing onto the sides of the brass holder. "Aye, I'm minded to strangle someone a'right, but 'tis only one wee Frenchwoman and that's only if she doesna get her arse out of this bed and dressed in the next five minutes."

Cinq minutes! Claudia's first impulse was to laugh, but slanting an upward glance at Jack's set and entirely serious face she thought better of it. Folding her arms across her breasts, she announced, "Five minutes, I fear it is *impossible.*"

He shook his head. "Oh aye, 'tis no only possible, 'tis verra probable, for I'm no goin' anywhere 'til I see ye risen."

"As you wish." Vaguely aware that some small, sick part of her had begun to enjoy their sparring, she let go of the covers to pat the vacant patch of mattress on either side of her. "Do you prefer the right side or the left?"

A low growl confirmed that he was neither tempted nor amused but to his credit he held his voice low and even as he said, "As you will."

She was on the verge of claiming victory when, in one swift motion, he reached down and ripped the bedcovers, quilt, blanket, and sheet, down to her toes. The icy chill of an autumn predawn penetrated her thin shift in seconds, raising gooseflesh on her bare arms even as her face heated with outrage.

"*Serpent! Couchon! Fils de chienne!*" Having exhausted her stock of apropos animal expletives, she snatched at the sheet, but he easily blocked her. "Only last night you promised you would not lay a knuckle on me."

Bending down, he brought his face to hers, so close that the tips of their noses all but brushed. "That would be *finger* and what I said was I'd no beat you provided you do as I bid, which, so far as I can tell, has yet to happen." Gaze locked on hers, he added, "Just as I gave my word to Milread that I'd have ye there in time to help her lay the cook fire."

"But I am injured, see?" Claudia lifted her left hand and wiggled her bandaged thumb.

Straightening to full, towering height, he answered with a scoffing sound low in his throat. "Ye'll maybe live, though to be sure I'll have a look at it before we're off. Either way, I gave my word that I'd see ye there and there ye will be. If I must carry ye thither and deliver ye to Milread in your shift, then so be it." On the mention of her shift, his gaze flickered to the vicinity of her breasts. "Ye'll find it a more pleasant trip, no to mention warmer, if ye'll but dress, aye?" He looked back up, a smile crinkling the corners of his eyes and heating the honey-brown irises to rich chicory.

Grands Dieux! Glancing downward, Claudia confirmed that her shift, or rather Evette's shift, was well worn indeed. Through the thin, cream-colored linen, her areolas shone pink as rose petals, the nipples stiffened to firm points from the chill. At least, she told herself, it was the chilly air that accounted for her embarrassing state. *Certainement* it could not be the sudden awareness that she was abed, and the nearest thing to naked, with a handsome and very virile Scotsman looming over her. Even more unnerving than the threat of being paraded nearly naked through the village was the prospect of once more being clasped against that broad, hard chest, of feeling those whipcord arms braced about her.

It was a wise woman who knew when to accept defeat. Claudia crossed her arms over her breasts and glared up at him. "You will permit me privacy in which to make my toilette?"

He hesitated, then nodded, a faint flush climbing his throat. "Verra well, use the chamber pot if ye must, but be quick about it and mind ye dump the filth in the privy beyond the house."

It took a full moment for his words to sink in and by the time they had, he'd turned to go. Too fuddled to find the English words to express her shock and outrage, Claudia grabbed for the pillow and threw it just as the makeshift curtain fell into place behind her gaoler's broad back.

S*itting at the kitchen table, his mug of tea growing cold in* his hand, Jack watched the dance of light and shadow upon the drawn curtain and promptly forgot to breathe. The splash of water, the rustle of soft feminine clothing as it fell about even softer feminine skin, a curse in French that like as not consigned him to Hell.

But she was too late, for Jack already burned.

From the time he'd stood over her bedside that morning and gazed down upon her sleeping form, he'd been a slave to one image, one fantasy. Black hair splayed across a pillow, a full pink mouth moaning his name, and gooseflesh rising on white, white skin as hands—*his* hands—slid the shift from her shoulders . . .

Whether sleeping like a bairn or doing something as innocuous as eating soup, Claudia Valemont was a temptress of the first order. Watching her delicately lap broth from her spoon the night before, he'd been hard put to choke down his own supper. Her sensuality was so much a part of her, so innate to her nature. He only hoped she might not realize the incredible effect she had on him, for once she did, she'd have him eating from her hand much as he'd trained his injured hawk, Lady, to do.

Damn, damn, *damn!* He slammed the cup down, sending tea sloshing, and pressed hard fingers to his throbbing temples, unhappily aware that other parts of his anatomy had begun to throb as well. Six months was a long time to suffer a cockstand, not to mention a feisty French lassie who couldn't get herself out of bed in the morning. Needing to vent some of the frustration building inside him, he lifted his head from his hands, fixed his gaze on the curtain, and bellowed, "Dinna make me come in there!"

T*he creaking floorboards felt like blocks of ice beneath* Claudia's bare feet as she hurried over to the washstand. Jack must have entered earlier and filled the pitcher while she still slept. Not certain how she felt about that, she poured the water—cold, of course—into the chipped crockery basin and used the cake of lavender soap left beside it to lave her face, neck, and other vital parts.

She was just drying off with the scratchy towel when from the opposite end of the room an annoyed male voice bellowed, "Dinna make me come in there!"

Zut, alors! Damn it! Taking up her comb, she plopped down on the edge of the bed and swiped the ivory teeth through her hair. *Merde,* shit, but the comb wouldn't budge. She'd been so exhausted the night before that she'd collapsed onto the bed before braiding her hair. Touching a hand to the back of her head, she confirmed that overnight the thick tresses had woven themselves into a rat's nest of knots.

"If ye're no out here by the count of ten, I'm coming to get ye." Sounding angry indeed, Jack began counting, "One, two, three . . ."

Infernal man. The comb still stuck in her hair, she found her gown and shoved it over her head. "*Je viens.* I come, I come," she called out and started back to the bed in search of her shoes and stockings, when something small and furry and sharp of claw scuttled over the tops of her bare feet. *"Ahhh!"* she screamed and hopped up on the bed just as the flash of white disappeared into a wormhole in the woodwork.

Paris had been infested with an abundance of mice and rats, too. As a child, she'd once seen a mouse dash beneath a housemaid's skirts and then run up the unfortunate woman's legs and ever since she'd harbored a terrible fear of the creatures.

Jack poked his head inside to find her standing in the center of the bed, arms wrapped about herself. "Och, but I see ye've met Heather."

Quaking on her perch, Claudia looked from him to the woodwork from within which she fancied beady black eyes were surveying her in preparation to pounce. "Heather?" Perspiration filming her forehead, she asked, "Y-you . . . keep vermin as . . . as p-pets?"

He shrugged. "I wouldna call her a pet, exactly, nor vermin either, but Heather and I, we've an understanding, ye ken?" He turned back to the wall and, crouching low, called softly, "Dinna be shy, my beauty, there's someone I want you to meet."

Holding out a palm, Claudia shrilled, "*Non, non,* let her stay as she is." Remembering the black-and-white cat she'd met the night before, she cupped her hands about her mouth and called out, "Here, kitty, kitty, kitty . . ."

Back to her and kneeling on the floor, Jack chuckled. "Ye'll no get any help from that quarter. Despite cats and mice being natural enemies, One Eye and Heather rub along tolerable well." Tone sobering, he added, "Unlike humans, animals hardly ever kill or maim without cause."

Wondering at his change of mood, she glanced down at him. "You let it, er, 'Heather' roam free?"

"Aye, most times I do." Her sinking spirits must have shown on her face, for looking back at her over his shoulder, he conceded, "I'll no tolerate harm befalling her, but if it'll set you at ease I'll put her in her wee cage when ye're about."

She briefly considered suggesting a mousetrap instead, but decided against pressing her luck. "*Merci.* Thank you."

"You're welcome." He turned his attention back to the task of retrieving the mouse from its hiding place.

Under other circumstances, Claudia might have been moved to laughter at the sight of a grown man, and such a *large* man at that, crooning baby talk to a wild beast. But seconds later, a tiny pink snout poked its way from the dark depths of the hole, followed by the rest. The mouse—Heather—all but leapt into Jack's open palm.

Standing, he stroked the white head with a single blunt finger, then deftly tucked the creature into his coat pocket.

Turning to Claudia, he stretched out a hand. "You can come down now."

Claudia hesitated. "Will it not come out?"

"Nay, she fancies my pocket. 'Tis like a wee warm nest to her."

Hoping Heather hadn't deposited any droppings in Jack's hand, Claudia took hold of it. Fingers wrapped about his broad callused palm, she stepped down. As she did, her comb, heretofore forgotten, fell free from the back of her head and clattered to the floor between them.

Jack stooped to pick it up. Examining it, he said, "That's a verra pretty comb ye have. Mother-of-pearl, is it?"

Jerked back to the present, Claudia assumed what she hoped was a nonchalant air and replied, "*Oui.* Yes. My mistress, she was most generous with her gifts."

"So it would seem."

Was that skepticism shading his voice or merely paranoia pricking her conscience? In truth, the full set of comb, brush, and hand mirror had been a present from Phillippe, a gesture of good faith in those early days when he'd set out to woo her.

Apparently satisfied with her answer, he lifted a snarled strand from her shoulder. " 'Tis a muckle mess but I dinna think we need cut it just yet. After you've finished dressing come out by the fire, and I'll see what I can do."

Startled by the offer, she could only stare. She'd been Phillippe's mistress for seven years and not once had he shown any interest in brushing her hair—although he'd pulled it a time or two.

"Dinna look so scairt," he said, sounding almost angry. "I willna hurt you."

Large and rough though his hands were, it had never entered her mind that he would. "I will be out in a moment," she said, marveling at how handsome he managed to look even when solemn-faced as a cleric. "And thank you," she added on afterthought, for it occurred to her that he needn't have offered to help her at all.

"You're welcome." He nodded and turned away to push through the blanketed enclosure. As soon as the flap fell back into place, Claudia grabbed for her stockings and shoes. She put them on quickly, a strange anticipation causing her to hurry.

She found him in the kitchen standing facing the fire, hands folded behind him, an earthenware pot of *something* bubbling from a grill set above the glowing embers. In preparation, he'd set her comb on the kitchen table next to his tea mug. Seeing their two personal articles lying side by side struck her as both homey and intimate.

Feeling awkward suddenly, she cleared her throat.

He unfurled the fingers of one hand from his opposite wrist and turned about to face her. "Have a seat," he said, gesturing her to a bench.

Grateful to face away from that unnerving amber gaze, she sat, tucking her legs beneath the table.

"Your problem, lass," he told her, taking position behind her, comb in hand, "is that ye want for patience." She was of a mind to tell him that what she wanted for were a full night's sleep and a decent breakfast, but all such tart retorts fled when she felt his touch at the back of her head. "Bend forward a wee bit. Aye, there's a good lass." He lifted a handful of hair from her neck, his roughened knuckles grazing her nape.

The contact, light as it was, took Claudia unawares. Tingling warmth shuddered down her from nape to tailbone, enervating some very sensitive spots along the path.

She must have moved, for instantly he stilled his hands. "Dinna be worrit. I'm no nearly as clumsy as I look."

Thankful he couldn't see her face, which suddenly felt on fire, she answered, "I am not worried. And I do not think you are clumsy. I am cold, that is all."

The last was a lie, for chill though the cottage was in the predawn, Claudia suddenly felt very warm indeed. Her flush flesh verily tingled with awareness. Her breasts, indeed the very blood traversing her veins, felt warm and liquid and heavy.

His hands left her hair to settle the shawl more firmly on her shoulders. "Better?"

Calluses grazed her skin in the barest of touches but this time Claudia steeled herself not to shudder. "*Oui.* Yes, *merci.*"

Juste ciel! Good heavens, but if a whisper of a touch could bring her to such a state, what havoc might a more lengthy exploration bring? Imagining those big rough hands, *hangman's* hands, no less, caressing her breasts, palming her belly and beyond, caused her to forget all about the chill. *Certainement* she no longer felt sleepy. By the time the fantasy progressed to big blunt fingers parting the folds of her woman's flesh and slipping inside, the dampness inside her thighs was all too real. An inner pulse jumped and so did she.

Jack stepped back. "I'm sorry, lass. I dinna like to hurt ye but that was a verra bad tangle."

Had he pulled her hair? More than willing to seize upon the excuse, she said, *"Continuez, s'il vous plait."*

He did continue, humming a soft tune beneath his breath as he worked away at her snarled hair with such patience, such gentleness, that he put to shame even Evette's expert ministrations. Before long, Claudia felt her eyelids growing heavy and her taut shoulders begin to relax. By the time he stepped back and announced, "Done," she was all but purring.

Sitting upright, she lifted a hand to the back of her head. Incredibly the long strands felt smooth and, most importantly, all present.

Stepping away so that she might rise, Jack chuckled. "Aye, ye're no bald, if that's what ye're worrit for."

The savory if unfamiliar scent rising from the cook pot reminded her that she was ravenous. Odd how she'd never cared for food until she'd been forced to go without. To lie awake fantasizing about the yeasty perfume of baking bread or the tart crispness of a freshly picked apple was torture pure and simple. In the course of the past few weeks, she'd developed a grudging affinity for those rioting, miserable masses on whose behalf Marie Antoinette was supposed to have declared, "Let them eat cake." Those same men, women, and children, faces sallow from hunger and from hate, who'd stood just outside Claudia's front gate, shaking their fists and chanting *"À la lanterne, à la lanterne!"* with such desperate frenzy that even now, a continent away, she trembled to think of it.

Pushing the memory to the back of her mind, she turned back to Jack and asked, "Do we have time to break our fast before we leave?"

He nodded. "Aye, we've a good hour before we need set out, but first the beasties must be tended."

"The *beasties?"* She cast her gaze about the cottage but sighted only the cat and Elf, heads buried in their respective food bowls.

He lifted his hand, ran his thumb in circles over his chin, considering. "There's the horses and Lady, the hawk, and the chickens' eggs to be gathered and Grizel to be milked. And of course they're sure to be wanting their breakfast, too."

"What of *my* breakfast?" Her stomach followed the question with an indignant rumble.

Eyes softening, he admitted, "Ah well, there's parritch and honey and tea and if Grizel cooperates there'll be milk as well. It'll be waiting for you when you come back."

"When I come back from—" The rest of her question ended on an oath for already Jack had taken hold of her arm and was steering her toward the cottage door.

"I'd feed the chickens first if I were you," he advised, releasing her arm to take down her cloak from where it hung by the door. "They're the worst tempered." He draped the cloak about her and then reached around her to open the door.

"B-but Jack, *j'ai faim.* I am hungr—" Before she could get the rest of the English words out, he laid his big hands about her waist and lifted her over the threshold.

Setting her down on the step outside, he shot her an infuriating wink. "Dinna fash, I'll keep your parritch warm."

And with that he shoved a basket of meal into her one hand, a lighted lantern into her other, and the door in her face.

Friendship is constant in all other things
Save in the office and affairs of love.

—William Shakespeare,
Much Ado About Nothing

I*t was dark still but the first pale promise of dawn lightened* the sky as a seething Claudia stepped off the stoop and onto the stone path. She followed it around to the back of the cottage, the basket looped over one wrist and the lantern held out to light her way. A small fenced patch of dirt yard backed onto the cottage; a half dozen or so feathered shapes moved about within. Following the squawking noise to the gate, she opened it and stepped inside, hefting the lantern high to navigate her way around several squishy, dark piles.

Crowned with a red comb and flaunting a spray of feathers, the rooster broke free from the clutch and came forward. Watching him strut up to her with ne'er so much as a backward glance for the hens holding meekly behind, Claudia set down her lantern and dug her hand into the basket. She must be tired, disordered indeed, for somehow the sight of those bandy legs and beady eyes brought to mind Phillippe. To be sure, her former lover had favored that very same garish scarlet for his coats.

Addressing herself to the cock, she said, "*Égoïste.* You, *monsieur,* shall wait until after your wives have eaten."

Dieu, but one night under Jack Campbell's roof and already she was conversing with fowl! Wondering if perhaps she was becoming a madwoman in truth, she filled her fist with grain and then reeled it back, intending to toss the first handful to the hens. Unfortunately, a blast of wind chose that very moment to rip through the yard, sending the seeds flying backward. Eyes watering, Claudia looked down to find herself covered from head to toe in feed—and the focus of seven pairs of beady black eyes.

Swallowing hard, she took a step back. "Now, now, *monsieur, mesdames,* there is no need to look at me so."

The fowl advanced an equal measure. There was several seconds' pause as each side took the other's measure, then the rooster let out a piercing screech and the chickens charged, wings flapping and feathers flying. Claudia dropped the basket, hiked up her skirts, and ran for dear life, nearly tripping over the lantern in her haste to escape.

Through the gate and back toward the house she sped, the crystallized cloud of her huffing breath the only thing she could make out clearly in the semidarkness.

"Ouf!"

The impact was akin to barreling into a brick wall. It knocked what breath she had left from her lungs and sent her sprawling backwards.

A strong arm whipped out, catching her before she fell. "Wheesht, woman, what am I to do with you?" Jack lifted his lantern so that the light shone full on her face. "It seems I canna leave you on your own for one wee minute."

Shuddering at the thought of those unblinking eyes, webbed feet, and oh so sharp-looking beaks, she lifted her face from one very firm pectoral muscle and sputtered, "*Les poulets* . . . the ch-chickens, they tried to . . . to kill me."

She shot a glance over her shoulder. Fortunately, avarice appeared to be the guiding principle of the animal as well as human kingdom. Pushing and shoving—or engaging in the chicken equivalent thereof—the beasts crowded about the dropped basket, gobbling grain as if it were their last meal. If Claudia might have had her wish, it would have been with coq au vin crowning that night's supper menu.

A deep rumble from the vicinity of her protector's chest caused her to swivel her head about. Damn him to hell, he was *laughing* at her. Outrage warred with vanity, for she knew she must appear not only ridiculous but also an utter mess.

Pushing away to drag a hasty hand through her seed-encrusted hair, she huffed, "F-first . . . you send me out to the mercy of those . . . those vicious beasts and now, now you mock me." Beyond angry, she reached out and gave him a goodly shove.

He didn't budge other than to swipe at his watery eyes. "You're right, I shouldna laugh, 'tis only . . ." Another tremor of a belly laugh choked off the rest of his apology. Recovering, he reached out to pluck something—a feather—from her hair. "Ah well," he said, twirling it about, "I expect it's safe to say ye've no seen a great deal of life outside of cities."

Still smarting from being the object of his mirth and not wanting to appear a complete idiot, she blurted out, "That is not true. In the summers we would leave Paris for the valley of the Loire." Judging she'd said enough, perhaps too much, she ended there.

"The Loire Valley, you say." Hefting a russet brow, he regarded her with steely eyes. "Isna that the river country where you French have all those grand big houses?"

"Well, er, yes," she answered, wondering just what she'd gotten herself into now.

"That must mean 'twas a noble household you served in?"

Seizing on what she hoped would sound like a plausible reply, she cleared her throat of seed dust and answered, "Ah *oui,* but the house of my mistress belonged to . . . to *her* family." Not a total lie, for Phillippe's father, *le comte,* had continued to enjoy robust health, much to his heir's chagrin. "And it was *petit.* Small. A cottage really." Only partly a lie, for the du Marmac summer residence had been of modest dimensions—for a château.

"Hmph," was all he said, then bent to retrieve the empty wooden pail he'd dropped in order to catch her. "Then ye'll ken how to milk a cow, aye?"

Claudia stared down at the bucket, her mind working. Queen Marie Antoinette had liked to play at dress-up, costuming herself and her ladies as shepherdesses or milkmaids as the royal fancy dictated. Owing to her position as Phillippe's mistress, Claudia once had received the summons to Le Petit Trianon at Versailles where she'd waited upon Her Highness at her celebrated *hameau.* Standing about with her fellow courtiers in a lace-trimmed kerchief and bow-bedecked overskirt while the queen, likewise garbed and perched on a stool, squealed in delight at the milk streaming into the chased silver pail had struck

Claudia as not only foolish but also deadly dull. Now, however, she found herself wishing she'd paid closer attention. Even so, the process had *looked* simple enough. If memory served her, all she need do was to take hold of the teat—abhorrent, repugnant thought—and manipulate the sensitive flesh until the contents flowed into the bucket. How difficult could that be?

Glancing up at Jack, seeing the skepticism etched into his every feature as he awaited her reply, she felt her hesitancy gel into firm resolve. Determined to redeem herself, to prove she wasn't so useless as heretofore her gaffes had made her out to be, she reached for the pail.

"Mais bien sûr," she said, wrapping her fingers about the handle and summoning a confident smile. "But of course."

Some minutes later, squatting on the three-legged stool and cursing a blue streak, Claudia had considerable cause to regret those words. It was the cow's fault, of course. The stupid bovine had taken a dislike to Claudia the moment she'd stepped inside the stall. Tail twitching, Grizel had kicked over the three-legged milking stool that Claudia had just set down, then eyed Claudia as if to say, "Your move."

The stool righted and the bucket positioned beneath the direction of probable flow, Claudia leaned in and grabbed hold of the teat with both hands. Careful to keep her cheek from brushing the beast's broad side, she pulled down. Grizel let out a piercing squeal and backed up. Wondering if she might be hurting her, Claudia took lighter hold and started to work the warm flesh. She knew a heady triumph when she felt the first trickle, and then a goodly stream, pass through her fingers to strike the inside of the bucket with an encouraging *ping, ping.*

The bucket close to three-quarters full, she was just congratulating herself on her hard-won victory when the horrible animal kicked out again. This time the flailing back hoof caught the pail, knocking it on its side and sending milk splashing Claudia's skirts, shoes, and the straw at her feet. *Merde!* She whipped out a hand and righted it, managing to save a third or so of the precious liquid.

Only too ready to quit the byre while she still had something to show for her labors, she grabbed the pail and lantern and backed out of the stall. Feeling like Job, or the female equivalent thereof, she trudged back to the cottage, the biting air drying her gown to prickly stickiness, the seeds that had somehow found their way inside her shoes feeling like full-scale boulders.

Somehow she was not really surprised to find Monsieur Campbell—Jack—watching her from the stepping stone outside the open cottage door, one hand curved about a mug of steaming tea. He slid his gaze down the length of her. "I dinna suppose you managed to get any into the bucket?"

"I *dinna* suppose I did," she mimicked, then shoved the pail at his chest and marched inside, the echo of his hearty laughter ringing in her ears.

C*laudia's day went downhill from there on. In the pearly* gray light of new morning, the inn taproom rang quiet as a churchyard, the tables and benches empty save for crumbs and dried spillage from the night before. The staleness of unwashed bodies, tobacco, and burned tallow still hung upon the air when Claudia and Jack stepped inside, but otherwise the low-ceilinged room seemed a different place entirely from the boisterous and dangerous place Claudia had first entered two days before.

Which was fine with her.

She'd spent the ride over in Jack's pony cart wondering how she would feel upon returning to this, the scene of her disaster. Not that the episode had been entirely unpleasant. There had been that moment, a few seconds at most, when she surrendered her knife and let herself fall into Jack's open arms and he'd held her close. They'd been strangers then, were strangers still, and yet how safe she'd felt, how protected. He *had* protected her, first laying his very life on the line and then his purse to pay for her room and board. Why? she wondered yet again, even as his friend, Milread's voice echoed in her mind, *Everyone's somebody tae Jack.*

And it wasn't only Jack who was deserving of her thanks. The day before, in the meeting hall, the barmaid had risen to speak for her although Claudia suspected that her doing so had put her out of favor with the innkeeper. Two people, two strangers, had put themselves at risk to save her life and so far

Claudia had yet to utter a single word of thanks to either of them.

And suddenly she felt very, very ashamed.

As if reading her thoughts, Jack bent his head to her ear and whispered, "Dinna fash, she's not one to hold on to a grudge." He inclined his head down the aisle between tables to where Milread sprawled on her hands and knees before the hearth, employing a small handheld brush to sweep ashes from the grate into the dustpan.

"We're verra sorry to be late," he called out, leading the way down the aisle. "Claudia had a bit o' trouble with the cow. And with the chickens," he added, smiling back at Claudia over his shoulder when she reached out to swat him.

Milread rose and turned to greet them, wiping her hands on the front of what must have once been a white apron. "Nay worries. The next coach isna due for another few hours." Gazing at Claudia, she said, "Plenty o' time for Mistress Claudia and I tae get better acquainted."

The Scotswoman topped Claudia by a good head and was built like an ox but if Claudia felt even the tiniest bit intimidated, she refused to show it. She pulled back her shoulders and inclined her head. *"Mademoiselle."*

The two women regarded one another, each taking the other's measure. And then Milread said, "I was just about tae make myself a cup o' tea. Will ye join me?"

"*Merci.* Yes, I believe I will."

The invitation plainly included Claudia only. Apparently taking the hint, Jack started edging his way to the door. "Well, I'd best be off. That chimney piece Duncan bespoke willna carve itself and forbye I promised auld Una I'd bring by one of my brews to ease her cough." To Claudia, he said, "Ye're no to go beyond the kitchen or the smokehouse nor to so much as visit the privy without telling Milread first until I come this eve to fetch you home. D'ye ken me?"

Humiliated that he'd not only brought up her status as his prisoner but then put Milread in the position of her keeper, Claudia only nodded and turned away. That she did indeed plan to seize her first opportunity to escape, whenever it might come, hardly seemed to signify. Jack Campbell didn't trust her and for some odd, inexplicable reason, that hurt.

Knuckled hands hidden inside the folds of her cloak, she

watched from the corner of her eye as Milread followed Jack to the door. The two Scots stopped on the threshold, voices lowered in conference. Occasionally one or both paused to peer her way but Claudia pretended not to notice. She was tired, she was humiliated, but beyond even that she was lonely. Lonelier than she'd ever felt in her life, for never had she felt more the outsider, nor farther away from all that was familiar and dear.

Lost to her own misery, she heard Jack take his leave and then the door close, presumably behind him. Footsteps padded back down the aisle toward her; a heavy tap on her shoulder had her whirling about.

"Shall we sit awhile?" Milread asked, though Claudia doubted it was truly a question. "Once the coach comes, we're sure tae be on our feet for the rest o' the day."

A short while later, her cloak hung on a peg by the door, the fire laid, and two mugs of steaming tea and a plate of bannocks set on the table before them, Claudia finally found the nerve to say, "*Mademoiselle,* about the other day, I wish to—"

Milread cut her off with a broad smile. "Nay worries, mistress, 'tis water under the bridge." She took another bannock from the plate and bit into it.

Taking a cautious nibble of her own flattened biscuit, Claudia swallowed and then said, "Call me Claudia, *s'il vous plait.* If you please."

Around a mouthful of biscuit, Milread asked, "Well then, Claudia, tell me how ye and Jack are rubbing along?"

Thinking back to their disastrous first evening together, Claudia allowed there was nothing to be gained by recounting the gory details, especially as they were all so patently unflattering to *her.* Reminded that Jack and Milread were friends—how good of friends she'd yet to discover—she said only, "He is very . . . quiet."

Milread cracked a laugh, sending biscuit crumbs sprinkling her square chin like snowflakes. "Oh aye, silent as a stone and deep as the sea, that's our Jack. And yet he's a regular chatterbox compared tae what he was when he was a lad." Expression sobering, she added, "At least after his puir maither's murder."

It was certain to be none of Claudia's business and yet that had never caused her to hold her tongue before. And so she didn't hesitate to ask, "Murdered?"

The smile left Milread's hazel eyes entirely. Tracing a broad finger about the rim of her cup, she confided, "Och, but 'twas a terrible thing. I dinna remember it all that well myself as I was but six or so. Jack would have been about eight or nine, his braither, Callum, four or five. They were on their way tae market, Maggie and the two lads, when a robber waylaid their cart. The boys wer'na harmed as she'd bade them burrow down in the straw at the back of the cart, but Maggie herself was killed, beaten tae death with a cudgel and, some say, ravished, too. Either way, they caught up wi' the bastard and strung him up in the commons just yonder."

Claudia felt her anger over that morning dissolve in a rush of genuine sympathy. "*Pauvre* Jack," she said, belatedly realizing she'd spoken aloud.

In Paris she'd witnessed her own mother guillotined in the square and thus she knew firsthand the pain of a parent meeting a violent end. That Jack had suffered such a tragedy, such a loss, at the tender age of nine tore at her heart.

Milread nodded and took a swallow of tea. "Aye, Callum seemed tae be fine afterwards, but Jack . . . it hit him hard. He didna speak so much as one wee word for nigh on a year."

Claudia had been too lost in sympathy to attend to all the details but now it occurred to her to ask, "Callum, this is a common name?"

"Aye, I suppose it is, though fortunate we are to have only the one." Milread made a face. "Callum McBride, the blacksmith's son and the selfsame sot who gave ye that wee shiner." She pointed a thick finger to indicate Claudia's bruised cheek.

Shocked to her core, Claudia nearly spat out the sip of tea she'd just taken. "That beast is Jack's brother?"

"Half-brother. They'd different faithers," Milread said and her shuttered expression told Claudia she meant to leave it at that.

But Claudia was determined to hear the rest. "Why did not Jack tell me this himself?"

Milread shrugged. "Why would he? Until t'other day, he and Callum had no spoken so much as a word to each other in nigh on ten years. They're no exactly loving brothers, ye ken, for since they were bairns Callum's harbored a terrible hatred o' Jack. And dinna ask me why, for in truth I've nay notion," she added, anticipating the question tickling the tip of Claudia's tongue.

Embarrassed to be so easily read, hoping she'd done a better job of concealing her true self the night before when she'd lied to Jack about being a lady's maid, she stared down at her plate. Toying with the remains of her biscuit as her mind worked to make sense of it all, she remarked, "Even for half-brothers, they do not much resemble each other." Perhaps there was some slight similarity about the bridge of the nose, the shape of the chin, but the likeness if indeed it could be called that ended there.

"Aye, Callum's always been skinny as a fence rail and with a face like a rat, no bonny and strong like Jack." Milread's voice ended on a sigh and a dreamy look hazed her eyes.

Wondering if she might have misunderstood the meaning of *bonny,* Claudia asked, "You think Monsieur Campbell handsome?"

"Aye." Milread's brow bunched in a scowl. "Ye dinna think so?"

Under pretense of taking a sip from her mug, Claudia asked herself that very same question. Before now she'd always defined "handsome" in terms of Phillippe's patrician features and slender physique. And yet there was no denying that Jack's rough-hewn looks held a certain appeal. He possessed a raw-boned sensuality, she'd allow him that, and his big, broad chest had felt nicely firm beneath her palms. The few times she'd seen him smile had confirmed that his teeth were straight and white and, more to the point, all present. And thinking back to that morning when his big hands, his *hangman's* hands, had worked gently away at her tangled hair, she was forced to admit that the tingling awareness his touch had triggered had little if anything to do with her contempt for how he earned his living.

Hating that he roused her, searching for faults, she answered at length, "Ah *oui,* of course, but do you not find him to be *un peu* large?"

Milread's wide mouth curved upwards; the look she slanted Claudia was positively wicked. "Ah well, I canna say as I've had the pleasure, but I ken he'd fill a woman up and then some."

Claudia nearly fell back in her chair. Her English might be imperfect at best, her command of Scots vernacular nigh on nonexistent, but she had no difficulty in comprehending Milread's meaning. Recovering her composure, she owned that a small, unworthy part of her couldn't help but rejoice that Milread and Jack were apparently not lovers.

Feeling more cheerful than she had all morning, she allowed, "*Alors,* I suppose he does have a nice smile."

Milread tossed back her flaxen hair and guffawed. "A nice smile, is it?" She slapped the flat of her hand onto the table, setting cups rattling. "Ye're a rare one, Mistress Claudia, and ye've some verra queer notions, but I ken we're goin' tae get on just fine."

It turned out that "getting on" with Milread proved to be the very least of Claudia's difficulties. As morning stretched into midday and midday into night, the Scotswoman showed herself to be as good-natured as her freckled face and ready smile portended—as well as gifted with the forbearance of Saint Jeanne. When in helping an overnight guest on with his boots, Claudia handed him his left boot first instead of his right, a mistake that sent him careening down the stairs, Milread only helped him up, checked for broken bones, and then went to fetch him a pint on the house. Likewise, when Claudia dropped an entire pot of hot stew smack in the middle of the tavern floor, Milread shrugged and went to the broom closet for a bucket and mop.

But after more than sixteen straight hours spent on her feet, not even Milread's bawdy tales and all-around good spirits could distract Claudia from the ache settling into her lower back or the sting of fresh blisters on her soles. Now it was nearing ten o'clock. Alistair had given the last call for drink some minutes before and the taproom was cleared of all but one man in the corner who'd fallen asleep over his half-full pint.

Taking advantage of the reprieve, Claudia set her broom in the corner and collapsed on the edge of a recently vacated and still warm bench seat. Her hair and clothing, indeed *all* of her, reeked of tobacco and grease, and she would have sold her chance for Heaven, if indeed she hadn't already, for a hot bath and the opportunity to wash her hair.

As it was, it seemed a monumental effort to even hold up her head. Nearby was Milread, whistling some cheerful tune as she swept away. Faced with all that energy, Claudia felt a grudging admiration take root in her breast.

Hoisting her throbbing head from the cradle of her open palms, she asked, "You work like this *every* day?"

Stopping to assess the two tidy piles she'd created, Milread answered with a shrug. "Ah well, it's no so bad once ye're used tae it. Harder than some jobs, maybe, but easier than others."

Throughout the day Claudia had wondered why it was that Milread meticulously sorted the droppings into two distinct piles, one of regular debris and a second of foodstuffs; the latter she parceled out and deposited in one of several small wooden boxes set about the taproom floor. Her question was at last answered when the barmaid left off sweeping to go over to one of the mysterious little boxes. She picked it up, lifted the lid, and angled the box so that Claudia could see within to the wooden block and, beneath it, the crushed form of what must have once been a mouse.

"Och, but ye're a fine fat fellow," Milread announced, lifting the block and holding the bludgeoned form by the end of its curling tail. "Ho, Bridie, come fetch your supper, ye lazy lass."

Lips smacking, the tabby cat called Bridie trotted up. Slanted green eyes fixed on the mouse dangling from Milread's hand, the cat braced itself and then leapt, neatly catching the tossed "treat" in midair. Looking inordinately pleased, Bridie trotted over to the nearest corner to savor her supper in private.

Reminded of her impromptu encounter with Jack's "Heather" and how tenderly he'd stroked the little white body before snuggling it away in his coat pocket, Claudia was glad he hadn't yet come for her so that he might be spared this spectacle. For herself she quickly averted her gaze, wishing she might as easily close her ears to the sickening *crunch, crunch.*

She was just about to rise and take up her broom once more when the main door swung open and Jack strode in. Despite her aching back and blistered feet, a trill of excitement shot through her, making that morning's humiliations seem a very long time ago.

A smile of welcome forming on her lips, she started up to greet him. "*Bonsoir,*" she said, painfully aware of how slatternly she must look, how unpleasant she must smell.

Coming up on her, his smile dipped into a frown. "Warming the bench, are we?" He reached out, wrapping a hand about her arm. "Well, come along with you. Like as no ye dinna deserve a morsel, but I'll feed you some supper anyhow."

His hold on her arm pinched but it was her pride that groaned in agony. Looking up into his set face, Claudia felt her smile sink along with her spirits. "But, I was only—"

"Having a well-deserved rest," Milread finished for her, coming up between them. Handing Claudia her broom, she said, "Jack, dearie, there's a full stewpot that's too heavy for me and Claudia tae lift. Would ye mind comin' wi' me tae the kitchen tae fetch it down before ye go?"

He hesitated, then released his hold on Claudia's arm. "Aye, I will." To Claudia, he said, "Since you're so in love with that bench, see you dinna budge from it until I come back."

She opened her mouth to snap out a reply, then clamped it closed again for there was no purpose to be served. For whatever reason, Jack Campbell had resolved himself to believing the worst of her. A cruel irony since, for the first time in years, she'd tried, really tried, to please.

Tears of frustration pricked the backs of her eyes, but through sheer force of will she held them back. Silent, she sank down onto the hard bench seat, her gaze boring holes in Jack's back as he followed Milread to the door leading out to the kitchen.

The door closed behind them and she was left alone with the snoring man, the cat, and what was left of the mouse; the latter suddenly struck her to be a kindred spirit of sorts. Thinking on how the poor, unsuspecting mouse had run headfirst into the trap, Claudia allowed she just might have more in common with those tiny, brainless creatures than she ever would have suspected.

A *narrow, covered walkway led from the tavern's rear door* to the kitchen dependency. Still fuming at the sight of Claudia taking her ease on the bench, Jack admitted to himself she'd looked maybe a wee bit tired about the eyes. And yet, on the other hand, far too fresh, too lovely, to have done much of any real work.

Milread's slamming the door brought an end to his conflicted musings. Turning about to regard her, he asked, "Well, what is it?" When she only stood glaring at him, one clogged foot tapping a tattoo on the paving stones, he added, "You could probably lift *me* if you were so minded, let alone a cook pot."

"Fie, Jack Campbell, I'm minded tae take down that pot and bang it right o'er your hard head. What devil is it that possessed ye tae speak so tae the puir lass?"

Jack couldn't believe his ears. "Puir lass! And d'ye take her part, then? What am I to think when I see her sittin' on her arse and watchin' you work like a slave?"

Face fierce, Milread rested her fisted hands on her hips. "Claudia labored long and hard today. 'Tis no her fault she's no been bred for such rough work."

"No bred for it, is she? And yet she's supposed to have kent service as a lady's maid in France, or so she said last night. How do you explain that?"

Milread shrugged. "Och, dressing hair and fluffing gowns 'tis no the same thing as laboring in a public house."

Jack bowed his head in grudging acknowledgment of the truth of those words. As much as he wanted to believe that Claudia Valemont was who and what she claimed to be, he couldn't see her as a servant, not even as a lady's maid. With her arrogant nose pointed north, back held ramrod straight, and delicate white hands soft as spun silk, she didn't look, speak, or carry herself as one who'd been beholden to any master.

"Wheesht, and d'ye no trouble yourself to wonder why it is ye're so hard on the lass?" He opened his mouth to protest that he'd never been anything but completely reasonable when Milread stalled him by raising a silencing palm. "'Tis written all o'er your face—ye fancy her."

"I dinna!" he protested even as he felt the telltale flames blister his cheeks and the memory of that morning's battle over the bedcovers rushing back to him.

The episode—and Claudia—had scarcely left his thoughts all day, for a bonny sight she'd been. Curled on her side, her profile had looked as finely wrought as that of a china figurine, her expression in sleep as innocent as a bairn's, the dark lashes sweeping the delicate indentation between eye and cheekbone, the mouth soft and pink and utterly kissable.

But there'd been nothing innocent or childlike about her breasts. Full, white, and womanly, the coral nipples winking at him through the thin shift brought to mind fresh summer peaches and, like the fruit, they'd made his mouth water. When she'd taunted him to climb in beside her, he'd been sorely tempted to call her bluff.

Milread's broad features narrowed into an expression of shrewd assessment. "What's more, I ken her wits maun be addled after all, for I could swear she fancies ye, too, puir wee idjut though that makes her."

He snorted at that, although buried inside his breast his traitorous heart gave a hopeful little lift. "If ye maun know, the lass loathes the verra sight o' me. According to Mistress Claudia Valemont, I'm a great, brainless lummox and a murderer betimes."

She answered with a chortle. "A lot ye ken o' women, Jack Campbell, and what ye do would fit inside a thimble wi' room tae spare. I tell ye she fancies ye."

He snorted. "Best ye stick to your cook pots and ale kegs, Milread, for ye'll ne'er make for a seer—or a matchmaker, either."

She clucked her tongue. "That may be, and yet I see a good deal more than some others I could name."

One eye on the door behind her, suddenly desperate to escape the scrutiny of those canny eyes, he said with feeling, "For the last time, the sooner that wee meddlesome woman is out of my house—and my life—the better it will be for all concerned."

To his chagrin, Milread only chuckled. "We'll see, Jack Campbell. We'll just ha' tae see about that."

*Fifteen-odd leagues away in Linlithgow, in a silk-hung bed*chamber of Aberdaire Castle, a vigil was under way. Gearald Edward Allen Drummond, seventh earl of Aberdaire, sat in a bath chair staring down at the wasted form in the bed, all that remained of his son, heir, and namesake. Until the week before, Young Gearald—Gerry—had been the hope of his house, his only offspring to reach adulthood and thus his final bid for forging the coveted alliance with the English.

But a freakish hunting accident had put an abrupt end to that lifelong dream. Now Gerry lay at last gasp, his lungs crushed from the weight of the horse he'd fallen beneath in an accident not unlike that which had maimed his sire. All the long week, the earl had cursed fate, had cursed the curse, even as he'd kept by his son's bedside, watching, waiting, for Gerry to recover enough breath to provide the answer as to whether or not he need bury his dream along with his son.

Not a patient man under the best of circumstances, the past seven days and nights had pushed the earl's tolerance to its very limit. Resolved to wait no more, he reached over and grabbed the boy by the collar of his nightshirt, hauling him up from the banked pillows.

Bringing his face down to the sweat-drenched one, he demanded, "Have you managed to get that whey-faced Sassenach bitch of a wife with child, Gerry? Answer me, damn you, did you at least do that?"

A light hand descended on the earl's shoulder. "He's tired, milord. We must allow him to rest."

Aberdaire twisted his head about and glared up at the physician, one of several "experts" he'd sent for from Edinburgh. The bastards had bled Gerry all but dry, covered his crushed chest with mustard plasters and poultices, and poured their teas and tinctures down his throat, but all to no avail.

"Dinna presume to tell me what to do." Aberdaire shook off the hand just as he shook off the notion that the doctor had any right to govern how his patient was treated. "He's dying, no tired. And he'll have plenty of time to rest once he's six feet under, but for now by God he'll answer me or else."

"Perhaps he will, milord," the doctor answered in his soft, monosyllabic voice, "but after he's had his medicine for the pain."

Staring deliberately down at his son's pasty face, the eyes wide and terrified, he snarled, "He'll have it once he gives me my answer or no at all."

Saliva bubbled forth from the corners of the boy's cracked lips. Aberdaire bent his ear close to the damp face and sought to decipher the soft rasping. "N-noo."

"Damn you, Gerry." He released the dying man to flop back onto the pillows with no more resistance than the corpse he soon would be.

Disgusted, Aberdaire wheeled about, turning his back on the bed so that he could better think. Brain ticking away like the ormolu clock set on the rose marble mantel, he called out, "MacDuff, where the bloody hell have you got to, man?"

His butler stepped free from the shadows that his all-black attire had allowed him to disappear into. "I am here, milord."

"Good, good." The earl raked a hand through his thick hair. Barring the white winging his temples and the passage of nearly fifty years, it was still the blue-black of a crow's wing. *I'm still young,* he told himself. *Would to God I were still able.* But self-pity was a luxury he'd never allowed himself nor had he the time to do so now. Shrugging it off, he said, "I need you to send a courier to Paris. Today, for there's no time to waste."

MacDuff took a halting step forward. "But milord, the situation in France is—"

"Dinna presume to tell me the situation in France. Do you ken you're the only one to read a newspaper?"

"Of course not, milord, 'tis only that—"

"Tell Gunn I'll pay him thrice his normal retainer—that should put some fire in his belly. And that I'll double—no, triple that sum provided he comes back with the prize."

"The *prize,* milord?"

"Aye." Aberdaire wheeled himself over to the window, shoved aside the heavy draperies that had been drawn to keep the light from hurting the invalid's eyes, and stared out to the boxwood-bordered lawns below. "Aye, something of mine I left behind in Paris nigh on five-and-twenty years ago. And now I'm minded to fetch it home."

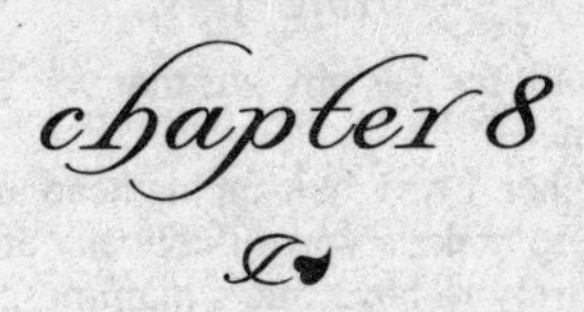

chapter 8

Passions are liken'd best to floods and streams:
The shallow murmur, but the deep are dumb

—Sir Walter Raleigh, *The Silent Lover*

"D*o you have a lover, Jack?"* *Claudia asked two weeks* later as they lingered over their breakfast before leaving for the inn.

Jack nearly choked on the healthy swallow of tea he'd just taken. "What the devil . . ." He plunked his stoneware mug down and stared across the table to Claudia.

Serenely sipping her morning tea heavily laced with honey and cream as she liked it, she sent him a blithe smile from over the rim of her cup. "An *amante,* a mistress. Someone who shares your bed?"

He speared her with a hard look. "I kent your meaning—I'm no daft. What I dinna ken is *why* it is ye care to know."

She glanced down at the puddle of spillage he'd made with his cup and a small smile touched her lips. "Oh, but I have embarrassed you."

"You hav'na," he shot back but already he could feel the heat creeping up past his collar.

She picked up her half-eaten oatcake and broke off a bite-size morsel. Nibbling at it, she said, "It is only that in France we speak openly of such things."

"This isna France." Appetite spoiled, he pushed aside his bowl of parritch, barely touched.

"*Non,* I suppose it is not." She sighed, lancing him a look that seemed to say, "more is the pity." Aloud, she said, "I was but *curieuse,* that is all, for it is obvious that you"—she hesitated—"appreciate women."

Jack glared at her, every hair on his head and body bristling. It was one thing to make a vow of celibacy and abide by it; another matter entirely to have one's manliness called into question—and before five in the morning!

"Well I dinna 'appreciate' lads, if that's what ye're worrit for."

"Oh, *non,* I did not mean to imply . . ." Another sigh brought Jack to the edge of his seat and then, "Ah well, perhaps it is best that we speak of it no more."

Her lush mouth curved into a full smile this time, one that touched her eyes. The latter shone like sapphires, but then why wouldn't they, fired as they were by the luster of pure, unadulterated *mischief?*

Jack folded his arms across his chest and dug in his heels. "Nay, we'll speak of it a'right. Neither of us is to budge from this table until I ken your meaning, the whole of it."

"Very well, if you insist."

She took a moment to moisten her lips, and Jack knew the sudden, strong urge to cover her mouth with his and taste her fully, deeply. To wipe away that oh-so-smug smile with his lips and tongue and teeth.

"When we first made our acquaintance in the tavern and my cloak, it fell open, your eyes they grew so wide, so big."

His eyes hadn't been the only body part that had grown big, but Jack would rather be stuck and spitted like a pig on fair day than admit it. Nor did he much care for being toyed with like a fish left to wriggle from the hook.

Determined to give as good as he got, he shot back with a question of his own. "If ye dinna wish to be stared at, why is it then that ye display yourself so?"

The slender hands fingering the oakcake soon sifted it to dust. Gaze lowered to the mess she was amking, Claudia said, "My English . . . I am afraid I do not understand your meaning."

For the first time since she'd been committed to his keeping Jack sent his gaze on a deliberate and leisurely perusal, starting with the very top of her black witch's head and ending with the milky mounds rising above that tautly laced, indecently low-cut bodice.

Holding his gaze there, just *there,* he felt his mouth lifting in a smile of its very own. "Oh, I think ye ken me well enough, but in case ye dinna . . ."

He reached out and she started, nearly toppling backwards onto the floor. *Wound tight as a spring, are ye? Well then, that's all the better.* Smile broadening, he held his hand so that the tip of his index finger hovered a bare hairbreadth from the soft flesh in question. "Like this."

Claudia shot a quick glance downward. When she lifted her eyes to him, the faintest trace of pink shaded her high cheekbones. "In France, this décolletage is considered modest."

"This isna France," he said for the second time, only this time his voice was softer, shakier. Drawing his hand away, he was reminded of the old adage about how those who played with fire ended up themselves getting burned.

And God, how he burned.

The tingling heat rushed his lower belly, then overflowed, flooding the reservoir of need between his legs where it pulsed and churned and all but groaned to be sated. He was hot, he was hard, and, above all, he was ready.

Like a man who'd labored too long beneath a hot summer sun, he shivered even as the inner heat burst forth into little beads of perspiration on his forehead, his back. Parched, he grabbed for his mug and pulled a long draught of the now tepid tea to clear the sawdust from his throat.

Swallowing—*hard*—he summoned his most high-minded tone and, hoping he sounded avuncular rather than just randy, said, "'Tis Scotland. In wearin' such a thing—and to a public house, nay less—ye risk no only lung fever but a great many other results that I dinna ken ye'd find verra pleasant." *No to mention ye're driving me mad.*

She lifted her chin a notch higher, her lush lower lip sticking out in defiance. Even so, he fancied there was a bit of a quiver to it when she said, "I regret that the sight of my body offends you, *monsieur,* but in truth I do not have anything but this to wear."

Bloody hell, what an idiot he was. He thought of her traveling bag, so light, so small. Too small to accommodate a gown, let alone the armoring of undergarments that went beneath one. Not only had he shown himself to be an ass, a brute, but also he'd managed to hurt her feelings into the bargain. *A fine day's work, Jack, and it isna even full light yet.*

Even though he already surmised her answer, to show her that he'd meant no harm, he asked, "No even in that wee bag of yours?" He jerked his chin toward the bed, its quilt pulled up, the traveling bag set at the foot.

The sudden sheen in her eyes as she shook her head made him feel the brute indeed. "*Non.* When I left France, I did so in haste and with little more than the clothes on my back."

Seeking to restore both the peace and Claudia's smile, smug or no, he held off asking why then it was that she kept her bag so close. Instead, he said, "I'll have a word with Milread. It may be that she has something you might wear."

"Mademoiselle Milread has been most generous with her offer to share her wardrobe such as it is but, if you have not noticed, she is much larger than I. The gown she gave me to try, it falls from my shoulders and drags upon the ground. There has not been time to alter it and even if there was . . ." Her violet gaze dropped to her clenched hands and she drew a long breath before admitting, "I am not so clever with my needle as I could wish."

A lady's maid-cum-seamstress who couldn't sew—further confirmation that Mistress Valemont was neither who nor what she claimed to be. And yet Jack tossed this latest bit of evidence atop his mounting pile of suspicions and moved on to the problem at hand. All that lovely flesh needed covering and quickly, for sure he wasna the only male in the village with a working pair of eyes. With her indecent French gown clinging to every delicious curve, the fabric growing more threadbare by the day, Claudia Valemont could coax a cockstand from a eunuch.

And there weren't any eunuchs in Scotland, at least none that Jack knew of.

She needed a dress. A decent dress, a modest dress, a *covering* dress. A dress that would, if not exactly hide those gifts God had so generously bestowed, at least camouflage them a bit so that any poor unsuspecting male drawn into her orbit might have some hope of going about his day without being turned into a babbling, lust-crazed idiot.

And by God, she would have such a dress even if it meant that Jack had to beg, borrow, or steal it off the back of some like-size female.

Or worse yet, *far* worse, see the inside of a dress shop.

The single dress shop on Selkirk's High Street wouldna do, he decided, for though Claudia's gown was worn to a rag, he could tell the fabric must have been verra fine when new. And she was small, so small. The gowns ready-made with the crofters' and town burghers' wives in mind would swim on her lithe faerie form, he felt sure.

There was any number of things he'd rather do with his day than ride hell for leather to Edinburgh and back again in time to fetch Claudia home from the tavern. Yet even as he debated with himself, came up with all manner of objections and counter objections, he knew he would go anyway.

Resolved, relieved, and perhaps even a wee bit pleased with himself, he swung his legs over the side of the bench and rose. "Dinna fash, lass. Betimes matters such as this have a way of working themselves out. Now finish your wee cake, or what's left of it, for we've the both of us a long and busy day ahead."

E*ighteen hours later, a stiff and saddle-sore Jack entered* the inn's taproom, a large box wrapped in brown paper and tied with cord tucked beneath one arm. Luicas, his apprentice and Milread's young brother, followed behind, his spindly adolescent's arms supporting a tower of smaller bandboxes that came up to the tip of his snubbed nose.

As Luicas's burdens evidenced, the foray into Edinburgh's shopping district had borne considerable fruit. He'd come back with not one gown but two, as well as a pair of soft kid slippers and sturdy half boots to replace Claudia's worn ones. There was also a heavy wool cape to see her through the Scottish winter, and sundry female fripperies—gloves, stockings, undergarments—it had occurred to him she might have need of.

"Well now, I wonder what all this can be about?" Milread said in a voice meant to carry to the room's far end where Claudia was vigorously knocking cobwebs from the corner. Putting down her own broom, she lanced Jack a conspiratorial wink, for he'd confided his plan when he'd brought Claudia to the tavern that morning.

Claudia propped the broom against the wall and came forward and despite the fatigue that came from undertaking a two-day journey in one, Jack felt both his body and his heart lighten at the sight of her. She'd tied her hair back with an old kerchief but a few stray tendrils had escaped to curl about her temples. A streak of something—soot—marked her left cheek and her color was high from her labors.

In a word, she looked beautiful.

"Jack? Luicas? What is all this?" Halting in front of him, she spread her hands to indicate the box Jack held as well as the towering stack Luicas had just offloaded onto a nearby bench.

Shy suddenly, Jack handed her the box. "I thought maybe ye could use this."

She hesitated then took it. "A gift . . . for me?"

"Well, it's certain it's no for me," Milread broke in, all impatience. "Open it and let's see what's inside."

The box seesawed in Claudia's arms, putting Jack once more in mind of how slender she was, how delicate. Heart drumming, he watched her set it carefully down upon a freshly wiped table, untie the cord with great care, and then lift the lid.

She looked up at him, face alight, and Jack suddenly felt ten feet tall rather than merely six feet four. "A gown. You bought me a gown!" She reached out to stroke the violet-colored silk then drew her hand sharply back. "Oh, but are you certain that . . ." She lowered her voice and, looking up at him, asked, ". . . You can afford it?"

Milread nudged her way closer to have a look. "Aye, for that would be real silk, would it no?" she said, her searching glance finding its way over Claudia's head to Jack's face.

The beginnings of a blush blistering his cheeks, Jack divided his gaze between the two women and snapped, "Well, I dinna exactly beggar myself, if that's what you're both worrit for. Nor will the Watch come abangin' on the door to carry me away for a thief or a coiner, for everything here was paid for with the King's own silver and gold."

Indeed, the four hundred pounds a year he received on retainer more than provided for his few wants and it had pleased him inordinately to put some of those funds to use in seeing Claudia properly outfitted.

The women relaxed visibly, and Milread turned back to Claudia. "Well, then, dinna just stand about. Go upstairs tae my room and try it on."

Claudia set the lid back on top, then ran her palms down the front of her soiled apron. "Oh, but I would not wish to soil it."

Milread looked from Claudia to Jack and rolled her eyes. "Just what we need about here, another fiend for cleanliness. Well, wash your face and hands if ye maun. There's a pitcher o' water set on the bedside table though where that bar o' soap Jack brought has got tae is anyone's guess."

"*Merci,* Milread." To Jack she said, "I will be but a moment." Taking hold of the box with both hands, she all but skipped over to the stairs.

Milread turned her attention to her brother, who'd subsided onto one of the benches and was yawning broadly. "Luicas, dearie, there's a mutton pie and a black currant bun kept warm in the kitchen. I dinna suppose ye might be hungry?" She reached out and ruffled his tousled brown curls.

"Leave off," he said, ducking and making a face, though his tired eyes had grown bright at the mention of food.

Over the lad's head, Jack and Milread exchanged knowing looks, for fifteen-year-old boys were always hungry.

"Oh aye," Jack said around a chuckle, "he's like as no starved. 'Tis been at least a full hour since he last ate." To the boy, he said, "Run along, lad. I'll no have your wasting away on my conscience."

The boy sprung from the bench and sped off in the direction of the backdoor.

Arms folded beneath her expansive bosom, Milread speared Jack a pointed look. " 'Tis a bonny gown, to be sure, but mayhap a wee bit grand for the tavern?"

Jack was not so naïve as to imagine for a moment that Milread meant to pass up comment. He thought over the answer he'd rehearsed, then said, "Aye well, 'tis only that with the lass to bide here through springtime, I thought she might find herself in need of something other than a workaday frock." Fresh inspiration struck and, seizing upon it, he added, "Why, there's church, for one. Ye canna expect her to wear ale-splattered skirts into the Lord's house."

"Indeed no." Milread nodded solemnly but her eyes danced as she said, "And then there's the *cèilidh* to celebrate the marriage of Duncan and Dorcas's wee Mairi on Thursday next. Such a gown would do grand for the dancin', d'ye no think?"

Shifting on the balls of his feet, he hedged, "I've no yet decided whether or not I'm going."

"Och, man, a bit o' fun would do ye the world of good." She

jerked her flaxen head to the staircase and, dropping her voice, confided, "And her, too. She's been twitchy as a cat all day, droppin' things right and left—more than usual even," she added when he only shrugged.

Jack had a notion that Claudia's "twitchiness" owed more to their morning match of wits than to a lack of dancing, but he held his peace, secretly pleased that he hadn't been the only one to leave the breakfast table muddle-headed and cross. Aware of his friend's searching gaze, he opened his mouth to reply that perhaps it wasn't the best of ideas to bring a prisoner of the Crown to a social gathering, when soft footfalls padding down the stairs caused both he and Milread to turn about.

Jack felt his heart rise up and slam into his chest with such force that, without thinking, he lifted a hand to cover it. Claudia stood in the alcove, lips parted in a soft, uncertain smile. She'd removed the kerchief and brushed out her hair. It fell about her shoulders in soft, glossy waves.

Her violet eyes looked soft, too, her gaze touching on his face before looking past him to Milread. "I think it fits, yes?"

The gown did far more than fit. She was lovely, absolutely lovely. And he'd been right about the color. Deep lavender, it brought out her eyes and did wonderful things for her pale skin and dark hair. And it was the latest fashion, or so the dressmaker on Princes Street had assured him. The low, rounded neckline, which he'd insisted be filled in with some lacy material for the sake of health and decency, not to mention sanity—*his*—descended into a fitted bodice that showed off its wearer's wee waist to perfection. In short, she glowed, and he wasn't the only one to think so.

Milread clasped her hands and, in a tone that was at once admiring and wistful, announced, "Delicate as a faerie princess, aye, Jack?"

"And you even thought of shoes!" Claudia lifted her flounced skirt to reveal low-heeled evening slippers—and a tantalizing glimpse of the slim ankles above them.

Jack swallowed hard. "Well, I'd no have you go barefoot," he said and then shrugged as though he hadn't spent a full quarter of an hour agonizing over whether to purchase these or the pair with buckles at the front.

"Thank you," she said and then, backing up a step, held her arms out from her sides to show off the Honiton lace cascading from the three-quarter-length sleeves to very best advantage. "How do I look?" she asked and her gaze, indeed all her focus, was riveted unmistakably on Jack.

Jack took note of the subtle lifting of the chin as Claudia awaited his response, and the sight of all that womanly confidence steeled his spine to resist. No doubt she expected him to offer up the praise that she no doubt felt to be her due. Well, he'd be damned if he'd give it to her, twice damned if he did or said anything to give her so much as an inkling of the sorry state he was in. He might be driven half mad with the lusting, his blood bubbling like liquid fire and his cock standing up like a dog begging for scraps, but he wasna so far gone that he'd let the wee witch make a public fool of him a second time.

"Humph," he grunted, keeping his gaze cool even as his sensitized flesh prickled and sputtered with the held-back heat. "I suppose ye'll do."

Oh she'd do all right. Do him in if he wasn't careful. That night, shifting position on his pallet for the umpteenth time, Jack acknowledged just why Claudia Valemont had been put into his path.

"To drive me mad, that's why," he whispered into the smoky darkness.

To torture and tease, to tempt and test, Claudia was the Delilah to his Samson, the Cleopatra to his Mark Antony. Like those ill-fated men who'd followed their hearts and lost their lives, if he gave in Claudia Valemont would end up making him very weak indeed. For once a woman like Claudia got her hooks into a man, he would be hers for life.

Even after she was long gone.

Until now his human acquaintances had been few and far between, his daily existence confined to the cottage he'd built and where he likely would die, but whenever the loneliness threatened to engulf him, he'd told himself this life he'd carved out for himself must be enough. He would make it enough.

Claudia's coming had changed all that. Being with her made him feel restless and edgy, made him yearn for pleasures he'd surrendered without ever sampling save for in the shadow land of his dreams.

He wasn't about to stand for it.

Peace came neither naturally nor easily to him, but at long last it had come and by God he meant to hold on to it, which meant holding out against her. Not only her fair face and lovely body, formidable opponents both, but also her lively mind. And then there were the rare but intense flashes of vulnerability, those glimpses into all she'd suffered and survived that made his heart tremble and twist and his knees go watery and weak until he could swear he felt himself melting into a puddle at her feet.

Unlike him, his beautiful nemesis was at peace with the world. He pulled himself up on his elbows and cast his disgusted gaze across the room to the drawn curtain. From behind its cover, the soft, regular purring—a less generous man might have called it snoring—announced that she was well and truly asleep.

Exasperated, he flopped onto his back, folded his arms behind his head, and closed his eyes. And that's when he heard it: a low moan, and then a strangled cry, coming from the vicinity of the bed.

"Nooooooo!"

The scream pealing forth was so piteous, so piercing, that Elf, lying next to him on the pallet, lifted her head and, ears pinned back, let out a howl of sympathy.

"Aye, lass," Jack said, laying a calming hand on the hound's tensed shoulder. "I suppose there's no help for it—we must go to her."

It was his habit and his preference to sleep naked but since Claudia had arrived to share his quarters, he'd taken to wearing his knee-length linen drawers to bed. Glad of them now, he got to his feet, fumbling in the darkness for the tinderbox. A stubbed toe, a bashed shinbone, and countless curses later, he found it atop the mantelshelf just as a sharp shriek of sheer terror shrilled from behind the bed curtain.

"I'm coming, lass. I'm coming."

He struck flint against steel, lit a candle, and carried the light over to the curtain. Sweeping it aside with the edge of his arm, he stepped inside. Candle held aloft, he wove his way through the maze of bandboxes and wrapped parcels to the bed where Claudia lay thrashing, dark head turning to and fro on the white pillow, one hand clawing at the wrist of the other as if seeking to break free of invisible bonds.

Afraid she would do herself an injury, he hurried to set the candle down on the bedside table and then reached for her. "Claudia. Claudia, lass, wake up."

Glazed eyes opening, she only screamed again and fought to push him away, her small hands slapping against his bare chest.

Hysteria on the scaffold steps was a common reaction among the condemned and by now Jack knew just what to do. He seized hold of her shoulders, the new white muslin night rail soaked through with sweat, and lifted her off the pillow. "Wake up, *now!*" he commanded and shook her hard.

She clamped her mouth closed and stared up at him, recognition gradually overtaking the fright in her eyes. Breathing hard, she managed to get out, "I-I thought y-you were the *borreau,* the executioner, come to carry me away . . . to the guillotine."

"I am an executioner," he said and, looking down into her damp face and dilated eyes, felt ashamed to own it. "But I've no come to take ye anywhere other than to the kitchen for a cup of chamomile tea if you've a taste for it."

She shook her head and scooted back against the headboard. Dragging a shaking hand across her brow, she said, "*Non, merci.* But sit with me a while?"

Suddenly mindful that they were both the nearest thing to naked, he took his hands from her shoulders and returned them to his sides. Wearing only her thin shift and with her raven's hair drawn into a loose braid and tied with one of the ribbons he'd bought for her, Claudia looked younger, softer, than she did fortified in her day clothes with their armoring of corset and petticoats.

He'd known she was vulnerable, terrified even, and yet when he sat beside her and she cast herself into his arms, he was completely unprepared. "Oh, Jack, I am so glad you are here."

Tenderness washed over him like a wave, carrying with it the desperate, self-destructive urge to lay both heart and head at her feet. Helpless to resist, he took her against his chest. "Wheesht, *mo luaidh, mo nighean dubh.*" My darling, my dark one. Unbidden, the Celtic endearments rolled off his tongue but then only because they came straight from his heart. With one hand he cupped the back of her damp head, using the other to trace slow soothing circles across her shuddering shoulders. "'Tis only a wee nightmare ye've had. But if it would help ye to speak of it, I'll gladly listen."

She drew back, hesitated, and then slowly nodded. "I was back in Paris. *Maman,* Phillippe, they had been taken already and now it was my turn."

Phillippe? A brother, he hoped, but didn't really think so. The jagged edge of jealousy was a sharp and unaccustomed sensation. He didn't like it one bit and yet even as he cursed himself for a fool, he vowed he'd get from her just who this Phillippe fellow was and, more to the point, what he'd been to her. But looking down to the small, shivering woman in his arms, he allowed that now was neither the time nor the place, so he shifted the question to the back of his brain and nodded for her to continue.

She turned her face up to his, eyes shaded with fear. "The tumbrel, they had it waiting and . . . and the ropes. I tried to run, Jack, I did, but my legs . . . they would not move. It was as if my feet, they were rooted to the ground."

"Hush, lass, ye're safe now. No one shall raise a hand to ye, I give ye my word."

A hint of a smile unearthed the dimple at the corner of her mouth. In the semidarkness, it winked at him even as she asked, "Not even you?"

Relieved to see it, for once he didn't mind her teasing and smiled back. "No even me, sorely though you do try me."

"*Bon,*" she said with a bob of her dark head. "For I bruise very easily."

"Aye, I mind that ye do." He reached out, ran his knuckles along the smooth plane of her cheekbone where the angry mark made by Callum's fist had finally faded away.

He'd intended only a light, friendly touch, but temptation was a wily thing. It stole up on a man and then struck without warning. Mindful of how soft her skin was, how close were their faces, he told himself he must draw back and move away. Instead he moved closer, let his hand glide down the long column of her neck to the delicate bones of clavicle and shoulder. He heard her catch her breath, registered the shiver that ran through her beneath the pads of his fingers, glanced down to her bosom, rising and falling beneath the thin shift, and knew instinctively that fear wasn't the cause of any of it. Hangman though he was, she didn't see him as such, at least not at the moment, and he was glad, so glad.

She lifted her face to his. Just a notch but it was enough. Her eyes, almost black in the shadows, melted into his, offering him her mouth if only he'd find the courage to take it. And he wanted to take it. God, how he wanted to. Even as conscience warred with desire, as fear fought with need, he ran his thumb along the seam of her moist lips, thought about what she might do if he dared to slip the digit inside. But it was the taste of her that he wanted, *craved.* One small sampling of the feast he was missing, and mayhap he might die a happier man. He slipped his hand to the back of her neck, wetted his dry bottom lip, angled his face . . .

And pressed his lips to the damp hollow of her temple.

Pulse hammering, he dropped his hand and drew back, tasting salt, tasting Claudia. His heart turned over, squeezed over on itself, and for the first time he acknowledged that the feelings rushing him went well beyond friendship, beyond even lust.

Shaking with reaction, he started up from the bed. "I should leave you to your rest."

She grabbed for his hand, the fear once more upon her and sharpening every feature of her face. "*Restez avec moi . . .* Stay with me . . . *please.*"

Jack stared down at the small white hand holding fast to his. It had been a long time since anyone—anyone human, at least—had reached for him. But even if it was only his hand that she touched and only safety that she now sought, she was dangerous just the same.

Because he was falling in love with her.

Brain brimming with the terrible truth of it, he shook his head. "I canna," he said as much to himself as to her. He swiped a hand through his hair, the fingers cold on his scalp and shaking with nerves and need. "Christ, Claudia, ye dinna ken what it is ye ask of me."

"Please, Jack, I do not want to be alone."

The simple plea proved to be his undoing. Though she still held on, slender fingers furled and surprisingly strong, he could shake her off like a fly if he so chose. But the bald truth was he couldn't bear to leave her any more than she could bear being left.

He released a heavy breath from the tight cage of lungs and

ribs. "Verra well, I'll bide for a bit, but if I fall asleep here beside ye, I'll no answer for it." Suppressed desire roughened his voice, made him sound gruff and sharp, but if Claudia noticed she seemed not to mind.

"*Merci.* Thank you." She let go of him and moved over to make room.

He hesitated, then eased in beside her, draping a corner of the quilt across his thighs. Back braced against the wall and legs stretched out, he patted his shoulder. "Lay your head."

She settled into his arms, tucking her head into the curve of his shoulder with the complete, unabashed trustfulness he'd found in animals but rarely in humans. The gesture warmed his heart. Unfortunately other bodily parts were warming as well, making him glad of the cold stones cutting into his back.

"This is nice, yes?" Yawning, she shifted position and a soft breast pressed against his pectoral.

Jack swallowed a groan. "Oh aye, lovely," he muttered more to himself than to her. "And will ye mind to come visit me in the madhouse betimes?"

She folded back sleepy lids to peer up at him. "Hmm?"

Frustrated desire roughened his voice, thickened his Scots burr. "Naything. Go to sleep."

For once not inclined to argue, Claudia closed her eyes and snuggled closer still. A moment later, a shapely and very bare leg kicked free of the covers. He slanted a look to the slender limb twining about him and bit back an oath. *Jesus, Joseph, and Mary.* Wondering if she wasn't torturing him on purpose, he angled his head and stole a glance at her profiled face.

A soft snuffling, part purr, part snore, sounded against his chest, putting his suspicions if not his body's yearning to rest.

Claudia slept.

But holding the warmth of her against his heart, inhaling the sweet perfume of her skin and hair, it was a long while before Jack found his own rest.

In an Abandoned Cottage on the Grounds of
Aberdaire Castle

"You've been away a long while, Gunn." MacDuff stepped from the shadowed corner and lowered the rain-spattered hood of his black cape. "Lord Aberdaire is most anxious to hear your news."

Looking into the butler's broad-boned face, the eyes colorless as glass and hard as stone, the courier felt a trickle of fear slide down his spine much like the rain that had found its way inside the collar of his greatcoat. Despite the foul weather that had dogged him since his ship had put into port, he'd ridden hell for leather over rutted and washed-out roads, going through a half dozen horses in his haste to return.

But now foreboding stiffened his tongue and caused his brain to cast about for any excuse to put off the inevitable bearing of the bad news. The latter he'd carried with him all the way from Paris, but never in the course of his nearly three weeks' journey had the burden felt so heavy as it did now.

MacDuff glanced about the cottage, lit only by a single lantern set on the crude dining table. Like everything else in the small room, the table and chairs were blanketed in thick dust.

"You hav'na brought the girl with you," the butler said at length. It was a statement, not a question.

"Nay, I hav'na," Gunn admitted, then sucked down a swallow of chill air before adding the rest of it. "I'm afraid she's dead, sir."

"Dead?"

Gaze drawn to the dirt floor and the toes of his drenched boots, he nodded. "I made inquiries of my contacts in Paris. The lass—Mistress Valemont—kept a house in the Faubourg Saint-Germain. Or more rightly I should say that her protector, a nobleman named Phillippe du Marmac, kept it for her. The month last, a mob rushed the gate, murdered what servants remained, and then ransacked the house."

"But how can you be certain she perished? Is there no possibility she might have escaped with her life, if no her possessions?"

Wishing it might be so, for his own sake as much as for the girl's, Gunn shook his head. "None, sir. Her body, I saw it with mine own eyes."

And a pitiful sight it had been, too. Apparently too impatient to let the guillotine do its grisly work, the rabble had strung her up from the lamppost at her town house gate. She hung there still, or rather what was left of her, weather-stained skirts flapping in the breeze.

In as few words as possible, Gunn told MacDuff the rest. When he'd finished, the butler drew a deep sigh and asked, "Given the condition of the corpse, how can you be certain it was she?"

"There are those who kent her well who've sworn it to be so. Her gown, her dark hair, her form—they tell me there can be nay doubt but it is Claudia Valemont."

"I see." MacDuff vented a long sigh, and Gunn supposed that the butler didn't relish relaying the grim news to his master any more than Gunn had relished relaying it to him. "Ah well, there is still the matter of the final installment of your payment." MacDuff slipped a gloved hand inside the folds of his cloak.

Gunn hesitated. He had a wife and three bairns to feed and the last few years had been lean ones, yet something inside him urged him to beg off. Though his wife would likely curse him for a weak-headed fool when he told her what he'd done, he found himself saying, "His Lordship has been most generous a'ready. 'Tis only sorry I am that I hav'na better news to bear him."

"Verra noble of you, Gunn. Most admirable, indeed. But you've been verra thorough, a'most *too* thorough, and I've strict orders from Lord Aberdaire no to let you leave this cottage without receiving your due."

The butler's colorless eyes fixed on Gunn's face, making him swallow hard and long to look away if only he might. But the black-swathed form drew one step closer, then two, blocking off his view of the narrow cottage.

"And Gunn, my lad, you *shall* have it."

The pistol's report was the last earthly sound the courier would ever hear.

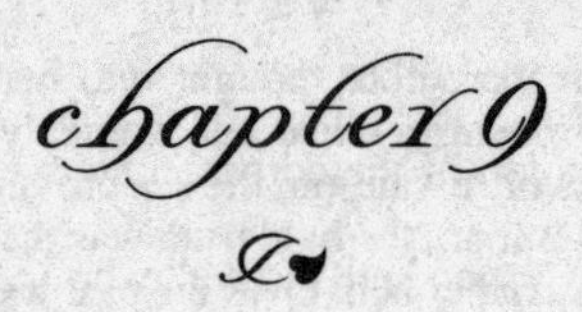

A genuine summer in each other's breast,
And spite of this cold time and frozen fate,
Thaw us a warm seat to our rest.

—Richard Lovelace, *The Grasshopper*

I*t had been years since Claudia had seen the inside of a* church let alone made her confession to a priest. The daughter of a courtesan, who'd become a courtesan herself, she'd attended countless salons, the opera and theater, and even the court at Versailles a time or two, but never before had she witnessed the celebration of the sacrament of marriage. The very notion of two people committing their lives to one another was itself a foreign thing, as strange and mysterious as the Scots people. Never had she felt more the fish out of water nor more grateful to have a friend, to have *Jack,* by her side.

Though she was at a loss to name the exact moment when it had happened, Jack and she *had* become friends. She'd ceased calling him Monsieur le Borreau and poking fun at his patois. For his part, he'd taken to bringing her mug of tea to the bedside so that now it was to the soothing aroma of chamomile and peppermint that she awoke. The calling off of hostilities made for a more peaceful existence, but it also left a curious void. Half the time she found herself fabricating excuses to seek him out, and the other half reasons to stay away. Fluttery and uncertain as she felt, it was hard to know what to say let alone how to behave. But there was one thing of which she was acutely, painfully certain.

She wanted to lie with him.

At first she'd tried telling herself that it must be boredom that had put such an incredible thought into her head. Or, if not boredom, then insecurity—had her womanly wiles really survived the horrors of revolution, the sea crossing, and a week of near starvation? But no, the bald truth was that she wanted him, the whole of him, in her bed. Over the past week, nightmares of those terrible final weeks in Paris had transformed into hot sticky dreams of rippling muscles, red-gold hair loosened to caress broad shoulders, and a lean masculine face registering the pleasure-pain of sexual release.

But it was his hands that her waking fantasies fixed on. Whether watching him carve out one of his beautiful mantel fronts or splint his hawk's crippled wing or unsnarl a child's kite string from the bow of a tree, all she could think was how very much she wanted to feel them on her body.

Jésus, but she must be damned indeed to entertain such thoughts, such *feelings* on her way to a church. She cast a guilty glance over to her *friend,* reins wrapped about one strong hand and seated next to her on the cart bench. Wearing a coat and waistcoat of russet-colored wool and buff-colored breeches that buttoned at the knee he looked very fine indeed. Silver-buckled shoes replaced his habitual boots and, miracle of miracles, he even had on a hat, a tricorne trimmed in blond braid. Simple tailored garments and yet Phillippe in all his finery had never looked half so handsome. And though Jack's hands sans gloves were rough, his manners as he tied the horse to the hitching post and then handed her down were as polished as those of any aristocrat.

Even at first glance, the village kirk was a far cry from the cathedrals Claudia had known in France, the square windows paned with plain thick glass, the gray stone façade pitted with age and devoid of gargoyle or grotesque. A single rounded turret rose above the pitched roof; housed within was the bell that would later toll to announce the celebration of the marriage of Mairi MacGregor to Fergus Fraser, the drover's lad, or so Jack had told her. After the service there would be feasting and dancing held at the inn. The latter she knew already for she'd helped Milread and the bride's mother, Dorcas, prepare food for two days now.

As they came up on the flagged stone steps arm in arm, Claudia realized that she was looking forward to the day ahead, not bored by the prospect of rubbing elbows with the "rustics" as she might have been but a few weeks before. In the course of serving in the taproom, she'd even begun to make a few friends. Callum was a frequent patron, of course, but by tacit agreement Milread always waited on him, and Claudia had schooled herself to ignore both his brooding gaze and occasional barbed remarks and go on about her work. But today was a holiday for the whole village as well as her. She didn't want to think about work. Most especially she didn't want to think about Callum McBride.

Feeling more lighthearted than she had in a long, long time, she slipped her arm free of Jack's to pass through the arched portal and into the narthex. Inside, the priest, whom Jack introduced as Father Angus, greeted them with a broad smile and a few good-natured jibes directed at Jack for his lengthy absence from mass. A pleasant-faced man of late middling years with a shock of white hair and a wrestler's stocky build, Claudia liked him instantly.

Incense scented the air inside the sanctuary. In honor of the occasion, the ends of the pews were festooned with bits of ribbon and plaid; a spray of dried heather and greenery interwoven with bright orange berries bedecked the simple wooden altar. She and Jack were just about to turn down the center aisle when she caught sight of Callum lounging by the baptismal font. He was engaged in whispering to a pretty, flush-faced brunette but, catching sight of Claudia on his brother's arm, his lazy gaze sharpened and his jaw clenched visibly.

Her hope that he might let them pass without comment was felled when he took abrupt leave of the girl and sidled toward them. Queasy unease churned Claudia's stomach but, beyond that, she was well and truly angry. In the old days, one whispered word in Phillippe's ear would have sufficed to see Monsieur Callum McBride tossed into the Bastille for the rest of his days. Not that she'd ever countenanced the brutal *lettres de cachet* whereby an aristocrat might have a member of the lower orders imprisoned without trial and often without cause; certainly she'd never considered bringing that "privilege" to bear on her own behalf. Even so, remembering who she was or rather who she'd been helped her to find the courage to face Callum head on.

Beside her she felt Jack tense and his big body move fractionally closer, his mint-spiced breath a warm draft on her chill cheek as he whispered, "Dinna fash, lass. You've no cause for fear."

She nodded and lifted her chin a notch higher just as her nemesis approached. The rank smell of stale spirits hovered about him but for once his hair was combed back and his face freshly shaven.

"Och, but it seems our wee gaolbirdie's come tae roost," Callum drawled, deliberately setting his spare body to block their path to the pews.

Jack took a broad step forward until the two brothers stood head to head. Callum was by no means short but Jack topped him by a good six inches.

"She's just as much right to be here as you, maybe more. Now stand aside." Jack squared his shoulders and Claudia could see he was more than prepared to barrel past.

"How now, lads, what's this?" Father Angus's black-cassocked figure materialized beside them, and Claudia had never been so glad to see a priest in all her life. "Still fightin' like cats, aye? Well, ye'll no be coming to blows in my kirk."

Livid, Callum's gaze shot to Claudia. "Do we let in thieves and whores tae soil it, then?"

Jack's fist came up at that but the good father's hand on his shoulder had him lowering it again. "'Tis the Lord's house, Callum McBride, and he welcomes all—even you. Now shut your mouth and take your seat before I forget I'm a priest and mind that once I was accounted to be the finest pugilist in the Lowlands."

Callum hesitated, brown eyes looking poised to pop in his too red face. "This isna finished, Jacko," he hissed, then stalked down the aisle to take his place in the pew beside his father.

Save for Tam and now Callum, nearly every man, woman, and child in the village turned around in their pews to look back at her, the foreign lassie who once again almost had brought the two brothers to blows. Some faces registered curiosity, one or two open hostility, but most looked on pityingly; the latter were the hardest to bear. Unlike the day of her sentencing when she'd had the luxury of shock to numb her, she was sensible to every glance, every whispered remark. Not since her flight from Paris had she felt so very desperate to get away from a place.

A faint color climbing upwards from his collar, Jack offered her his arm once more. "The service will be starting soon."

Feeling the heat climbing her own throat and cheeks, she shook her head. "I should not have come. I will wait for you in the cart. No, back at the cottage . . . I can walk. . . ."

Trembling, she lifted her lavender skirts and turned to leave but Jack's hand on her upper arm stayed her. "Bear up, lass, and hold your head high. You've naught to be ashamed for." Sliding his hold to her hand, he turned down the center aisle, towing her along.

Mindful of how very loud her new slippers sounded striking against the stones, she whispered, "Please, Jack, I swear I will not try to escape, only please, *please* let me leave. Can you not see I am not wanted here?"

"That's no true. No true at all." He halted before one of the center pews, made the sign of the cross before the altar, and then held open the gated door for Claudia to enter. Painfully aware of the congregation's collective gaze fixed on them, she slipped inside.

Only when they were seated side by side on the curved bench did he say, "*I* want you here."

She turned her head to regard him. "You do?"

Gaze trained ahead, he nodded. "Aye, as Father Angus said, I may keep a pew but it's been a while since I've seen the inside of it." Still staring straight ahead, he stretched out his hand. Strong and warm, it closed about hers and this time she'd no thought of pulling away. "Stay beside me, Claudia."

For one of the few times in her life, Claudia was at a loss for words. She settled back against the curved wood, content to let her hand lie in his. The seat felt hard against her spine, the church so cold that her exhaled breath caused little clouds of steam to mushroom from her mouth, but she found she didn't mind.

Jack Campbell wanted her beside him.

Spirits soaring to giddy heights, she kept her gaze fixed on the altar throughout the service as the vows were said, the rings pledged, and the sacrament given, but throughout it she allowed her mind to ramble free. The bride was beautiful and heart-wrenchingly young, as was the bridegroom. No more than sixteen if they were a day, Claudia thought with something akin to amazement, then realized that she'd not been all that much older when Phillippe du Marmac had taken her to his bed. She'd lost not only her innocence in that bed but also her hopes and dreams. Seven long years of blistering assaults on her woman's pride had followed. To endure, she'd armored her heart against feeling too much, wanting too much, until it had become as callused as Jack's hands.

But these past weeks with Jack had softened her. For good or for ill, she'd started to care again, not just for herself but for others as well. Would Jenny's broken arm mend? Would old Una's cough respond to Jack's latest remedy? Would Lady, Jack's crippled hawk, ever learn to hunt on her own again?

Bit by bit, day by day, she was becoming part of a community. Although it was desperation that had brought her to this village and force that held her, she would forever cherish her time among these simple Scots whom, she was fast learning, were not so simple at all.

But she couldn't stay, of course. Be it next week or next month or the month after, eventually she would escape and find her way to her father. Until now, paternal acceptance had seemed an end in itself, the Happily Ever After to close the storybook on all her woes. But now she found herself wondering what life as the daughter of a Scottish earl might be like. She supposed that in time Lord Aberdaire would want to arrange a marriage for her. Though she would not wed blindly—foremost her future husband must be decent and kind—but likewise she could not expect love. A marriage of convenience was the standard for persons of her station. The best she could hope for would be friendship and mutual respect and perhaps children, although having never conceived in seven years, she rather supposed she was barren. Perhaps a widower with a ready-made family, a kind-hearted man who would overlook her bastard birth and lack of maidenhead to provide a mother for his children. In time she might find contentment in such a union but certainly not passion.

But if she and Jack were to come together, there would be passion the likes of which she'd always dreamt of, longed for. He might not compliment or court her with flowery phrases as a Parisian gentleman would, but he wanted her even as she wanted him. She could see it in his eyes, the way those amber embers followed her about a room when he fancied she didn't notice. Should they continue to deny themselves simply because he was her gaoler and she his prisoner? Or, for that matter, because together they had no future?

Life was dangerous. Life was short. Had she not changed clothes with Evette back in Paris to slip undetected from her house, she might even now be moldering in an unmarked grave. So far in her short stay in Scotland, she'd been attacked once and very nearly condemned to die. Was it so very wrong then to reach for a little happiness, to take one small sip from passion's cup before resigning herself to whatever else fate hurled her way?

She didn't think so, but then again she didn't greatly care if it *was* wrong. Jack, however, was cut from very different cloth. He was moral. He was good. And beyond that, he possessed a conscience the size of the palace of Versailles.

He cannot hold out against me forever, she told herself, taking heart from the thought that moral and good and honorable though he was, he was still human—still a man.

And woman of the world that she was, surely she could find *some* way to surmount his gentlemanly scruples. With luck, that night's celebration, a *cèilidh* they called it, would provide her with a perfect opportunity to do so. Aside from the present service—and one couldn't very well undertake a seduction in a church, although planning one, well, that was another matter—it would be her and Jack's first social outing together.

And Claudia was always at her best at a party.

E*xcepting the ill and infirm, the entire village turned out for* the wedding feast, which began late in the morning and promised to last well beyond midnight. The ale and mead and whiskey flowed and the groaning board was covered with platter upon platter of hearty Scottish fare. At nine o'clock that evening, when most revelers declared their bellies to be on the verge of bursting, the trestle tables and benches were cleared and pushed against the walls to make room for the dancing.

Jack stood at the far end of the room, nursing a tankard of ale and following the dancers with his eyes, one lively, lavender-skirted lassie in particular. Face flushed and hair flying, Claudia had taken to the ancient Celtic reels as though she'd been born to them. One or two missteps were all it took before she was executing the complicated sequences in perfect time with the music.

Himself born with two left feet, Jack couldn't help but admire her seemingly effortless grace and boundless enthusiasm as well as envy the continuous stream of surefooted, eager males who materialized to partner her. Lost to his brooding, he scarcely registered that the music had paused until, as if conjured by his wishful thoughts, Claudia stood before him.

Beaming, she caught at his hands. "Dance with me, Jack."

Slightly panicked, he shook his head. "I dinna dance."

Perfect ebony half-moon brows arched in a show of disbelief. "But how can this be? You are Scottish, are you not?"

"Only half," he answered without thinking.

Giddy laughter greeted that statement. She gave his hand another reckless tug. "Then let the Scottish half come out to dance with me."

Icy fear crawled down his spine, childhood chants of *idjut, gomeral,* and worse names betimes echoing in his mind. He backed up a step and jerked free. "You'll no be laughing when I come down on your wee foot and make you a cripple."

She started to remonstrate with him when Luicas poked his tousled head between them. Bright-eyed and rosy-cheeked, he turned to Claudia and asked, "Are ye promised for this dance, Mistress Claudia?"

Claudia darted a glance to Jack. He thought he saw disappointment flicker in her gaze but, before he could be certain, she lifted her chin and answered, "It seems that I am not, *monsieur.*"

Taking the hand she offered, Luicas looked so flushed with triumph that Jack tensed his grip on his tankard until the curved handle threatened to snap. "Then ye are now." In the midst of leading her away, he must have felt Jack's gaze boring into him for he turned back to ask, "That is if ye dinna mind, Master Jack?"

Jack did mind, he minded terribly, but what choice had he other than to say, "Go on wi' you, then."

Subsiding onto the bench to watch them take their place in the queue along with the other dancing couples, he felt a terrible, irrational jealousy take root in his gut. Wee Luicas had only begun shaving the spring last but seeing his hand resting on Claudia's waist made Jack itch to wipe the grin from that fatuous, freckled face—with his fist.

"Och, but dancing's thirsty work." Milread flopped down on the bench beside him and reached across for his tankard. "No all that different from shaggin' but then ye dinna do that, either." She hid her smirk in the tankard's broad rim.

"Dinna be shy," he said with deliberate sarcasm. "Help yourself."

She set the tankard down and swiped a hand across her mouth. "My, my, but yer a testy one. If ye dinna mind my askin', what bug is it that crawled up yer arse?"

"Dinna mind me," he muttered, feeling at odds with the world. Glancing over at her, it struck him that something was different. "Your hair," he said. "You've done something to it." And then, by way of offering an olive branch and because it was true, he added, "It's verra becoming."

Smiling, she patted the crown of flaxen curls piled atop her head, a pale blue ribbon cunningly interwoven among them, and a few wisps left loose to soften her square-shaped face. "Claudia let me have one o' her ribbons and then showed me how to fix it. She's a way with hair."

And people, Jack thought, marveling anew at how she'd managed to charm the breeches off not only Luicas but every male in the room as well as win over most of the women, but then she seemed to possess an innate knack for putting people at ease. Even Peadair and Pol, curmudgeons both, were beaming at her besottedly from their seats by the settle.

Milread reclaimed his attention by laying a sound punch on his arm. "Go on and dance wi' the lass, ye great gomeral."

Realizing he'd just been caught slack-jawed and staring, he said, "You ken I canna dance."

She started up from the bench. "Maybe it's time ye learned. Past time, if you ask me. But since ye'll do as ye please tae spite my wise words, I'd just as soon go and see if Alistair needs another keg from the cellar as bide 'ere and watch ye mope."

"I am *not* moping," he called out to her retreating back but seeing the crowd closing in he felt the oddest urge to lay his head in his hands.

His friend was right, of course. He was moping, and he was as sick of doing so as he was of his own company. He waited until the reel drew to its final figure, then stood and started working his way toward the floor. Not to claim Claudia for the next dance, he wasna that brave, but mayhap he might offer her a glass of cool ale or invite her to go for a walk with him? He kent how she hated the cold but thinking on her lovely flushed face and the damp hair clinging to her temples, he told himself that perhaps a moonlit stroll in the fresh, clean air might find favor with her.

But drawing up on the floor, Jack's heart stalled along with the music, for a quick scan of the dispersing couples confirmed his worst fear. Claudia was missing.

Claudia's life in Paris had lacked for meaning but never for amusements. More than once she had strolled along the garden paths of Versailles, drunk from champagne fountains, and nibbled on the choicest of delicacies. And yet never before had she enjoyed an evening more than she did that night.

But when she missed yet another turn and in so doing trod on poor Luicas's toes, she allowed that perhaps she'd enjoyed herself a bit too heartily. Shouting to be heard above the music and laughter and stomping feet, she made her excuses to the boy, firmly refusing his repeated offers to escort her back to Jack.

Stepping off the dance floor, she made her way through the crowd toward the bench where she'd last seen him. Along the way, she found her progress frequently stalled by men and women stopping her to offer a sip from their mugs or to coax her back onto the floor. Head spinning, she smiled and kept on. The realization that her head continued to whirl even now that she'd stopped dancing in circles confirmed that the drink she'd imbibed between dances had begun to creep up on her. Warmed by the villagers' overtures of friendship as well as the exercise, she'd drunk from each offered mug. And then of course she'd been fortifying herself for what she hoped would happen once she and Jack returned to his cottage. Dutch courage, she thought it was called, though the cool ale had tasted most refreshing going down. She only hoped she would be spared sampling it coming up; otherwise her plans for the evening—for Jack—would have to be postponed.

She'd been drunk only once before—a surfeit of champagne to deaden the pain of a particularly humiliating encounter with Phillippe. Even after emptying her stomach's contents into the chamber pot, she'd been wretchedly ill all the next day, a violent headache strumming her skull and her throat scraped raw from vomiting. It was not an experience she would care to relive, certainly not on such an important night.

Perhaps if she could take in some fresh air, disaster might yet be averted. Or better yet, could she find Jack and ask him to take her home early? Would it constitute a breach of etiquette to leave now, she wondered even as she held on to the edge of a table and rose up on her toes to scan the crowd.

How tall these Scots were, how solidly built, and yet none were so tall or so beautifully proportioned as was Jack. Cursing her own lack of inches, she was just about to strike out for a better perch when she caught sight of Jack on the edge of the dance floor, his solemn-eyed gaze unmistakably fixed on the pretty, sloe-eyed brunette she'd seen that morning flirting with Callum. Now the girl seemed to have eyes only for Jack and, judging from his rapt, earnest, almost stark expression, he must be bedazzled indeed.

Gaze narrowed, Claudia assessed her competition. The child couldn't be more than seventeen and so blooming and fresh as to make Claudia suddenly feel like a crone—and a jealous crone at that. All at once, the whine of the fiddle and the soulful chords of the *clarsach,* or Scots harp, threatened to rend her heavy heart; the pounding of the drum called a *bodhran* fired through her throbbing head like a cannon boom. The air lay too thick and heavy for breathing; pipe smoke clogged her lungs and the greasy smell of cooked meat made her stomach roil.

A blessed blast of cold prompted her to tear her tortured gaze away from Jack and the girl to the door. She'd been cold for weeks and yet the air cutting in from the cocked door suddenly seemed blissfully inviting. A breath of fresh air, that was all she required. When she returned, her stomach and head would have settled, as would her heart.

I will be back before he even realizes that I have gone, she promised herself, and turned to direct her unsteady steps toward the door.

*Seated at the head of the bridal table, hands joined, the par-*ents of the bride surveyed the dance floor with satisfied smiles.

"Och, but she's a bonny lass, is she no?" Dorcas said around a happy sigh.

Gaze alighting on his daughter and new son-in-law leading off the other couples in the next reel, Duncan gave his wife's hand a firm squeeze. "But of course she is and how could she help but be when she's the verra image of her maither."

Dorcas turned to him and swatted at his arm although she was pleased, he could tell. "I wasna speakin' of our Mairi, though o' course she's beautiful, for she's her faither's bonny blue eyes, does she no? But nay, I was speakin' of the French lassie." She shifted her gaze to scan the benches, chiefly occupied by those too weary, too drunk, or too old to join the dancing. "Matters between her and Jack look to be progressing apace."

"Wheesht, woman, the drink must have addled your wits, for he's at one end of the room and her at the other and so they've been for most o' the evening."

Dorcas lanced him a smug smile. Men, what dear wee fools they were when it came to matters of the heart. "But 'tis my verra point, husband. His eyes hav'na left her so much as once since the dancing began. Why ye've only tae mark how brooding and miserable he looks tae ken he's half in love wi' the lass a'ready."

"No so brooding as that one." Duncan jerked his chin to where Callum stood sulking in his solitary corner, a mug of ale in one hand and a dram of whiskey in the other.

For the first time that day, Dorcas's smile fell. "Aye, there's another whose eyes hav'na left the lass all the day, but it isna love that causes them tae burn so bright, I fear."

Grim-faced, Duncan nodded. "Aye, he's a troublemaker, a drunkard, and a brute like his da. He's sure tae come tae a bad end and soon. I only hope he doesna take Jack down with him."

Dorcas reached for her cup of mulled wine to knock off the sudden chill at her back. "Aye, there'll be a reckoning between those two ere long, I can feel it. And the French lassie, poor wee innocent though she is, I fear she'll be at the heart of it."

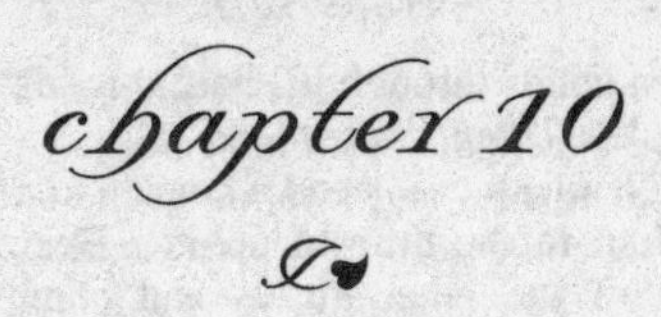

> With how sad steps, O moon, thou climb'st the skies!
> How silently, and with how wan a face!
>
> —Sir Philip Sidney, *Astrophel and Stella*

U*nfortunately Neilli, the brown-haired lass who'd thrown* herself in Jack's path to claim him for the next dance and another of his Campbell cousins twice removed, couldn't recall exactly when she'd seen Claudia and Luicas step off the floor. Somewhere between the Highland Fling and the Sir Roger de Coverly, she thought, but couldna be certain. The one piece of luck was that Luicas had not disappeared along with Claudia—had he, Jack would have happily strangled him without benefit of rope—but instead had sought out his master in the crowd. Between the two of them they made a thorough search of the taproom, then the remainder of the inn, but in the end their quest only confirmed what Jack felt already in his gut: Claudia was nowhere within.

As he bounded down the inn stairs from his fruitless search of the upper floor, Duncan's admonition of what Claudia could expect should she be caught attempting to escape—hangit from the neck 'til dead—came back to him in a quick frozen flash. The very thought of her lovely lithe body swinging from the hemp sent ice water shooting through his veins at the same time that it fired his resolve.

He had to save her, whether from Callum or from the gallows or from herself hardly mattered as the end result would be about the same. Dead was dead and though he didna think Callum would go so far as to kill her in cold blood, knowing his half-brother as he did, if he got to her first Jack doubted she would very much care to live afterwards.

He ran rough hands through his hair, dug his fingers into his pounding temples. *Think, Jack, think.*

To escape, Claudia would need a horse and a fast one and he doubted she'd spare the time to unhitch Beelzebub from the cart. As most of the other guests had come on foot from the kirk, that meant she would have to go into the stable where the coach horses were kept—and the scene of her disastrous first attempted theft. If she were caught thieving this time nothing Jack could say, be it fact or falsehood, would save her.

After giving orders to Luicas to keep a discreet watch within, he lit a candle from the rush lights on the hallway table and struck outside to search. The air was frosty cold, the sky above a milky white swirl pregnant with impending snow. Before him, his exhaled breaths crystallized in little clouds of steam as he hurried down the paving stone path that snaked away from the inn proper to the outbuildings that lay just beyond.

He was halfway to the stable when the moon slid free from a bank of clouds, illuminating a slender silhouette on the part of the path that turned off not to the stable but to the byre across the yard from the kitchen.

Cupping his hands about his mouth to funnel the sound, he called, "Claudia. *Claudia!*"

The figure whipped about, hair catching on a gust of wind. "Jack," she called back and a slender thread of white—a hand and arm—waved in the air.

Encouraged that she didn't run from him, that she actually seemed to be *hailing* him, he nonetheless sprinted toward her, the motion and wind sending his candle's flame streaking like a shooting star.

"Claudia." Reaching her, he held the candle out to his side with one hand and hauled her against his chest with the other.

To make certain she was real, not an invention of moonlight and his own desperate thoughts, he pressed her close, slipping a hard hand down the elegant arc of her spine to the small of her back. But the heart beating against his chest felt real enough as did the silky, wind-whipped hair crowning the head tucked beneath his chin.

Breathing hard, looking out across the dark patch of deserted yard, he said as much to himself as to her, "You're a witch, Claudia Valemont, sure as you're a woman. I dinna ken what devil it is that could have possessed you to, to—"

"But Jack," she cut in, her voice a muffled blur against his coat front, "I only thought to take a walk."

Take a walk? A *walk!* As excuses went it was shallow as a puddle. He would be daft to believe her and yet somehow he did. Even so, the urge to shake her was enormous, summoning the willpower to resist it nothing less than a monumental feat. To put himself out of temptation's path, he released her and stepped back.

His gaze slipped over her much as his hand had done, checking for damage, checking to make certain she was real. At some point during the dancing she must have lost or removed her lace fichu for it was missing now. Rising from the scooped neckline, the high slopes of her breasts shone like alabaster in the moonlight. Holding himself back from trailing a finger down that enticing cleft was even harder than not shaking her, he decided. And then there was the matter of her nipples, standing out firm and full as small berries beneath the tabby silk of her bodice as if begging to be noticed.

In the midst of his lusting, it struck him that, along with her gown's collar, she was missing her cloak. Practicality took precedence over desire and anger, at least for the present, and he shoved the candleholder into her hands and started on the pewter buttons of his coat.

"You'll catch your death," he chided. He shrugged free of the coat and, reaching behind her, bundled the warm wool about her shoulders.

"But now you will be cold," she protested with a small shake of her head.

"Nay, I'll not be," he said with perfect honesty, for the shock of her going missing, the desperate hunt about the tavern and grounds, and now the relief at finding her safe had brought the perspiration trickling from his pores. And then of course there was the nearness of Claudia herself; even under the best of circumstances, the latter tended to make his temperature spike and his blood heat.

But the prospect of some departing wedding guest catching sight of them and construing the worst—that she'd meant to escape or, more damning still, that he'd been helping her—sent a wave of chilly dread crashing over him. If he had half a brain, he'd whisk her out of plain sight—and harm's way—and quickly.

"Come along." He took back the candle and, laying firm

hands on the tops of her shoulders, turned her about in the direction of the byre.

"Where are you taking me?" she asked, twisting her head to look up at him even as her slippered feet stumbled over each other to keep up with his longer gait.

"Someplace more or less warm and dry and private where I can hear myself think—and you talk."

"Oh" was all she said and, although he tensed himself for an argument, amazingly she didn't give him one. Indeed, she didn't offer up so much as another word, only looped an arm about his waist and pressed against him.

Not that he minded. Even now, when she'd as good as frightened him out of his few remaining wits and he had every reason to be mad as hell, he liked having her close. More than liked. One wee glimpse of those moonlight-bathed breasts was all it had taken to bring his confused cock leaping to life. Even now he was hard and swollen, aching and stiff, and it was sorry he was that he couldna claim the camouflage of his coat to cover up the proof of what he already kent to be God's own truth.

He wanted her but, beyond that, he loved her. When he thought she'd gone missing, he'd felt his heart twist and torque until he felt sure a part of it must have broken off entirely. The call to find her and bring her safely back had bordered on compulsion, more an act of absolute necessity than of duty or even honor.

But he meant to tell her none of this. His objective in leading her into the byre was to get answers, not give them, and until he was satisfied as to why, just why, she'd struck off on her own without so much as a by-your-leave, neither one of them was going anywhere.

The byre was a relatively small wattle-and-daub structure that backed up onto the kitchen and served to shelter the chickens, sheep, and pigs that supplied the inn with eggs, milk, and ultimately their flesh. Usually the latter touched Jack's heart with sadness and not a little anger but at the moment he was too caught up in the maelstrom of his own private emotions to think beyond Claudia. It was as if the world, *his* world, had reduced itself to the petite person of Claudia Valemont and what she would say or do within the next few minutes would decide whether it continued to turn on its axis or became stymied in the bog.

He yanked open the byre door, going in first to light their way. She followed him inside without argument or question, setting him to wonder once again at her uncharacteristic complacence even as he pulled the warped wood closed behind them with a shuttering smack. Mindful of the dangers of so much straw and dry wood and his own trembling hands, he used his candle to light the globe lantern hanging from a peg inside the door, then snuffed out the candle and pocketed it.

Only then did he trust himself to turn about to face her. Folding his arms across his chest for protection—hers—he demanded, "What the devil did you think you were about, to go striking out in the dark and by yourself?"

She answered with an expansive shrug, an utterly Gallic gesture that would have knocked his coat from her shoulders had she not already slipped her arms inside the sleeves. "I have told you, I was warm from the dancing, the people, the fire. I wished for some air, that is all."

Given her brittle tone, though, he suspected there was more to it, a great deal more indeed, and he meant to hear the whole of it, for if she was at risk for escape, better he learn so now than later. "Then why did you no come and find me? I would have gladly brought you."

She was standing just far enough from the light that most of her face was cast in shadow but not so much that Jack missed the telltale worrying of her bottom lip with her teeth; the mannerism, he'd learned, meant she was thinking and thinking hard.

Another shrug and then, looking away from him, she said, "I saw you speaking with that . . . that little girl. I did not wish to disturb you."

Puzzled, he leaned one shoulder against the wall and cast his thoughts back to earlier that evening but still couldn't recall conversing with any children. Most of the bairns had either fallen asleep or been put to bed upstairs before the dancing had even begun. The only person of any age that he'd spoken to beyond a nod or a word in passing was Milread. Och, but he supposed there had been Neilli, though the latter had been no idle chat.

"If you mean the lass with the nut-brown hair, I suppose wee Neilli might be considered a girl by some as she's no quite seventeen but—"

"*Certainement* you and . . . and 'wee Neilli' seemed to be *enjoying* yourselves," she broke in, black brows arched and the eyes beneath them narrowed to reproachful slits as though he were the one whose behavior wanted for explaining. "Why, I am surprised you even noticed I was gone."

Not quite certain how the tables could have gotten so turned and in such a short span, he shoved away from the wall, closing the distance between them in three stomping strides. "Oh aye, I noticed. And it was a rare merry time of it I had, too, tearing about the inn's four corners in search of *you.*"

In the midst of his tirade, suspicion tickled the edges of his mind like a feather. Might she be jealous, he wondered, then dismissed the notion as ridiculous. He was not the sort of man to rouse a woman to jealousy—or anything else for that matter. Freakish height and breadth aside, he was an executioner. *Monsieur le Borreau* she called him, though she hadn't in a while.

"As for Neilli, I only stopped to speak to her because I thought she might have seen where you'd got to, but all she could say for certain was that you'd disappeared in the middle of the dancing."

"Oh," she said, mouth forming a near-perfect circle to match the vowel.

For a talkative woman such as Claudia, the response was suspiciously short. For the first time it occurred to him that her silence, what she didna say, might be a good deal more telling than words.

He was making a mental note of that insight for his future dealings with her when point-blank she asked, "Did you think I had run away?"

He started to deny it but stopped himself, reasoning that if he was going to demand honesty from Claudia, he must expect to give it in return. "When I couldna find you, what was I supposed to think?"

Jack's admission sent a spray of chilly water shooting down Claudia's spine and, despite the warmth of his coat wrapped about her, she shivered. She was being foolish, foolish and sentimental. Of course he didn't trust her nor should she blame him. She'd been lying to him for weeks, was lying still. And yet how it stung to see the doubt, the mistrust, flaring in those amber brown eyes.

She gulped down the hurt even as earlier she'd gulped down the ale. Biting her lip, she asked, "Would you care very much if I had?"

His gaze, incredulous, shot to her face. "Of course I would care," he replied, sounding highly insulted. 'Tis my duty to—"

"That is not what I asked. I asked would you *care*. Would you miss me?"

He hesitated. "Aye, lass, I suppose I would, no to mention I wouldna much care to be called upon to hang you."

Why whenever they came to the cusp of closeness must he flaunt the grizzly means by which he earned his living, almost as if he were trying to push her away? She opened her mouth to ask as much when the music of a harp filtered through the closed barn door. The young woman's voice that accompanied it rang clear and true and plaintively sweet.

"'Tis 'The Ballad of Barbara Allen,'" Jack told her and she nodded because, incredibly, she'd heard it once before—not that Miss Chitterly's rather studied delivery had ever struck such a soulful chord in Claudia's breast as did this Scottish lass.

Inspiration struck and, remembering she'd been planning all day for them to make love, and not war, Claudia reached for his hands. "Come, dance with me, Jack."

Jack's pulse thrummed beneath the pad of her thumb. "What, here?"

Still holding on to him, she shrugged. "Why not? There is no one to see us."

"Because I'm a great clumsy clod, that's why not."

Thoroughly vexed and more than a little tipsy, she stamped her foot into the straw. "Why must you always speak of yourself so? You move most gracefully." *And silently,* she added to herself, thinking of the many times she'd turned about to find him standing just behind her.

"For a great hulking beast, you mean."

Unashamed by her desire, she let her gaze slide from his face over his breadth of shoulders to his chest and the flat ridges of his belly. "You are large, yes, but your body is strong and beautiful."

He lifted her chin on the edge of his hand, forcing her gaze back up. Stark, hungry eyes bore down into hers. "Dinna mock me, Claudia. Not now."

He wanted to be touched, she realized, this hangman whose own touch he hoarded for bringing death but never pleasure. "I but speak the truth as I see it, *monsieur.*" A giggle slipped out and she admitted, "For I have drunk too much to lie. The ale, I fear it has gone straight to my head."

He dropped his hand from her face. "In that case, I should see you home."

She shook her head. "In a little while, yes, but not yet. Dance with me first. There is a dance I used to dance in Paris called the waltz. Do you know it?"

He shook his head. "I dinna ken much of dancing."

Ah, so she'd been right. Ignorance of the steps and a fear of appearing foolish were at the core of his repeated stubborn refusals. Hastening to reassure him, she explained, "The waltz is much simpler, much slower than a reel and is danced between one man and one woman only." Only just realizing she still held on to his hands, she guided his right beneath the bulky coat she still wore. "You have only to rest your hand at the center of my waist like so," she assured him when, flushing, he started to withdraw it, "and with the other take hold of my hand."

She brought her own hand out from his coat's overlong sleeve to rest on his elbow and felt him flinch as though she'd touched him with a hot poker instead of her own light and suddenly chill fingers. Noting how rigidly he held himself back from her, she had to hide a smile. *Pauvre* Jack, he didn't know what he was in for.

"Now what?" he asked, his stiff jaw and stoic eyes making her think of a man about to face the torturer.

"Now, *monsieur,* we dance. A simple one-two-three, step in, step close. See how we are making a small circle?"

Staring down at their moving feet, he nodded as if mesmerized.

She let him take her through a few more turns before offering, "*Très bien,* very good, but perhaps smaller steps and do not lift your feet so high. It is not so much a step as it is a glide."

Gaze still fixed on the floor, he asked, "People in Paris dance like this in public?"

She couldn't help laughing but mostly because it felt so wondrous, so right, to be in Jack's arms. "The waltz comes from Vienna, not Paris, although it is very popular there as well and danced in all the finest ballrooms of the city, or so it once was," she amended and amidst the thrill of being in Jack's arms, her heart gave a little dip.

"You hail from a verra queer country, Mistress Valemont," he said, but at last he'd left off staring down at the floor to look at her. There was even a flash of a smile in his eyes, and she could sense some of the tension lifting from his shoulders and arms.

Encouraged, she leaned closer. She'd never bothered with buttoning his coat and now the tips of her breasts brushed against his chest. "The two of us like this, it is nice, is it not?"

He didn't answer beyond a shy nod but his body spoke volumes. Try as he did to hold himself back, she felt the hard pressure of his arousal against her belly, felt her own body's answer in the aching swell of her breasts and the sticky dew forming inside her thighs.

They completed a few more circuits until, like a clock winding down, they stopped all at once, their feet ceasing to either step or "glide." The lesson at an end, it was nothing short of madness to linger let alone to touch yet Jack couldn't seem to stop from doing either. As if it had developed a will of its own, his hand slid upwards from her waist, traveling over the hard casing of whalebone corset to the soft underside of her breast.

She closed her eyes and tilted her head back. "Hmm, I love the way you touch me."

Only then did he realize that he was flicking the edge of his thumb over the peak of her breast and that it was his attentions and not the chill air that had caused her nipple to harden into a firm little point.

Dropping his hand before it could pillage further, he bit back an oath. "Christ, Claudia, I shouldna be touching you at all."

Her eyes shot open and her lower lip protruded in such a way that Jack ached to draw it inside his own mouth, to suckle and taste, to nibble and tease. "Why not?" she asked, all innocence, as if she hadn't a clue to the chaos she was creating.

Myriad replies leapt to mind. Seizing on the one with which she would be least able to argue, he said, "Ye're my prisoner."

"Ah *oui,* that is so, and because I am, the law gives you the right to beat me." A wicked smile touched both her mouth and her eyes and she went on, "Hmm, what was it? Ah yes, as many as twenty strokes, I think?" She made a face, then shook her head, sending an ebony curl fanning over his chest. "And yet you may not dance with me, may not touch me in kindness? This Scotland of yours is a most strange country, *monsieur,* a most strange country indeed."

Och, but the little minx had recalled his verra own words to tease and fuddle him. "Be that as it may . . ." Resolved to be strong, he started to set her from him.

She caught his hand and pressed it to her once more. Her silk-sheathed breast, warm and buoyant, filled his palm. "I want you to touch me," she said, and the earnestness in her eyes, the desperation edging her voice told him this wasn't a game to her, at least not any longer. "I've dreamt of it and of . . . of touching you, too." She flattened both hands against his chest, the palms massaging his pectorals in slow, sensual circles.

Jack felt himself hardening at her touch, not just his nipples but his cock, too, though he hadn't thought the latter could get any harder. He wondered if she felt it pressed against her belly; as close as they stood, surely she must. If she did, she must ken how near he was to sweeping her off her feet and laying her down on the straw-covered floorboards. From there it would be but a short step to sin, to taking her amidst the scents of straw and manure and sweat, his ragged breaths and Claudia's small soft moans mingling with the stirrings of the animals.

But even on the precipice of jettisoning his honor and his vow, some small part of his brain refused to shut off. Until now, he realized, he'd been more than a little disdainful of those who gave in to their carnal desires. Arrogance masquerading as virtue, fear as chastity. But gazing at Claudia, seeing the desire he felt reflected in her eyes, imagining all the things he wanted to do to her and have her do to him, he finally, truly understood what it meant to be wanting and weak and . . . human.

Humbled, he drew his hand away from her breast, then gently lifted hers from working its butterfly magic on his chest. Turning it over, he pressed a kiss into the blister-bitten palm and said, "We canna do this, Claudia. It's no that I dinna want ye, lass," he hastened to assure her when he saw the raw, wounded look leap into her eyes. "I do, more than you can begin to know. It's only . . ."

A blast of cold air whipped inside the byre, causing the lantern light to flicker and blink. That and the sudden jolt of shock on Claudia's face caused the remainder of his apology to dry up in his throat. He swung about to see Alistair standing inside the half-open door.

"Verra cozy," he remarked with a chuckle, looking from Jack to where a mussed Claudia stood just beyond him, his coattail reaching beyond her knees.

Jack felt his face heat. How much had the innkeeper overheard let alone seen? If the rumor were to get out that he'd seduced Claudia or she him, for sure she'd be removed from his keeping. That she might be made to serve out the remainder of her sentence in the tollbooth, subject to gaol fever and the advances of the randy warder, sent a quiver of fear shooting straight through him.

Minded that they'd stopped before doing anything strictly wrong, he schooled his features to impassivity and said, "Mistress Valemont was just giving me a lesson in dancing. The waltz," he added for good measure, trusting that Alistair wouldn't know just how intimate a dance that might be. "What is it you want, Alistair, or is it that you missed me?"

Scowling, Alistair reached into the breast pocket of his patched frock coat and pulled out a crisp vellum square. "This came on the morning mail coach. I meant tae gi' it tae ye earlier only—"

"You thought you'd have a wee look at it first," Jack finished for him and snatched up the letter.

Muttering about ingrates and ne'er-do-wells and barmaids who couldna be trusted to keep their skirts down, Alistair shambled off, throwing the door closed behind him.

Jack stared down at the letter in his hand. He took note of the seal of the Crown, recognizable despite its having been broken already, as well as the franking with "On His Majesty's Service" and "Immediate" marked in bold red letters, and felt the heavy press of responsibility and something akin to dread descend upon him.

"It is not bad news, I hope?" Claudia came to stand beside him, studying his profile, which no doubt registered the grimness of his thoughts.

To avoid looking at her he kept his regard on the letter, taking his time in refolding it along the original creases. At length he said, "A highwayman found guilty of putting a bullet through the heart of the earl of Aberdaire's courier is to hang on Friday next, and I'm called to see the sentence carried out."

Though he still didn't so much as glance at her, he felt her frozen stare cut through him like a blast of wintry air.

"The courier of Lord Aberdaire?" she repeated, a tremor to her tone as if the man or his master were a personal friend.

"Aye, so it reads."

"Must it be you?" He fancied he heard desperation in her voice. To be sure, it held an edge that he hadn't heard in some time. "Edinburgh is a large city, it is not? Surely there is another who—"

"Aye, there is and yet it must be me. The condemned, he petitioned the judge to ask that I be the one."

Only weeks earlier Jack would have puffed up with pride that his professional reputation for offering a quick, clean death had traveled so far and wide. Now all he felt was numb—and so very cold inside.

Knowing he could hold off no longer, he turned to face Claudia. A blind man couldn't have missed how she shrank from him. *Monsieur le Borreau,* she was no doubt saying to herself, and that he couldn't fault her for thinking of him as such only increased his misery tenfold.

From deep within him, a long buried bitterness rose, cutting through the coldness, melting it like salt sprinkled on an icy path.

Fixing his gaze on Claudia's suddenly pale, stricken face, he said, "Dinna look so downcast, Mistress Valemont, for now I've nay choice but to take you so far as Edinburgh after all."

*Callum stood at the forge, brooding on his night's disap*pointments. At first he'd thought it a stroke of fortune when he'd seen the Frog bitch wander off during the dancing. He hadn't hesitated but had followed her from the taproom to the outside but, as his foul luck would have it, so had Jack.

Jack, always Jack.

When they'd disappeared into the safety of the byre, Callum had returned to the taproom and tried to drown his disappointment in drink. On his way to refilling his tankard yet again, he'd bumped into Alistair. It seemed an important letter had come for dear old Jack and the innkeeper meant to give it to him that night. Thinking on what he, Callum, would do were he to get a hot little piece like Claudia Valemont in the dark and alone, he'd been quick to point Alistair to the byre. But his hope that Jack might be caught in some disgrace had died on the vine, too. Upon his return, all the innkeeper could say he'd interrupted was the two of them *dancing!*

Callum's disappointment had tasted bitter as gall. To choke it down, he'd swallowed enough whiskey to fell a small horse. Still sleep had refused to come, until around midnight he'd stumbled into the smithy adjoining his father's cottage to see if exhaustion and sweat might not coax it along. And so he stood before the heated forge, stripped bare to the waist beneath the leather apron, sweating out his night's whiskey and hammering away at the dents from an iron bar even as he sought to hammer out the years of frustration and hurt.

"What the fook d'ye think ye're about?"

More annoyed than startled, he turned to see his father, Tam, standing in the doorway and dressed in a nightshirt and cap. A candle trembled in one raised hand, sending light streaking back and forth across the room.

Wild and free as the Frog bitch had danced.

But whereas the woman pulsed with life, his father looked dry as old bones, the few remaining threads of gray hair tucked beneath the knitted nightcap and the yellowed flesh stretched so tautly over his face that every crevice, every bone jutted out like a Highland crag.

It canna be much longer now, Callum thought. The prospect made him neither happy nor sad, and he turned back to the furnace where the blistering heat had rendered the metal bar as soft and malleable as a woman's flesh.

"Go back tae bed, Da," he said, even as he hauled back the hammer and struck another series of sharp, satisfying blows.

But instead of leaving, Tam padded over to the forge. The candle he held had burned low in its pewter holder, its untrimmed wick hanging limp and lifeless as an old man's cock, little tears of tallow slipping off the cord to splash into the reservoir.

Callum the boy had shed tears aplenty, but Callum the man didna cry, not ever. In his dreams Mam still cried, though, and begged and screamed. It was the screaming he minded most. Since the Frenchwoman's coming, he'd taken to hearing it during his waking hours sometimes.

Coming up on him, Tam yelled, " 'Tis three o'clock a'most. Ye dinna work half so hard in daylight." His bloodshot eyes narrowed. "Ye maun be up to some mischief, and I mean tae know what."

Above the clanging, the *screaming,* Callum shouted, "Leave it be, auld man."

Red face working, Tam shook a fisted hand. "D'ye dare speak tae me so, tae gi' me orders in my own forge, whelp?"

The name touched off an explosion inside Callum's head to rival Mam's screams. He swung about, the hammer raised in one clenched fist. "Aye, I'll speak tae ye as I please, *do* as I please, for we both ken I've earned the right and if either o' us need mind his step, 'tis ye, auld man, no me."

Tam shrank back, the pupils in his faded eyes grown so large as to give the illusion of being empty sockets. "I dinna ken ye. Ye maun have drunk sae much as tae make ye daft, for I canna make heads or tails of any of it."

Voice pitched above the din, Callum joined his voice to the screaming inside his head. "Och, but ye ken me, Da. Ye ken me just fine."

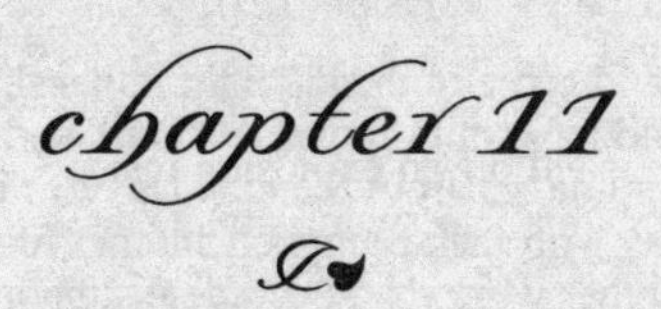

Chapter 11

O wad some Power the giftie gie us
To see oursels as ithers see us!
It wad frae monie a blunder free us,
An' foolish notion.

—Robert Burns, *To a Louse*

Three Days Later

They set out for Edinburgh in the pale gray predawn: Jack, Claudia, Luicas, and Elf. Seated inside the pony cart next to Jack, Claudia avoided his gaze by keeping hers trained a few yards ahead to the rump of the dappled gray mare the boy rode and the dog gamboling alongside. She was no judge of horseflesh but she thought the horse looked to be a calm creature, far less feisty than either Jack's bay hitched to the cart or the tinker's horse—or so she hoped.

For on the back of that very horse she meant to steal away from Edinburgh to Linlithgow—and freedom.

Aberdaire Castle, her father's seat, lay some fifteen miles west of Edinburgh, or so said the pleasant-faced coachman who'd stopped inside the taproom for a pint the week last. Once she reached Aberdaire's sanctuary it would be over, for no one would think to look for a runaway lady's maid-cum-seamstress-cum-horse thief within the stone-and-mortar walls of an earl's castle. Not even Jack.

Once they arrived in Edinburgh, her opportunity must come sooner or later, for it stood to reason that he and Luicas could not watch her night and day. At some point they would have to leave her to carry out their unsavory trade. She only hoped that her chance would come in the daylight rather than at nighttime when she would have only moon and stars and the occasional street lamp to guide her from the city. Day or night, she would leave, for to stay with Jack Campbell another four months, even so much as another week, had become insupportable.

To want a man more than one was wanted in return—this was not wise. To want a man hired to kill, who was but one step above an assassin, was nothing short of madness. To begin to fall in love with such a man, to bask in the luxury of forgetfulness for long, blissful stretches of time, was a betrayal of the worst kind, tantamount to turning her back on every one of her countrymen who had felt the sharp bite of the guillotine's blade.

Jack didn't cut off people's heads. He hung them—a less grizzly death for the onlooker, perhaps, but no kinder to the poor victim, possibly less kind, or so she'd heard. Despite his protestations to the contrary, deep inside him he must harbor some remorse, some fledgling shame; otherwise why would he have worked so very hard the previous evening to keep her from attending the packing of the tools of his trade?

Thinking of herself as one who must choke down a bitter tonic in order to be cured of a fever, Claudia had doggedly followed him and Luicas outside to the byre, determined to see all, to see the very worst. Once inside, she'd steadfastly refused to leave, until Jack had become resigned, defiant even. One by one he'd withdrawn each article of death from the storage cupboard, calling on Luicas to recite its proper function before packing it inside the traveling trunk.

"Luicas, prithee explain to Mistress Valemont the nature of that which I hold in my hand."

The boy turned to Claudia, fresh face beaming with the desire to demonstrate just how very much he'd learned. "'Tis a pinioning strap, mistress, tae hobble the hands o' the condemned and the knees as well so he canna step back from the line."

Jack's eyes, hard and flat as stones, trapped hers. Handing the strap to the boy, he asked, "And why is it that he must not step away from the chalk mark?"

Taking it to wrap in flannel for the journey, Luicas answered, "Why, on account o' that bein' where the two leaves o' the trap come together, Master Jack. 'Tis verra important the client fall through fast and straight, for betimes a rope can take a man's head clean off sure as that great blade the Frogs are usin' o'er in France. Oh, beg pardon, mistress," he offered at Claudia's involuntary gasp.

Jack's gaze flickered from Claudia back to the boy. "You may leave us, Luicas. I'll finish here."

Luicas hadn't needed to be asked a second time. A brief bow to Claudia and then he was off like a shot.

Jack and Claudia regarded each other. "That was cruel," she said even as she wondered how, even now, she could want him so much.

Behind Jack's amber eyes, flames leapt. "I seek only to feed your curiosity, mistress, for in the course of these past weeks I've kent it to be a hungry beastie indeed."

For once lacking a retort, she turned to go. "I will leave you to your . . . your preparations."

Jack had been kneeling by the trunk but now he shot to his feet beside her, his voice soft but his every word edged with steel. "The man I'm called to Edinburgh to hang also shot and killed a young maither of five from another parish though 'tis only for the courier's murder that he stands condemned." Defiant amber eyes bore into hers, daring her to look away. "When I settle the noose about his neck, when I walk away and pull the lever that will send him into eternity, will you weep for him, Claudia?"

Tears stung the backs of her eyes, clogged her throat, but she refused to shed them just as she refused to look away. "*Non,* I will not weep for him." She pulled a hard, choking swallow. "But I will weep for you, Jack."

It was then that she'd promised herself that when Jack Campbell returned from Edinburgh, he would do so without her.

The jostling cart, the hard bench, and even the tedium of the journey itself were slight discomforts compared to the scathing pain of self-reflection. She'd made a fool of herself the night of the *cèilidh,* throwing herself at Jack like a common strumpet in her cups. Better she go now while there was yet time, before she was moved to offer him not only her body but also her heart—and thereby become as helpless against him as that of the poor wretch whose neck he would wring on the morrow.

Would Lord Aberdaire attend the hanging of his servant's murderer? she wondered yet again. Were she and Jack on speaking terms, she would ask him, for she'd no wish to repeat her experience in London when she'd arrived on her father's doorstep only to learn he'd left already. But even if he had, this time she would insist on waiting for his return, for not only had she run out of places to run but also the heart to take her there.

She risked a sideways glance to Jack. Red-gold hair pulled back in his customary queue to reveal the clean, strong lines of his face, he didn't look any happier than she was about their silent standoff. In fact he looked quite miserable, she decided, noting a deep purplish crescent carved beneath the amber eye revealed in profile.

Knowing that she was soon to leave him forever made it easier to forgive the episode in the byre. Underlying the simple wish to part on good terms was the deep and desperate need to capture every look, every touch, and every spoken word and imprint them on her memory for all time. What time they had together she was determined to use to learn all there was to know about him, not the shadow side of his trade but the little everyday things . . . starting with the mystery surrounding his middle name.

Being the one to offer the olive branch was a new and uncharted role for her, but she resolved to throw herself into it with as much enthusiasm as a breaking heart could muster. Lest she lose her nerve, she averted her gaze to the warm, flannel-wrapped brick upon which she rested her feet and asked, "Jack—this is a Scottish name?"

Jack, too, had been mentally replaying the previous evening's episode and kicking himself for his calculated cruelty. Not that Claudia was entirely blameless—she had, after all, insisted on following him out and then refused to leave. But in trotting out the tools of his trade before her innocent eyes and then forcing on her the specifics of their use, he'd gone far too far. Owing to the dubious gift of hindsight, he'd come to see his bad behavior for what it was, a desperate and ill-conceived bid to soften her, to force her into admitting that perhaps he wasn't quite the monster, the *criminal,* she'd made him out to be. And, in so doing, he'd acted the monster in truth.

She must hate him well and truly.

And so it was the lovely silken sound of her voice, more so than the question itself, that jolted him, setting off a fuse of pure, unadulterated gladness to explode inside his chest.

Shifting to face her, he answered, "Nay, 'tis English as was my father." Glad to find his voice steadier than either his hands or his head, he added, "His Christian name was John but he was called Jack. When I came along, he was long gone, but my maither had me baptized Jack, no John. I think she missed sayin' his name."

She looked up at him, violet eyes clear and showing none of the heat of their quarrel. Christ, but he wanted to kiss her, fully and passionately as he had come so verra close to doing the night of the *cèilidh* when at the last moment he'd regained his principles—and lost his nerve.

She smiled and his heart turned over. "I like Jack. It suits you. But what does the 'H' in 'Jack H. Campbell' signify?"

He peered out to the road ahead and pretended not to hear. As glad as he was to have her speaking to him again, he couldn't help but hope that her curious mind might soon fix upon some other unknown.

No such fortune, for but a breath or two later, she asked, "It is a family name?"

He shrugged. "In a way."

"Infuriating man." She threw her arms into the air. "Will you not answer me this . . . this one so simple question?"

At that very moment, the cart's front wheel hit a rut in the road. Jack's heart leapt into his throat even as he shot out his free hand to hold her back before she could go tumbling over the side.

He released her and swiped a hand through his hair, which he felt certain would be snowy white by the time her sentence was served in full. "Christ, woman, have you no heard, 'curiosity killed the cat.' The same can be said for prying French lassies though hard as your head is, I dinna suppose I should be worrit."

"Forgive me." She returned one hand to the side of the cart, with the other she found his arm. Hers was the lightest of touches, but it burned through his layers of clothing to mark his flesh like a brand. "Only Jack, I still want to know what that 'H' stands for."

He hid a smile and as much to prolong the touch as to tease her, he asked, "Why?"

"Because . . . well, because I want to know everything about you."

"Oh, aye, a fascinating specimen am I." She must have

glimpsed his full name on the summons he'd received. He sighed, unsure of whether to feel flattered or violated, but either way he resigned himself to telling her. She'd seen the worst of him, his darkest side. Certainly a mere name couldn't put her off more. "Verra well, but ye must give your word ye'll no laugh."

"Cross my heart." She lifted her hand from his bicep to sign the cross over her bosom.

Her delectably soft, full bosom. Remembering the feel of her breast beneath his palm, of how good, how *right,* it had felt to hold her against his chest, his thighs, he drew a deep breath, released it very slowly, before confessing, "Hamish."

The gale of laughter she emitted nearly caused him to drop the reins. But, Dear Lord, it *was* good to see her smile, to hear her laugh even if it was at his expense. Better a clown than a monster, he decided, even as he pretended annoyance and said, "You laughed."

"I did. I am sorry but it is so . . . so dreadful. 'Amish," she tittered, a hand fanned out to brace either side of the impossibly tiny waist that but a few nights before he had spanned with his two hands.

"*H*amish, not 'Amish. Please, Claudia, 'tis bad enough without your leaving off the 'H.' And 'twas my maither's faither's name, if ye must know."

A thought struck him. He'd been curious before but then so much of her history was sketchy or missing altogether that the issue of names had seemed the least of it.

But now that she'd introduced the topic of names, it seemed the perfect time to ask, "What of Claudia? It's a lovely name to be sure," he added when he saw her high brow furrow into a frown, "but it doesna sound verra French."

"Ha! A lot you know. Claudia is very French indeed although my given name, the name I was baptized with, is . . ." She hesitated and he waited with bated breath until she ducked her head and admitted, "Clothilde."

"Clothilde?"

She nodded. "It is a most unfortunate name, I know, as bad as Hamish or perhaps worse. Even as a child I refused to come when called by it and so on my sixteenth birthday Maman's present to me was that I might be Claudia instead."

He thought for a moment, then turned his head to smile at her. "I like Claudia better."

Her brow smoothed and her mouth softened into a wistful smile. "So do I, Jack. So do I."

They reached Edinburgh as the soon to be slumbering sun was dipping low beneath the horizon, casting a smoky pink haze over the spired skyline. The tollbooth to which Jack was called lay just off of that part of the Royal Mile known as Canongate; the rooms kept in readiness for him were clean and commodious but, more to the point, they were close to his work. Even when the warder sent the prisoner's particulars on ahead, Jack always visited with the condemned on the eve of the execution to see for himself. Not to draw out the prisoner's suffering—that was God's prerogative—but because he prided himself on being precise, careful. In order to determine the optimal striking force for the falling body and the distance required to achieve it, not only weight and height but also body mass must be taken into account and Jack trusted no one but himself.

But now he had Claudia to consider. She'd fallen asleep an hour before they reached the city. Glancing down at her dark head resting on his shoulder, he tried again to reconcile the urge to take her with him to the tollbooth with the equally strong urge to shield her from any experience that might bring up past horrors. Although the night terrors were coming fewer and farther in between, she still sometimes awoke screaming, muttering snippets of phrases in French and English that, pieced together, painted an ugly picture of her final days in France.

Tucked into the old medieval quarter of the city, the Rose and Thistle Inn on Blackfriars Street seemed the perfect compromise, but a brisk walk to the prison and yet far enough away from it that Claudia need never so much as glimpse the iron gates. True to its era, the façade featured an outside staircase, overhanging upper stories, and crow-stepped gables. A thatch of ivy blanketed one side of the age-mellowed stones and swinging from a chain above the door was a small painted sign depicting a rose and thistle and the accompanying English words. *She'll be safe here,* he told himself, and willed himself to believe it.

He reined in at the cobbled courtyard, and Claudia raised her head from his shoulder to cast him a sleepy half smile. "We are arrived?"

Deprived of the pleasant weight, he turned to regard her. Hair mussed and violet eyes still heavy with sleep, she looked young and soft and vulnerable, the sight of her enough to make his heart ache for what could never be.

"Aye," he said, resisting the urge to touch her smooth cheek, "I didna want to wake you."

"And what of you?" Sitting upright, she busied herself with smoothing imaginary wrinkles from her cloak and gown. "You have driven all day without once stopping to rest."

Her tone was almost . . . wifely. It left him flummoxed but pleased, too, warmth radiating from his chest so that he scarcely noticed the chill air. Even as he acknowledged that nothing could ever come of it, that she might care for him even a little left him feeling light-headed in a way that had nothing to do with fatigue.

Hoping not to make too great an ass of himself, he reached back to where Luicas lay curled up about Elf, boy and beast fast asleep amidst the baggage. The boy had given in to fatigue roughly an hour before and, after hitching his mare alongside the bay, had climbed inside to get some rest.

Nudging the lad's shoulder, he said, "Wake up, wee Luicas, for we're here."

The boy bolted upright, dull gaze sharpening as he took in his surroundings.

Less enthused was Elf, who promptly laid her head back down on the coil of rope and closed her eyes.

"Look sharp, lad," Jack said with a laugh, already starting down. "There'll be time aplenty to explore later, but for now you'd best get busy with the bags, aye?"

He handed over the reins to the waiting ostler and then turned to lift Claudia down. The feel of her slender waist beneath his hands brought back potent memories, and it was only through sheer force of will that he managed to set her down and take a shaky step back to safety.

The smell of beeswax was strong when they stepped inside the inn's oak-paneled foyer. The innkeeper, who introduced himself only as Tweedie, greeted them warmly as did his wife, a pie-faced matron of middling years who wore her salt-and-pepper hair tucked beneath a neat white cap.

Jack doffed his tricorne and stepped forward. "We're in need of a room. Have ye one to let?"

The innkeeper opened his mouth to reply but his wife answered for him. "Oh aye, that we do. We were full up the night past but we've several vacancies as of this morning and even if we hadna we wouldna think of turning away such a bonny couple and at such an hour, would we, Tweedie?"

On the words, "bonny couple," Claudia let out a little gasp. Casting her a warning glance, Jack wondered if perhaps he should have prepared her for the fact that, during their short stay, they would be posing as husband and wife. The Rose and Thistle was, after all, a proper tavern, which was why he'd brought Claudia to it in the first place. But along with the guarantee that the bed linens would be fresh and the washing water changed once a day, "proper" meant that no "lewdness" or "mischief" was tolerated within the sanctity of its whitewashed walls—an unmarried man and woman sharing a single bedchamber would violate both counts.

Dark eyes bright, Mistress Tweedie sallied over to Claudia, on whose delicate cheekbones patches of pink had already begun to climb. "Och, but ye're wife's a bonny thing, Master Campbell," she announced, as though Claudia were not standing beneath her very nose. "Foreign looking, but a beauty all the same."

"French," Jack answered when he glimpsed the telltale flash of fire in his "wife's" narrowed violet eyes.

"Well, doesna that explain it," she gabbled on, and just as Jack was wondering what the devil she might mean, she burst out, "It maun be a love match, then. Dinna be shy, dearie," she added, speaking to Claudia directly for the first time since they'd entered and shooting her a broad wink. "Ye'll no be the first blushing bride I've clapped eyes on nor the last, God willing." Glancing back to her husband, standing silent as a post, she confided, "Tweedie says I can sniff out newlyweds a league away."

Jack heartily doubted that Master Tweedie ever got the chance to say much at all, but he summoned a noncommittal smile all the same. "Ah well, about that room . . ." he prodded, still hopeful of getting Claudia behind closed doors *before* the explosion.

Reminded of her duty, Mistress Tweedie clapped her chubby

hands. "Dinna stand about, husband, but show them straight up. The green room, I should think, for it has a bonny view o' the courtyard and a cunning little dressing room tucked into the one side—the verra thing for a blushing bride," she confided to Jack, with a sharp stab of her elbow into his side. "I'll send Lettie up wi' a tray after ye're settled, for I'll wager ye'll be wantin' tae sup alone."

Claudia's and Jack's repeated attempts to assure her that such extravagant generosity was appreciated but wholly unnecessary—they would gladly take their supper in the dining room along with the other guests—fell on deaf ears. Too weary to argue further, Jack admitted defeat and said that supper in their room would be grand. Ignoring the violet daggers Claudia aimed at him, he gestured for her to follow the innkeeper up the carpeted stairs.

The green room was aptly named, for green velvet drapery swathed both the bed and window and there was even a stencil of ivy festooning the border between wall and ceiling. As soon as Tweedie left them alone, closing the chamber door behind him, Claudia rounded on Jack. All traces of sleep had vanished from her eyes, which now looked to be as sharp as tacks and more than fit for piercing straight through him.

"You allowed her to think we were wed!"

The outraged look she lanced him wasna verra flattering. Seeing it raised his hackles as well as resurrected the hurt. He wasna good enough for her, he kent that well enough and yet must she rub his nose in it?

"She supposed we were and I wasna about to gainsay her. 'Tis a proper tavern, Claudia, no like Alistair's. Were I to tell her the truth, we'd soon find ourselves tossed out into the street."

"But in France—"

"This is *Scotland,*" he said through set teeth and then stalked off to the far corner under the guise of unpacking his shaving things. "But if ye'd rather, I'm sure I can find you an empty cot in the tollbooth," he offered, slamming his shaving cup and then his razor down upon the walnut washstand. She looked so crestfallen, so perilously close to tears, that he instantly regretted the harsh words. "Claudia, lass," he said, leaving the unpacking to come to her side. "Let us no argue. I've to leave for the prison directly after supper. Aye," he said in answer to the surprise in her eyes. "They'll be keeping a room ready for me."

Wrenching off her cloak, one arm catching in the lappet, she cut her gaze up to him. "Will not the innkeeper and his wife find that rather odd behavior for a lusty bridegroom?"

"It may be," he allowed, reaching behind her to extricate the tangled limb, "but I'll no be the first 'bridegroom' with business to attend. Forbye I'll be back for dinner tomorrow afternoon." Determined to get the rest out before he lost his nerve, he quickly added, "I thought we might climb to Arthur's Seat to watch the sunset. That is, if ye'd like."

"Arthur's Seat?"

"Aye, 'tis a sort of wee mountain in the park behind Holyroodhouse. 'Tis a steep climb but well worth it for it gives a bonny view of the city and the Crags, too."

"I . . . I would like that very much," she said, and he wondered at the sudden wistful look she sent him before she turned away to hang her cloak in the wardrobe.

Regarding her, he said, "I thought you might wish to do some shopping while I'm"—he hesitated—"away. There are some bonny shops on Princes Street and along the Royal Mile." When she only shifted her shoulders, he added, "I mean to leave Luicas behind to see to your needs."

She blanched at that. "To guard me, you mean?"

Luicas's entrance, their saddlebags slung over one spindly shoulder and Elf in tow, saved him from answering. Grateful for the reprieve, Jack turned to address the boy. "Luicas, set that down and come hither. I've a charge for ye."

Ever eager to make himself useful, the boy slid the bags from his arm and set them on the bench inside the door before coming forward. "What is it, Master Jack?"

"I'm off to the tollbooth after supper. I'll need you to stand watch o'er Mistress Valemont until I return on the morrow."

The lad's face fell. "I'm tae stay behind, then?" At Jack's nod, the corners of his wide mouth drooped lower still. "B-but who . . . who will help you tae test the trap and . . . and tae stretch out the rope and—"

"I expect I'll manage on my own this once, lad," he said, laying a consoling hand on the boy's shoulder, for it was hard to be young, harder still to be young and yearn to be grown.

Luicas brightened. "Can we no take Mistress Claudia tae the

prison wi' us? She could take tea wi' the warder's wife until we're through?"

Glancing beyond the boy to Claudia's suddenly ashen face, Jack rushed to reassure her, "Nay, wee Luicas, 'tis best for all concerned that Claudia stay behind and you with her." At the boy's crestfallen look, he added, "'Tis a weighty charge I'm giving you, lad. Edinburgh is a large city and full o' foul and dangerous characters, and I'm relying on you to keep her safe for me."

Squaring his narrow shoulders, Luicas nodded in solemn recognition of the trust. "I'll no fail ye, Master Jack. The lady shall no leave my sight, I swear it on my da's grave."

"There's a good lad." He dug into his sporran and counted out a wad of ten-pound notes, which he handed to the boy. "Tomorrow after breakfast, you're to take Mistress Claudia out to the shops and purchase whatever it is she fancies." Again that twitch of apprehension, that spine-tingling sense of impending danger. Heeding it, he added, "But mind you keep to Princes Street and the Mile and dinna go wanderin' off to where you might come to harm."

Looking resigned if not happy, Luicas pocketed the bills with a nod and then announced his intention to go below to see that the horses were being properly cared for.

During the latter part of the interchange, Claudia had drifted over to the window to gaze out onto the courtyard below. She'd been caught up in lamenting that sunset she and Jack would never see together but at the sound of the door falling closed, she turned about.

"Why do you look so sad, Jack?" she asked, torn from her own misery by his wistful look.

"Ah well," he allowed, coming to join her at the window, "'tis only that I was minded just now of how verra young he is and how in another year or so he'll have come to see standing watch o'er a beautiful woman as more a pleasure than a duty."

The compliment, as unexpected as it was unsought, took Claudia completely unawares. In the salons of Paris, poets had penned sonnets celebrating her beauty and painters had vied for the honor of capturing her image on canvas, but none of those accolades had meant half so much as did Jack's simple compliment.

She wouldn't have thought she had a shy bone in her body

but once again Jack proved her wrong. Pretending interest in a jagged fingernail, she attempted to regain her equilibrium. "Thank you," she murmured, for what more was there to say?

It was Jack's turn to look away. "You dinna have to thank me for only speaking what is true."

A knock outside their door put an end to their awkwardness. Jack left her to answer it.

A round-faced young maid appeared in the hallway outside, a tray in hand. "Supper, sir," she chirped, her sloe-eyed gaze looking Jack up and down, or so it seemed to Claudia. "Where shall I set it?"

Jack shrugged. "That wee round table by the fire, I suppose."

Full hips swaying like a bell, she stepped over the threshold and crossed the patterned carpet to the hearth. She set the tray down and bent to lift the lids off the covered dishes, but shoving away from the window, Claudia waved her off.

"I will serve my *husband,*" she said very firmly and the girl only shrugged and turned to go.

Jack reached into his sporran, handed the girl a coin, and then held the door for her. "Such a gentleman and sae generous," she simpered, making a show of slipping the money inside her low bodice. "If ye need anything, anything a-tall, ye've only tae ring and ask for Lettie. That's short for Lettice," she added with a grating little giggle. Catching Claudia's withering gaze, her smile fell and she bobbed a quick curtsy and scurried out into the hall.

Yanking off pewter lids and then slamming them back down, Claudia remarked, "I suppose you think she is 'beautiful' too?"

Infuriating man, he only rolled his shoulders and said, "Well, I wouldna say she's ugly." Coming up on the table, he held out a chair for her.

Reminded that jealousy would only spoil what was to be their final hour together, Claudia sank into the floral-cushioned seat. To cover her gathering tears, she averted her eyes and began assessing the contents of the supper tray. Mrs. Tweedie had, it seemed, thought of everything, down to the chilled bottle of Flemish wine that had just been decanted.

Wishing she were indeed the blushing bride the innkeeper's wife believed her to be, that she and Jack might have a lifetime of suppers and sunsets ahead of them, she looked up to find him watching her from his chair across the table, an unfathomable expression on his handsome face.

To break the uneasy silence, she exclaimed, "Wine, how lovely." Nerves on edge, she reached for his pewter goblet. "A toast, I think, to the shortest marriage that ever was."

She'd meant to be amusing but the tightening of Jack's jaw and the wounded look in his eyes told her she'd been anything but. "I'll need to keep a clear head for the morrow."

"Jack, I—"

"And," he cut in, gaze hard, "I'm minded I work best on an empty stomach." Removing its cover, he set his plate down on the floor and then whistled to Elf, who bounded over. "If you'll excuse me . . ." He pushed away from the table and, to Claudia's dismay, rose.

Listening to the dog's gobbling, she looked on in stricken silence as he went over to the washstand where he stripped off his shirt to wash his face, arms, and all that lovely expanse of gold-dusted chest.

Hating that they would part forever in anger, she started up. "Jack—"

"Not a word," he ordered, his glaring expression framed by the shaving mirror.

She watched in stupefied silence as, dressed once more, he gathered up his few things, called a sated Elf to his side, and then walked out the chamber door without so much as another word.

T*he supper wasn't excellent but it was good. An entire beef* roast, jacket potatoes, new peas, and a pudding for dessert although Claudia scarcely had the appetite to stomach more than a few bites. Past caring that the wine was Flemish and not French, she poured herself a second glass, finished it, and then poured herself another. Not because she wished to become drunk—setting out on the morrow with a heavy, throbbing head would be disastrous—but because she desperately needed to sleep.

And to do so, first she must deaden the pain.

But despite the three glasses of passably decent wine and a mattress and pillow stuffed with feathers instead of dried heather and bracken, Claudia lay awake to see the sun rise over the spired skyline.

And to weep for all those sunsets that would never be.

H*is duty discharged, Jack stood before the cracked* dresser-top mirror and stared at his hooded self for a long, long moment before pulling off the cover and tossing it on the scarred dresser top to join his discarded gloves. He ran both hands over his face, scratchy with budding beard and clammy with sweat, and asked himself yet again why it was he should feel so damned bad.

It had been, by everyone's reckoning, a verra successful morning. Bull-necked and barrel-chested, the condemned had fired through the trap like a shot. Afterwards the warder and the guards and even the prison surgeon had complimented Jack on a perfectly executed drop. Once their praise would have meant something to him, had him beaming with pride and bursting with self-worth, but now all he felt was edgy and restless as if his very skin trapped him like an ill-fitting coat, pinching in places, too loose in others.

The highwayman he'd turned off had been a nasty sort and wanted in five counties for nigh on ten years. Jack had met him twice, the night before when he'd come to the condemned cell to take his measurements and then that morning on the scaffold steps. Both times, the prisoner had sworn that, though he'd killed before, he'd had nothing to do with the courier's death, and both times Jack had reminded himself that he was an executioner, not a judge or a jurist and certainly not a priest. And yet if he were honest with himself he'd have to admit that he always felt better when they confessed.

But it was over now. Half of him couldn't wait to return to the inn and Claudia but the other half dreaded the thought of facing her. She'd lived through the Terror in France, had seen men, women, and even children murdered en masse, and because of that experience she painted all executioners with the same broad brush. Useless to point out to her that those he met on the scaffold were condemned not for their birth but for the foulness of their deeds. And yet the crisp line he'd drawn between the two conditions seemed to bleed together more and more with each passing day.

But now he was tired; he didn't want to think anymore let alone argue his point. He didn't want to argue at all. What he wanted was a shave and a bath. He wanted a meal, too, but beyond all else he wanted Claudia. Not that he would allow himself to hold or caress her—since the night of their "dance lesson" he'd told himself that such familiarity must be strictly off-limits. But to hear her voice, see her smile, perhaps touch her hand in passing—any of those simple pleasures would be balm to a soul that suddenly seemed not only bruised but well on its way to rotted.

In truth, he felt as if his entire person were coated with some invisible slime. Taking advantage of his solitude, he lifted his arm and drew a surreptitious sniff. He didn't smell bad, or at least he didn't think he did. Before leaving the inn the night before, he'd washed himself and though the water in the basin had been cold, the soap he'd brought with him, evergreen and mint, had been strong. Even so, he moved to the washstand and sloshed water into the bowl to wash his hands. Not because they'd got dirty—he'd worn gloves, after all—but because the symbolism of it appealed to him. But now something felt different, something felt *wrong. Not enough,* he decided, and started sluicing his face and neck, too. "More," he said, this time aloud, and tore off his drenched shirt to scour his chest and belly and arms; his oxters and his shoulders and finally his hands again until he stood shivering, panting, raw, the pitcher and bowl now as dry as one of Elf's well-gnawed bones. *What the devil is the matter with me?* he asked of both the wild-eyed man in the mirror and the wolfhound perched on the cot behind him, even as the truth came crashing down on him.

It was Claudia, of course. He wanted to be clean for her.

But staring at his dripping reflection, he allowed he wanted it for himself, too.

> The best-laid schemes o' mice an' men
> Gang aft agley,
> An'lea'e us nought but grief an' pain,
> For promis'd joy!
>
> —Robert Burns, *To a Mouse*

S*eated at the breakfast table the following morning, Claudia* finally admitted she couldn't afford to delay the inevitable any longer. Heavy-eyed and muzzy-headed though she was, with a heart that was somewhere betwixt *breaking* and *broken,* it was time she put her plan for escape into motion.

Nerves strung taut as wire, she looked across the saltglaze tea service to Luicas, blithely mopping up the last of the clotted cream with what she accounted to be his third scone. The sight of all that innocent, fresh-faced, *unsuspecting* youth caught at her heart, making her loathe herself almost as much as the trick she was about to play upon him. Certainly it would be kinder, gentler, to wait upon her chance and then slip away from him on the crowded Edinburgh streets, but it also would be infinitely more dangerous. By the time she found her way back to the inn—and to the mews backing onto it—young Luicas could have raised the hue and cry, or worse yet, his master.

Jack. Thinking on their strained leave-taking the day before, her heart gave a painful lurch. She'd spent the long, sleepless hours dividing dusk from dawn asking herself if she shouldn't leave him a note at least, some explanation to ease his mind—and salve her own conscience. In the end, she'd decided against doing so. A clean break would be the best way, not to mention she hadn't the faintest idea of what she'd say to him.

The grandfather clock in the hallway below knelled. Claudia glanced up sharply, feeling each toll vibrate inside her breast. Half past ten—she dare not dally any longer. One eye on the boy, she dipped her little finger inside her cup, testing the temperature. The chocolate had been scalding when she'd poured it earlier but had cooled to tepid, which for her purpose made it ideal.

Taking advantage of Luicas's rapt attention on his breakfast, she lifted the cup and upended it over herself. "Ouf!"

Predictably Luicas leapt to his feet, fumbling for the napkin that he'd forgotten was tucked beneath his chin. "Ye're no burnt, are ye?"

She had the fleeting thought to pretend that she was so that she might send him off in search of a physician or, barring such high drama, at least butter from the inn larder but decided against it. He might just as easily panic and go to fetch Jack from the prison and then where would she be?

Far more prudent to stick to her original plan such as it was. Accordingly, she took up her napkin and dabbed at the muddy brown streaking the bodice of her cotton floral print. "*Non,* only clumsy and wet. But I cannot go out to the shops in such a state. I shall have to change my gown before we leave."

Relief registered on the boy's face. He really was a very good boy, she thought, and looking into his earnest gaze, so like his sister's, she felt her heart give another guilty little dip.

He nodded and then resumed his seat, one eye on the untouched scone on her plate. "Are ye goin' tae eat that? No that I'm still hungry, mind, but seems a shame tae waste it."

"*Non, non* you have it," she assured him, scraping her chair back from the table to rise. *Pauvre* Luicas, little did he know that, if she succeeded, food would not be passing his lips again for several hours.

Feeling as if her legs were of no more substance than the orange marmalade Luicas had smeared on his scones along with the cream, she somehow managed the trek from the breakfast room to the bedchamber—and the wardrobe within. A plain but handsome piece, the walnut armoire had the curious—and in this case, highly convenient—characteristic of resting flat on the floor sans pedestal or feet. Throwing the double doors open wide, she pretended to rummage through, an absurdity given she possessed only two other gowns, Evette's sprigged muslin and the lavender silk, the latter far too formal for a shopping expedition.

She'd worn the gown the first and, she supposed, last time for Mairi MacGregor's wedding. That night in the byre Jack had come so very close to kissing her that his breath had brushed her lips, a caress in itself. The memory sent her heart slipping even lower in her chest where it crashed like a carriage run into a tree. To cover the pain, she summoned a smile and prepared to play her part with however much heart she still had left.

"Luicas, *chéri,*" she called back, schooling her voice to sound sunny and light. "Will you come here, *s'il te plait?* I require a man's opinion."

That she'd called him a man alone sufficed to have him vaulting from his seat and into the bedchamber, the napkin still tucked into his collar. Belatedly jerking it free, he joined her to stand before the open wardrobe.

She gestured within to the two gowns, hanging side by side on their wooden pegs. "Which shall it be?" she asked and, when he moved closer, stepped back to stand directly behind him.

"I canna say as I ken much about females' clothing but . . ." Sticking his head half inside the opening, he squinted in concentration, sucking cream from his thumb. "Maybe if ye was tae take them out soooooo . . ."

Calling on all her might, Claudia had reached out with both hands and given him a goodly shove. Taken unawares, the lad lurched all the way inside. Heart racing, she slammed the doors closed behind him and then fumbled to turn the key in the lock.

"Lemme out! Lemme out!" An assault of pounding caused the wardrobe to sway.

She bit her lip, hating what she'd done, hating herself even more. Above the din, she called, "Do not be alarmed, Luicas. There are several wormholes in the back. Last night while you slept I used the knife from supper to widen them. You will be warm, yes, but you will not suffocate, and in a few short hours your master will return to set you free."

"Tae kill me, ye mean," he shouted back, then laid another salvo inside the locked doors.

Reminded that Jack would indeed return, Claudia snatched up her cloak, the handkerchief-wrapped brooch, and the tied parcel of her mother's saved letters she'd brought along; the latter two articles she shoved into her battered valise and then started for the chamber door.

One foot on the threshold, she couldn't resist calling back, "*Adieu, cher* Luicas. And please do not be angry with me, for it is only that I must go home now."

Tears clogging her throat, she pulled the chamber door closed behind her, locked it against the boy's muffled cries, and then hastened to the stairs.

The Royal Mile was thronged with midday traffic, both horse-drawn and pedestrian, as Jack made his way to the inn, Elf keeping to his side. With each step he took, his sense of foreboding grew keener as did the anxiety gnawing at his belly, the sixth sense that something was terribly, terribly wrong. More than the unfathomable tumult of emotions swirling inside him, he feared for Claudia. Why oh why hadn't he bowed to the dictates of his inner wisdom and brought her with him to the tollbooth where at least he might have kept her safe? Why oh why had he left behind a boy to do a man's job?

Because ye've gone saft, Jacko, an inner voice, *Callum's* voice, crowed.

Soft though his head might be, it wasna nearly so soft as his heart. Whoever Claudia Valemont was, if indeed that were her true name, she'd gotten to him, penetrated the protective casing it had taken him decades, nay, a lifetime, to build, and the invasion had left him as soft, spongy, and stupid as a snail denuded of its shell.

True, he'd hated the prospect that taking her with him to the prison would in some way transport her back to her solitary night in the village tollbooth and before that to a Paris torn asunder by revolution. Owing to the carnage she'd witnessed there her fear of executioners, of *les bourreaux* as she called them, ran deep.

And perhaps, just perhaps he hadn't cared to drive home the point that he was, in fact, one of them.

Choking down the fear that his selfishness might have cost Claudia, and cost her dearly, he quickened his step until he was skirting a run, his cloak flying behind him. A costermonger pushing along his cartload of roasted chestnuts wheeled out in front of him and then slowed to a near standstill or so it seemed to Jack. He barreled around it only to find his progress further stalled by a plump housewife waddling at snail's pace, market basket in hand, and a loaded-down dray crawling by. Suddenly it seemed as if the entire city of Edinburgh had turned out to thwart him. Determined, he darted around the cart, so close he felt the back of his cloak brush against the horse's hide. Ignoring the driver's curses, Jack checked to make certain Elf was still with him. She was and so he sped ahead, turning off into a narrow wynd that he remembered as emptying out onto Blackfriars Street. Blinking owlishly, he stepped out from the darkened close into the sunlight. A half dozen or so long determined strides brought him to the inn steps. By the time he reached it, taking the stone steps to the entrance two at a time, the sweat was running down his back in warm rivulets.

The inn's common area was cool and quiet in the pale light of late morning, it being past breakfast but not yet time for dinner. A smattering of voices trickled out from the open parlor door. On his way to the stairs, Jack hesitated, and then backed up a step to peer inside. A trio of guests amused themselves within, two frock-coated older gentlemen puzzling over a chessboard and a somberly dressed matron in gray serge, bloodless lips moving as she read silently from the open Bible in her lap, but no Claudia. Smoothing a hand over his wild hair, Jack turned to go, hoping to leave before anyone saw him.

"Oh, my word, Master Campbell, we dinna expect to see you so soon," Mistress Tweedie shrilled. The innkeeper's wife stood just at his back, a tray with three very full glasses of sherry balanced on the flat of one broad hand. "But wherever is your bonny bride? Och, but I thought she said she was tae meet up wi' ye? Dearie me, but ye've gone white as a sheet. Will you take a glass of sherry tae warm yourself, then?"

Ignoring the three pairs of curious eyes at his back, he shook his head and forced himself to ask, "How long ago was it that she, ah, set out?"

A frown splitting her brow, Mistress Tweedie took her time in considering the question until Jack was tempted to grab her by her plump shoulders and, tray and all, shake the answer from her. "Hmm, no long after ten, I expect," she began at last, "for Lettie was just finishing clearing the breakfast dishes. Herself came into the front hall—your dear wife, no Lettie—and asked me tae send 'round tae the stable for her horse."

Heart skipping beats, Jack nodded. "I see," he muttered and, God help him, he did. "Thank you."

He stepped aside to make room for her to enter but instead the damnable woman clung to him like a leech, setting down her tray to follow him out into the hallway.

"I told the lass she ought not tae venture out on 'er own, that she'd do better tae bide here and wait for you. Och, but these modern young women are too headstrong by half. But it's maybe that she's only taken a wrong turn and gotten herself lost but shall I call for a constable just in case?"

A constable! Jack had made it so far as the stair landing but at the mention of constables, he made an about-face. "Jesus Christ, no!" Over the thundering in his ears, he added more calmly, "What I mean to say is that she's maybe returned a'ready and ye've just no seen her come in."

She opened her mouth to answer, then promptly snapped it closed. But the look she sent him spoke volumes, confirming what he'd already surmised: there wasna much that went on within her inn's four walls that Mistress Tweedie missed.

Clinging to fragile hope nonetheless, Jack turned about and barreled up the stairs. Thundering footfalls brought him down the narrow hallway to the door of the chamber he'd let. It was locked, he discovered upon trying the brass knob, and he fished beneath his cloak for the key inside his coat pocket. Bringing out the key to fit it into the lock, he was alarmed to discover his hands were shaking. *Claudia, lass, what have you done to me,* he asked himself for what must have been the hundredth time since he'd begged off the warder's hospitality of wine and biscuits to return early. Despite his fumbling, the key hit home. Senses on the alert, he turned the knob, praying he might be mistaken, knowing in his heart of hearts he was not.

Even before he stepped inside, he knew what he would find—absolute stillness, eerie, bone-rattling quiet. Gone were the familiar sounds he'd come to associate with Claudia: her soft melodic humming, the tapping of her teacup against its saucer, the general whirlwind that seemed always to surround her. She brought so much life to a room that it was impossible not to take note of her presence—or to mark her absence.

And even as he acknowledged that she was gone—gone for

good and not just for shopping—idiot that he was, he couldn't keep from calling out, "Claudia. Claudia, I'm back."

He crossed the little sitting room, quiet as a kirkyard, and entered the bedchamber, suspiciously neat, hollow with emptiness.

Halfway inside the bedchamber, he heard it. "Mphm, mphm, *mphm!*"

The warbling seemed to be coming from within the wardrobe. The key stood in the lock. Even before he turned it and got the double doors open, he knew it wasn't Claudia he would find within.

Wilted as a plucked violet, Luicas fell into Jack's arms. Catching him, Jack said, "Luicas, lad, what the devil . . ."

Dashing a thin hand across his streaming brow to dislodge the wet threads of hair, Luicas stepped back, tears bubbling forth from his reddened eyes. "I-I'm s-sorry, Master. Mistress C-Claudia, she . . . she . . ." His voice broke off on a sob.

Fresh panic plowed Jack like a fist in the gut, but he forced himself to remain outwardly calm as he said, "Easy, lad. Take a deep breath, and then tell me what has happened to Claudia."

The boy obliged, sucking down air as though it was still in limited supply. "Just before we was tae go out tae the shops, she spilled chocolate down the front o' her frock. The flowered one wi' the little rosebuds sewn along the neck."

Fear clawing at his entrails, Jack seized the boy by the shoulders and gave him a hearty shake. "I dinna care what it was she was wearin,' only get on with it."

"She bade me come o'er tae the wardrobe and help her decide which gown tae put on." Daring a look up into Jack's face, he admitted, "And so I did and turned my back for just the minute, and she gave me a goodly shove—for a wee woman, she's verra strong. The next thing I knew, it had gone all close and dark. And then I heard the key turnin' in the lock and mistress weepin' and sayin' 'twas past time she went home."

Home? Jack dragged a hand through his tangled hair, struggling to find some sense in it all. Back to France—that couldna be, not when she'd risked so much to leave.

"Think Luicas, think. Did she say anything, *anything* at all, to hint at where she might be headed?"

Luicas dragged his bottom lip through his teeth but at length he shook his head. "Nay, master. 'Home,' that was the whole of it."

And then it was as if the scales suddenly fell from Jack's eyes and the cobwebs cleared from his brain. Inside his head, Claudia's own silky voice called him back to that very first day they'd met when she'd followed him outside Alistair's to launch her desperate plea. *I must find my way to Linlithgow,* she'd said. *It lies just west of—*

Of Edinburgh, he finished for her now, and letting go of the boy to rush the door, he couldn't credit that he hadna reckoned it all ere now.

Home. I am coming home.

Crouched low over the mare's mane against the wind's bite, Claudia repeated the words as if they were a mantra, a magical incantation to ward off the sick, sinking feeling that she was making the very worst mistake of her life. For try as she might, she couldn't shrug off the sense that every patch of frost-parched ground she covered, every craggy slope she urged her horse to climb, carried her farther from, not closer to, all that she'd come to hold familiar and dear.

More than once, she'd almost turned the mare back around to retrace her path but now it was too late to do other than stay her chosen course. A signpost she'd encountered at the crossroads a mile or so back had confirmed she was already more than halfway to her destination. Only seven more miles to the town of Linlithgow and from there she reckoned another few miles at most to Castle Aberdaire. Since sighting the signage, she'd allowed her horse to lapse into an easy trot. No need to exhaust either the mare or herself when her present pace would carry her to her destination before nightfall and in good time.

In fact, loosely constructed as her escape plan had been, everything was progressing amazingly well. Her heart had quailed when, upon descending the inn stairs that morning, she'd encountered the ever-vigilant Madame Tweedie in the hallway below. But when Claudia had said she was off to meet her husband, the good wife had beamed at her and insisted on sending a servant boy to fetch her horse for her. Only after she was mounted with the reins firmly in hand had Claudia dared reveal her true destination, asking the ostler in a whisper if he would be so good as to direct her. The boy's eyes had widened at that, no doubt thinking Linlithgow to be a long way for a woman to ride alone, but he'd only shrugged and pointed the way.

Even though she'd never before been to Edinburgh, a lifetime spent in Paris had left her with a knack for navigating bustling city streets, and she'd experienced next to no difficulty in finding her way to the Royal Mile. Her greatest challenge had been in controlling the beast beneath her on the heavily trafficked streets, for her previous riding experiences had been limited to the open fields and parklands of Phillippe's family estate.

But barring a few minor mishaps, she'd soon enough found herself on solitary country lanes, rambling alongside fields littered with bracken and the husks of harvested crops as she made her way westward, skirting the Firth of Forth. Occasionally an errant cow or sheep crossed her path, a drover or farmer in chase, but otherwise she'd met up with no one. She was too far from the coastline to see the water, but she fancied there was the tang of salt in the air. There was even a glint of sunshine in the gray-washed skies above and the roads were blessedly dry. She'd be in Linlithgow within the hour, she felt certain, and then somehow she'd find a way to have Jack's mare returned to him. The creature was costly but, more to the point, she'd come to understand how deeply he felt for the animals under his care—no point in adding to her mounting pile of sins by stealing his beloved horse as well.

Lost in her thoughts, when she first became aware of the pounding echo she shrugged it off as the beginnings of a headache. But no, the steady drumming came from behind, not within, and seemed to be growing both closer and louder until it seemed to shake the very earth beneath her horse's hooves. Another traveler, no doubt? Tamping down panic—she couldn't expect to be the only one out and about on such a fine day—she slowed her horse to a walk in order to venture a backward glance.

At first sight, the brownish black dot bobbing along the horizon might have been a visual illusion caused by her staring directly at the sun. Or perhaps some distant landmark she'd fail to notice ere now? Only, like the expanding pupil of a startled eye, the dot was growing ever larger until all at once it lost its circularity and assumed the shape of a single horse and rider.

The sun broke free from its cover of clouds to limn both man and mount in golden light so that the rider's bared head seemed to burst into flame. Recognition slammed into Claudia then and though she'd all but brought the mare to a standstill, she had to clutch the saddle to keep her seat. This was no anonymous rider but Jack, Jack Hamish Campbell, charging toward her at full gallop, black cape catching the wind like the sail of a pirate ship.

A treacherous trill of relief shot through her even as she turned about and dug her knees into the mare's sides. She'd purposefully taken the mare and left Jack Beelzebub because she'd feared the larger, more spirited bay would be too much for her. Now she regretted that decision and regretted it heartily. The mare might be light and strong enough to best the bay in a short race, but for the longer haul she hadn't the stallion's staying power just as Claudia hadn't a prayer of holding her own against a seasoned rider like Jack.

And yet some small stubborn part of her balked at being so easily conquered. She reached back and laid a stinging slap on the mare's muscular hindquarters. Unaccustomed to such rough handling, the horse let out a shriek and bolted forward. Her loosened hair slashing at her face, Claudia crouched low over the saddle, dug in her knees, and hung on for dear life.

Only a few yards behind her now, she heard Jack calling to her to halt.

"*Jamais!* Never!" she called back without turning around and struck the reins across her mare's sweaty shoulders.

The wind picked up, carrying a stream of Celtic curses to her ears. There was no help for it. He was gaining on her. Soon bay and mare were running neck to neck and nose to nose along the rock-strewn path, their exhaled breaths forming nearly identical crystalline clouds. Claudia knew she should keep her gaze ahead but she couldn't resist a quick sideways peak at her pursuer. Nostrils flaring and sweat streaming the sides of his strong set face, Jack turned to look at her. Gone was the soft-spoken man who was never too busy to return a fallen bird to its nest, deliver a tonic to a rheumy old woman, or untangle a child's kite from the branches of a tree. Eyes gleaming feral and dark as chestnuts, white teeth bared in determination, and normally neat hair flying about his face and shoulders like a crimson flag, this Jack was for all intents and purposes a stranger to her. And for the first time since that day more than two months before when she'd stepped inside his cottage, Claudia was well and truly afraid of him.

"Rein in before ye break yer bluidy neck. Or I'm minded to break it for ye," he demanded, fury thickening his burr into a full brogue.

Before she knew what he was about, he shot out a hand and caught at her horse's bridle. Foolishly she slackened her grip on the reins, which he wrenched from her, too.

"Give those back!" She leaned across the gap between the horses and reached out.

Jack's eyes widened. "Mind the road, ye wee idjut!"

She whipped her head about and saw that they had veered off into a small copse. The trunk of a massive birch loomed just ahead, and the frenzied mare was headed directly for it. Claudia screamed and grabbed for her saddle's pommel, the only thing she'd left to hold on to.

But Jack had both sets of reins firmly in hand and, cursing furiously, he somehow managed to cut a sharp left. They whizzed by the tree with bare inches to spare, Claudia's cape flying out to catch on bark before they shuddered to a teeth-slamming halt.

Shaking with reaction, head whirring from the speed at which she'd been traveling and the nearness with which she'd come to dying yet again, she watched Jack leap from the saddle and come over to her. She gasped when he reached for her, powerful hands closing about her waist in a far from gentle hold.

With the immediate threat of crashing into the tree removed, Claudia's thoughts turned inward. Close, she'd come so very close. Seven miles more, ten at most, and she would have gained the sanctuary of her father's castle where, she told herself, nothing bad would ever touch her again. Bitter anger swallowed up every other emotion, enabling her to forget that only a short while before she'd been on the brink of turning back.

"*Non!*" She kicked out with her foot, still caught in the stirrup, and when that didn't work, shoved at Jack's shoulders.

"Suit yourself." He released her and she half fell, half slid from the saddle onto the spongy peat turf.

Panting, perspiring, she stared up at him and from somewhere found the breath to ask, "H-how . . . how did y-you f-find me?"

Arms akimbo and legs spread in a wide stance, he stared

down at her. "Och, but even an unschooled clot-head such as myself can reckon one and one sums to two, though it took me a while, I'll grant you that." The look of loathing he lanced her sent a chill of dread shooting down her spine. "When Luicas was minded of how you'd said you were going 'home,' I didna think it was back to France you'd meant." He laughed then, and the harsh, biting sound of it made Claudia wince. Turning away to rummage through his saddlebag, he continued, "Then I was minded that it was to Linlithgow you'd first asked me to take ye. But to be sure, I had a wee chat with the lad who'd saddled the mare for you—and then pointed you the way. So you see, mistress, ye're no quite so clever as you like to think."

Claudia didn't feel clever. She didn't feel clever at all. Feeling the futile tears begin to form in her eyes, she fumbled beneath her cloak for a handkerchief. When she looked back up she saw Jack advancing on her. An arrow of sunlight shot through the treetops, setting off the glint of metal in his one hand and, in a flash of pure blinding panic, she realized what he carried was a set of wrist shackles.

She shook her head, seeking even now to dislodge all the memories associated with that particular implement—Maman, Phillippe, and most recently that day two months before when, hobbled hands gripping the prisoner's bar, she'd looked back to a sea of stern-faced villagers and prepared herself to die.

"Oh, Jack," she said in a half scream, half moan, dimly aware that the tears were flowing freely now. "Oh, please, no." She backed up, her back striking the mare's damp side, but the horse wouldn't budge.

And neither, it seemed, would Jack. "Give me your hands," he said, already reaching for them.

Dumb with horror, she shoved them behind her, continuing to shake her head though her throat had gone too dry to voice further protest.

Indecision flickered across his face, giving her a moment's hope, but then steely resolution returned and she knew all was lost. "Now Claudia," he began reasonably. Another step brought him to stand directly in front of her. "Dinna make this any harder on yourself than it need be."

Reaching behind her, he caught her left arm. When she resisted, he tightened his hold, forcing it around to the front. Still struggling, she struck out with her free hand, but it was no use.

Hearing the metal cuff clamp closed, feeling the cold finality of the steel banding her wrist, she suddenly saw why it was that wild animals so often gnawed off their trapped limbs rather than submit to capture. Panicked, she reached out with her free hand and dragged her nails down the side of his face. He cried out and reared back even as his hand, powerful as any manacle, grabbed bruising hold. Another few seconds of wrangling while he maneuvered her arm above her head and then the second metal cuff closed about that wrist, too, signaling her defeat.

Great chest heaving, Jack stepped back. Swiping a hand down his bloodied cheek, he said, "You're no one to make things easy, are ye?"

Finding her voice at last, she took a step toward him, chains clinking. "I am not a good horsewoman. If you do not free my hands, I will not be able to keep my seat."

"Nay worries on that score," he answered, already moving to tie the mare's reins to those of the bay. "You'll be riding with me."

If we judge of love by its usual effects,
it resembles hatred more than friendship.

—François, Duc de La Rochefoucauld, *Maxims*

J*udging from Claudia's stiff posture, slender back held ram*rod rigid to keep from brushing against him, she did not relish the ride back to Edinburgh. But for Jack the journey proved to be pure, unadulterated hell especially when, just before entering the city gates, exhaustion finally bested pride and she fell back against him. It was bad enough he'd spent the past few hours inhaling her light rose scent, her loosened hair spread across his chest like a silk fan. To also have her slender torso molded to his belly and chest and her firm little rump wedged inside the vee of his open thighs was torture pure and simple. Despite the brisk air and the chill brought on by the setting sun, his cock and balls burned hot as cinders.

To ward off desire, he focused his thoughts on the myriad ways she'd wronged him. That she'd lied to him alone sufficed to put her beyond the pale. But she'd also bamboozled his apprentice, stolen his horse, and then ridden off without leaving behind so much as a note. That he hadn't merited so much as a few scribbled lines of farewell cut deepest of all. He should hate her, he *did* hate her, and yet he wanted her still, more now than before—and that made him hate her all the more.

Even so, a league or so from Edinburgh, he'd stopped to take off the manacles. Not because he felt guilty, well, at least not much, but because he didn't want to draw any more unwanted attention to them. Far better for the Tweedies, indeed all the inn's occupants, to believe that he and his "wife" had simply had a lovers' quarrel than to begin to suspect the truth.

Or at least that's the reason he gave himself as they rode into the cobblestone inn yard. He dismounted, hurled the reins to the sleepy-eyed hostler, and then turned back to lift Claudia down. But instead of setting her on her feet, he tossed her over his shoulder.

"Set me down, you . . . you swine." She punctuated the demand with a kick that went no further than the air.

Jack laughed a bitter laugh and shifted her to hang sack style over his left shoulder. For the benefit of the boy, who stood staring at them open-mouthed, the reins all but forgotten in his hand, he said, "Now is that anyway to address your lord and master? Are ye no happy to be once more in my arms, my sweet?" He started up the steps to the entrance, Claudia making use of her freed hands to pummel his back.

Gaining the landing, he reached for the brass doorknob even as the knob turned and the door swung back. Mistress Tweedie must have been watching for them at the window. Chubby hand braced on the doorframe, she looked from Jack to Claudia slung over his shoulder.

"Why, Mistress Campbell," she shrilled, angling her capped head to address Claudia's upturned one as Jack stepped past her. "Good heavens but what a fright ye gave us all, ridin' off by yourself like that." Looking past Claudia to Jack, she gushed, "Will you and the missus be taking supper in your rooms then, Master Campbell? I've a lovely leg o' mutton saved back from supper and jacket potatoes and apple tart for desert."

Balancing a seething, squirming Claudia in his arms, Jack answered with a firm "no" even as Claudia called out a "yes."

"Pray dinna trouble, Mistress Tweedie," he said, reaching for a rush light from the demilune table set next to the stairs. "My 'wife' and I will be retiring."

"But surely a bite of supper first and then—"

"Good night, Mistress Tweedie," he called back, already halfway up the stairs.

"Jack," Claudia protested, slamming a knuckled hand into his shoulder when he kept on. "I am hungry. I have not eaten all day."

"And whose fault might that be?" he demanded, stalking down the hallway to their room.

On his orders, Luicas had left the door to their chamber unlocked. He shouldered it open and stepped inside. Reaching around Claudia's flailing feet, he slipped the candle in the wall bracket and then pushed the door closed with a satisfying slam.

The dressing room door opened simultaneously and Luicas stuck his tousled head out, Elf holding to his side. "Mistress Claudia, ye're back!" he announced, beaming with happiness and relief as though he hadn't spent his morning roasting inside a locked wardrobe on account of her.

Jack, however, was in a far less forgiving mood. Stalking toward the bed, he barked, "Leave us and dinna even think about coming out again until morning."

The boy's smile dropped with the swiftness of a falling brick. "G'night, then," he said and, ducking back inside, pulled the door closed.

Coming up on the bed, Jack threw a wriggling Claudia down upon the mattress, so hard that she bounced up like a ball of India rubber.

She pulled herself up on her elbows, eyes flashing. "You promised you would not beat me."

"And you promised ye wouldna run off, so I suppose that makes us both liars." He came down on top of her, pinning her to the mattress. A palm braced on either side of her, face bare inches from hers, he hissed, "Tell me, Claudia, what's in Linlithgow that you maun risk your neck to get there, and dinna give me that *shite* about dressmaking. I've seen your handiwork with needle and thread—ye'd no last so much as a day."

Eyes mutinous, she tried pushing at his chest. "I do not owe you an explanation."

"Och, but ye owe me. Were it no for me and the lies I told about your addled wits you'd be rotting on the end of a gibbet ere now."

"*Ah oui, Monsieur le Borreau*, you would like that, would you not?"

For the first time in more than a month, she'd called him the name, and he was stunned at how much hearing it hurt. To anchor his anger, he grabbed hold of her wrists. "Who are you?"

"You already know who I am."

Tears shimmered in her eyes; normally the promise of them

would suffice to soften him but frustrated desire and hurt had joined forces to swallow up all other feelings, most especially pity. These past two months he'd treated her with kindness and consideration, had begun to gift her with his trust, and still she'd played him for a fool, haring off the moment he turned his back. Now he meant to break her, not her body but her will, and if they must tangle and snap at each other like a pair of wild beasts, then so be it.

"I ken yer name, witch, if indeed Claudia Valemont is your true name, but I dinna ken *you.*" He stretched her arms as far above her head as they would go, reveling at the feel of his thumbs sinking into soft, delicately veined skin.

"Bête! Couchon." She tried kneeing him, but he caught her before she could get her leg up. To ward off further attack, he shoved a knee between her legs, spreading them wide where they could do no harm.

She was little and she was light but she fought him with all she had and like a cat with claws unsheathed she proved herself to be a formidable opponent. Sweat streamed the sides of his face, salting the fresh scratches on his cheek.

"The day of your sentencing, you said your sire was an earl—a *Scottish* earl. Why, Claudia? Why would you say such a thing if it wer'na true?"

Head lashing the pillow, she cried out, "I told you, I told you, I did not wish to die."

"And then there's the wee matter of your hands." He grabbed one now and turned it on the pillow above her head to regard the ring of newly formed calluses rimming the flesh where her fingers joined her palm. "Until two months ago, these hands had ne'er done so much as a day's labor. Had they? *Had they!* What really brought you to Scotland, Claudia? Damn you, answer me!" he demanded when she only pressed her lips together. Firm, full, and infinitely kissable, that lovely, *lying* mouth was the portal to all the answers he sought. "Verra well," he said, a sudden treacherous calm claiming him. "As I willna let ye up until I have the truth and ye willna see your way to giving it to me, I suppose we're in for a long night of it."

Claudia was still struggling when the shock of his mouth coming down on hers caused her to go stock-still. His was a kiss meant to humble, not arouse, and yet at that first bruising assault she felt the resistance draining from her limbs. She stopped fighting his hold, stopped fighting him, and melted into the moment. The scrape of Jack's unshaven jaw against her cheek. The bright crimson stripes where she'd scored his cheek. The earthy aroma of sweat and musk and man mingled with the evergreen and mint of the soap he'd used. After the first crushing onslaught he gentled, both his kiss and his grasp. His mouth was firm on hers, steady and sure but not hurtful, and the thumbs that had been pressing into her pulse points now moved over the insides of her chafed wrists in slow, soothing circles.

She moaned into his mouth, some foolish endearment intertwined with his name. He tasted nice, delicious even. Some combination of cinnamon and mint, she thought, with perhaps a pinch of anisette. And though she'd promised herself she'd fight him tooth and nail, when he ran his tongue along the seam of her lips, she sighed and opened for him like a flower.

He slipped inside, delved, explored. With his tongue he teased the sensitive underside of her lip, touched the tip to hers, then plunged deeper. There was anger in his kiss still but there was tenderness, too, and passion such as she'd dreamt of, prayed for, but until now never truly known. The combination was a heady mix of magic and madness, and Claudia couldn't think beyond the heat.

Still kissing her, he released her wrists, filled one palm with her breast, hesitated, sighed, and then gently squeezed. Pleasure, or rather the promise of it, streaked through her, ending in little teasing tongues of flame that lapped at her lower belly and brought her womanhood to full throbbing life. At some point her legs had become wrapped around his torso. She felt cool air brush her stocking-clad calves, the draft reaching up to her bared thighs, and the hard, hot heat of him pressed against her belly and knew that despite their quarrel, despite her lies and his fury, she wanted to take him inside her.

"Oh Jack, *chéri,* I . . ."

She broke off, hating that there were clothes between them, worse yet that there were secrets. Bared skin and bared souls, that was how it should have been, could be still, if only she might find the courage to give him the answers he sought.

When he finally spoke again, his voice sounded a soft, hot vibration against her ear. "Who are you?"

She lifted herself to meet him, inviting the hardness, the fury, the *heat.* "Does it matter? Why must it matter?" To divert them both she arched her back, tempting him with her mouth and all the rest of her.

He kissed her again, this time just a brush of his closed lips across hers, but it was enough. "I canna help if ye willna trust me with the truth." He pulled back to stare down at her with amber eyes that were now more wistful than angry. "Trust me, Claudia."

And it was then that something deep inside Claudia Valemont broke. Tears gushed, so hard, so hot and heavy, that looking up into Jack's face was like peering through a watery screen. Rivulets running into the hair at her temples, she squeezed her burning eyes closed, scarcely registering the moment when he rose up and lifted her onto his lap.

Against his chest, she sobbed, "I am Clothilde Antoinette Valemont. *Ma mère* . . . my mother was Célestine Marie Valemont." She drew a shuddering breath, bracing herself to continue. "And my father is Gearald Drummond, the earl of Aberdaire."

"Y*ou're faither is the Black Earl?" He'd begin to suspect as* much and yet her admission shocked him all the same.

They were still sitting on the edge of the bed, Jack's long legs stretched out before him and Claudia lying across his thighs, her head pillowed in the crook of his arm, the curve of her flushed, tear-stained cheek at once the sweetest and saddest sight he'd ever beheld.

She lifted her head a notch to look up at him. "Yes, but why do you call him so?"

Jack hesitated, wondering how much to say. Sticking to indisputable fact, he said, "Ah well, 'tis only that the Drummonds sided with the English against Bonnie Prince Charlie and the Jacobites in the Forty-five. 'Tis said that, like his sire, Aberdaire considers himself to be more English lord than Scottish laird, but then that's maybe no a crime, I suppose."

"And for that Lord Aberdaire is called the Black Earl?"

He reached down and lifted a strand of hair from her shoulder. Rolling it about his finger, he answered, "That and the color of his hair, the same blue-black as yours." In reality the moniker owed as much due to the earl's reputation as to his hair color, but he hesitated to malign a man he'd never met based on rumor alone. Instead, he teased, "Scottish as well as French—nay wonder you're so stubborn. How did that ever come about?"

Their enmity forgotten, she smiled through her tears and shifted to sit beside him. "Maman was born in Bourgogne—Burgundy—but she lived in Paris most of her life. It was there that she met my fath . . . the earl. Only he was not yet an earl but a young Scottish lord touring the Continent. They met at the opera; he invited her to join him in his box and they became lovers that very night. The rest, it is an old story. I was conceived and then he returned to Scotland. *C'est tout.*"

"How did you live?"

He could feel her stiffen as she answered, "Maman was very beautiful. It was not long before she attracted the attention of another nobleman, the duc d'Andromaque. She became his mistress and we moved into a big house on the Place Vendôme." Eyes downcast to the small feet that didn't quite touch the floor, she said, "That must shock you?"

He shook his head, touched her face to reassure her. "My faither was an English dragoon posted to the Borders. Like your parents mine met and fell in love, or at least she did." He pulled a long swallow before adding, "He left my maither to go back to England before I was born. She only married Tam to give me a home and a name."

"And yet your surname is Campbell, not McBride?"

He nodded. "Aye, which suits Tam and me both, as I wasna any more anxious to own him as my sire than he was to call me son." Minded that he'd meant to learn about her, not give away himself, he said, "So I was right in thinking you've ne'er labored as a lady's maid?" He'd always known she was beyond his touch, far too fine for the likes of him, but only now did he realize how doomed, how ridiculous his foolish, fledgling hopes really were.

"Oh, Jack, how disappointed you sound. How sad you look. You make me wish I might say yes." Embarrassed by his own transparency, he started to demur, but she only shook her head. "I *had* a maid, Evette, though she was more like a sister to me than a servant. We grew up together, even slept in the same bed as children though we had to take care not to be discovered, of course."

Gently he said, "You miss her very much, I think."

"*Oui,* I do," she answered, eyes growing moist. "I begged her to come with us to England but she was to wed Pierre, the footman, and her life she said must be in France with him. And so one morning very early she and I exchanged clothes, for we are of a size. She sat at my window in my favorite yellow gown and with her light hair hidden beneath a black wig while I slipped from the house, pretending to be her. I carried a market basket over my arm and hid my hair beneath a cap and so I made my way to the farmer's cart that was waiting to take Maman and me to Calais and . . . and to the ship. Only Maman . . . they had taken her the week before and . . . and cut off her head . . ." Shoulders bowed, she seemed to grow smaller before his very eyes.

"Hush, you're safe now." Reaching around her to trace slow, soothing circles on her back, he wondered at the miracle that, after what had befallen her mother, Claudia could bear to have him touching her. "You dinna have to go on, mind. If it's too painful . . ."

She lifted her chin a notch as she did when she was girding herself to be brave, to be strong. Poor Claudia, only now was he coming to appreciate just how brave, how strong, she really was.

She shifted around to face him, turning world-weary eyes up to his face. "No more secrets, *chéri.* I want to tell you all of it. I only hope that when I have finished, you will not hate me too much."

"I could never hate you," he told her and meant it though the skeptical look she sent him caused a little trickle of fear to slide down his spine.

"We shall see," she whispered and then looked away to gather herself before taking up her tale. "At first we told ourselves Maman would be safe—she was only a *courtisane* and of common blood. But her protector was a duke and after he and his family were taken, we knew it was but a matter of time before they came for her and perhaps me as well. We began to m-make plans for l-leaving but . . . but we waited t-too long. Too long . . ."

She'd begun to shake. He could hear her teeth knocking together and that frightened him almost as much as did the wild, hunted look in her eyes.

He tightened his arm around her, began to rock her as if she were a small child. "Oh, Claudia, oh, sweeting, I'm so sorry."

Gaze fixed on the wall beyond him, she continued, "I watched, you know. The day they bore her to the scaffold, I was standing in the back of the square. Her gown was torn and dirty and her hands were bound, but when her turn came she held her head high and climbed the steps to the scaffold without once faltering. Someone threw an egg; it struck her just below the eye. She begged the indulgence of the *borreau* and withdrew a handkerchief from her pocket—Maman was never without her handkerchief—and wiped the blood and yolk from her cheek. Then she turned back to him and nodded and he beckoned his assistant forward to arrange her hair."

She'd been staring over his left shoulder, but now she turned her face up to his. "Before placing the head in the lunette, they cut the hairs away from the neck so they do not interfere with the blade, did you know?"

He did, of course, but was too ashamed to say so.

She nodded, seemingly satisfied with his silence. "She laughed then, high enough so that I could hear her all the way in the back, and called out, *'Ce n'est pas nécessaire, Monsieur Sanson.'* It was then that she lifted off her wig with a flourish and tossed it into the lap of one of the *tricoteuses* knitting in the front row. A hush fell then for her real hair was clipped close to the scalp and so white that at first she appeared bald. Until that day, I had never been permitted to see her without her powder and her paint and her wig." Mouth trembling, she looked up at him as new tears slipped down her cheeks. "I was her daughter, Jack, but I never really saw her."

Jack felt his heart squeeze in on itself in his suddenly too tight chest. Arm about her shoulders, he crooned, "Hush, sweeting, ye're safe now, safe in my arms." Dear God, how he hoped and prayed that might be true.

He thought of the myriad disasters that might have befallen her earlier that day, a woman travelling alone on the open road, and felt a sharp shaft of fear quiver down his spine. As for Aberdaire, the earl was an unknown entity and Jack resolved then and there that, father or not, Claudia would not face His Lordship on her own.

Wishing he might draw her against his body and shelter her for all time, he pulled her even closer. "Does Aberdaire ken you're in Scotland?"

She reached up and swept a hand beneath her one eye, then the other, smearing the tears. "I cannot be certain that he knows I still live. When I arrived in London and learned from his housekeeper that he had left for Scotland, I did not leave my name."

"And yet you've no sent word to him, no in all this time? Why not, Claudia?"

Even as he asked the question, he realized he was selfishly glad she hadn't. Whatever happened now, the cherished memories of the past two months were his for all time.

"It was bad enough that I was penniless and a refugee but to come to him as a condemned horse thief would be . . . unthinkable. *Certainement* he would refuse to own me if he were ever to find out."

"Well, he'll no find out from me, I swear to you," he vowed, taking her cold hand in his and pressing it to his lips, all the kiss he now dared give her. "And if it's on Linlithgow and Castle Aberdaire that you've set your heart, I'll see you safe there."

"But will you not get into trouble, Jack? Before you could have said I escaped but now . . . if someone were to see you taking me—"

"Nay worries," he broke in and forced a smile as though his heart were whole instead of chipping into tiny bits at the surety of losing her. "Mind I'm like One Eye the Cat—I've nine lives at the verra least and like as no a tenth in waiting."

"Oh, Jack, you are so good to me. I do not know what to say, how to thank you."

He'd promised himself no more kissing, but when a smile broke through her tear-streaked face as she turned it up to his, it seemed the most natural thing in the world for him to match his lips to hers. This time the kiss was sweet. *She* was sweet. And soft. And willing. All he need do would be to ease her onto her back and . . .

Disgusted with his own weakness, mortified that he'd been on the verge of taking advantage of her distress, he tore his mouth away and set her from him. Hands on her shoulders, he held her at arms' length, willing his head to clear of impossible dreams. "Christ, Claudia, I'm sorry. We mustn't. *I* mustn't . . ."

Fierce violet eyes met his refusal. "Why must we deny ourselves? I know that you want me, Jack. I can see it in your eyes, feel it in your touch."

"Oh aye, I want you." He stroked a finger down the side of her face, following the track of a half-dried tear. "So much that betimes it hurts my heart just to look at you. To be close to you day upon day and know I hav'na the right to touch you is torment such as I wouldna wish on my verra worst enemy." She opened her mouth to protest again, but he laid two fingers across the sweet lips he could still taste on his own. "But be that as it may, I willna take advantage of a woman placed in my charge. 'Tis bad enough I've kissed and fondled you . . . and you an earl's daughter."

"An earl's *bastard,*" she corrected when he took his hand away. "And thus no better born than are you."

He still held her hand. Tracing a thumb over the delicate thread of blue vein cutting diagonal across her slender wrist, he said, "Even if you dinna have so much as a drop of noble blood and were the servant you made yourself out to be, I'd no defile you."

"Oh, Jack," she said, biting her kiss-swollen lower lip. "I thought surely you must know." She laid her free hand on the side of his face, her fingers feeling like snow on his flush skin. Holding his gaze with her own sad soulful eyes, she confessed, "You cannot defile me, *chéri,* for I have no innocence left to lose."

chapter 14

> Take mee to you, imprison mee, for I
> Except you enthrall mee, never shall be free,
> Nor ever chast, except you ravish mee.
>
> —John Donne, *Batter My Heart*

F*eeling as though a dagger was being twisted deep inside* her heart, Claudia rose to cross the room to the window. Behind her, bedsprings keened as Jack got up to follow her.

Coming up behind her, he laid his big, warm palms on her shoulder. "Who is it who hurt you, lass? You've only to tell me his name and he's as good as dead."

The same words issued from another man's lips would have sounded a hollow boast, but this was Jack and, coming as it did from him, the oath stood as a simple statement of fact. Claudia thought she might drown in the warmth rushing her heart. That he assumed she'd been ravished only spoke to how dear, how noble, how very *good* he was.

"Oh, Jack," she said on a sort of strangled half laugh, half sob. Feeling far older than her five-and-twenty years, she reached across her and covered one of his hands with hers. "I am so tired of pretending, of hiding—especially from you."

"Then dinna hide, *mo chride,* my heart, but tell me all. I promise to listen and no to judge you."

"Very well, then." She swallowed deeply against the chalk dryness coating her throat and, her hand still atop his, admitted, "I am—was—a *courtisane* as was my mother before me. But there has only been one man," she hastened to add because suddenly it seemed so very important that he not think too badly of her.

Powdered and painted, coiffured and patched, she'd been paraded about fashionable Paris like one of her mother's prized poodles. She'd been just a month shy of seventeen when she'd met Phillippe du Marmac at a levee held by one of her mother's friends and so painfully naïve, so easily dazzled that even now she bit her lip in shame to think of it. Dashing, young, and the heir to the du Marmac title and fortune, he'd easily swept her off her feet. A house in fashionable Faubourg Saint-Germain, a carriage and driver, and a generous quarterly allowance had purchased him exclusive rights to her body and bed.

Gently but firmly Jack turned her around to face him, and she would have gladly surrendered an eyetooth to be able to look somewhere, anywhere, other than his knowing amber gaze. "Once you called out a name in your sleep—Phillippe. That was him, aye?"

Shuddering to think what else she might have called out, she nodded. "*Oui.*"

"Did you love him, Claudia?"

Startled by the question, she nonetheless answered without hesitation, "*Non,* there was never any love between us. Passion at first, lust if you prefer, but never love."

Nor friendship nor respect nor even so much as simple caring, she realized, and the sudden, unexpected lump rising to the back of her throat felt as large as a brick of coal.

"That's verra sad."

Regarding him through the lens of misty eyes, she said, "*Oui,* I suppose that it is."

"Where is he now?"

"Dead. Executed in the Place de la Révolution the month before Maman." *Pauvre* Phillippe, he'd been yet another victim of the guillotine and his own noble birth. Odd that it was now that she could find it in her heart to mourn him.

"I'm sorry." He kept his hands on her shoulders and his gaze locked on hers. "He was a gentleman, your Phillippe?"

Truth telling must be as contagious as the smallpox, for one damning admission only seemed to lead to another. "An aristocrat and the eldest son of a *comte.* But please, do not call him *my* Phillippe."

Her voice broke off as a montage of humiliating memories fired through her mind. Phillippe, one hand grabbing a fistful of her hair as he forced her down onto her knees. The sickening smoky sweetness of his cheroot just before he pressed the burning tip to her breast. The prick of gooseflesh and shame as the last veil of her clothing fell away, leaving her standing naked and vulnerable before his hot, gloating gaze.

"He used you ill, didn't he?" In the glow from the peat fire and the room's single candle, Jack's gaze bore into hers.

She opened her mouth to deny it but the expression on his face told her that her own must be as transparent as glass. Hating that her throat felt thick, she pulled a long, hard swallow. "He used me as I deserved to be used. As one who accepts such an arrangement must expect to be used. As a *putain,* a whore, must expect to be used."

He slid his hands from her shoulders and tightened his arms about her. "You're no man's whore."

She opened her mouth to protest but before she could he took it with his own, his hands delving into the thick tangle of her hair. "Jack?" she said as soon as she could breathe again. "Then you do not mind that I am not a virgin?"

His forehead resting against hers and eyes closed, he hesitated, then answered, "No so long as you dinna mind that I am."

She started to laugh, then stopped herself when she saw the tight press of his lips and the raw vulnerability etched into his every feature. She pulled back to look at him. "You are teasing me? You are not serious?"

But the sudden blush bathing his face and throat told her that he was very serious indeed. In dismay, she felt his hands leave her and saw that he meant to turn away. "Forgive me, *chéri,* I do not mean to embarrass you. It is only that . . . Why did you not tell me before?"

He cocked a brow, regarded her. "Well it's no exactly the thing a man brags about, is it? Forbye I thought you must a'ready suppose I was, for you mentioned often enough how it was that I slept alone."

Hating that she'd hurt him even if it had been unwittingly, she slid a single finger across the moist seam of his beautiful mouth. "You do not kiss like a virgin."

He made no move to return her touch but stood eyeing her warily as a deer might regard a hunter with bow braced. "I said I was a virgin, no a monk. And should you be wondering do I fancy lads o'er lasses, the answer is no."

She smothered a smile. "I had not thought so but thank you."

Now that the shock was wearing off, she was coming to view

the prospect of all that untried masculinity as highly erotic. A deep and almost unbearable anticipation gripped her, making the girlish passion she'd once felt for Phillippe seem tepid and very, very shallow.

Intense amber brown eyes bore down on her. "Will ye have me, lass? In your bed, I mean?"

"Jack, are you . . . are you certain?"

He answered with a swift nod. "Aye, certain I've been a horse's arse, a bloody fool. And if ye'll but give me leave, I'll show ye just how verra sorry I am."

"Oh, Jack." She launched herself at his chest.

His arms closed about her, holding her tight for a long, long moment. Then he slipped an arm about her waist, another beneath her knees, and lifted her. Cradled close against his chest, she could feel the heavy drumming of his heart, the heat of him through the linen of his damp shirt, as he carried her over to the bed.

Gently he laid her on the center of the mattress, then joined her. A palm braced on either side of her, legs straddling her skirts, he said, "Ye'll have to show me what to do, but only the once." His earnest expression dissolved into the lopsided grin she'd come to love. "I'm a fast learner, ye ken."

Overcome by emotion, she stroked her hand down his lean, hard cheek. "Oh, Jack. If either one of us knows about loving, it is you."

Damn, but he should have thought to undress her first, not to mention take off some of his own clothes, at the very least his boots. For himself he might have managed but Claudia's clothing was far too complicated to remove with her lying down. He had the swift vivid image of tossing her cloak and skirts up about her waist but dismissed it just as swiftly. It was their first time together. He wanted it to be perfect, or at least as perfect as he could manage to make it.

With a sigh, he stood them both up again, hesitated, removed her cloak, and then started on her gown. "Too many eyes and hooks," he muttered, struggling with the queue of silk-sewn fastenings fronting her bodice.

His hands, the same hands that could without a tremor arrange a noose about a man's neck, shook like those of a palsied old man. With anticipation, yes, but also with nerves. What he was about to do would betray a lifelong vow, but since meeting Claudia, his conscience had withered to a fragile thing, no match for the robust fierceness of his wanting. His cares, past and future, forged into a single-minded focus: he simply had to be with her.

She seized hold of his hand, her grip surprisingly strong for one so small, and brought it to rest low on her belly. Gaze holding his, she said, "Would you believe, Jack Campbell, that beneath these layers and layers of skirts, I am not wearing so much as a scrap of lace?"

He might be a virgin, but he wasn't such a daft idiot that he couldn't read the sultry invitation in her voice. "Is that so?" he whispered back and pulled her to him for another kiss while he caressed her through her clothes.

With his help she stepped free of her gown, shed her corset, her quilted petticoat, and finally her fine lawn shift. Her breasts were unbelievably beautiful, high and firm and flawless save for a small, cylindrical white scar just above her left nipple. Perhaps someday he'd ask her how she'd come by it but for now his attention, indeed all his focus, was riveted on her legs. Sheathed in silk stockings of sheerest white, they were even prettier than he'd imagined them to be, her ankles and calves trim, the thighs above the lace-trimmed garters pale as moonstone.

She was so lovely, so very fine. So far he'd done little more than kiss her and yet his cock was so stiff it strained the panel of buttons fronting his breeches, his balls heavy and swollen with the force of his need. And the only thing more powerful than his desire was his fear.

He shook his head. "*Mon duinne,* I dinna ken what it is I'm supposed to do, how to please ye."

"I think you do." Taking hold of his wrist, she brought his touch to bear on the plump mound between her thighs.

He hesitated, then began stroking her. Crisp curls teased his palm. Before it had seemed rude to stare at her there but now he did so—openly. "You're the same blue-black as a crow's wing here, too," he remarked with a kind of wonder, thinking that the erotic etchings he'd once seen in a book, detailed though they'd been, couldn't begin to do justice to female beauty—at least not to Claudia's.

Bracing a hand about her waist, he slicked the pad of his thumb down the dewy cleft dividing her mons. She moaned and backed up against the edge of the bed, spreading her legs wider. He entered her with first one finger and then two, sliding back and forth, stretching her wide.

Several times, he stopped to whisper in her ear, "I'm no hurting you, am I?" and each time she only shook her head and reached out to reclaim his hand.

Wet and warm and welcoming, the musk on his fingers made his mouth water and his groin pulse with a steady rhythmic ache. He wouldn't have thought it possible but he felt himself growing even harder, thicker.

"My turn," she said, and reached for him, long slender fingers starting on his shirt buttons. "I have wanted to do this for a long time," she told him, freeing the second to last button. "Ever since that night when I cried out in my sleep and you came to me and I saw you. Do you remember?"

He pulled a hard swallow. "Aye, I remember. You were in your shift and all I could think of was how much I wanted to take it off you."

"I wish you had." She slipped the shirt over his shoulders, pulled the tail from the waist of his breeches, ran her palms and fingers over the dusky flat discs until his nipples stood straight up. "I would not have stopped you, you know."

He did and though part of him regretted that they hadn't made love sooner, in his heart he knew he'd been right to wait, for back then he'd only just begun to love her. Now she was in his heart, she *was* his heart, and even though he was breaking faith with himself by making love with her, nothing in his life had ever felt so right.

"I will not stop you now." She started on the panel of buttons fronting his trews.

Desperate as he was to be free of them, he caught at her hand. "I'm a great beast and ye're delicate as a faerie. I dinna ken how we can come together wi'out my hurtin' ye."

She smiled up at him, warm and welcoming, even as she took him in her hand. "It has been a long time for me but I do not think you will hurt me." With her thumb, she teased the great bulging vein that seemed to thrum in keeping with his very heart.

"I'd rather die than hurt you." And wishing he might take

away all the hurts of the past, he bent his head to her breast and laved the little white scar with his tongue.

She gasped, then arched against him, a hand threading through his hair, drawing him closer. He took her nipple into his mouth and gently tugged even as he reached down to fondle her other breast.

"Lovely, so verra lovely," he murmured and reached around her waist to lift her up and lay her on the emerald counterpane, a striking backdrop for black hair, violet eyes, and white, white skin.

She opened her arms. "Come to me, Jack. Come to me now. I do not care if it hurts; I only want to hold you inside me."

Jack didn't wait to be asked a second time. He kicked off his boots and then peeled off his pants. Coming down on top of her, he braced a knee on either side of her and slid a hand between her already parted thighs.

"Och, lass, but ye're slick as marsh grass."

"It is you who have made me so." Violet eyes, clear of tears now, unshadowed by second thoughts, looked up into his. "I am wet, Jack, only because I want to take you inside me so very much. Because I want *you* so very much."

Her small, sure hand closed about his shaft. She guided him to her, saving him from fumbling. He felt a brief, hesitant pressure as he entered her, her narrow channel balking against his breadth. And then she lifted her hips and ground against him, taking him all the way inside.

For a long moment, the miracle of it held him still as he sought to hold on to the myriad sensations rolling through him. His penis, the tip exquisitely, almost painfully sensitive, the shaft pulsing with life and chafing for movement. The musk-scented heat that rose up between them like steam. Claudia's rapid-fire breaths punctuated with tiny, impatient moans as she wiggled beneath him.

And then without conscious thought, he began to move back and forth, inside and out, slowly at first, but then with increasing confidence. Sweat slicked his brow, his back, and the insides of his thighs. He slid one hand beneath her buttocks and lifted her against him. Before long they were retreating and advancing together in perfectly matched movements, his every thrust seeming to carry them both higher and higher toward the crest of some unseen crag.

"Christ, Claudia, you're hot as a furnace."

"That is good, I think?" She tossed back her head and smiled even as her inner muscles fisted about him.

Oh, it was good all right, almost too good. Biting the inside of his lip to keep from crying out, he answered, "Whatever it is ye're doing, you wee witch, dinna stop."

"I am holding you as tightly as my body will allow and I promise I will not stop, not even if you beg me to." She slid her hands about his hips, pressed her palms to his buttocks, urging him closer, *deeper.* "Look at me, *chéri.* I want to see your eyes when you come."

At some point he'd squeezed his eyes shut though he hadn't realized it until now. Opening them now, he gazed down. Christ, but she looked just as he'd imagined her so many times only perhaps even more intensely, more blindingly beautiful. Raven hair splayed across the white pillow, eyes wide as saucers and almost black with desire, mouth pink and swollen from his kisses, she was the embodiment of his every fantasy, his every dream. And, for the present if not the future, she belonged only to him.

Emotion welled inside him. Desire, to be sure, but something else, something less fragile and far finer than the physical pleasure he was taking in the joining of their bodies. He'd never been much with words, but this pleasure, this unbearable closeness demanded to be voiced.

"Claudia," he said, pulling himself up on his arms to look down at her. "Is it supposed to be like this? I never thought it could be like this."

She regarded him with wide, feral eyes, kissed his jaw, his throat. "*Mon Dieu,* neither did I."

Bowing to primal instinct, he reached down between them, rubbing his thumb over the hard little nubbin just above where they were joined. Claudia's breath caught on a rasp; she arched, pitching her slender hips in silent demand. And because he could deny her nothing, because he ached to be inside her for not only now but always, he pulled all the way out and then drove into her, sheathing himself in one shuddering thrust.

"Oh, *Jésus,* oh, Jack!"

Her keening cry, her inner muscles convulsing about his shaft very nearly proved to be his undoing. But as much as he hated to leave her, he knew that he must, for there was one part of his vow he still refused to break: he would not beget a bastard.

And so he withdrew and rolled onto his side, spending his seed on the mattress where it could do no harm. "Sweet Jesus," he moaned when at last he found his voice. Looking down, he saw that he was gripping the edge of the bed so hard that his knuckles had gone white.

Claudia's small hand touched his shoulder. "Jack, *ça va?* Are you all right?"

"I'm still alive, if that's what ye're askin'. Beyond that . . ." He rolled onto his back and gathered her against him. "Christ, Claudia, that was—"

"Perfection," she finished for him and settled her head on his damp shoulder. "Now I see why in France we call it *le petit mort,* the little death."

Breathing didn't come easily but somehow he found the energy to smile. "If this is dyin' than sure it is I'm the merriest corpse that ever was."

Now that his heart had ceased beating like a drum, a delicious languor had begun to roll over him. "Thank you." He pressed a kiss onto the top of her head and closed his eyes, content to listen to the sound of their commingled breaths and the spit and hiss of the fire devouring the peat bricks within the grate.

But even in the presence of all that peace, his mind refused to shut down completely. "Claudia?"

"Hmm?"

Wondering how to ask, he stroked her slender back, his thumb mentally counting down each fragile vertebra from occiput to tailbone. "What you said just now . . . Did ye ne'er take any pleasure in the act before with . . . him?"

Even now, he couldn't bring himself to speak her former lover's name. The bastard might be dead, a headless corpse moldering in an unmarked grave, yet Jack had never been so jealous of anyone in all his life.

She pushed up on one elbow, dark hair streaming over one milk white shoulder. Looking into his eyes, she gave a resolute shake of her head. "*Jamais.* Never."

He released the breath he'd been holding and admitted, "If I were a better man, I'd say I was sorry and mean it. But I'm not and so I must tell you that I'm no sorry."

She sighed. "Perhaps I should be but I am not, either. In all the years I was with him, not once did I find my release in his touch. He was impatient; he did not take his time with me. He hurt me sometimes, many times. In my heart I hated him for his cruelty but mostly I hated him for not giving me the pleasure that other women I knew found with their lovers. But now I think that perhaps it was not all his fault, that my body must have been holding back, saving itself for . . . for you."

He exhaled heavily, his heart suddenly feeling too big, too swollen, for the tight casing of his chest. "You dinna feel I've soiled you, then?"

"Oh, Jack, oh, *chéri.*"

Tears spilled down her face; at a loss, he reached up and caught a fat droplet on the edge of his thumb. "Claudia, sweeting, what is it? What's wrong?"

She shook her head at him, dashed a hand over her wet cheek. "*Mon chéri,* do you not see? You have not soiled me. You have washed me clean."

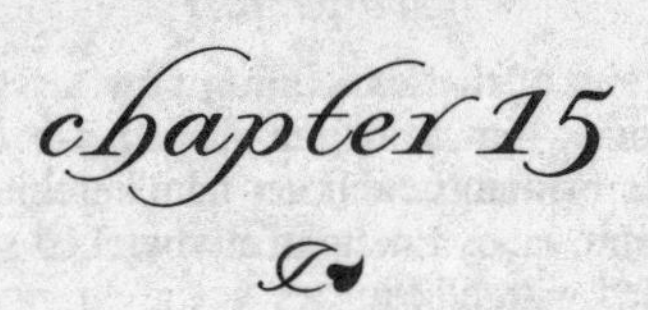

Gie me ae spark o' Nature's fire,
That's a' the learning I desire.

—Robert Burns, "Epistle to John Lapraik" No. 1

The next morning, Jack sent Luicas home with the cart and mare. He wanted time alone with Claudia, of course, but beyond that he was loath to involve the lad in what amounted to abetting a prisoner to escape. Not that he and Claudia struck out for Linlithgow that day, or the day after, or the even the day after that. The excuses to linger came fast and furious, much like the snow that fell obligingly outside their chamber window. And then, lo and behold, the following day was Christmas. Since Claudia had come to Scotland, one day had slipped into the next until she'd lost count altogether and had forgotten all about the winter holidays. Not so Jack.

"There's one more yet," he told her and, reaching beneath the covers on his side of the bed, withdrew a small, elaborately wrapped box. "Open it," he urged, pressing it into her hand, as impatient as any child on Christmas morn.

Though it was nigh on ten o' clock in the morning, they were in bed still, where they'd spent the better part of the three previous days and nights, propped up against the banked pillows and, thanks to the warmth of a roaring fire, naked beneath the covers.

Claudia accepted the box, one of several he'd already bestowed on her, and holding it up to her ear gently shook it. "When did you do all this?"

"The other afternoon when you were napping, I went out for a wee ramble."

Jack's "wee ramble" had led him to the shops on Princes

Street. The fruits of that expedition now lay spread about the mussed bedcovers—a set of fan-shaped hair combs sparkling with amethyst brilliants, a linen handkerchief trimmed with silver-gilt bobbin lace, a delightfully wicked set of scarlet silk garters threaded with black.

Letting the anticipation build, she slowly untied the silver bow and lifted the lid. Inside was a small swan of cobalt-colored glass, a lovely trifle. Upon closer inspection, though, she saw that the swan was hollow and was in fact a vial for holding scent, a light rose fragrance to replace the bottle she'd brought with her from France, now all but gone dry.

"Oh, Jack, *chéri,* you think of everything." Delighted, she lifted the stopper and passed the bottle beneath her nose.

"Not that you need it," he told her, reaching across to take it from her when she would have dabbed some of its contents at the base of her throat. He set it on the bedside table on his left then shifted to her. "You a'ready taste like flowers."

If Claudia thought to ask him what flowers tasted like, the pert question flew from her head the second he threaded his arms beneath hers and pulled her back against him. Leaning forward, he kissed the side of her neck, his tongue laving the little pulse point below her ear.

"And your skin's like silk. Warm silk," he whispered, his own warm breath grazing the wetness as he reached around her to take her breasts in hand.

"But, *chéri,* I feel so guilty," she said even as she leaned back to savor the sensations of him nuzzling her neck, of his callused palms weighing her breasts. "I have not so much as one *cadeau,* gift, for you."

"Not one, aye?" Chuckling, he grazed his thumbs over her nipples, still pebble hard and puckered from his recent kisses that morning. "But I count two at the verra least."

Closing her eyes, Claudia smiled to herself. Her Jack hadn't lied about being a fast learner. Though he'd lost his virginity but four days before, already he was engaging in love play with the finesse of an accomplished seducer.

He eased her from his shoulder and laid her down on the mattress, the sheet riding low on her waist. A decent woman would have pulled it back up, but Claudia had learned the futility of trying to be someone and something she was not. And so when he slid his big body down the front of her, not stopping until the crown of his red-gold head was level with the vee between her thighs, her first thought, her *only* thought, was to kick the remaining covers aside and spread her legs even wider.

"Tell me, *mo chride,*" he said, parting her woman's flesh fold by fold with exquisite care. "What does this feel like?"

Claudia had considered herself to be the inquisitive one but over the past days Jack seemed to have developed an insatiable desire to know everything about her, right down to the nature of the sensations he could create by running his thumb down the slick, blood-warmed cleft between her thighs.

Only too happy to satisfy his curiosity as well as the rest of him, she didn't hesitate to answer, "Like champagne bubbles tickling one's nose, only on the inside and . . . and much nicer."

"Champagne bubbles, aye?" Lifting each of her feet to rest on his shoulders, the doubtful look he sent her suggested he didn't find the comparison at all complimentary. "Do you like it?" he asked, lowering his head once more.

Champagne or the rather amazing thing he was doing to her with the point of his tongue? "Yes. Yes, I like it very much," she said, aware that perspiration had begun to film the backs of her knees and that a heavy liquid warmth had settled inside her thighs.

Slipping one finger inside her, then two, he asked, "And when I kiss you here, and lick you, and suckle that wee rosebud of yours 'til you cry out, is it champagne bubbles then?"

Fingers deep inside her, he drew her clitoris between his lips and gently nipped. Claudia nearly came off the bed, gasping as pleasure that skirted pain streaked through her like a bolt of lightning from the top of her spine to the tips of her suddenly curling toes.

Recovering, she managed to shift her damp head side to side on the pillow. "*Non,* more like fireworks, *nice* fireworks, exploding inside me."

He lifted his head and beamed up at her as if fireworks met with his approval. "That explains it, then."

"*Comment* . . . what . . . what does it explain, *chéri?*"

"How it is you can be both so scalding and so slippery wet."

This time she lifted her head from the pillow to scowl down at him. "*Monsieur,* if you liken me to marsh grass one more time I am going to get up from this bed." It was an idle threat, of course. Short of an explosion—a real one—she wasn't going anywhere.

"Wheesht, if you maun know, I was minded of the morning dew on a rose petal." He contrived to look wounded though his clever fingers continued to strum her heated flesh like a musician playing his instrument.

A sharp rap outside their door had Claudia collapsing back against the pillows, a groan of pure frustration breaking forth from her lips. "Must we answer it? Can we not pretend to be sleeping still?"

But Jack was already springing from the bed. He paused to wrap a blanket about his hips before bounding to the door. Looking back at her over his shoulder, he grinned. "I'd a'most forgot, I've one last wee giftie for you."

Sitting upright, Claudia reached for her shift, balled up beneath her pillow. Shoving the wrinkled garment over her head, she said, "Jack, no more gifts. You will beggar yourself."

But Jack's last wee giftie, perhaps the most precious of all, proved to be a very full, very hot bath. Claudia had barely reached for her cloak to cover herself when the chambermaid, Lettie, entered with another maid. Between the two of them, they rolled in an enormous hipbath set on casters.

Too ecstatic even to be angry at the way the girls' gazes slipped over Jack's naked chest and lower to where his erection caused the blanket to tent, Claudia hurried over. Bending to trail a hand in the deliciously warm water, she registered the chamber door clicking closed.

Once more alone with Jack, she straightened to tug off her cape. Tossing it into a nearby chair, she whirled to face him. "You did all this, for me?" she asked even as she stared down at the whirls of steam rising from the copper rim.

A shy nod served as his only answer. "You're pleased then?"

"Pleased? *Pleased!"* Oh, Jack," she cried, launching herself into his arms so that he lost hold of the blanket, which fell to the floor. "You are so good to me." Rising up on her toes, she sprinkled kisses over his stubbled jaw, his flushed throat, his clavicle.

Threading his fingers through her tangled hair, he smiled down at her. "Ah well, lass, maybe I canna give you fine things and servants to wait upon you, but a hot bath I can manage."

He was so big and warm-hearted, so generous and kind,

Claudia felt her heart overflowing with love even as her eyes threatened to overflow with bittersweet tears. "Oh, Jack," she said, catching his hand and pressing a kiss into the callused palm. "You give me so much, *chéri,* everything I need, all I could possibly want and more."

He rolled his broad shoulders, but he was pleased, she could tell. "In that case dinna stand there, woman, but get in whilst it's hot. I'll wash your back for you."

"Yes, you will," she said, already tugging the shift over her head and then off. "And then, *cher* Jack, I will wash yours."

Sometime later, Claudia leaned back against Jack, the warm water sluicing their freshly scrubbed flesh. The tub was narrow and not terribly deep but at her insistence he'd joined her. Now he leaned against the hooded back, long legs bent at the knees and Claudia tucked between them.

Resting her head back against his chest, she released a sigh of pure contentment, for what once she'd taken for granted now seemed the most decadent of luxuries. "In Paris, I used to bathe in milk twice a week."

He lifted a hand from the water, amusing himself by trailing a little stream from her breast to her belly. "Seems a daft thing to do."

"It is supposed to keep the skin soft and supple," she said, her breath catching when, beneath the water, he slid his hand along the inside of her thigh.

"In your case, it must have worked." Chin resting atop her head, he asked, "D'ye ever miss your old life, in Paris, I mean?"

Claudia ran a finger down his forearm draped along the tub's curved edge as she considered the question. A month before, the mention of Paris would have stirred a sharp pang of homesickness as well as a hornet's nest of fierce emotions at having been forced to flee. Now, however, she found she felt only a vague sadness.

"Parts of it. The city is beautiful always but it is at night that she comes alive. But I do not miss it as I did before." Pleased that the horrors of her last months in the city, those last weeks especially, need no longer blacken her memories of happier days, she almost added, *Before I met you,* but stopped before she did.

"Mayhap you'll go back someday?"

She thought of the tumbrels bearing their shackled victims to the Place de la Révolution, the pitiless mob hurling obscenities and rotted fruit, the street dogs lapping the blood pooling in the square and despite the warm water and the heat of Jack's big body engulfing hers, she shivered. "I do not think so."

He lifted his head, angling it to look down at her. "I'm sorry for what happened to your maither." He hesitated, and against her back Claudia could feel the vibration of his heart picking up pace. "My maither, she was killed, too."

She hesitated, then admitted, "I know."

"You do?"

She nodded. "Milread told me. She said that she was murdered by a highwayman and that . . . that you and your brother were there."

"Aye," he said around a sigh and settled back once more, sending a current of water shifting about them. "But I dinna remember much, anything really. 'Tis like a great black hole in my brain, a cloud covering o'er the sun. Only bits and pieces from just before and . . . and after. How hot the sun felt burning through the back of my shirt. The hair ribbon Mam wore—'twas the same bonny blue as the sky that day. The fly that kept landing on the bridge of my nose nay matter how many times I swatted it away. And then afterwards the smell of the blood, so strong I could taste it on my tongue. And Callum beside me, arms wrapped about himself, howling like a banshee." He drew a deep, ragged breath. Pressing a kiss onto her shoulder, he teased, "But tell me, Mistress Curiosity, how it is that you kept from making mention of it all these many months?"

Glad he wasn't angry with her, she replied, "I was waiting for you to tell me in your own time. I can be patient when I must."

"Can you now?" He swept her freshly washed hair over her shoulder and leaned forward to brush his mouth along the nape of her neck. "Well, I for one am *growing* verra impatient . . . impatient to finish what that wee knock on the door interrupted."

Indeed, beneath the water Claudia could feel his arousal abutting her backside as well as her body's answering call. The cooling bathwater suddenly seemed boiling, the throbbing inside her thighs pounding apace with Jack's heart.

Even so, she'd never have a better opportunity to ask him the question that had been lurking on the edges of her mind for the past three days and nights. "Jack?"

"Hmm?" he said, curving a hand to the side of her breast.

"Why is it you never took a lover before me?"

His hand stilled and his whole body beneath hers went tense. She was about to withdraw the question when he answered, "I told you, like you I never kent my father."

She ran a hand down his forearm, the wet hairs forming a brownish-red queue along his pale flesh. "It is hard, I know, to grow up without a father, without a name. Though perhaps easier in Paris than here?"

In Paris, bastards had been as plentiful as boats on the Seine or tulips in the gardens of the Tuileries. The few playmates she'd had growing up, all children of her mothers' friends, hadn't had fathers either so that the circumstances of her birth had never been a subject to remark upon. But Scotland was a very different world. The clan system may have died on Culloden Moor, but for most Scots, "broken" men and women though they were, familial bonds remained strong.

Beneath her, Jack shifted position, sending water lapping the tub's sides. "It got easier as I grew older. I was twice the size of most lads my age and after splitting a few lips and denting a skull or two, they learnt to keep their less flattering remarks about my maither to themselves. But I kent what it was to be a bastard, and swore to myself and maybe God, too, that I'd no inflict such a state on an innocent bairn."

A wiser woman would have left it at that but Claudia being Claudia she had to ask, "And yet you never married?"

"Ah, well, there's no all that many fathers eager to wed their daughters to a bastard and one who's the hangman at that." She started to protest that he was a fine man, handsome and strong, clever and kind, when he interrupted to admit, "And maybe, too, I was no all that eager to risk my heart only to have it broken."

They were silent for a while, the imminent journey to Linlithgow weighing heavy on their thoughts, the wash water growing tepid about them.

At length, Jack said, "I wish ye might stay to see the springtime."

I wish I might stay forever, Claudia thought, glad he couldn't see her face. Her brief time with Jack had shaped her into a better, finer person; their lovemaking these past days had exceeded every fantasy she'd ever entertained. He never rushed, never hurt her as Phillippe had, but always took his time. Exploring the juncture of her neck and shoulder, the texture of an inner thigh, the folds of her woman's flesh were journeys in themselves, not means to an end. He liked to call her his "wee witch" and said he felt the most fortunate of men to be in her thrall; but she was sure if she stayed on, it was inevitable he would tire of her. Jack might not have a dishonorable bone in his big beautiful body, but then he'd only just begun to explore his physical side. She'd yet to meet the man who could be satisfied with one woman indefinitely. Phillippe's dalliances had drawn little feeling from her beyond a vague anxiety for the security of her future. But loving Jack as she'd come to, she'd be hard-pressed not to scratch out her rival's eyes. Far better to leave with an intact storehouse of beautiful, unblemished memories than to stay and court the risk of them becoming tainted with regrets.

Sounding as if his mind had traveled far, far away, he said, "Every spring I take Elf and head north to Loch Rannoch—'tis in the Highlands, in Perthshire. From the distance, the crags look to be fair near the same deep blue as the water and sky, and the woods are so thick with pine that the scent clings to your clothes long after you come away. Ah, lass," he said, his voice dropped to a bare, rough whisper against the shell of her ear, "I dinna have the words to describe the beauty of it but trust me 'tis a bonny place, a place like nowhere else on earth."

Like nowhere else on earth. The more cynical Claudia of a few months past would have pointed out that, as he'd likely never been outside of Scotland, he was hardly in a position to make that claim. But her short time with Jack had changed her and there would be no turning back even if she'd wished to. He'd worn down the sharper edges of her nature, not with force but with patience and kindness, gentleness, and caring. Because of him, she would go to Linlithgow and to her father a kinder and better person.

But now she wanted not to go to Linlithgow and her father but to the Highlands with Jack, to his special place. And if she couldn't do so physically, at the very least she could accompany him there in her mind.

And so, twisting about to look into his face, she stroked a hand down his lean, hard cheek and said, "Tell me, *chéri,* what is it about the Highlands, this place, that you like best? If you could show me only one thing, what would it be?"

He answered with a fierce shake of his head that sent water flying from the ends of his loosened hair. "You'll think me daft."

"Tell me. Tell me, please. I want to know." She smiled encouragement and tucked an errant lock behind his ear, the tip of which was wreathed in bright red. *Cher* Jack, only he could manage to make blushing seem not only manly but also erotic, for now that she knew just how far down his blushes extended, she couldn't seem to stop herself from saying and doing things calculated to coax the lovely color to come.

"Verra well." He picked up a lock of wet hair from her shoulder and, studying it intently, said, "The wildflowers."

"Heather, you mean?" Could it be that of all the legendary scenery the Scottish Highlands boasted, he wanted her to stay to witness the blooming of what was at best a wildflower, at worst a weed?

He shook his head. " 'Tis no in spring but in late summer and early fall that the heather blooms. But in springtime there's bell heather, which is more reddish than purple and fair near the same color as . . . as the woman's flesh inside your thighs. And there's twinflower, the funnel-shaped petals as delicate and pinkish white as your skin, and an orchid called creeping lady's-tresses—'tis a'most the color of your eyes, lass. Och, but just the thought of it all clears my mind."

Throat so thick, so knotted with emotion that she could barely swallow let alone get the words out, she asked, "You would take me there, to your special place?"

"Aye, I would." The brand of a blush was still upon his cheeks, but the eyes he lifted to hers were golden and clear. "I'd strip you bare and then I'd lay you down on the grass so that your fine black hair was spread out like a fan. And then I'd take the flowers we'd gathered and one by one I'd wreathe them about your hair and lay them upon your breasts, your belly, and the black curls between your thighs. And then I'd come into you. And when we cried out our pleasure we'd do so full and free, for there'd be no innkeeper, no chambermaid, to hear us, only the water and sky and the fields and crags and the great God above."

"Oh, Jack, I wish . . ." She stopped because she didn't know what more to say, didn't dare go on, so she took his face between her hands and brought her mouth down on his for a swift, hard kiss. Drawing back, she whispered, "Make love to me, Jack." *Make me forget I must leave you.* "Let us pretend that it is spring and not winter and that the green counterpane on our bed is the green of the field and that the little vial you bought me holds not the scent of roses but of wildflowers."

He nodded, eyes solemn, and then reached out a hand to steady her when she stood to step over the bath's edge. Water pooled onto the knotted hearth rug at her feet but Claudia scarcely noticed for all her attention was fixed on Jack.

Like Poseidon rising from the sea's crashing waves, he climbed from the tub to stand beside her, his swollen sex standing proudly out from the crown of dark auburn curls at his muscular thighs. Without a word, they came into each other's arms. Hands about her waist, he lifted her high against him and then brought her to slide slowly down the length of him much like the droplets of water sliding down their bodies. Hands joined, they hurried toward the bed, where they came together in a tangle of wet limbs and sodden sheets and low, eager moans. Claudia could hardly wait to take him inside her again, to show him with her lips and tongue, with her fingers and hands, what she was too much of a coward to convey with words. And this time when her satisfaction came, it came from deep within her, the muscles clenching and releasing with such force that she forgot dignity, forgot pride, and threw back her head and cried out, *"Je t'aime,"* again and again until her throat was scraped raw and her voice hoarse.

Much later, as they dressed to go below for the midday meal, she could only be grateful that Jack didn't ask after the words' meaning . . . for they were the French for "I love you."

With nowhere to go and no tasks to claim them, they spent most of the rest of Christmas day and then night in bed. Between lovemaking, they held each other close and talked of both everything and nothing at all. Pleasantly exhausted, more sated than she'd ever thought to be, Claudia lay with her back to Jack's chest and her buttocks to his thighs. His arm draped across her waist, she couldn't be sure where she ended or he began nor was she entirely sure that if she rose her legs wouldn't fold beneath her. Not that she cared to stir. For the first time in her life, she was exactly where she wanted to be.

Thinking him to be asleep, more than halfway to somnolence herself, she started when without warning he spoke out from the darkness, "Claudia?"

"Hmm?"

"Earlier, d'ye mind how you were sorry you hadna a gift for me?"

"Yes."

"There is one I would claim of you now. Not a gift so much as your word on something." He smoothed his palm over the flat plane of her belly. "If by chance we did make a bairn together, I want your promise that you'll send for me so I can care for you, the both of you."

Claudia felt as though the air had just been squeezed from her lungs, and the sensation had nothing to do with the fact that her body was folded into Jack's. Neophyte to sexual congress though he was, he'd shown remarkable restraint, withdrawing each time they'd joined to release his seed outside of her. Not that there was need for such caution. In the seven years she'd been with Phillippe never once had she missed her courses.

"I'm barren," she confessed, biting her bottom lip, surprised that what had always proven to be such a convenient condition now could hurt so very much.

She hadn't wanted Phillippe's children but that wasn't the same as not wanting children at all. There had been times before the Terror when she had chanced upon families picnicking on the lawn of the Tuileries, children tossing bits of bread to the ducks or floating toy ships on the miniature lake, and the yearning, the *emptiness,* would rise up to strike at her from nowhere.

But Jack was not so easily put off. "All the same, I'll have your word on it before I close my eyes. Promise me, Claudia. Promise me that if you find yourself in trouble, you'll send for me." In a milder tone, he added, " 'Tis the only boon I'll ever ask of you and no such an unreasonable request, mind?"

Grateful to be facing away from him so he couldn't see the tears slipping from the corners of her eyes, she swallowed hard and then said, "*Oui,* I would send for you."

For the first time since they'd lain together, she'd told him a lie.

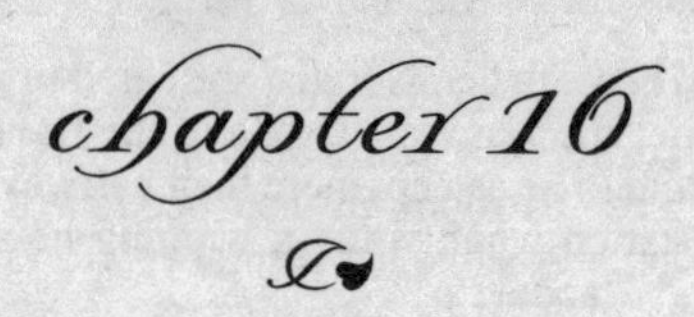

Had we never loved sae kindly,
Had we never loved sae blindly,
Never met or never parted,
We had ne'er been broken-hearted!

—Robert Burns, *Ae Fond Kiss*

Eventually their idyll had to end. They couldn't remain holed up in their room at the inn forever, delectable fantasy though that surely was. Even Mistress Tweedie began to wonder aloud if didn't they have a home of their own to go to. The day after Christmas, Boxing Day, the sun emerged from hiding, setting the snow to fast and furious melting. By the second day, the air was almost balmy and by the third the roads sufficiently clear to permit safe travel. They set out on horseback after breakfast, a light meal of tea and toast that neither could find the appetite to eat, Jack on Beelzebub and Claudia on a gentle gelding they'd hired from a lending stable to serve in the stead of the mare.

Linlithgow lay fifteen or so miles west of Edinburgh, the town's center clustered around a marketplace known as the Cross. As they left behind the narrow streets and stone-arched bridges to skirt the loch, they fell silent, each falling victim to the press of their own private thoughts.

Perhaps he will stay awhile. . . . Perhaps he will return to visit me sometime, Claudia thought even as she allowed the unlikelihood of either occurrence. She and Jack were creatures from two very different worlds. He wouldn't feel any more at ease in a noble household than she first had felt in his tiny village, and he had too much pride to try.

Jack's thoughts ran a similar course. *How can I bear to leave her?* warring with *How can I do otherwise?* Within the four walls of their rented room, in their bed, she'd made him feel like a king, but returned to her natural environment, she'd once again see him for what he was: a coarse lummox, a hangman, an embarrassment. No, leave her he must, for he'd too much pride to stay and ape the gentleman. To do so would only heap more misery upon them both and taint the past week with shame and regret. The latter prospect was beyond even his bearing, the threat alone strengthening his resolve to leave once he'd satisfied himself that Claudia would be well cared for. As soon as he had, he would be on the road headed back to Selkirk, perhaps as soon as that night.

Castle Aberdaire lay on the southern shore of Linlithgow Loch, a fine stretch of shimmering lake gilded by the unseasonably brilliant afternoon sun. When Claudia and Jack reached the main entrance arch, the Aberdaire coat of arms emblazoned on a shield at the pinnacle of the wrought-iron gate, her courage deserted her.

She reined in her mount. "A moment, *s'il vous plait.*"

Jack drew up next to her. "What is it, lass?"

I am a coward, she might have answered, but instead only shook her head. "I feel that once we pass through these gates, nothing will be the same—that *I* will not be the same. Ah, but you must think me foolish."

He reached across to clasp her hand in his. "I dinna think you're foolish. A wee bit scairt maybe and with good reason but no foolish."

Through her kidskin glove, she could feel his warmth, his energy, pooling into her. She held on tight, threaded her fingers through his, and wished she might never have cause to let go.

Regarding their interleaved hands, she said, "I have prepared myself for this for months now. No, for my whole life, I think. When I came of age to leave the nursery, Maman insisted I have a British governess. Almost as if she had seen into the future and knew that someday I must come to Scotland and the home of my father." She tried for a smile, but it quavered on her lips. "And now that I have, I am afraid to take these last few steps."

He squeezed her hand. "Bear up, lass. 'Tis like visiting the toothpuller—best to get it over with quick, aye?" He flashed her a smile that belied his claim of ever having required the services of the toothpuller, just as his sad eyes belied his brisk, cheerful tone. "Come along with you, otherwise I'll be taking tea with His Lordship all by my lonesome." He released her hand and urged his horse into a canter, leaving Claudia no choice but to follow him through.

The crushed shale drive seemed to stretch on forever, winding as it did through fallow fields, a game park, and then a series of terraced lawns. Ahead, the castle's rounded turrets and battlements came into view above the tops of the leafless trees, the stones a gunmetal gray that seemed to Claudia to repel the sun's golden glow.

I am home, she told herself again and again, though she'd never felt less at home in her life.

As they drew nearer, assorted structures dotted the snow-patched lawns, fanciful follies built to resemble Greek temples and Chinese pagodas and grottoes whose fountains of frozen water had just begun to thaw.

Their journey ended in a circular, brick-lined drive. Jack dismounted, and then came around to help Claudia down. Two grooms dressed in matching livery materialized from the direction of the stables they'd passed to take their horses. Jack hesitated. Hand fisted on the reins, he eyed the approaching groom as if they were cattle reevers instead of servants in the sage-and-gold livery of an earl.

Reminded that he wasn't accustomed as she was to having servants wait on him, Claudia laid a light hand on his arm. "It is all right. They will take them to the stables and care for them."

"Mind you water and walk them *before* you feed them," he said to the younger of the two, then surrendered Beelzebub with a grudging air and followed Claudia across the courtyard.

Elf had been keeping pace beside them but as they came up on the curved stone balustrade, a carved lion guarding either side, she let out a low growl.

"Come on with you, lass," Jack coaxed, tugging on her collar. "They're naught but stone."

Still looking far from happy about it, the dog followed them up the stone steps to where, like the lions, two footmen in livery and elaborately curled wigs were stationed sentinel fashion on either side of the massive double doors.

"We're here to see His Lordship," Jack informed them and though they exchanged glances, no doubt taking in his simple coat and ungloved hands, they stepped back to allow them admittance.

The butler who met them inside the great hall was a man of middling years and undeniable Scottish ancestry, though his impeccable black attire seemed out of keeping with his stocky pugilist's build. "You are expected?" he asked, though the colorless eyes that raked over Claudia and then Jack clearly conveyed that he knew they were not.

Claudia shook her head. "*Non,* but—"

"You've a card, then, madam?" He held out a white-gloved and very square palm.

Claudia shook her head, throat scraped so dry that she could barely get the words out to answer, "*Non,* but I have this." Hands shaking, she reached inside her cloak for the brooch that had not left her possession since she'd departed France. Slowly, carefully she freed it from its handkerchief wrapper and dropped it into his open hand.

The butler looked down at the object resting in his hand and then back at her. Plainly unimpressed, he passed it back to her. "I dinna ken how it is you've come by the Aberdaire clan brooch but a card, madam, would be a considerably more helpful means of stating your name and purpose."

Drawing strength from the knowledge that Jack stood at her back, she hoisted her chin, squared her shoulders, and said, "You may tell His Lordship that Mademoiselle Claudia Antoinette Valemont awaits his pleasure. And that she will not leave until she has seen her father."

S*trong emotion, Claudia suspected it must be shock,* brought ruddy color rushing the butler's cheeks, the opaque eyes looking black as obsidian, the irises eclipsed by startled pupils.

Recovering his aplomb, he nodded. "Verra well. His Lordship is in the east wing. I will conduct you there." He started to turn away when Elf sounded a low snarl. Slowly, very slowly, he turned about to glare beyond Claudia's shoulder. "The beast remains here," he said and, given the direction of his gaze, Claudia couldn't be sure whether he meant the wolfhound or Jack.

Jack stepped forward, speaking for the first time since they'd gained the hall. "The dog accompanies the lady, as do I."

The butler hesitated, then inclined his head. "For now," he said, then turned away to strike out beneath the vaulted archway.

He set a brisk pace. Matching it meant that Claudia registered only a fleeting impression of what must once have been a medieval great hall, its stone walls hung with ancient tapestries and the severed heads of a variety of game animals. The latter's glassy-eyed gazes seemed to follow them up the circular stone stairs, the walls of which were so close that, mounting them, Claudia was reminded of the tollbooth in Selkirk. She shivered and looked back over her shoulder to Jack. His beautiful mouth was set in a grim line and his eyes looked as sad as she felt, but when he caught her gaze, he smiled and sent her a reassuring wink. She smiled back as if her heart weren't breaking and quickly turned around before he could see that it was. He was being so brave, so noble, the very least she could do was to behave in kind, though a traitorous part of her cried out that she didn't want him to be brave or noble at all.

They were coming into the newer part of the castle. Iron-studded doors, rounded arches, and flagged stones gave way to classical columns, ornate plasterwork, and Italian marble. In the gallery, ancestral portraits of seven generations of black-haired, lean-faced Aberdaire earls and their countesses filled the niches between the Corinthian columns.

My ancestors, Claudia thought with a sort of strangled awe, and an odd little shiver trailed her spine for none of them could be said to look happy.

All the while she was aware of Jack at her back. He didn't touch her, of course, nor speak so much as a word, but she felt his steady regard like a reassuring hand pressed to the small of her back, urging her on, refusing to let her falter.

Je t'aime. I love you, Jack, her mind screamed, and she mentally scourged herself for not finding the courage to tell him before they left Edinburgh. Now she might never have the chance to do so, might never even see him again after this day.

The butler's abrupt halt before a paneled mahogany doorway cut off Claudia's ruminating. He knocked once and, after receiving permission to enter from the sharp male voice within, opened it. The drawing room they stepped inside was lavishly appointed and furnished in the French fashion. Gilded pier glasses flanked the far wall, and a massive crystal chandelier crowned an elaborate plasterwork ceiling of vulturelike birds intertwined with scrollwork *A*'s.

But it was to the black-haired figure in the gilded bath chair that Claudia's gaze was drawn.

"Miss Claudia Valemont, milord." The butler stepped to the side of the door.

Long, delicate hands worked the chair wheels on either side, bringing the earl toward her. *My hands,* Claudia thought, and felt the chill of his silver-blue eyes on her like a bucket of snow dumped down her back.

"What the devil . . . Is this some manner of jest?"

The name, *her* name, obviously meant something to him. Praying that her shaking legs would sustain her, she swept a low curtsy.

Rising to look the earl straight in the eye, she answered, "It is no jest, my lord. I am Claudia Valemont, lately come from Paris, France, and I have reason to believe that you are . . . that you are my father."

"Impertinent chit," he said, dismissing her claim with a wave of his slender, blue-veined hand. Peering beyond her to the hallway where Jack stood in the open doorway, he demanded, "And who the devil is that . . . *person?* No my son, I trust," he added, sarcasm plainly evident.

Ashamed she hadn't thought to introduce Jack on her own ere now, Claudia could barely bring herself to meet his gaze as she said, "Allow me to present Monsieur Jack Campbell of Selkirk, my lord."

Jack started forward, stopping a pace or so inside the door. "Milord," he said and though he didn't bow, he inclined his head with statesmanlike grace.

Claudia's heart turned over; never had she been more proud to be with him than she was at this moment. How foolish she'd been to think for a moment that he would be out of place here. Jack's quiet dignity, his effortless bearing, allowed him to more than hold his own in any company be it in a cottage or a castle.

Aberdaire, it seemed, was less impressed. He spared Jack no more than a fleeting glance before calling to his butler. "MacDuff, some wine, I think, for our *guest.*"

Earl and servant exchanged a knowing glance. "Verra good, milord," the butler replied. He went over to the rosewood wine table and, his back turned to them, poured ruby liquid from the chinked crystal decanter. Turning around, a single glass in hand, he crossed the carpet to Claudia.

Stunned that the earl had not offered Jack refreshment as well, Claudia meant to refuse the glass held out to her. But the manners of a lifetime were not to be broken in a day and so she reached out to take it.

As if reading her mind, Lord Aberdaire drawled, "Alas, MacDuff, I fear we are remiss. Master Campbell must be thirsty as well." Gaze narrowing, he said, "Pray have one of the servants see him and his hound to the kitchen for a pint and a meal and then find him a bed above the stables."

"Aye, milord, I will," the butler replied, his voice overriding Claudia's gasp. He scraped a low bow and then started backing his way toward the door, beckoning Jack to follow.

Outraged, Claudia stepped forward. "My lord, there is some mistake. Monsieur Campbell is not my servant."

The earl's gaze flickered over her, settling on her face. "Have no fear. Should your claim prove valid, whatever he is to you, he will be suitably rewarded for his pains in bringing you to me."

Throughout Jack had remained the picture of composure, his hands folded behind his back, the right one clasped about the wrist of the left, and broad back held straight as a lance. But by now Claudia knew him far too well to miss the muscle ticking in the side of his jaw as he said, "I want for no reward save that of knowing milady has her rightful place."

"Prettily said, Master Campbell, but you may leave us just the same. I find myself wanting time alone with my . . . with Miss Valemont."

Claudia opened her mouth to protest on his behalf once more, but Jack's warning look had her holding her peace. "I thank you for your hospitality, milord." Turning back to Claudia, for the first time since entering the drawing room, he bowed. "Milady, I will take my leave of you . . . for now." He let his gaze linger on her for a long moment before turning to follow the butler out into the hallway.

Listening to his footfalls sounding down the corridor, Elf's nails clicking on the tiles as she followed her master out, Claudia's heart answered with a resounding wrench, and it was all she could do to keep herself from turning about and running after him.

The earl's voice called her back. "What proof can you bring to substantiate your claim?"

Dragging her gaze away from the doorway, Claudia remembered the brooch. "This, my lord." She hesitated then passed the pin to him, careful to keep her fingers from brushing his hand. "My mother gave it to me, along with your letters to her, before the gendarmes came for her. She said to keep it with me always. That it belonged to my father. That it belonged to *you.*"

Holding the brooch between his thumb and forefinger, he was silent for a while. At length he said, "Anyone, a servant, could have taken this and the letters, too. Judging from the newspaper accounts, it sounds as if it's bloody chaos over there."

She bowed her head, remembering. "It is, milord."

"And yet you escaped. How did you manage it?"

"I changed clothes with my maid, milord, in order to slip from the house and make my way to Calais. There I met the fishing boat that would take me to Dover. My jewels, which I had sewn into my cloak, all went for my safe passage to Dover. All save the brooch."

"Clever girl," he said, and Claudia fancied there was a grudging respect in his voice. "Come closer and let me have a good look at you."

So many times she'd imagined this reunion, dreamt of it, prayed for it. Yet now that it had come, now that she was alone with the man who had sired her, she wanted nothing so much as to turn and flee. Another dream lost, she thought, even as she stepped forward.

"Verra well," he declared and flagged her toward a gilt-backed chair. "You're not as beautiful as she was, nor as tall, but you've the look of her. In all these many years, I've yet to encounter another woman with eyes that particular hue of violet—until now." He reached for his wine goblet, set on the table beside him. "A toast, I think, to reunions."

Claudia lifted her glass in a silent salute and then took a small sip. The sherry tasted bitter but then likely it was the bitterness of her loss she tasted.

Regarding him across the expanse of room, she felt slightly ill and far from triumphant. "Maman . . . my mother is dead, milord. She was taken on—"

"Enough," he barked, his voice so ferocious that she started in her seat. "Nay need to belabor the gory details. 'Tis enough to ken that she's dead, though I could have guessed as much, otherwise why would you have come?"

Why indeed, Claudia thought, and took another sip from her glass.

"But now that you have, you'll do."

"Do, my lord?"

"Aye, the Marriage Mart, of course."

The phrase was unfamiliar to her but the cold foreboding settling into the hollow of her stomach was all too recognizable. "My lord?"

"Surely you dinna expect me to let a perfectly presentable daughter of marriageable age go to waste, now do you?"

"B-but I am not of legitimate birth."

He tossed the brooch onto the marble-topped wine table as if it were no more than a trinket. "An impediment in some quarters but one that may be surmounted provided the dowry is fat and the bridegroom desperate for funds." Laying a hand on either curved arm of his chair, he leaned forward. "My late wife was never a well woman. Only one of the children she bore me survived to adulthood. My son and namesake and your half-brother, Gearald, took a tumble from his horse two months' past. He died the week after and without issue." A look of contempt crossed his sharp features as he added, "Nay heir but a milksop miss of a wife who's been nothing but a drain on my nerves and purse."

Ironic that she'd always wanted a brother, and she'd had one all along only to lose him before they'd even met. "I am sorry for your loss, my lord."

He waved a hand, dismissing the sentiment. "The point is I've nay legitimate heir to carry on the line." He cast his gaze down to his legs, their withered contours covered with a plaid blanket. "And nay hope of begetting one now. Until today, I'd almost resigned myself to having the title pass to my nephew's boy. Almost."

Despite the fire blazing from the marble-manteled hearth, Claudia shivered. The inside of her mouth felt pasty and dry; to quench her thirst, she took another sip of wine. "I am afraid I do not understand."

Shrewd eyes regarded her over the steeple of tented hands. "The Scottish primogeniture laws are considerably more flexible than those of England. As a Scottish peer whose heir is deceased, I may declare any child of my blood, male or female, legitimate or no, as heir to my title and lands." He lifted one hand from its rest and wagged a thin finger her way. "And it just may be that I choose you."

Claudia's head spun as she considered what he was offering her. In France, the Salic law prohibited females from inheriting a peerage, and she'd always thought a similar code was observed in England. But this was Scotland, as Jack had told her so many times, and things were different here. If Lord Aberdaire were to name her as his heir, one day she would be a countess in her own right, command this household and vast lands of her own. It was more than she'd imagined in her wildest fantasies, a glittering future that only a fool, a royal fool, would refuse.

But Jack's face kept flashing before her mind's eye. She remembered the look of raw wonder in his amber gaze when he'd entered her that very first time, of how her own heart had melted even as her body had yielded to accept him. She thought of the passion and laughter and tenderness they'd shared that week, the friendship and mutual respect they'd forged over the past two months. Emotions as varied and confusing as the hotchpotch soup he'd concocted for their first meal together churned inside her. But of one thing she was certain: she loved Jack Campbell. Such a love was worth several kingdoms; forfeiting one earldom seemed a paltry price to pay.

Lifting her gaze from the wineglass she'd been turning in her hands, she said, "While I am humbled by this great honor you do me, I fear I must refuse."

"You little fool." The earl's fist smashed onto the tabletop, sending the brooch skittering over the edge. "Have you any notion of what it is you're so blithely giving up?"

Despite the woozy headache drumming her temples, a strange and wonderful calm enveloped her. Meeting his furious gaze head-on, she answered, "Yes, my lord, I believe I do. But even if I did not, I fear I would be of little use to you for, you see, I am not a virgin."

That got his attention and hers, too, for she hadn't intended to open that particular Pandora's Box. Wondering why she'd revealed so much of herself, thinking that her speech had sounded a bit thick, she bit her lip.

Pallid cheeks flushed, thin mouth growing thinner yet, and cold eyes narrowed to slits, Aberdaire railed, "It's that great animal who brought you here. Jack . . . Jack Campbell, yes, that was his name. You've lifted your skirts for him, hav'na you? Hav'na you! No, dinna trouble to answer, for of course you have. Like begets like. If you're half the whore your mother was, you wouldn't be able to resist a cock that big."

She wanted to rise and walk out, but shock held her pinned to the seat and, in truth, the room had begun to reel. Reclaiming her voice, she struggled to keep her thoughts apace with her thickening tongue. "In France I had a protector, a nobleman. Such . . . such is the lot of an illegitimate girl with . . . with no dowry and no father and whose *mère* . . . mother makes her way as a *courtisane*. I lived as his mistress for . . . for . . ." How long had it been? Unable to recall now, she settled on, "*Many* years, my lord, until he was taken and . . . and killed. And compared to Jack's, his 'cock' as you call it, was quite modest," she concluded, as breathless as if she'd just finished a footrace.

The earl was shaking his head at her but, strangely, he seemed more pleased than angry. "Och, but your Célestine's daughter, right down to your foul whore's mouth. Another obstacle, but, like the condition of your birth and your whoring ways, not necessarily insurmountable."

The sound of a throat being cleared brought both their gazes back to the door, where MacDuff stood. "The wine, milord, I trust it's proving satisfactory?"

"Most satisfactory," the earl agreed. Casting a meaningful look at Claudia, his thin mouth turned up into what might have been a smile. "I think someone may be ready for a wee rest, is that not so, my dear?"

Claudia opened her mouth to answer that she meant to leave

and leave now only no such coherent reply came out. The wineglass, still more than half full, slipped from her numb hand, the wine spilling out over the patterned carpet like blood. Watching the stain come closer and closer, fathomless as any sea, she was vaguely aware that at some point she'd slipped from the chair's edge to the floor to join it.

The earl's chuckle floated above her; she heard the faint creaking of his chair's wheels as he rolled toward her. "Before you escort her to her chamber, allow me to present Lady Claudia *Drummond*. My daughter."

Fleas hopped about the loft, flies buzzed, and the scent of manure was strong in Jack's nostrils. Setting down his saddlebag on his straw-stuffed pallet and stripping off his coat, he reminded himself that he'd made his bed in far humbler places than this. Knowing how Tam loathed the very sight of him, to keep the uneasy peace he'd often taken himself from the house to the byre and slept amongst the soothing smells and sounds of the animals. Sometimes he'd bide there for days on end until his mother's pleading finally brought him back inside.

Just as Claudia had tried to plead for him today.

One look at her face had told him that she'd been genuinely shocked by his reception. Jack, however, had been expecting it. While Lord Aberdaire had been none too subtle about putting him in his place, a place he'd foolishly allowed himself to forget, he couldn't fault his lordship's reasoning. If Claudia was to be accepted as a daughter of the house, she must sever all ties with her past, her recent past especially. It was time for him to bid her good-bye, to free her to live the life to which she'd been born. Delaying the inevitable served no purpose other than to heighten the heartache.

And yet something beyond his own selfishness held him back from slipping away while he had the chance. That something, or rather someone, was the earl. Even for a man who prided himself on his English-style sangfroid, he'd seemed unnaturally calm for having a long-lost daughter walk through his door. It was almost as if he hadn't been all that surprised by Claudia's sudden appearance. Something was amiss—Jack could feel it like a draft at his back, raising the hairs on his nape to full prickling attention.

He'd leave, all right, but not before he assured himself that all was as it should be.

*Claudia awoke on a mattress so soft that for one brief sec-*ond she thought herself to be back in her bed in Paris. Cracking open an eye she found that the room, though richly appointed, was most definitely not hers. The draperies, bed curtains, and counterpane were done in claret-colored brocade, not the airy cotton print she'd favored, and the carpet was Turkey, not Aubusson as hers had been.

She had to find Jack.

It was an effort of will but she managed to haul her head from the pillow and pull herself up on her elbows.

"You slept well."

Even before she managed to focus her gaze across the room, she recognized the steely voice as belonging to Lord Aberdaire.

Scraping her dry tongue over her bottom lip, she said, "The wine, it was drugged?"

He wheeled himself toward her. "An unfortunate but necessary tactic. Will you take some water?"

She shook her head—a mistake that sent the room canting back and forth like a coach lantern. Pressing hands to her hammering temples, she asked, "What is it that you want of me?"

"As I've told you before, unworthy creature that you are, I mean to make you my heir. In light of Britain's policies toward Scotland, it behooves me to make certain that an Englishman, not a Scot, sires my future grandchildren. A Sassenach son-in-law, preferably one with a seat in the House of Lords, will fill the bill nicely."

"You cannot force me to marry against my will."

"Debatable." He snapped his fingers and MacDuff emerged from the shadows carrying a mahogany lap desk. In answer to her unspoken question, the earl said, "You will find paper, pen, ink, sand, sealing wax—all the implements required to compose the letter that will bid farewell to Master Campbell and send him on his way."

"Send Jack away!" she said, all but forgetting her spinning head in the rush of outrage. "I will not."

"Och, but you will and gladly, for my butler is a man of many and varied talents, are you not, MacDuff?"

"I like to think I ken my duty, milord."

Shifting his gaze back to Claudia, the earl continued, "MacDuff is being overmodest, I'm afraid, for in his salad days he was a topnotch pugilist. But more to the point, his sire once was employed in the Tower of London—as a torturer. A tender father was MacDuff Senior and careful to pass on all the finer points of his trade, is that no so, MacDuff?"

"Aye, milord, 'twas honest work even if a wee bit messy at times," the butler answered with a grin and, distraught though she was, Claudia couldn't help but notice that his earlier refined accent seemed to be slipping.

Though the haze of the drug they'd given her had yet to wear off, looking between the two men, she felt a scream building in her throat. "You are not only a monster, milord, but also a coward to threaten me so. I may not be brave but nor am I a fool. If I am maimed, disfigured, I will be of no use to you on 'the Marriage Mart,' as you call it."

Aberdaire shook his head; he appeared to be genuinely surprised. "Oh no, my dear, you mistake me entirely. It's no you I'll set MacDuff to practice his considerable skills upon but your lover, Master Jack Campbell."

A*t some point, Claudia must have passed out, whether from* shock or the effects of the drug she couldn't be sure. She came to, coughing and sputtering, to the noxious fumes of smelling salts being passed beneath her nose.

Only when she'd regained her faculties sufficiently to pull herself up into a sitting position did Lord Aberdaire continue. "'Tis the big strong ones that incapacitation weighs heaviest upon, is that not so, MacDuff?"

"Aye, milord, 'tis oft the way of it."

The earl shook his head. "It was a terrible trial to me, the loss of my legs. But for a man such as Master Campbell, a man who has kent what it is to possess the strength of ten men, life as a cripple would be . . . unendurable. Enough to drive one to take his own life, I should think?"

MacDuff dutifully nodded. "I've kent it to happen, milord."

Addressing Claudia directly, Aberdaire said, "You really should reconsider your position, m'dear. When those broad shoulders are crooked and those long legs crushed, Campbell will be of scant use to you . . . in bed or anywhere else."

"Stop! I will do it." Tears streaming, she twisted about to reach for the pen and paper from the lap desk the butler had placed beside her. "But first will you answer me one question, my lord?" she said, blotting a tear from the sheet of foolscap.

He inclined his head.

"Before your son died, when you learned that revolution had come to France, that aristocrats and all who served them were being seized and fed to the guillotine, did you ever think of my mother and me and wonder what might have become of us?"

Expression placid, he shook his dark head. "No, I did not. Not once."

Seated on the edge of his pallet, Jack stared at the letter, without doubt penned in Claudia's fine flourishing hand, and though it had to be the third time he'd read it, he still couldna believe the proof of his eyes.

Mon cher *Jack,* it began—that much sounded like Claudia. *I trust you will find it in your heart to forgive me for committing to paper that which a braver woman would find the courage to say to your face.* Ha, as if Claudia had ever been afraid to speak her mind. *We must part, chéri, as we have known we must from the very beginning. We are creatures from two very different worlds and now the time has come for me to take my rightful place in mine. To do so, I must bid* adieu *to you and to the friendship we have shared these past weeks.* "Friendship" she called it!

I hope you will accept this money purse as your just due and this letter for that which it is, my final farewell. Know that in the coming years I will think of you often and fondly as I hope you will of me. Je t'aime, *Claudia Valemont Drummond.*

Je t'aime. The French for *I love you.* She'd spoken the words before, in the throes of her release, thinking he hadn't understood. But he'd kent her then as he kent her now. Just as he kent that it was Aberdaire and not Claudia who wanted him out of her life. What had he threatened her with, done to her, to coerce her into writing it?

If he has harmed her, I will kill him. With my bare hands, I will kill him, Jack vowed even as he looked up from the note to the grinning footman who'd delivered it. Forcing a smile, he asked, "Might that wee leather bag be for me?"

Coins jingled as the servant handed him the purse. "Aye, man, 'tis for ye. Fifty Scotch pounds—no a bad take for shagging a lord's daughter."

Temples pounding, Jack accepted the purse and made a show of weighing it in his palm. He loosened the string, pulled out a gold sovereign, and tested it between his teeth. "As sweet as the fruit between a woman's thighs, laddie. Sweeter, mayhap." He dropped the coin back into the purse, tightened the cord, and then slipped the purse inside his sporran. Rising, he asked, "Now if ye'll be so good as to point out which window is the lady's, I'll blow her a kiss on my way out."

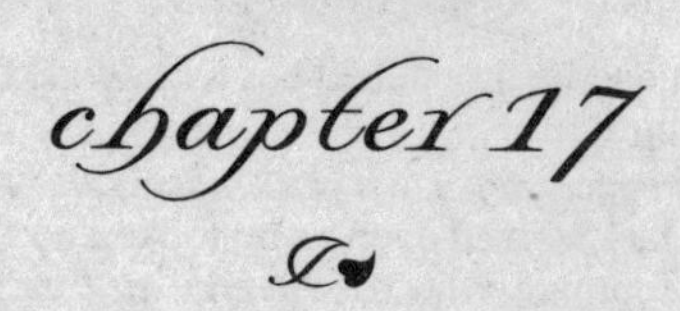

O farewell griefe, and welcome joye.
Ten thousand times therefore;
For nowe I have founde mine own true love,
Whom I thought I should never see more.

—"The Bailiff's Daughter of Islington," a Scottish ballad

Claudia sat at the small supper cart that earlier had been wheeled into her chamber by the stone-faced housekeeper who'd refused to meet her gaze. The effects of whatever it was they'd dosed her with had worn off shortly after she'd written Jack the farewell missive the evening before. The deed done and Jack gone as of that morning, she doubted they'd drug her further. Still she hadn't been able to bring herself to touch a morsel or a drop from the trays that had arrived at regular intervals throughout the day. To quench her thirst she'd resorted to drinking washing water from the pitcher. It was cool and it was clean and all in all she'd congratulated herself that she'd been clever to think of it.

A pity she hadn't been clever when it had counted. Had she bothered to learn something of his lordship (she'd given up even thinking of him as "Father") before wandering inside his castle gates like a lamb to the wolf's den, she might even now be back at the inn with Jack, safe and warm, cherished and loved. They'd be in bed at this hour or perhaps sharing a bath or a meal—not that they'd eaten much over the past week but . . .

That morning she'd stood at her chamber window and watched him ride out from the courtyard. *"Adieu, chéri,"* she'd called out through the leaded glass and for a flash of a second when he'd turned his horse about she'd fancied he'd looked up at her. But that was absurd. The castle would have myriad bedchambers, and hers was easily thirty feet above ground level. He wouldn't have seen her just as he wouldn't have had cause to look back. The terse little note she'd been made to pen him had taken care of that. No doubt he was even now cursing her for a conniving whore who'd bedded and used him only long enough to win her freedom—and the proverbial pot of gold. If only he might know the truth, if not now then someday.

Oh, Jack! She cast a swollen-eyed glance down to the contents of her tray, the dishes prepared in the French fashion. She'd gone so far as to break the soufflé with her fork—it was light and fluffy as a cloud and baked to a light golden color. The salmon, too, was cooked just the way she liked it, the flesh flaky and moist. The wine was French, too, from Reims, and there was even fruit and Brie cheese for dessert. She wondered if, like a Christmas goose, she was being fattened up for the kill—or in her case, the wedding.

Lord Aberdaire must be mad, that was the only explanation that made anything approaching sense. Crazed with grief over the loss of his son or, more properly, his doomed schemes for the succession of his dynasty.

Heavy footfalls sounding down the corridor interrupted her brooding. She cocked an ear, listening. No doubt it was the sour-faced matron come to collect her dinner things. For the first time in more than twenty-four hours, her hopes surged. Now that Jack was safely away, there was nothing to be lost by her trying to escape. All she need do once she was free of her room was to slip outside, find her way to the stables, and steal one of the horses—surely the third time must be the charm. If she were fortunate, she might even catch up with Jack on the main toll road passing through Edinburgh.

More optimistic than she'd been all day, she rose, snatched the wine bottle from the tray, and cut across the room to the marble-topped washstand. Under normal conditions she would have said it was a sin to waste such an excellent vintage but reminded that desperate circumstances require desperate measures, she upended the bottle into the washbasin. Empty bottle in hand, she hurried about the room, extinguishing candles and wall sconces until the only light came from the sliver of half-moon outside her window. She fumbled her way back to the chamber door, flattened her back against the wall next to it, and held her breath.

The footsteps stopped just outside her door. There was a half-second's pause, and then the tinkling of tiny bells. No, not bells but *keys,* she decided and lifted the wine bottle above her head. Heart striking against her chest, she listened as several more keys apparently were tried and rejected; finally she heard the lock click home. Nerves frayed to threads and mouth dry, she watched the door creak slowly open, fraction by fraction until a large foot insinuated itself inside.

The form that followed she saw only in silhouette but it looked far too large and broad to belong to the housekeeper, sowlike creature though she was. But there were plenty of other servants in the castle, and Claudia hadn't a second to waste. She launched herself forward, aiming the bottle high for the back of the interloper's head.

With lightning speed, he whipped about, the bottle missing him by inches and slipping from Claudia's clammy grasp. Thrown off course, she careened forward. Strong arms banded about her, hauling her against a hard, muscled chest. She drew a sputtering breath—and inhaled the crisp, clean scent of evergreen.

In the darkness, Jack hissed, "Wheesht, woman, if I'd kent you meant to brain me, I'd have thought twice before coming to fetch you." Before she could answer, he brought his mouth down on hers for a swift, hard kiss.

When she could breathe again, she whispered, "How did you manage to find me?"

Despite the season, he wore no coat over his shirt, which was damp and clinging. She slid her hands over him, the broad shoulders bunched with muscle, the hard biceps of his arms, the tautly muscled belly, making sure he was real, making sure he was indeed there and not a fiction of her fraught mind.

"Before I left, I had one of the servants point out which room was yours. Then I waited 'til dark and came back through the east entrance. Fortunately for me 'tis guarded only by His Lordship's dogs, which are no verra well fed—that man really ought to mind how he treats his animals. A few strips of meat tossed from my saddlebag and we were all fast friends."

She smiled against his shoulder. "But how did you get inside?"

Raising his hand, he sucked on the knuckles. Although it was too dark to see the damage, Claudia caught the faint metallic scent of drying blood.

"I took the keys off the butler. He dinna care to give them up at first but I, er, persuaded him 'twould be a verra good idea if he did." Flexing his hand, he elaborated, "He's tied up in the kitchen along with the housekeeper and one of the footmen." He set her from him and reached for her hand. "But we've no time to waste. I've the horses waiting beyond the stables but I've nothing more to feed to the dogs."

"Do not worry." Glancing across to the shadowy shape that was the abandoned supper cart, she smiled into the darkness. "I have something from His Lordship's chef that they will appreciate just as well."

That night Lord Aberdaire's guard dogs dined very well indeed. Having made it past the canine gauntlet with nary a snarl raised except for Elf's, Jack and Claudia rode hard and fast for the next three hours, stopping in Edinburgh only long enough to water the horses, and whenever possible keeping clear of the main roads. When there were no signs of pursuit, they dismounted to walk the horses, keeping to the cover of a hedgerow-bordered field, Elf only too happy to lapse into a stroll alongside them.

Hands tucked inside her cloak to guard against the cold, Claudia said, "It seems my father has decided that I am more trouble than I am worth."

Jack made a scoffing sound low in his throat and threw an arm about her. "A lot he knows but then I suppose a title and a brain box dinna necessarily go together."

Wise words indeed for it had been her craving for acceptance, for respectability and position, that had caused her to turn a blind eye to the pot of gold that lay within her grasp all these many weeks.

Wondering what she had ever done in her miserable life to deserve the devotion of this kind, good man, she wound an arm about his waist and said, "You risked much to come back for me."

He stopped walking and turned to regard her. It was not yet light but the moon was full and brilliant, as were the stars, and in the shaft of pure white light that fell over them she could see the fierce caring written into every weary line of his tired but handsome face. "I'll warrant 'twas no more than you risked when you wrote that wee note telling me to leave," he said, voice soft and gaze softer still. "Aberdaire must have held something over you, something verra dear, for you to write such a thing."

Oh, yes, Jack, something very dear indeed. She tightened her arm about his waist. "Someday I may tell you, *chéri,* but not today. Not today." When he only nodded and kept on, she couldn't resist asking, "But what of you? How could you be so sure he forced me?"

He hesitated, considering. When he turned to her again, the moon was no longer just above them and his face was a mask of shadows, but she could hear the smile in his voice when he answered, "Like you, *mo chride,* I may answer that someday but no today. No today."

"Luicas, lad, drink up," *Callum urged from across the trestle* table. "Ye're fallin' behind and there's plenty more where that came from." He picked up their empty whiskey glasses and held them high. "Ho, wench, look sharp. These fishes are swimmin' out o' water."

From across the crowded taproom, Jenny scowled. "Hold on to your breeches, Callum McBride. "Wi' Milread abed upstairs wi' the head cold and Claudia still away, ye'll ha' tae wait your turn."

At the mention of his sister's name, Luicas ducked and flattened his shoulders against the booth's high back. "She doesna like me tae drink strong spirits," he explained, a guilty flush riding high on his cheeks. "Nor does Master Jack. He says 'tis deeds that stand as a man's true measure, no how much whiskey and ale he can stomach."

Jack, always Jack.

"Does he, now?" Schooling his features so that his hatred would not show, Callum reached inside his coat pocket and pulled out the pewter whiskey flask he kept with him for just such emergencies. After a quick look about to make certain Alistair's back was turned, he poured a generous measure into their two glasses.

"Och, but your sister's no here tae see, is she, nor Jack, either. And as they say, when the cat's away . . ." At Luicas's blank, bleary-eyed look, he explained, "What I mean is that wi' your master still in Edinburgh, there's nay reason ye shouldna have a bit o' fun, now is there? A bit o' fun and a bit o' talk, that's all we're havin', aye, Luicas?"

The boy nodded solemnly and took a cautious sip. It was only his second drink but already his fair cheeks bore a ruddy flush.

Anticipation thrummed through Callum; hiding it, he settled

back against the seat. Sipping his drink as though he had all night, he confided, "I'm no a traveling man like ye and my braither are, Luicas. Tell me, d'ye fancy Edinburgh?"

"Aye, I do." Thin shoulders squared as though he was feeling manly indeed, Luicas reached for his drink. Bolder now, he took a long swallow. Eyes watering, he managed to choke down the whiskey. "The little I've seen o' it, that is."

"How so, lad? 'Twas yer second time there, was it no? Is yer master such a slave driver that he doesna gi' ye leave t' amuse yourself?"

"Nay, 'tis no like that at all," Luicas answered without hesitation, and inwardly Callum seethed at how quick the brat was to leap to Jack's defense. "I was tae take Mistress Claudia out tae the shops along the Mile and such but as it came about . . ." Here he paused, spiny shoulders dipping forward, and then admitted, "But we . . . I ne'er got beyond the inn."

"The inn?"

Luicas nodded and then, looking dejected still, bent to slurp more whiskey. "On account o' Mistress Claudia bein' wi' us, Master took a room on Blackfriars Street and left me there tae guard the lass and take her about. Only . . . only . . ." Face growing rosier by the second, he set down his glass and burst into silent tears.

"Only what, lad? Come now," Callum soothed as the thin chest rose and fell in mute sobs. Biting back his distaste, he reached across the table and laid a consoling hand on the shuddering shoulder. "It canna be so bad as all that."

"Oh, 'tis, Master Callum, 'tis worse," he wailed, covering both hands over his streaming face. "For I let him down, ye see. Master trusted me tae guard the lassie, but I . . . she . . . she got away."

Heart pounding, Callum could scarcely contain himself. "She escaped, d'ye mean?"

Luicas dragged his sleeve beneath his snotty nose. "Aye, locked me up inside the wardrobe and then took the horse and left for . . . for Linlithgow I think it was." Sniffing back tears, he brightened and then reached for his glass. "He brought her back, though, Master did."

The expression of hero worship on that young face was enough to make Callum want to retch, but he forced himself to say only, "He did, did he?"

"Aye, went after her on Beelzebub and carried her straight

back." The boy's expression darkened and, after downing the last of his whiskey, he leaned in to whisper, "In the three years I've been wi' him, ne'er once has he laid a hand upon me but by the sounds comin' from their room, he maun ha' beat her but good."

Jack beat a woman? Callum couldna credit that the lily-livered bastard would have the stomach for it and so he asked, "Ye saw him *strike* her?"

"No exactly," Luicas admitted. Casting his gaze downward, he traced a finger about the spillage from his drink. "But I heard 'em in the next room, her especially, for she let out such piteous moans."

"Ah, moans, ye say?"

The boy nodded vigorously. "Aye, and such sighs and whimpers, puir lady, as tae make me sorry for her in spite o' her lockin' me up. And then there was the creakin'."

"Creakin'?"

"Aye, the mattress I suppose it was, for he'd thrown her down upon it, and him atop her, and when last I did see 'em they were thrashin' about like a pair o' wild beasties. Puir lass," he said again, this time around a broad yawn, "I hope he didna hurt her tae bad though she shouldna ha' run off as she did."

Hiding a smile, Callum tipped his glass back and finished off his own whiskey. "Nay, Luicas lad, ye've the right of it. She shouldna ha' run off."

Jack and Claudia rode throughout the night and following day, not stopping until they reached Selkirk to refresh themselves and the horses at an inn on the cobbled High Street. Jack's village was but an hour's ride from Selkirk proper, and his cottage lay less than a league beyond it. Once more in the saddle, Claudia looked across to him, riding beside her, and marked how the lines of fatigue seemed to be lightening with every mile traveled. Claudia, too, was eager to reach not only their journey's end but also the cottage; the latter, she realized with a start, she'd come to view as her home. Though neither she nor Jack had made mention of how the change in their relationship would affect their domestic arrangements, she suspected that the blanket cordoning off the bedroom area would come down that very night. And that when she slipped beneath the starched sheet and quaint quilt, Jack would join her.

Lost in happy anticipation of the night ahead, refusing to think beyond the immediate present, Claudia was mentally cataloging familiar landmarks when, without warning, Jack reined in.

"What is it?" she asked, wondering why they were stopping in the middle of the thicket bordering his property, and thus almost to their destination.

Nostrils working, he answered, "Smoke. A great fire, for mark how the air's thick with ash."

Now that she thought of it, her eyes had begun to water a short while back, but she'd attributed it to the combination of fatigue and chimney smoke, the latter when they'd ridden through the village.

He relaxed, the worry lines smoothing from his brow. "Och, but what an *idjut* I am. 'Tis the thirty-first of December. It must be the Burning Out of the Old Year."

"The Burning Out of—"

"An old custom that dates to ancient times, like as no to the Druids. To drive out evils and bring fertility to the crops and cattle for the coming year, a great bonfire is lit at half-past nine on the last night of the old year. Now, of course, 'tis little more than an excuse for merrymaking, for bringing on the drums and the dancing and the whiskey." Turning back to look ahead, he said as if thinking aloud, "They must be eager indeed, for though 'tis dark, it canna be more than five." He hesitated. "Will you be wanting to go, then?"

Claudia didn't hesitate at all. Smiling, she shook her head. "No, Jack, tonight I want only to be with you."

B*ut as they cleared the copse and came out onto the hillside,* it was silence and not drums and laughter and stamping feet that greeted them. Their hilly perch afforded a bird's-eye view of the glen below and from it they saw that the cloud of bitter black smoke funneling heavenward came not from the open field but from Jack's cottage.

"Hold here," he shouted to Claudia and then urged Beelzebub down the sloping path, Elf running behind.

Claudia didn't hold, of course, though she followed down at a slower pace, the air growing blacker and heavier the closer she came to the cottage. By the time she reached the charred remains of the fence post, the air was so thick with smoke that she had to take the linen handkerchief Jack had given her to cover her nose and mouth.

Jack's cottage was wreathed in orange flames and black smoke, the burning roof spitting cinders onto the scorched yard like a hissing cat and sparks popping from the chimney flue like kernels of roasting corn. Squinting through the haze of smoke, Claudia sighted Jack just ahead. Her heart lurched when she saw him slide from Beelzebub's back and hit the stone path running.

"Jack!" she screamed when she saw he was headed for the burning cottage. "Jack!" One foot tangled in her horse's stirrups, and, cursing, she fought to free it.

She half slid and half fell from the saddle, her cloak twisting about her as she hit the charred ground and rolled. Shoving herself up on scraped palms, she found the handkerchief on the ground beside her and then scrambled to her feet.

He was halfway to the cottage now, Claudia's cries for him to stop no doubt drowned by the fire's roar and Elf's wild barking. Ever at her master's side, the dog leapt up, grabbing a great mouthful of his clothing to pull him back. But nothing, it seemed, would stay him.

"Jack!" Claudia called out again, but if he heard her, he gave no sign of it.

Choking on smoke, the linen handkerchief now black, she ran after him, dodging fiery arrows as she called his name, the ground searing the soles of her shoes.

Futile though it was to think she could stall him, reaching him, she caught at his arm, the little protective square of blackened linen fluttering to the ground.

He shook her off much as he had the dog, turning on her with fierce, feral eyes. "Go back, Claudia."

The flames flaring from the windows and door brought to mind a furnace, the temperature so intense Claudia felt as if her skin were melting like wax. "Jack, y-you must not . . . g-go in there," she said around a spell of coughing. "The roof . . . it c-cannot hold."

A flaming missile shot toward them. Cursing, Jack launched himself at her, carrying them out of harm's way just as the fire hit home in the very spot where they'd stood.

His breath a rasp in her ear, he said, "I must. One Eye,

Heather, Lady—they'll die otherwise." He shook her off and started forward again to the blackened front steps.

Frantic, she cried, "It is you who will die. *You,* Jack." Rushing up behind him, she grabbed his arm with both her hands and all her might.

"I must . . . I must save them," he said and jerked free.

Sinking to her knees on the scorched grass, tears streaking her gritty cheeks, she screamed, "*Je t'aime, Jack.* I love you, Jack! I *love* you!"

It was then that the resistance, the fight, left Jack Campbell. The animals trapped inside that burning building were, barring Milread, the only friends he'd ever known and his sole family since his mother's death. The books he'd gathered over the years were, in their way, old friends, too. And then there was the cottage itself, the haven he'd built for himself with his own hands and the only true home he'd ever had. But when he looked back at Claudia, when he saw the love shining from her reddened eyes and the tears cutting through her soot-caked cheeks, he knew he couldn't take so much as one more step toward that burning building. She'd said she loved him, and suddenly he knew that whatever else happened he wanted to be around to hear her say those words again and again, day after day, for the rest of his long, *long* life.

And so even as the tears for all those dear lost little lives fell fast and furious, even as great choking sobs wracked his chest, he took a step toward her, then another and another until she was in his arms, or rather he was in hers.

"Come away, *chéri,*" she said, wrapping her slender arm about his waist. "Come away and do not look back."

Leaning into her strength, he managed a nod and arm in arm they picked their way through the singed yard to safety. They were almost to the fence when Elf's frantic barking had them raising their bowed heads.

Eyes tearing, Claudia pointed to the hillside ahead. "Jack, *chéri,* do you see that?"

"Aye, I do." Blinking stinging eyes, he could just make out the queue of bobbing bright lights snaking toward them. But as the lights drew nearer, he saw that they hailed not from the ravenous inferno at their backs but from the lanterns of the half dozen or so men making haste to reach them.

At the head of the pack was Duncan. Reaching them first, he said, "When Dorcas first said she smelled fire, I told her she maun be daft, but that woman has a nose like a bloodhound." Gesturing with his empty water bucket to the men at his back, he said, "Point us tae the well, lad, and if it isn't burned yet we'll offer what aid we can."

Jack shook his heavy head and prayed that Duncan and the others crowding around them would attribute the tears wetting his cheeks to the smoke. " 'Tis too late."

Duncan's high brow lifted and in a carrying voice he said, "Och, we're Scotsmen, are we no? We'll no be bested by a wee fire, at least no wi'out a fight, will we lads?"

A hearty cheer went up. Looking about him at the earnest faces of the neighbors who'd turned out to help—Duncan, Peadair and Pol, his cousin young Rabbie Campbell, and even Alistair—and then at the sweet, sooty countenance of the wee woman holding steadfast at his side, Jack felt a lump thicken his throat.

He released Claudia's hand, turned back to the blazing cottage, and poked an arm through the thickening wall of smoke. "Verra well. 'Tis that way, just beyond the house to the left."

Duncan's mouth curved into a smile. "Ye heard him, lads. Tae the well!"

S*tationed at the well, neck cloths tied about their noses and* mouths, the men formed a bucket brigade and for the next hour they fought a losing battle with the flames. Jack had accepted their help on the condition that he and he alone assume the most dangerous position: that at the very end of the line and nearest to the burning cottage.

Standing safely behind the fence where she'd sworn to Jack she'd stay proved to be the hardest promise Claudia had ever had to keep. Fingers digging into the charred wood fence rail, she watched her beloved, stripped to the waist and broad shoulders and back gleaming with sweat, hurl bucket after bucket of water upon the hungry flames.

And still the fire raged.

When the cottage door exploded in fiery hail, knocking back everything and everyone in its path, Claudia had never felt so helpless in all her life. And when, frantic, she at last spotted Jack's large form limned in angry orange light striding toward her, she could have fallen to her knees and wept with gratitude and relief.

"Oh, Jack," she cried, wrapping her arms about him and vowing never again to let him go. "Oh, Jack, thank God."

"It's gone," he said simply, pulling down his makeshift mask, and to her relief he dropped his bucket to the ground and wrapped both his arms about her.

Arms linked, they turned to watch the fire in its final throes. The exhausted men joined them in keeping silent vigil, watching in mute horror as the cottage exploded into fiery hail and the proud standing walls of wattle and daub withered to stumps. And when the roof puckered and then caved in with a great, rushing roar, signaling that it was well and truly over, then and only then did Jack let himself turn away.

Duncan cleared his throat, a signal to the other men to fall back. Dividing his gaze between Jack and Claudia, he said, "I suppose ye'll be wanting some private time, so the lads and I will take our leave now. But if it's a place to stay ye're in need of, Dorcas's and my door is open."

Alistair came up, mopping his brow. "And I, er, suppose Milread wouldna mind if the lass were tae share her room at the inn for awhile."

Jack swiped the back of his hand across streaming eyes, then nodded. "You're a rare friend, Duncan. And I thank you as well, Alistair."

Gaze knowing, Duncan said, "Dinna do anything foolish, lad. The law is here for a reason, ye mind."

"So I used to believe," Jack replied and the bitterness burning into those words shocked even him. "But now I'm no so sure."

Milread had agreed to mind the animals while they were away. But as accustomed to laying fires as she was, she'd not be so careless as to neglect to bank one before leaving.

Duncan clapped Jack on the shoulder. "Och, lad, a cottage can be rebuilt but once a life is lost, 'tis lost forever." He stooped to pick up his bucket and lantern and then turned to go.

One by one the others took their solemn leave. Jack waited until the last man had departed, then he turned to Claudia and fell into her open arms.

"Oh, lass, what a muckle mess it all is," he said, voice breaking.

And then he laid his head into the curve of her shoulder and sobbed out his heart's hurt while Elf stood by and licked the top of his sooty hand. Later, when the storm of feeling had subsided, he refilled their buckets and together they walked about the smoking rubble to douse the last of the sputtering flames.

The cottage and all within were lost, of course. The byre, too, had burned to the ground, except for the remnants of door, its split boards bearing the marks of the mare's hooves. They'd been fortunate to find both horse and cow wandering the field a short distance off; both animals now were safely tethered with Beelzebub and the gelding.

Claudia looked up from brushing off the blackened spine of a book and, cocking her head, said, "Jack, did you hear that? It sounded almost like . . . like a cat."

Beyond weary, he upended his bucket over the smoking remains of the charred chimney piece before answering, "Aye, I thought I heard it, too, but to be sure 'tis only our wishful fancy and weariness and mayhap the wee brownies out to trick us for disturbing their nests." He started for the well to refill the bucket.

"Meow."

This time they both spun about to see One Eye, black fur pockmarked and white paws grayed with soot, come bounding toward them from the direction of the chicken coop.

"One Eye!" Jack cried, dropping the bucket and running toward the cat. "Och, but I'd never thought to set eyes on you again."

Obviously happy to see him, too, One Eye dropped the furry morsel he'd been carrying between his jaws at Jack's feet. Too relieved to scold him for hunting, Jack bent to pick him up when he saw that the dropped "morsel" still moved.

"Heather!" Claudia exclaimed, taking the unspoken word straight from his astounded mouth. Apparently too caught up in her enthusiasm to recall that she was supposed to be terrified of mice, she bent and scooped the little beast into her open palms without a qualm.

Cradling the cat in his arms, Jack pressed an unashamed kiss atop the beast's singed head. "You're a hero, One Eye. I dinna ken how it is you did it, but I'm that proud of you, lad."

Their spirits were dampened, though, by the discovery of the hawk's cage, the metal melted and holding nothing beyond a few burnt feathers.

"Oh, Lady, my puir lass," Jack said, fresh tears sliding through the grime on his cheeks.

He used the handkerchief not to wipe his eyes but to wrap about the scalding metal. In that way he carried what was left of the cage to the vegetable garden, where he found a shovel not too badly melted and, using it, scooped out a hole in the charred hearth.

"Soar high, my Lady," he said, knocking the last shovel of dirt atop the little mound and then bending to smooth it with his hands. "For as Father Angus says, in Heaven all things are made right and all hurts healed, and I maun believe that one wee crippled wing willna present half so much of a challenge to God as it did to me."

Holding his cat in her arms and his mouse in her pocket, Claudia felt the hot tears slipping down her own cheeks. Blinking them away, she followed him back to the front of the yard, pretending interest in the view ahead to give him privacy to compose himself.

They stood side by side for a while longer, surveying the devastation which, even now, Claudia could scarcely credit. Shaking her head, she said, "Can you be certain this was not a chimney fire? Perhaps Milread forgot . . ."

Scouring his face with the corner of his shirtsleeve, Jack shook his head. "The byre burnt, too, yet there's nay sign of a fire trail betwixt the house and it." Lifting her lantern to look beyond him, Claudia saw that he was right, the path and grass that bridged the two foundations were more or less unmarred.

"'Twas no accident, this, but arson pure and simple," Jack said, broad arms opening to span the desecration, all that remained of his cherished home.

"Who would do such a thing?" But even as Claudia voiced the question, the all too apparent answer rose up. "Callum," she said, shaking her head, for if she'd ever wondered at the depths of Jack's brother's obsessive hatred, the proof stood all about her now in the broken cottage walls and steaming rubble.

"Aye. If I had any doubts, I'm done with doubting now." He reached into his pocket and withdrew a small scrap of fur, charred about the edges. Face registering distaste, he held it out for her to see.

"A rabbit's foot? But what—"

" 'Tis Callum's 'good luck charm' or so he likes to say," Jack answered, pocketing the severed limb once more. "He never goes anywhere without it, yet I found it just now on yonder path. And inside about the area of the hearth, I found what looks to have been a pile of cloths reeking of pitch."

"But if he's hated you his whole life, why choose now to . . . to do all *this?*"

His face set in grim lines, he took the lantern from her and then her hand in his and started steering them up the path and away from the wreckage. "I dinna ken the answer to that yet, *mo chride,* but before this night is o'er I mean to find it out."

chapter 18

The fires of hate, compressed within the heart,
Burn fiercer and will break at last in flame.

—Pierre Corneille, *Le Cid,* 2.3

F*laxen hair tied up in curling rags, eyes and nostrils rimmed* in red, and wearing a voluminous men's dressing robe with patched pockets and multicolored sleeves, Milread rushed forward to greet the grubby-faced new arrivals and their animal menagerie crowding her bedroom. "Och, but tell me it's not so. The cottage—"

"Lost," Jack finished for her, face grave. He set One Eye down upon the floor to prowl and in as few words as possible, apprised her of all that had taken place since he and Claudia had first seen the fire.

Listening, Milread stuffed her fist into her mouth to stifle a sob. "I was just there, this verra morn tae milk Grizel and tend t'other beasties." Tears brimming, she looked from Jack to Claudia. "And I didna so much as lay a twig in that grate, I swear tae ye I dinna."

Claudia came up on the barmaid's other side and gave her shoulders a reassuring squeeze. "We know you did not, *chérie,* but someone . . ." She hesitated, glancing over to Jack, "Someone did."

Milread thought for a moment and then her hazel eyes, heavy as they were with cold, opened wide. "Callum?" When they nodded in unison, she said, " 'E's a devil, I'll grant ye that, but surely 'tis low tae sink, even for him?"

"Mayhap," Jack said and left it at that.

Milread looked from Claudia to Jack. "How can I help?" she

asked, and Claudia's heart warmed at the knowledge that not only was this good, kind soul Jack's friend but hers, too.

He raked a hand through his grime-streaked hair. "Most of my savings went with the fire, but I've a bit set aside in an Edinburgh bank. It will take some days to get to it, though. In the meantime, I'll be needing somewhere to stable the horses and the cow."

"Dinna be worrit about that. Grizel's milk will more than pay for her board and we've plenty o' empty stalls in the stable." Jack started to protest that he didna want Alistair's charity, that he could *pay,* but Milread only shook her head, sending a curl unraveling from its wrapper. "Och, I give that man charity every time I take him between my legs. Leave Alistair tae me."

Jack reached down to stroke Elf's head where a patch of fur bore the fire's scorch. "I ken it's a lot to ask but Elf and One Eye—"

"Will stay right here in this wee room wi' me."

"Thank you, lass." Jack hesitated, then said, "There is one more I need you to keep safe for me," and something in his voice prompted a thread of apprehension to weave its way down Claudia's spine. He turned to her, eyes earnest and square jaw set, and said, "I need you to bide with Milread for a while."

Claudia shook her head. "Wherever it is you are going, I will go, too."

He shook his head. "Nay, you willna."

She dug in her heels. "You have no right to tell me where I may and may not go, Jack Campbell."

"Aye, I do. You're still my prisoner, mind."

She slammed the flat of both hands against his chest. "Why, you, you—"

"Though even if you wer'na, sure as if we'd been by a priest joined, 'tis your loving me and me you that gives me the right. That selfsame right you brought to bear in keeping me from going inside the cottage I claim now in calling on you to stay."

"But you are going, into a different kind of fire but perhaps one that burns just as dangerous." Tears pricking her eyes, she leveled her gaze on the amber eyes peering out from the blackened mask and said, "You are going to confront Callum."

It wasn't a question nor did he deny it. "I've lost much this night—Lady and my books and the money are but the start of it. For ten years that cottage has been no so much my haven as my hiding place, somewhere I went when I needed to pretend that ugliness, that cruelty, that the great wide world beyond didna exist, that it couldna touch me. But now it *has* touched me, Claudia, no just the ugliness but the beauty also. *You've* touched me. And whether for good or for ill, I've done with pretending and with hiding, too. This reckoning between my braither and myself, 'tis a thing long overdue."

"Then let me come with you, let me—"

"Hush, *mo chride,* and hear me out." Hands on her shoulders, he held her away from him. "Of all I've lost and stand yet to lose, the one thing I couldna bear is for aught to happen to you. Please, Claudia, say you'll bide here with Milread until I return. To do what I must calls for a clear mind, and I canna have that if I'm worrit that some harm may come to you."

Claudia had thought she hadn't more tears to shed but the wetness on her cheeks told her she'd been wrong about that, too. "And you think I could bear it if something happened to *you?"*

"Wheesht, woman, and do you think to get rid of me that easy?" Through the soot, his mouth lifted in the lopsided smile she'd come to love, and that same smile now wrenched her poor heart in two. "Now that you've said you love me, I mean to be around a good long time if only so I can give you cause to say it again and again."

"Oh, Jack," she said, and seeing that his mind was made up, she did the only thing she could do. She laid a hand on either of his gritty cheeks and pulled his face down to hers for a long, soul-searching kiss.

The sound of Milread clearing her throat had them drawing apart once more. "Och, but it'll be morning and the pair o' ye still standin' in the middle of my floor sighing o'er who's tae go and who's tae stay."

Jack pressed a kiss onto Claudia's forehead and then stepped back. "She's right, mind. There's nay point in my putting it off any longer." He started toward the chamber door.

"Hold! No so fast." Milread padded over to the far side of her bed and bent to cram a hand beneath the mattress. After a moment's poking around, she withdrew a flintlock pistol and small drawstring bag. Walking over to Jack, she handed both to him. "I'm no sayin' tae use it, mind, but if the need should arise . . ."

"With luck I'll bring it back tae ye as shiny clean as it looks to be now." He tucked the pistol into his belt and dropped the bag of lead balls into his sporran. Then he engulfed his childhood friend in a hug. "You're a braw lass, Milread," he said, upon breaking away, "and the verra best mate a man could want for."

Milread cracked a grin but, looking on, Claudia didn't think her suddenly tearing eyes were due to a head cold. "So ye keep telling me, though all my rare charms ha' yet tae snare me a man under fifty."

The McBride cottage was a good forty minutes' walk from Alistair's but with nearly three decades' worth of wrongs to redress and a temper spiking to boiling with every step taken, Jack arrived in half that time. The door wasn't locked nor did he bother with knocking. The fetid smell of roasting flesh fouled his nostrils the instant he stepped over the threshold, and he had to steel himself not to gag. It had been more than ten years since he'd last set foot in this place and yet, looking about, it might have been but a day. The dust lay thicker, perhaps, and the eating table and chairs looked to be even more littered with dirty dishes than he remembered, but the essence of the place, the invisible blackness that blanketed its four walls like a shroud, was just the same.

His back to the door and Jack, Callum squatted before the hearth, using a long-handled wooden fork to prod the carcass of whatever hapless beast he'd spitted. Some manner of bird, Jack thought, then turned away and brought the cottage door closed with a slam.

"How now, brother, but this is a rare honor," Callum said, setting the fork down and rising. Starting toward him, he wiped his palms on the front of his trews. "Join me in a wee dram whilst supper cooks?"

By the looks of him, he'd had more than one wee dram already. Nor did Jack miss the heavy reek of smoke that clung to his person as surely it did to his own.

Jack shook his head. "I found something that belongs to ye and I'm minded to return it."

"Och, did ye now? And what might that be?"

Jack took the rabbit's foot from his coat pocket and held it out. "'Tis yours, is it no?"

Callum shrugged. "It may be but as I lost mine some time ago, I've had tae search out a new lucky charm." He tapped a finger to the feather peaking out from his shirt pocket.

Jack tossed the foot onto the table beyond Callum. "I think you lost it earlier this eve when you laid torch to my cottage."

Callum shook his head, greasy dark hair slipping forward over one glittering eye. "Wheesht, ye maun be as daft as that Frog bitch ye bide wi' for I've been here all the day and night. If ye dinna believe me, ye've only t'ask Da."

The reference to Claudia had Jack fisting his hands at his sides. Tamping down his temper for the moment, he said, "As if Tam could be trusted to speak true even if he wer'na drunk as David's sow."

"Och, but let us bury the hatchet, aye, Jacko? Even if Mam did spread her legs for a Sassenach soldier, we're still braithers after all."

Jack took a step forward, causing Callum to back up an equal measure. "Shut your mouth, Callum, or I'll shut it for you. You're a scourge on Mam's memory, no fit even to speak her name."

"No fit am *I?"* Callum's smile flattened and his gaze went as blistering hot as the melted metal birdcage Jack had buried earlier. "But let us no stand about haverin', my brother, for supper's a'most done and there's plenty for two." Gaze glittering with malice, he found his smile again and said, "There's those who'll say hawks are for flyin' and no eating, but I say a bird's a bird."

Jack felt as if an invisible fist had plowed into his solar plexus; his breath left him in a whoosh. The empty cage, the plucked bird roasting on the spit, the glossy feather, gray barred with black, in Callum's pocket—suddenly it all made perfect, horrific sense. *Lady!*

"You bastard!" Jack launched himself forward, locking both hands in a death grip about Callum's skinny throat.

Gasping, Callum reached up to tear Jack's fingers away, but Jack was past pain, past caring, past thinking beyond the grief. He held on that much tighter, his big thumbs moving unerringly to the fragile windpipe.

Callum's breath came out as a rattle. His legs folded beneath him and he sank to the floor. Rather than relinquish his hold, Jack went down, too. Callum was no match for Jack's strength but he was wiry and agile and as slippery as an eel. Somehow he managed to roll onto his side, and determined not to let him go, not this time or ever again, Jack rolled with him. They ended up on the flat circle of stones just outside the hearth, the fat falling from the cooking carcass into the fire causing the burning peat to sputter and pop. A hoarse shout of raw anguish tore from Jack's throat and, forgetting caution, he reached out to recapture his stranglehold.

Panicked, Callum had sent his one arm flailing about the floor by the fire and too late Jack saw why. Somehow Callum had got the cooking fork in hand. The three prongs were as sharp as knife blades and when Callum brought the fork upward and over, Jack knew he had bare seconds to wrench it away.

"Stop it, the both of ye!"

Tam's voice coming from the arched alcove of the bedroom startled them both, but it gave Jack just the advantage he needed. Reaching up, he tore the makeshift weapon from Callum's grasp and tossed it into the flames. On his knees, he rose to stand, hoisting Callum up with him. Pinning the slighter man to the far wall, he folded his free hand into a fist and barreled it straight into his brother's face. Blood spurted; teeth flew. It felt so bloody good, so long overdue, that he hauled back and prepared to hit him again.

"I said *hold!*"

The pistol's loud report had Jack whipping about, one hand already going to the loaded weapon at his own belt. But Tam had trained the smoking pistol on the ceiling, not him; plaster and pieces of thatching fell about his head and bowed shoulders like snow.

Callum had slumped against the wall but at the sight of the pistol he came forward. "Kill him, Da, kill him," he urged, all but dancing on his toes. "Ye've time tae reload, and I'll go and bolt the door so he canna get away."

Tam lowered the weapon to his side and shook his head. "Nay, I willna."

Callum's bloody face bunched into a scowl. "Then give the pistol tae me, ye codless auld sot, and let me do it." When his father only shook his head, he turned on Jack, eyes seething with hate. "If it wer'na for ye, Mam would be alive. She'd be alive. 'Twas her love for ye that killed her sure as if ye'd held the club in your own hand."

Rage spent, Jack shook his head. "You must be mad."

Callum's face fell. "If I am, 'tis because I mind that day like I ken the lines on the palm o' my own hand."

Tam's voice cut in, low and feeble. "I was aulder than she, auld enough tae be her da." He walked over to the table, set the pistol on its edge, and pulled out a chair for himself. Stiffly he lowered himself onto the caned seat; it seemed to Jack that he'd aged a good decade since he'd first come into the room. "Aulder than she and yet no so auld that I dinna ken what it was tae feel, tae *want.* And, God help me, I wanted her. Sweet Maggie, they called her then, the bonniest lassie this side o' the Tweed."

"Shut up, auld man," Callum spat but Tam only ignored him.

Fixing his gaze on Jack, he said, "She only marrit me for the bairn's sake, for your sake, but it was for love and love alone that I took her to wife though she'd ne'er sae much as looked my way."

Pacing about the room, hands held over his ears, Callum chanted, "Ye're ruining it, ye're ruining it. Ye're no supposed tae tell. Only I'm allowed tae tell."

Tam's gaze remained fixed on Jack, but Jack kent that it was the past he saw, not the present, and suddenly he was seeing it, too. The horse's hooves pounding toward them. Mam on the cart seat, the reins in hand, looking back over her shoulder to him and Callum and telling them to climb into the straw piled in back. "Mind you cover your heads, too," she'd urged. "That'll be your faither come after us, and he's sure to be in a rare mood."

Your faither, your faither, your faither . . .

Tam's voice brought Jack back to the present. Turning world-weary eyes on his stepson, he asked, "Have ye ever wanted a woman sae bad ye could taste it? Sae bad ye could taste her on your tongue long after ye'd closed your eyes in sleep?"

Jack swallowed hard, feeling the back of his throat knot. "Aye, I have," he answered, thinking of Claudia as he'd last left her, her sweet, soot-stained face turned up to his for a farewell kiss. He shifted hard eyes to Tam. "But no so that I'd kill for it."

Tam's cracked lips parted in a smile then. Later Jack would remember that he'd looked almost relieved. "We'd had a rare wrangle the night before. I'd struck her hard, knocked out a tooth. When I woke up that morn, she was gone and so were her pistol, the pony cart and the both o' ye."

Jack nodded for he remembered it now. He remembered it *all.* How the hairs at the back of his neck had prickled like pins as, at Mam's urging, he and Callum had hurried through their breakfast of parritch and honey. How he'd left Callum to crawl to the front of the cart and, hugging Mam's waist, had begged her not to halt but to keep on. But she'd only wrenched his wee arms away and, sterner than she'd ever spoken to him before, bade him go to the back with his brother and hold his peace. Cocking the little pearl-handled pistol she'd brought along, she counseled, "Whatever you hear, whatever you see, dinna say a word, *mo chride.*"

Dinna say a word, a word, a word . . .

Jack slipped a hand inside his coat and held it at his waist, the smooth metal of Milread's pistol caressing his palm. "The man on horseback, shouting to us to halt, that was you, wasna it?"

Tam nodded, tears splashing his wrinkled cheeks; standing behind his chair, Callum had gone silent. "She was my wife—*mine.* Even if she ne'er loved me, that didna give 'er the right tae leave. And so I borrowed my neighbor's horse and caught up wi' the cart on the road tae Kelso. I begged her tae come back wi' me, promised I'd nay raise a hand tae her—or tae ye—ever again, but she wouldna soften. Said the night before was the verra last time and that no faither would be better for ye than one who was a drunkard and a brute."

Jack's fingers curved about the pistol. Slowly, carefully, he started to pull it free from his belt. "And so you killed her?"

Tam nodded. "Mind I didna set out tae, but when she wouldna see reason, when she held out that wee pistol and told me tae back off or else, I went daft. I grabbed her by the hair and pulled her down from the cart. But even after I'd got the pistol away from her, she fought me like a hellcat, and before I kent what I was about, I threw her down upon the grass. Somehow my walkin' stick found its way into my hand. When she started up, I struck her hard, again and again and again until she stopped screamin', stopped thrashin,' and lay still as a stone." He paused, his knobby throat working. "Her skirts had got bunched about her waist. She had long slender legs and lovely full white thighs and when I told her I loved her and put my cock inside her, she was still warm."

Jack had the pistol in hand now; he didn't bother to hide it. The tears swimming in his eyes were almost blinding but even so at such close range he could hardly miss. He trained the flintlock on his stepfather and cocked the hammer.

Tam didn't flinch. "It wasna until I'd finished and was doin' up my breeks that I saw the pair o' ye standin' by the side o' the cart, straw stickin' out from your hair and clothes. Callum started screaming, but I figured he was too little to understand much o' what had passed. Ye, on the other hand, were a problem. I couldna be sure how much ye'd seen, for ye just stood and stared, your wee mouth clamped tight as a trap."

Dinna say a word, a word, a word . . .

Like a curtain being drawn back from a Christmas tableau, Jack saw it all, the scene he'd blocked out for two decades, in panoramic view and grizzly detail. The crimson blood smeared on bright green grass. Tam bending down to lay a handkerchief over Mam's staring gaze. The flies flitting about her still form even as, perched in the bows of the berry tree, a mistle thrush launched into song.

Hatred burned like acid in Jack's belly. He had never felt such loathing, such contempt, in all his life. "And coward that you are, you let another man, an *innocent* man, take the punishment that should have been yours."

He had the pistol trained on Tam. He would kill him, of course. The only decision left was whether to fire into his head or his heart. His heart, Jack thought, the verra organ of his own body that throbbed as if with a mortal wound.

Tam wet his lips but otherwise didn't make a move, neither to rise from the chair nor to reload the pistol that lay within easy reach. "Aye, a drifter who'd stolen some apples and then nodded off tae sleep in our byre. I found him when I got back and 'twas like the answer to a prayer. I smeared some o' the blood on his clothes, changed my walking stick for his staff. But there was still one problem left: ye."

"Me?"

"Aye, for ye'd seen everything, and I couldna trust ye tae keep yer peace. At first I thought tae come into your room one night and smother ye wi' a pillow, but then I was minded that a good half o' the village a'ready thought ye were daft. Even if ye were tae start talkin' again, who would believe ye?"

Dinna say a word, a word, a word . . .

"Afterwards I told myself I'd make amends by being a proper faither tae ye. Only every time I saw ye starin' up at me wi' those big golden-brown eyes, *her* eyes, I thought my head would split and my heart would burst."

Jack's index finger settled over the trigger. He'd killed countless times before, launched murderers into eternity with a single pull of the gallows' lever. This time it was a pistol trigger he would pull back on.

"Say your prayers, old man."

"Jack, *non!*" It was Claudia, standing inside the cottage doorway. Beneath the smudges, her face had gone very pale.

Beside her stood Milread, wringing her hands. "Dinna do it, lad. He's no worth it."

Jack shook his head. "Leave me be, the both of you. You heard him—he killed my maither. He killed Mam."

Claudia started across the room toward him. "But if you kill him, it is you who will hang."

The pistol in his hand began to waver. "It willna matter, for justice will be done."

"It will matter to me. *You* matter to me." Pushing past Callum, Claudia came to stand at Jack's side. "If you kill him in cold blood, you will be no better than him." She laid a light hand on the arm holding the flintlock. "Jack, *chéri,* if it is truly justice that you seek, then let us send for Duncan. Let him stand trial for his crime in a court of law."

Callum left his father's chair and ran to Jack's other side. "Dinna listen tae her, Jacko. Be a man and do it. Do it now!"

Tam heaved a heavy sigh. "A rope or a bullet makes nay difference tae me, for I've naything left tae live for."

And suddenly Jack realized that was the very best argument of all. Tam did indeed have nothing to live for. But Jack did. He had Claudia and who knew but they might even find a way to forge a future together. If he'd learned anything this day it was that life was precious, too precious to squander on a moment's madness. He uncocked the hammer and lowered the pistol to his side.

"Coward!" Callum shrieked. Face bathed in fury, he backed

away toward the table, but Milread was already there, picking up the discarded pistol before he could reach for it.

Jack pocketed his weapon and wrapped his arm about Claudia. "You're no much for obeying orders, are you?" he said, then pressed a grateful kiss atop her head.

Turning her tear-streaked face up to his, she admitted with a sigh, "Disobedience, it is a fault of mine, I fear, and one of many you will have to accustom yourself to once we wed."

Despite the horrors heaped upon him in the course of . . . was it only twenty-four hours . . . Jack found his own smile. "Did you just propose marriage to me, Mistress Valemont?"

The corners of Claudia's soot-blackened lips lifted. "Yes, Monsieur Campbell, I believe I did."

Thinking of what he'd almost done, all he'd come so close to losing, Jack felt his whole body begin to tremble. Turning his back on his stepfather and Callum, he whispered in her ear, "I need to be with you," though in truth he was past caring who might overhear. "As soon as we've seen Tam to Duncan—"

Across the room, a shot rang out. They broke apart and spun about to see Tam, blood gushing from the bullet hole at his temple, fall from the chair seat to the floor.

"Saints preserve us!" White-faced, Milread made the sign of the cross.

Jack dashed across the room and went down on one knee beside the prone form. Out of habit, he felt for a pulse though in truth there was no need to do so for the gaping hole in his stepfather's temple confirmed what he knew already: Tam was dead.

Callum, gaze like glass, slumped in the chair his father had just vacated. "It wasna supposed tae happen this way," he said with a shake of his matted locks.

Jack picked up the little pearl-handled pistol. "This was Mam's," he said, more to himself than to Callum. "A gift to her from my father before his leaving."

Staring ahead, Callum nodded. "Aye, he always kept it upon him. I suppose ye'll be wantin' it?"

Jack hesitated, then let the pistol slip from his grasp. The past was dead, finished. Mam would live in his heart forever, he would honor her memory forever, and so he was in no need of a memento. Though his heart was still heavy with hurt, and would be for some time to come, he suspected, he felt lighter, *freer* than he could remember ever having felt.

Claudia crossed the room toward him. "Come away, *chéri.*"

She held out her hand. Jack took it, pressed the cold palm to his lips, and then rose. Arm in arm, they walked past a stunned Callum and made their way to the door, Milread in tow.

"What a day," Milread exclaimed as they crossed the threshold and paused on the stepping stones outside to gather themselves before continuing on to fetch Duncan. "But if any good can come of so much bad, it seems some has." She cast a significant glance between them and grinned. "It, uh, looks like the pair o' ye have finally opened your eyes tae see sense—and one another."

"Aye, I suppose we have," he admitted, reaching out to tuck an ebony strand of Claudia's hair behind her ear.

Claudia looked up at him and the love, the compassion, shining forth from her gentle gaze was a potent enough tonic to begin to heal even the deepest of hurts. "It *was* Callum who torched your cottage, was it not?"

"Aye, it was."

Milread blew out a heavy breath. "Then we've at least one rook tae roost in the Selkirk Tolbooth?"

Jack hesitated, then shook his head. "Nay, let Callum be. Forbye 'twould be my word against his and even if he were judged to be guilty, it would not bring back my cottage or Lady. Let his punishment be that he must live with who he is."

"But Jack," Milread protested, brow forrowing, "Ye canna mean tae let him get off with such a thing. Why, ye ken how it is with him. What's tae keep him from striking out at ye again?"

Jack glanced at Claudia, hesitated, and then cleared his throat. "It may be that I'll no be staying around long enough to find out."

"Leave the village!" Milread looked well and truly shocked.

"Aye," he answered, fixing his gaze on Claudia. "There's a great wide world out there, and suddenly I'm minded to see a bit of it . . . that is if a certain wee woman willna mind pointing me the way."

Eyes moist, Claudia laid her small hand in his and squeezed. "I think she may be persuaded . . . once her sentence here is served, that is."

They continued down the path in silence. Just as they were

about to step out onto the roadway, a bugle sounded from close by.

Jack cocked his ear, listening. "That Duncan is a wily old fox," he said in response to the women's questioning looks. "It must be that he's sniffed out the trouble and sent his men on ahead to aid us."

His words seemed to be borne out when, a few minutes later, a man whom he recognized as the bailiff met them at the fork in the road. Looking directly at Claudia, he said, "I arrest you in the name of His Majesty, King George the Third."

Fear frissoned through Jack's body. Setting Claudia behind him, he stepped forward. "On what charge?"

"Attempt to escape and thereby violate the terms and conditions of her sentence as set forth—"

"Och, man," Jack broke in, torn between fury and relief. "There must be some mistake or is it ye havena working eyes? This is Claudia Valemont standing just beyond me. Does she look to be escaping to you?"

The bailiff's eyes narrowed. "The alleged escape attempt took place this week past and in Edinburgh no Selkirk."

Jack opened his mouth to deny it when Callum strolled up to join them. "Aye, 'tis so." Turning to Jack, his broad smile revealed the bloody gap where his front tooth used to be. "And thanks tae your apprentice, Jacko, we've a signed statement swearing it was so."

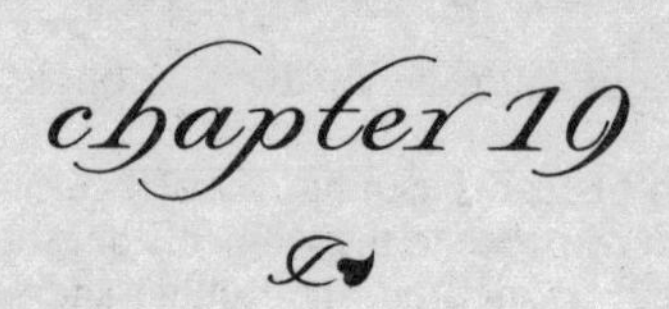

The last, the dreaded hour is come,
That bears my love from me:
I hear the dead note of the drum,
I mark the fatal tree.

—"Gilderoy," a Scottish folk ballad,
attributed to Thomas Campbell

The Selkirk Tollbooth
One Week Later

Jack stood on the tollbooth's portico, the gray drizzle that promised soon to turn into snow misting about him. How many times had he stood thus, on execution eve, waiting for the warder to admit him? How many times had he visited the cell of the condemned with his measuring tapes and his scales and his ready assurances? How many times had he passed a wife or mother, a sibling or sweetheart, trembling and teary-eyed in the corridor on their way to or from their farewell visit with the condemned, invariably bearing a food basket, blanket, or some cherished object meant to bring comfort at life's last? No matter how weary or rushed he might be, Jack always made it a point to stop and reassure them that, nay worries, death would come quick and painless. But now it was Jack who trembled, who feared, who carried the basket of food and the blanket that he prayed would bring if not solace then at least some respite from the misery, for now it was his beloved, his Claudia, who stood condemned to die.

When he'd seen the sworn affidavit bearing Luicas's mark at the bottom, he'd scarcely been able to credit the proof of his eyes. Could the boy be so bitter over the wardrobe incident that he would do Claudia such a mischief? But between bouts of crying and snatches of sentences, Luicas had explained that Callum had invited him to the taproom and, once there, had set about introducing him to his first whiskey. First and last, he swore up and down, for when he'd made his mark on that wee paper, official looking though it was, he'd thought it to be the tavern bill of fare.

Damning as that document was, Duncan was too fair a man to condemn Claudia on it alone. But when the rider dispatched to Edinburgh returned with Mistress Tweedie's sworn statement in his pocket, the magistrate had had no choice but to uphold his original pronouncement. "Hangit by the neck 'til dead," he'd said with a bang of his gavel, though those with seats at the front of the room later remarked that his eyes had seemed suspiciously dewy.

But tears, be they Luicas's or Duncan's or even Jack's own, couldna help Claudia now. Action was what was called for and he could only pray he might find the cunning and the courage to do all that was required of him.

Beginning . . . now. Eschewing the heavy iron doorknocker, he used his fist to hammer away, reveling in the bruising pain to his split knuckles. A moment later, he heard the bolt sliding back from the opposite side of the door. He straightened his shoulders and his features just as the door swung back.

Red-rimmed eyes and a gust of spirits-soured breath greeted him from across the threshold. It seemed Wallis the warder and one of Callum's mates had already started in on the whiskey.

He glanced to the wicker basket Jack clenched in one tight fist, to the plaid blanket slung over his other arm, and cracked a snaggletooth smile. "Come tae see the Frog lassie, I'll warrant. Gi' 'er a good-bye kiss for me, aye?"

Jack and Wallis were of an age but years of a steady diet of whiskey had whittled away at the warder's flesh until he was little more than a skeleton covered with great tufts of thick dark hair. Jack could have knocked him down with near to no effort and made his own way to the condemned cell at the back of the building, but once there, he would need the rusted ring of keys hitched on Wallis's belt to unlock the cell door. Wallis kent it, too.

"I need to measure her," he said, a bald-faced lie for by now he was as familiar with the terrain of her body as he was with his own flesh. With his hands and eyes he'd memorized every curve and angle, from the soft buoyancy of her breasts to the long elegant column of her throat and the fragile blades of shoulders and the knobs of her spine.

Wallis stepped back for him to enter. "Five minutes."

"Surely you can do better than that?" Jack reached into the pocket of his coat for the whiskey he'd brought.

An eye on the flask, Wallis licked his lips. "A'right, ten then."

He grabbed for the flask, but Jack held it just beyond his reach. "Twenty and I'll throw in a gold guinea for your trouble."

Wallis nodded. "Done."

Jack handed him the flask, but held back the coin. "*After* I've seen her."

He followed Wallis's shuffling footsteps down the narrow corridor leading to the prisoners' ward, passing empty cell upon empty cell until they came to the one where the condemned was brought on execution eve. Through the Judas window in the curved cell door, Jack saw her. She sat perched on the edge of the crude bench, dark head bowed, her normally straight shoulders fallen forward. The key grating in the lock had her snapping her head up, dark tangles falling back to reveal the stark pallor of her face.

"Jack!" She shot from the bench, a welcoming smile pulling at the corners of her bloodless lips.

Feeling his heart twist in on itself, Jack shoved past Wallis to step inside. "Claudia," he said, for what more could he say?

The cell was little more than a hole, measuring four feet by six, scarcely enough room to hold the straw pallet, wooden table and chair, and the bench Claudia had just vacated. Two long strides were all it took to have her in his arms.

"You came. I prayed that you would but . . ." Her voice broke off and she buried her face in his chest.

The cell door scraped closed. Ignoring both it and the snicker at his back, he said, "Of course I came."

Gently he disengaged her from his arms and went to set his burdens on the rough-hewn table. Turning back to her, he laid a hand on each shoulder, holding her at arms' length while he took silent inventory. Crescents shadowed the undersides of her eyes but there were no bruises, at least none he could see.

"How do ye fare, lass?" Inane question—how well could a woman contemplating her imminent death possibly be? "Wallis, he hasna hurt ye?" he asked even as he wondered what he could do about it if he had.

"No one has harmed me," she said, and he let out the breath he hadn't known he was holding. Her gaze strayed to the shadowed corner where a slop bucket sat, flies buzzing about the mouth. Even in the frail light trickling in through the crescent of the barred window, he could see the pink staining her cheeks as she admitted, "I was ill earlier, but I am well now. Now that you are here."

He brushed back her hair and pressed a kiss upon her damp forehead. Her face still bore a few smudges from the fire and he made a mental note to see she had water to wash with before tomorrow. "There's nay cause for shame. Loosing one's bowels is a common thing."

She dropped her gaze to his chest. "It is vain of me, I know, but I hope I will not be sick tomorrow. I would like to die well"—she paused to smile—"perhaps even with style—as my mother did. Will you help me to do that, *chéri?*"

When answering proved to be too painful, facing her all but impossible, he busied himself with setting out the contents of the hamper: bannocks and cured salmon, a soft cheese rolled in oats, called crowdie, and Milread's own buttery shortbread for dessert.

"You should eat something. Ye'll need your strength for the morrow."

That drew a small chuckle. Expression almost mirthful, she joined him at the table. "Does it take so much fortitude, then, to swing from the rope?"

Jack's throat felt as thick as though he were the one strangling. It was a minor miracle but somehow, from somewhere, he found both the voice and the courage to turn to her and explain, "When I pull the lever, the trapdoor beneath your feet will open and you'll drop into the pit beneath the scaffold. Ye willna swing." *No if I can help it.*

Chewing her bottom lip, she mulled over that information a while, then said, "So only those who take my . . . my body from the pit will see me after—"

"Aye, it is so."

She took a deep breath and then slowly exhaled. "In Paris, it was not uncommon for those at the front of the crowd to rush the scaffold for some memento from the dead. It is said that a countess had her little finger cut off and taken for a trophy." She shuddered and so did he.

To anchor them both, he took firm hold of her shoulders. "On my honor, I promise ye, no one will lay a hand on ye, lass, save myself and . . . and Luicas."

"*Merci.* Thank you. And tell Luicas that . . . that he is not to blame himself. All this, it is not his fault."

He hesitated, then nodded. "Now ease your mind and sit down to your supper."

Surveying the bounty, she still smiled but made no move to take the single chair. "It is the custom, is it not, to prepare the condemned all his favorite foods for a last meal? But even if I cared to eat, I do not think escargot and *saumon au poivre* are to be found in the kitchen of a Scottish prison." She let out a brittle laugh.

"Will you at least take some wine, then?"

Her dim eyes brightened. "There is wine?"

"Aye, there is," he said, already pouring a measure from the uncorked bottle into a porcelain cup. "It's no French but then it's no punked, either. Milread showed me where Alistair keeps his private stock."

Accepting the cup, she took a small sip. Wine in hand, she drifted over to the small window where light dribbled in through the heavy metal bars. Lifting her face to it, she said, "You have been good to me, *chéri.* Not just this but . . . but these months past. I think now that I had never before known such happiness."

Coming up behind her, he laid the blanket he'd brought over her shoulders. "You canna begin to ken what it does to me to see you like this, *mo chride.*" He took her cup and set it down on the bench, and then took her in his arms. "And to know that 'tis I who brought you to it. If I hadna borne you away from your faither's, if only I'd—"

"Sh, no regrets," she whispered, laying two cold fingers across his lips. "I would have found some other way to escape. *Non, chéri,* if my life must end, I am glad that it will end with you at my side."

"You could plead your belly, say ye were wi' child. The law forbids executing a woman who's breeding."

She shook her head. "And in a month or two, when the lie is discovered, what then?" Looking about, she shrugged. "Life in such a place as this . . . Can death be worse?" She shivered and pulled the ends of the plaid closer together. "I am almost looking forward to the morrow."

He wrapped the plaid about her shuddering shoulders and took her against his chest. " 'Tis nerves as much as the chill that makes you tremble so." He'd meant only to offer comfort and his body's warmth, but already his flesh was preparing itself to provide a great deal more. "Let me warm you, *mo chride.*" He pulled a hard swallow. "Let us be together this one last time."

She shook her head. "I am filthy."

She tried to step back but he held her against him. "Nay, ye're perfect. The loveliest lassie that ever was."

Beneath the shelter of the blanket, small cold hands slid over his chest. "How is it that one can feel so alive and still be but one night from death?"

"We're all dyin' starting from the day we're born," he told her and, taking her hand, guided her over to the table. Pushing the food to the far end, he cleared a spot and then, bracing his hands about her waist, lifted her up.

"I willna take ye on the filthy straw," he whispered and, his back to the door to shield them, he pulled the blanket about them both.

Within its shelter, she shoved up her skirts and parted her legs to take him. He stepped inside, slid a hand inside her splayed thighs, found her with his fingers. She was warm and moist and throbbing with desire—with life. Desire for him, the very man who tomorrow would be her executioner.

Despair lent their lovemaking a desperate ardor. Claudia's small deft hands, cold no more, were working the buttons at the front of his trews. She took him in her hand, guided him to her. He slid a buffering hand beneath her buttocks to lift her even as he thrust hard and deep.

"I love you, Claudia. I'll love you forever."

Hands anchored to his shoulders, she dug her fingernails into his flesh, marking him as tomorrow he would mark her. "Then do not leave me. Stay inside me." She threw back her head, ground her pelvis against his. "I want to feel you come inside me. Please, Jack. There can be no fear of conceiving a child I will not live to bear."

He reared back, then plunged into her again. "I willna leave ye, lass. God help me, I canna leave ye even if it were otherwise."

He would have liked to have held back, to prolong their joining until they reached the threshold together, cried out together, but there wasn't time. Every passing second brought their inevitable parting that much nearer. Claudia knew it, too. Fixing violet eyes on his face, she directed her inner muscles to squeeze and release, squeeze and release, caressing him until he could wait no more.

He withdrew one last time and then drove into her. His seed spurted deep inside her, hot and heavy and heady as freshly cut hay. Pleasure, release, crashed over him like a wave, leaving him gasping and lost as a drowning man floundering beneath the dark, inky water.

Even after the last ripple had died out, he stayed inside her. Laying his damp forehead against hers, he said, "You didna come. I want to make you come."

She shook her head. "There is not time."

He reached down to withdraw from her but kept his hand there, just *there*. "There's time. I'll make time."

Her skirts were bunched about her waist at the front. Beneath the shelter of the blanket, he ran his hands up and down her damp thighs, played his fingertips along the thick trickle of milky fluid, using it to lave the slick, sticky folds of her woman's flesh until they were slicker and stickier still. When she was ready, he sunk hard fingers inside her, first one then two then three. Again and again he plunged and withdrew, probed and kneaded, until he felt her inner muscles clench and unclench like a fist and she moaned that she couldn't bear it, that he must stop, even as she clawed at his hands and lifted her hips to drive him deeper still.

And just as her release was upon her, just as the muscles of her thighs were stretched taut and quivering as bowstrings, he bent and covered her with his mouth. He felt her climax thrum his lips and tongue, drank in the tangy nectar of sweat and satisfaction, then rose up and kissed her full on the mouth so that she could taste it, too. And finally he held her shuddering body tight against his as though he might really keep her safe for all time instead of for these few stolen moments.

She lifted her face to his. "Oh, Jack," she said, then kissed his jaw, trapped a trickle of sweat on the tip of her tongue and followed the trail down the side of his neck. Taking his face between her hands, she smoothed her palms down the damp bristled flesh that he'd meant to shave for her. In the midst of the caress, her features froze and her body stiffened.

"Mon Dieu!" She pulled out of his embrace, yanking down the front of her gown with clumsy, shaking hands.

Jack whipped his head about to see two red-rimmed eyes and a thick bridge of nose framed in the cell's portal. Wallis sniggered. "I thought yer kind liked to wait 'til *after* they was dead."

Rage—raw, explosive, and lethal—ripped through Jack and for the second time in as many weeks he kent what it was to want to kill someone for the pure, primitive, *personal* pleasure he would take in the act.

It was for Claudia's sake that he forced down the anger. Ignoring Wallis, he whispered, "Dinna fash, *mo chride.* I'd my back to the door and the blanket about us the whole time. He couldna see so much as he'd have you believe." She nodded and he helped her to arrange herself, then refastened his breeches. Ignoring the leering gaze at his back, he pressed a chaste kiss onto her forehead. "I must leave you."

She touched his cheek. "*Oui,* I know you must." The eyes that so many times he'd seen bright with teasing mischief regarded him now, solemn and resigned.

It was the hardest thing he'd ever done, harder even than not killing Tam the week before, but he took his hands from her, turned away, and walked to the cell door that even now was groaning open. On the threshold, he weakened and turned back.

She shook her head and touched a shaky hand to her mouth to blow him a kiss. "Go, *chéri.* And do not weep for me. It is not *adieu* until the morrow. For this night, we will say only *au revoir.*"

It wasn't until Jack stood outside the prison gates that he registered the wetness on his cheeks and realized he was crying and had been all along.

• • •

It was a fine day for a hanging, the skies above clear of either snow or rain. Looking out onto the sad-faced villagers who'd turned out to watch, Jack sighted Alistair at the back, his ale cart set up to take advantage of the drawn crowd though precious few of the onlookers held tankards. Most, like Dorcas and Mairead and Peadair and Pol, held handkerchiefs and rosary beads instead.

Da dum, da dum.

In reality there was no one at the drums this day as there had been all those many years ago when as a boy Jack had stood watching the man falsely accused of his mother's murder swing from the gallows. But the drumming resonated through him all the same, each regular, rhythmic beat building toward crescendo inside his skull. Too late he realized that it wasna to exact justice but vengeance that he'd become a hangman in the first place, that every neck about which he'd cinched the noose had stood as a surrogate for Mam's murderer. Only the culprit had been under his verra nose all along, even had lived under the same roof, which made Jack's life, at least until Claudia's coming, one great laughable lie.

Da dum, da dum.

Jack pressed a shaking hand to the small of Claudia's back and guided her into position beneath the beam. Avoiding her gaze, he dropped down on one quivering knee to the trapdoor beneath her feet, aligning the tops of her small toes to the chalk mark he'd trusted no one but himself to draw.

Perfect, everything must be perfect.

She'd filled out since that first time he'd clapped eyes upon her all those many weeks ago, but she was still light as a feather, more bone than flesh. For her to drop hard and fast as required meant he must fix weights to her feet. He did so now, cinching the leather strap about her ankles and then securing the small sandbags to it. He'd weighed them a good ten times the night before and then another ten this morning.

Perfect, everything must be perfect.

To focus his mind on his task, on Claudia, he closed his ears to the sounds of shuffling and weeping going on below. Rising on jellied legs, he tested the knots once, twice, and then thrice.

She fretted her bottom lip, looked about the scaffold, and

then out into the crowd. "Luicas, he is not here to bid me bon voyage?"

"Be still, *mo chride,*" was all he said for he didna dare say more.

Her mouth trembled but the violet eyes meeting his were dry and impossibly brave. "I am glad it is you. If it must be someone, then I am glad it is you."

He hadn't been able to bring himself to have them cut off her hair and so he'd ordered that the ebony strands be braided and pinned beneath the stiff white cap. Early that morning he'd sent Milread on ahead to help her with it not because he couldn't have done it himself but because he didn't trust himself to see Claudia so soon before and still do all that was needed.

Hands shaking, he reached up to place the noose about her neck. "Bend your head for me," he said as he'd said to countless victims on countless occasions before, only now his heart pounded and his palms sweated, for this was Claudia. The sight of the rope coiled about her slender throat like a viper poised to strike all but froze the blood in his veins. Cinching the knot, he leaned in and whispered, "Have courage, lass, and all will be well," but in truth it was his courage, his *faith,* that was wanting.

"So much rope, Jack?" A smile flickered across her drawn face, and she reached up with her hobbled hands to touch the slender column of her throat. "And I have but a little neck."

"For pity's sake, Claudia, dinna make it any harder than it is."

She nodded. "*Pauvre* Jack, it is hard to part, is it not? Fewer than three months, it seems such a little while to be happy but we were, were we not?"

He swallowed hard, his throat as thick and parched as if it were he who stood wearing a collar of hemp. "Aye, I've never been so happy." *Nor will I be so again.*

"The end will come quickly, will it not?" For the first time since she'd mounted the scaffold, a quiver of fear found its way into her voice.

Praying it was the truth he spoke, he said, "I'm verra precise. You'll no feel a thing." His gaze fixed on hers, his palms at the top of her shoulders. "But mind you stand exactly as I've placed you, toes to the line, and whatever happens dinna move so much as a muscle. And for Christ's sake, dinna fight the rope."

From the crowd, Callum lifted his ale tankard and called out, "Get on wi' it or give o'er tae those o' us who can." A trickle of applause echoed the sentiment—Callum's cronies, Jack supposed.

Fingers shaking, he laid the white handkerchief over Claudia's face, knowing he would never again look upon it. "When you are ready, call out to me."

He backed away to take position by the pulley. Blood pummeled his temples in a roaring rush, and he could swear he heard his heart drumming inside his ears. Laying his gloved hand on the lever, he waited for her signal and prayed to God he wouldna pass out before she gave it.

Da dum, da dum.

It seemed an eternity but, over the Latin of Father Angus's prayers, at last she called out, "*Je suis prête*. Jack, I am ready."

Please, God, please, God, please, God . . .

Taking a deep breath, Jack threw the bolt home.

And sent the woman he loved hurtling into the black hole below.

So this was death. The afterlife was black as pitch—she'd expected that—but it also smelled musty. And felt prickly. Far too incommodious to be Heaven but then too cool for Hell. Purgatory, then, that murky middle ground where lost souls like hers were sent to wander pending Judgment Day. Only there was no room to wander, or even to move more than an inch or two. Indeed, the very "sky" seemed to scrape the crown of her head.

A cracked whisper tickled the edges of her ear. "Mistress Valemont. Claudia. Psst, are ye a'right?"

Hands reached out from the darkness to whisk the cloth from her face. Squinting, Claudia found herself nose to nose with Luicas. She could just make out the whites of his eyes floating within the frame of his frightened face.

"Luicas, did they hang you, too?"

"Wheesht!" He clamped a clammy hand over her mouth. "D'ye want them tae hear us?"

Dizziness waved through her as she caught a flash of steel, the terror sending her stomach somersaulting. Fighting the sensation, she managed to move her head in a shake and he took his hand away.

The dagger's blade sliced through the bindings at her wrists. Freed, Claudia reached up to touch the stinging flesh banding her throat. Never before had pain been so welcome, for it meant she was alive. "I am not dead?"

He snorted. "No at the moment but ye will be, and me along wi' ye, if we dinna get ye out o' here and quick." He set to work on the rope hobbling her ankles.

Eyes adjusting to the darkness, she saw her landing place for what it was, a brick pit amply lined with straw. The noose lay in a harmless coil in her lap. Picking it up, she felt along the frayed edges.

I'm verra precise.

And it was then that she understood. The rope had been cut through partway. Subjected to her body's weight and that of the sandbags strapped to her feet, it must have snapped just as she dropped from view.

Luicas's whisper, edgy with tension, sliced through her amazement. "There's a wee door at the back for drawing out the bodies. It lets out into the basement o' the bridewell. We'll have tae crawl through one at a time and then make for the woods. There's horses saddled and waiting in the stand o' trees beyond the tollbooth gate."

She gave a quick nod. "*Oui,* but what of Jack? When it is discovered that I am missing . . ."

Not meeting her gaze, he answered, "He'll meet up wi' us at the border. Now come along, mistress, we've nay time tae waste, and Master'll have my cods on a spit if I let ye come tae harm again."

Three hours of hard riding brought them to the taproom of a public house not far from Lockerbie. Luicas had suggested they stop to refresh the horses and themselves, and Claudia had readily agreed. So far in the nearly two hours since they'd arrived, no pursuers had presented themselves but then neither had Jack. With luck, their respite would afford him time to catch up. But knowing him to be a seasoned horseman, Claudia couldn't help thinking he should have overtaken them ere now.

She turned to Luicas and asked yet again, "You are certain he knows our direction?"

He lanced her a look of weary patience. "Aye, mistress, 'twas the master himself who mapped our route and bade me halt here." His voice was steady but his usually rosy complexion was pale beneath the windburn, and the shadows carved beneath his dulled eyes suddenly made him seem far older than his fifteen years.

He is worried for Jack, Claudia thought, and felt the light meal she'd just taken weigh on her stomach like a stone.

She pulled the hood of her cloak low over her brow and kept to her stool in the corner while Luicas went to bespeak her a room, for at Jack's direction, they were to rest by day and travel by night, at least until they crossed the border into England. It was the middle of the week and late afternoon. The few patrons huddled about the hearth were too busy minding their trenchers and pints to pay the newcomers more than a passing glance. The two barmaids lounging on either side of a yet to be spiled cask showed even less interest. Watching the one yawning openly reminded Claudia of how very tired she was. It suddenly seemed a monumental task to support her heavy head and so she let it fall forward, the barmaids' conversation filling her head like the droning of insects.

"A hangman tae be hangit? Och, but that's rich."

Claudia snapped up her head. Heedless of her hood falling back, she cocked both ears to listen.

"Aye, I had it no an hour before from my cousin who had it from her husband's braither's wife's braither—Ned's a coachman and just down from Selkirk—that he helped a prisoner tae escape, a French lassie."

Claudia's every nerve cried out to her to leap up from her bench and question them, but she kept her seat, scooting to the very edge to better hear.

"'Tis said they were lovers. A hard price tae pay for dippin' his cock in French cream, I'd say."

They shared a chuckle, then the first woman asked, "Any word on the whereabouts o' the Frog bitch?"

Her friend shook her greasy head. "She disappeared sure as she dropped off the face o' the earth."

"Good riddance tae bad rubbish, I always say, though more's the pity she couldna ha' gone missin' before she brought the puir man sae low."

"Aye, and 'tis said he's a looker, too. Big strappin' fellow with red hair. If I'd had the chance, I'd ha' showed 'im Scotland can give as good as France any day—nay, better."

"Ah well, 'tis past regretting now," said the other around a sigh that froze the blood in Claudia's veins. "His cock and the rest o' him will be food for worms soon as they can find another hangman tae do the job."

By the time Luicas returned, fear had leached through Claudia's shock. Bolting up from her seat, heedless of who might be watching, she grabbed his thin shoulders and started steering them both toward the door. "He meant to take my place on the scaffold all along, is it not so? Is it not so!"

Tears welling, he managed a nod. "Aye, but he made me swear no tae tell ye for fear ye'd turn back."

Shoving him away, she started outside.

Catching up to her, he whispered, "Dinna do it, mistress. They'll only hang the both o' ye."

"Calm yourself, Luicas, we will not be returning to Selkirk." The boy's features relaxed into a look of near relief, which Claudia knew would be short-lived. "We will go to Linlithgow—to Aberdaire Castle."

They rode for two days, stopping only to trade their horses for fresh ones and to pay the tolls along the way from the dwindling stock of coins Jack had given Luicas. Filthy, saddle sore, and dizzy with fatigue, Claudia stood alone on the castle steps, having left Luicas in charge of the horses, which the groom had hesitated to take.

The two footmen posted inside the vaulted doorway she recalled from before but, judging from their blank stares, she guessed they did not recognize her, confirming that she looked at least as bad as she felt—perhaps worse.

As she approached the entrance, the taller of the two stepped forward. "If ye're lookin' for work, servants' entrance is 'round the back."

Lifting her chin and staring him down as though her face and clothing weren't encrusted with grime, she said, "I am Lady Claudia, His Lordship's daughter. And if you do not open this door at once and admit me, I will make very certain that you both live to regret it."

The brows beneath the powdered perukes lifted and their flat gazes sharpened in recognition. "Christ," exclaimed the taller of the two, "it is her."

His companion shot out an elbow and knifed him in the side. "Shut up, ye wee idjut, and get that door."

Lump in her throat as the doors groaned open, Claudia couldn't help but recall the very first time she'd stood on that threshold. Jack had been with her then and thinking of what he would say if he were here now, she paused before entering.

"Once they have cooled down, our horses will require water and food, as will the boy. See that he is taken to the kitchen and given refreshment at once." And with that, she swept past them.

The earl's butler, MacDuff, greeted her inside the great hall. Sangfroid slipping, he stared at her, mouth agape. "Lady Claudia!"

She answered with a quick nod. "Lord Aberdaire, he is in residence?"

He inclined his head. "Aye, milady, in the solar. As soon as you've bathed, I'll—"

"Now," she broke in, already pushing past him.

The earl was indeed within the solar, open shears in hand, bending over a hothouse rosebush, when MacDuff led her to the doorway.

"My lord," Claudia said, not waiting for MacDuff to announce her. She stepped inside, schooling herself not to think about the last time she had seen them, taunting her from the edge of her bed.

Lord Aberdaire looked up from the rosebush he'd been clipping and his features froze. "So you're back," he said, then punctuated the statement with a sharp snap of the shears.

The felled limb, rosebud and all, dropped onto the parquet tiles. Silver-blue gaze fixed on Claudia, Aberdaire set the shears down upon the silver tray that the attendant footman held out.

"Leave us," he said, a directive that for once encompassed MacDuff, too.

By mutual consent they waited until both butler and footman had bowed themselves out of the room and the door had closed on silent hinges.

Only then did the earl say, "Why have you come back?"

Knowing there was nothing to be gained by subterfuge, Claudia met his ice blue gaze and answered, "Jack, Monsieur Campbell, he is to be executed."

"For the crime of abduction, or has he committed yet another felonious act since stealing you away?"

Claudia's gloveless hands, hidden in the folds of her cloak, balled into fists. "Jack has committed no crime. I went with him of my own free will, as you must know. I was sentenced to hang, and he arranged for my escape. Now they mean to hang him in my place."

"And I suppose you've come to beg me to intervene on his behalf?" The expression on his face reflected just how unlikely an outcome that would be.

Claudia could almost hear Jack's voice whisper in her ear, *Have courage, lass, and all will be well.* Yes, she would have courage, for Jack's sake as well as her own, and God help them both.

She squared her aching shoulders and lifted her chin. "It is not to beg that I have come, my lord, but to bargain."

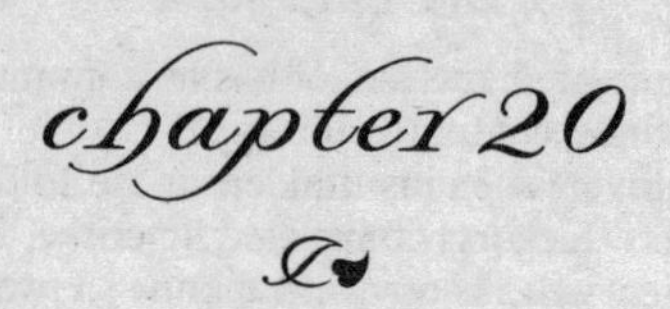

How like a Winter hath my absence been
From thee, the pleasure of the fleeting year!
What freezings have I felt, what dark days seen,
What old December's bareness everywhere!

—William Shakespeare, Sonnet 12

The *sliding back of his cell's window hatch had Jack jerking* his head from the pillow of his palms. Squinting at the sudden brightness, he rose from his seat on the bench to see Wallis's broad forehead and two beady eyes framed in the Judas hole.

"Supper already, Wallis? Och, man, but you're sure to be spoiling me. I'm still stuffed from that grand dinner you served up the last time."

It was a standing joke between them, for "dinner," indeed all Jack's meals, consisted of one bare oatcake and a pint of watered-down ale. The food baskets that Milread and Dorcas MacGregor had brought him had been confiscated shortly after his visitors left. The saving grace was that the irons shackling his wrists to the stone wall permitted only the sparest of movements, making it impossible to work up much of an appetite. Unfortunately what the short chains also wouldn't permit was for him to lie down comfortably. Sleep, when it came at all, did so in small, random snatches, but he coveted those escapes from reality, brief as they were, for it was in his dreams that Claudia came to him.

Claudia, lovely face flushed, catching at his hands for him to dance with her. Claudia, black hair whipping about her shoulders as she urged the mare faster still. Claudia, eyes tender and smile soft, as she opened her arms for him to come to her that very first time. That she was free and safe—nothing else mattered, he told himself. When his time came, as it must soon do, he would hold the memory of that sweet countenance in his mind's eye and die if not a happy man then at least one with few regrets. For as Master Shakespeare had writ, " 'Tis better to have loved and lost then never to have loved at all." And Jack had loved Claudia and loved her well. He loved her still.

But in a few more days it would all be over, for surely they'd have the hangman down from Edinburgh any time now. Jack's only remaining hope was that whomever they brought wasna a ham-handed bungler but someone who'd turn him off proper and clean—he deserved that much, he thought.

Wallis's voice called his rambling thoughts back to the present. " 'Tis your lucky day, Campbell, for ye're free tae go."

For the first time in five days, or was it six, Jack allowed himself to feel well and truly annoyed. "Verra funny, Wallis, but you'll have to pardon me if I'm too tired to play your little game."

"It's nay game, Jacko."

Jack looked up sharply. Callum's voice had replaced Willis's as had his brow and narrowed eyes in the window. "What the devil—"

"It seems ye've friends in high places, Jacko. The bleedin' earl of Aberdaire saw fit tae intervene on your behalf, and now the charges agin ye've been dropped."

For a long moment, shock held Jack still, for Claudia's father was the last person he'd expect to help him.

He was still asking himself why when Callum's voice cut in on his thoughts. "Tender braither that I am, I've come tae give ye a proper sendoff. Me and a few o' the lads."

Before Jack could answer, the cell door groaned back and Callum and his cronies crowded inside, their lanterns held high to reveal eyes burning bright with anticipation. "His hands are hobbled a'ready. Verra convenient," Callum remarked, holding his own lantern to shine full on Jack's face. "Verra convenient indeed."

The drawing room door closed, signaling the exit of Claudia's "chaperone," although the earl's housekeeper, Mistress Dunlevy, really served as more of a guard than a duenna. But as much as Claudia had come to detest the woman over the past week, at the moment she was honestly sorry to see her go. For the door barely had met its frame when, wedged into the cushion next to her, Lord Haversham reached for her knee.

Claudia shoved his hand away and scooted to the far end of the divan. "You are forward, sir."

The viscount favored her with a broad smile. The latter was nothing short of a mistake for it served to emphasize yet another of His Lordship's unfortunate features: large uneven teeth set into a generous expanse of puffy bleeding gums. But as unappealing as she found that smile, indeed all of him, to be, the very worst were his eyes. Small, squared, and squinted, they reminded her of a sheep, as did his frequent bleating laugh.

"And how, fair lady, might I be otherwise when I am confronted with such celestial beauty as to give fair Venus cause for envy were she to, ah . . . that is to say . . ."

"Were she a living person and not a mythological deity?" Claudia suggested gamely.

"Ah, wit as well as loveliness. You are a rare treasure, my sweet, and how eager I am to unwrap your secrets in a sennight's time," he added with a wiggle of his single eyebrow.

Despite the warmth from the fire, his thinly veiled reference to their wedding—and more to the point, wedding *night*—drew a shudder from Claudia. In a week's time, six more days to be precise, Viscount Haversham would own her just as surely as he owned his horse or the calf pads strapped beneath his silk hose, or the silly high-heeled pumps he favored. He would exercise a husband's right to touch her, to demand that she touch him. Claudia had yet to contemplate either eventuality without having the express urge to retch—or flee.

Already on her feet, she said, "I am afraid I must take my leave of you, my lord, for suddenly I do not feel at all well."

Haversham dutifully rose to stand beside her. "My lady, I shall count the minutes until I next find myself in your sweet presence." Taking her hand, though she hadn't offered it, he slathered a wet kiss on the top, the little suckling noises he made putting her in mind of yet another barnyard beast—this time, a pig.

"Perhaps you would do better to count in hours," she said

and, snatching her hand away, rounded the tea cart and made a rush on the door.

Passing through it into the hallway, she nearly collided with Lord Aberdaire on his way inside.

"Claudia, where are you haring off to? I specifically told Mistress Dunlevy to leave you and Lord Haversham alone."

"I have a headache," she answered automatically though it was far from a lie.

His thin lips twisted in a scowl. "Practicing to be a wife already, eh? Well, go on with you, then. Only see you show a civil face to your bridegroom tonight at supper."

Biting back the sharp retort that a free Claudia would have given, she nodded and turned toward the staircase and the respite of her room.

One more week and then good riddance! Aberdaire expelled a heavy sigh and then wheeled himself inside the drawing room where a scowling Haversham was wearing holes in the Turkey carpet, a glass of brandy held in one ring-adorned hand.

Sighting the earl, he exclaimed, "The chit is cold, *cold* I tell you."

Drawing up on him, Aberdaire shook his head. "Dinna be an ass, Haversham. She's a bastard and half French. If she's even half the whore her mother was, you'll be getting the best of the bargain." At Haversham's raised brow, he elaborated, "You'll have to get an heir off her one way or the other. Who knows, but you may find my little Claudia so bold and buxom in bed that you can send that whey-faced mistress of yours packing and save yourself the cost of her keeping."

Looking somewhat mollified, Haversham finished off the rest of his brandy and then went to the sideboard to pour himself another. Piggy face reflected in the pier glass, he said, "Then I trust you've no objection to my sampling the wares?"

Aberdaire hesitated. It was an open secret that Haversham beat his mistress and that when in London was a frequent visitor to Mother Damnable's, a nasty Covent Garden brothel that catered to clients whose tastes ran to flagellation and defloration—not that the earl need fret that Claudia's maidenhead was at risk.

He shrugged. "I suppose there's no harm in a nibble or two of forbidden fruit. Only mind you leave no marks, Haversham, at least not where they're liable to show. I'll no stand for having the validity of this marriage called into question by accusations that she's been coerced."

"Just so." Excitement flushed Haversham's baby cheeks; turning away from the mirror, he sent the earl a gummy grin. "I'll want to save some surprises for the wedding night, won't I?"

Poor Claudia, Aberdaire thought, gaze settling on his future son-in-law's dimpled hands, the thick fingers grasping the brandy snifter edged with long, sharp-looking nails. The chit might be a troublesome baggage with a serpent's tongue and a will like Damascus steel, but given what her future held, Aberdaire almost felt sorry for her.

Almost.

M*ilread stepped back from her "patient" and shook her* head. "Two ribs broken, maybe three."

Sweating with the strain of holding his arms away from his battered sides, Jack bit back an oath. "Just bind them, will you?" Every breath brought him to his chair's edge, but he refused to give in.

Milread vented a heavy sigh then bent to her task of winding the strip of cloth tight about his torso. "'Tis a fool's errand, Jack," she said, coming around to the front of him to tie the ends into a neat knot. "One man canna take on an army."

Grateful to be able to lower his arms, he eased himself back against the slatted chair. "Aberdaire hasna an army, only a handful of nincompoops in satin breeches and powdered periwigs."

"Be that as it may, ye're still only one."

"I was only one before, and I got her out then."

The breath he drew to brace himself before standing proved to be a mistake and one that cost him dearly. Blades of piercing pain stabbed his sides, bringing fresh sweat breaking out on his forehead. Biting back a wince, he leaned a hand on either chair arm and hauled himself up, the room seesawing as he gained his feet.

Milread rushed to lend him her arm and to his shame he was obliged to lean heavily on it. "Aye, that ye did," she said once he'd nodded that the dizziness had passed, "but this time they'll be on their guard—and you weak as a kitten. How ye'll even manage tae keep your seat long enough tae ride out o' this inn yard let alone forty odd miles is anyone's guess."

"I'll manage." His movements as stiff and mechanical as those of a wind-up toy, he released her arm and reached for his shirt, hanging over the back of the chair.

Milread had managed to soak out the worst of the bloodstains though there was no helping that the one sleeve had a long rent down the side. He'd buy a new shirt in Linlithgow, he supposed; until then, he'd keep his coat on.

Taking pity on him, she stepped behind to help him on with it, feeding his arm through the sleeve. In a suspiciously quavering voice she said, "If ye should, uh, happen upon Luicas whilst ye're in Linlithgow, will ye do something for me?"

"Aye, anything. You've only to ask it," he said, grinding his teeth as she helped to guide his other arm through the sleeve.

"Tell him I . . . love him and that . . . that I want him tae come home."

Slowly he turned about and reached out to chuck her chin. "I will, lass. And dinna look so downcast, for I mean to bring the both of them back safe—or die in the trying."

S*eated on the edge of his unmade cot, Callum swiped the* torn knuckles of his right across the stream of snot leaking like blood from his left nostril. He'd thought that the bashing they'd given Jacko in the tollbooth cell might finally curb his craving for revenge but like a child nibbling at sweets, it had only sated his appetite for the time.

Bruised and battered though Jacko was, in time his heart like his body would heal and he would be whole again. And so it wasna enough, no nearly. Turning his tear-swollen eyes up to the drooping ceiling, Callum allowed he wanted more. He wanted it all.

Broken—Callum would settle for nothing less.

I*t was late afternoon the following day when Jack rode* Beelzebub into the main courtyard of Aberdaire Castle. He'd taken a room at an inn in town but had halted there only long enough to bathe his face, comb his hair, and put on the fresh shirt he'd bought to replace his ruined one. Not that he thought for a moment that Claudia would fault him for his appearance but, above all, he mustn't let Aberdaire or his bully of a butler see just how badly beaten he really was.

Everything hurt. It hurt to breathe. It hurt to hold off breathing. Yesterday he'd sneezed and he'd been sure his busted ribs would explode and join the little fractured stars swirling before his eyes. Even his jaws ached from the effort of clenching them against the pain.

Grateful for the whiskey Milread had insisted he carry with him, he took the flask from his pocket and drew a small sip to gird himself for tackling the task of dismounting. The liquor scored his throat but it would, he kent, lessen the pain in his limbs and trunk. But no spirit, no matter how strong, could begin to numb the raw, renting anguish he'd felt ever since that afternoon when he'd learned the terrible news. Claudia was to wed.

After taking another measured swallow, he capped the flask and tucked it back inside his pocket. Thus fortified, he braced himself to climb down, hoping he might do so without falling flat on his face as he had earlier. Fortunately this time he navigated the distance from saddle to cobblestones and then from drive to stone steps without incident. Sliding one hand along the baluster, he gained the portico, staggering past the two startled footmen to enter.

"Where is she?" he demanded of the butler once he'd gained the great hall.

"The Lady Claudia is not at home to you nor are you welcome here." MacDuff, Jack noted with some relish, still sported a small bandage across the bridge of his nose, which, when last they met, Jack had busted. "Now kindly take your leave."

Voice raised in the hope that, wherever she was, Claudia might hear him, Jack said, "I'm no leaving, kindly or otherwise, until I've seen her."

Claudia was hiding out in her room from Lord Haversham and making a show of working on her needlecraft under the gimlet gaze of Mistress Dunlevy when she heard raised male voices funneling up from the great hall below. Jack? Even as she told herself her ears must be deceiving her, she threw aside her embroidery and shot from her chair.

She was out the bedchamber door and haring down the hall to the curved stone stairs, the portly housekeeper huffing to keep up. But no, her hearing hadn't played tricks on her for there he was: Jack, her Jack, his broad back to her as he argued with MacDuff. Caution, indeed even the terms of the bargain she'd struck to gain his release were for the moment forgotten in the onslaught of pure joy rushing her at the sight of him. She vaulted from the stair landing and hurried toward him, the heavy skirts of her crimson brocade the only thing keeping her from breaking into a full, undignified run.

"Jack," she said, not able to contain herself even as the sense struck her that something with him wasn't quite right.

Slowly, as if overnight he'd reached the age of Peadair or Pol, he turned to her. The sight of his face caused to her freeze in midstep, the smile slipping from her lips. Bruises in variegated shades of green, purple, and plum stained the left side of his face. The eye above was swollen shut; his mouth was swollen, too, the bottom lip split in several places.

"Jack, *mon Dieu,* what has happened to you?" Glimpsing the butler's watchful gaze, she said, "You should not have come."

He started toward her, gait stiff and none too steady. "So I've been told but now that I have is there somewhere we may be private?"

She glanced to MacDuff and then the housekeeper, who'd just gained the hall and was marching toward them. "Leave us," she said, a directive meant to encompass them both.

MacDuff's icy gaze settled on her face. "Milady, are you certain that is wise?"

Holding back a shiver, she lifted her chin to regard him. "But of course. Surely you would not wish Monsieur Campbell to carry back tales that I am kept prisoner here?"

She punctuated the latter with a light laugh, but her warning was all too clear, for MacDuff inclined his head to Mistress Dunlevy, who shrugged and shuffled back toward the stairs.

"This way." MacDuff led them to a small sitting room of Tudor-style furnishings and traceried windows set just off the hall. "See you dinna overstay your welcome, Master Campbell," he said, then backed out, pointedly leaving the door ajar.

As soon as she judged the butler to be out of earshot, Claudia turned to face Jack. "You are free, are you not? They did set you free?" she asked in a low voice, fearful that his bruised face might mean he'd escaped instead.

"Aye, they did. And for that it seems I am in Lord Aberdaire's debt and"—he paused, gaze searching hers—"yours as well."

Schooling her voice to coolness, she said, "Ah well, a life for a life—we are as you say in English 'even' now. But, *mon Dieu,* what has happened to you?"

He shrugged, then immediately his features contorted as though even that small movement caused him great pain. "Since he couldna have the pleasure of seeing me hang, Callum brought his mates around to the tollbooth and gave me a proper sendoff."

"Oh, Jack." She waved him to a chair, a heavy brocade affair with gated legs, but he shook his head although he looked poised to drop at any minute.

"I stopped off in the town before coming here. At the inn, I heard you were to wed some Sassenach lordling. Is that true, Claudia?"

"Yes, Viscount Haversham, this Thursday next. It is to be a small ceremony in the castle chapel and then we will leave for London."

His bruised forehead bunched in a scowl. "Is this some manner of bargain you struck with Aberdaire so that he'd intercede on my behalf? If it is, you should ken I'll no have you selling yourself for my sake."

Recalling the part she'd sworn to play, she tried for a gay laugh but it came out brittle as old bones. "Selling myself? But I am sure I do not know what you mean."

"Do you love him, then?"

"Lord Haversham comes from one of the oldest families in England. I am told the title was conferred by the Conqueror himself. Given the circumstances of my birth, I count myself fortunate the viscount will have me."

One hand braced to his left side, he closed the distance between them. "That's no what I asked. I asked do you love him?"

She fisted her hands at her sides to keep from reaching for him. "You know that I do not."

He slowly raised his hand to touch her. Claudia knew she should move away and yet, weakling that she was, she held her place and let his rough, busted knuckles stroke down her burning cheek, even that slight contact sufficing to melt her resolve along with her knees.

Gaze on hers as his hand slid along the column of her neck, he asked, "Do you love *me?*"

Choking back a sob, she said, "What does it matter? We come from two different worlds, Jack. That we thought to be together in a world of our own making was a foolish dream, *chéri,* for outside of our hearts no such place exists." She bit her bottom lip, trying not to cry, and because she was weak, turned her face to press her lips into his wrist. "This must be *adieu.* Promise me, oh, promise me you will leave now and not come back."

"I willna." He reached for her again but this time she found the strength to back away so that his outstretched hand met with only air. "I'm staying at the Hawk and Dove on High Street. Every day, every night between now and Thursday next, I will wait for word from you."

She shook her head. "Then you will wait in vain, for I will not send for you."

Beneath the mask of bruises, his expression hardened. "Dinna be a fool, Claudia. If you go through with this marriage, you'll have sacrificed yourself, sacrificed *us,* for naught. Knowing what I do of your background and birth, of your recent history since coming to Scotland, do you really expect Aberdaire will let me live once you and Haversham tie the knot?"

She shook her head, panicked mind reeling. "If you leave, you will be safe. It must be so, it *must.* Go home, Jack. For both our sakes, go home and forget you ever knew me."

"Heed me, Claudia. That you love me and I you makes you mine more than any vows said before a priest. And so it willna matter a whit if you've a wedding ring upon your finger or no, for if you dinna send for me, make no mistake—I *will* come to claim you."

Heart in her throat, she turned to regard him for what must be the last time. "You are mistaken, *monsieur,*" she began, seizing on her fear for him to strike all traces of warmth from her voice. "I am fond of you, of course, but love . . ."

The betrayal in his eyes tore at her heart. Unable to bear it, she swept past him to the door. The kindest, safest thing she could do at this point would be to persuade him to hate her. And so on the threshold she turned back and prepared to deliver what would amount to the coup de grâce, the final, fatal blow.

"I am *une femme du monde,* a woman of the world, Jack. For

such as I, *la nuit, tous les chats sont gris.* At night, all the cats are gray."

From his study window, Aberdaire monitored the courtyard below where a stiff-legged Jack Campbell remounted his horse and then walked it back down the drive. Though he detested weakness in all its forms, it was fear that the earl hated most, and yet to himself he admitted that MacDuff's announcement of Campbell's impromptu appearance had shaken him and mightily. Why was it that the bothersome brute simply would not go away?

Frustrated, he brooded on possible ways and means of accomplishing Campbell's permanent disappearance but in the end discarded them all. MacDuff had made a hash of dispatching Gunn, such that the body had been found on the road bordering Aberdaire's property instead of buried as he'd directed. They'd been fortunate to arrange for a scapegoat to take the blame, but he'd told himself he must tread warily from thereon. This was rural Scotland after all and not London's East End. A second body turning up in as many months would be bound to draw suspicion.

Yet he'd kent enough of men and human nature in his nearly half century of living to recognize determination when he saw it. Jack Campbell was nothing if not determined and not for a moment did Aberdaire deceive himself into believing he meant to allow next Thursday's marriage ceremony to carry on.

He was still lost in grim contemplation when MacDuff's heavy knock sounded outside his study door.

"What the devil is it now?" he barked.

The butler came to the door but backed off from entering. "There is a . . . a person to see you, milord."

"Whoever it is, send him away."

A young dark-haired man of wiry build and shabby clothes insinuated himself inside. Christ, but MacDuff must be growing daft to be bringing tinkers into the castle and to his very study door at that!

"The tradesmen's entrance lies at the east gate," he snapped, and then started to turn his chair back to the window.

For the first time since entering, the young man spoke. "I'm no a tradesman, Your Lordship," he said, a thatch of greasy hair sliding over one deep-set eye, "though I have come t' offer ye my services."

Callum had followed Jack to Linlithgow, where he'd found the township abuzz with gossip about the impending marriage of the English Viscount Haversham to the earl of Aberdaire's French daughter, Lady Claudia. *Lady* Claudia. So the Frog scut was an earl's by-blow—he supposed that explained her hoity-toity ways.

As for what Jack was doing in Linlithgow, that was just as easily reckoned. The bitch had got him wound about her little finger and now that he'd had her he hadna the sense to move on to greener pastures—which suited Callum just fine.

"We're fully staffed at present but, if you wish, you may leave your name with MacDuff. Should a vacancy occur—"

Callum narrowed his gaze on the crippled man. He'd come too far to turn back now. "Och, but I'd hate tae have tae cool my heels in town, milord, for who knows but I might just let it slip out that 'til a fortnight ago, *Lady* Claudia was spending her days working in a tavern and her nights shagging my hangman braither."

Predictably Aberdaire wheeled about. Lean face ashen and features drawn tight, he demanded, "Who are you?"

From the doorway, the butler answered, "Allow me to present Master Callum McBride." He hesitated. "Jack Campbell's brother."

"Half-braither," Callum corrected, determined once and for all to step free from Jack's shadow.

The earl's silvery-blue gaze slipped over him and Callum forced his shoulders back from their usual slump. "Well, Master McBride, you've the Devil's own nerve to strong-arm your way inside my castle and then attempt to blackmail me. But fortunately for you I admire boldness when I see it. What I dinna admire is stupidity. Your actions, while ill conceived, have just enough of the former to interest me. What service is it you propose to render me?"

Callum licked his lips, schooling himself to answer slowly, carefully, for he'd never have another such chance. "If I ken Jack, and believe me, Your Lordship, I do, he'll die before he sees *Lady* Claudia wedded tae another. He'll die, d'ye ken me?"

"Only too well. I take it you're offering to hasten that happy event?"

"Aye, that I am—for a price." He took a gulp of air, girding himself before blurting out, "One thousand pounds, and ye need ne'er trouble yerself about Jack Campbell again."

With such a sum, Callum could live like a king. He could live anywhere. Since Tam's suicide, the gossip had made the rounds, and the village where he'd meant to live and die now felt more like a prison than a home.

Thanks to Jack. Always Jack.

And so even more than he wanted the money, he wanted his revenge—and this time he would have it. The very best part, the pearl beyond a price, would be witnessing the look on his half brother's face just before he fell down dead at Callum's feet. If he could manage to make him beg and squirm a bit before, so much the better.

The earl's voice called him from his thoughts. "That's a great deal of money, Master McBride."

Callum snorted. "Is it now?" Pointedly he looked about the study, taking in the fine velvet drapery, the gilt-trimmed furniture, the gold and silver that seemed to fire and flash from every conceivable corner. "For some, milord, but no so great a sum for others, aye? And then again 'tis a verra great service I mean tae be rendering ye."

The earl continued to deliberate. Watching him lace and unlace his long-fingered hands, Callum felt his heart drum and his bowels tighten for suddenly it seemed as if the hopes of a lifetime, *his* lifetime, were pinned on Aberdaire's next few words.

"It's a verra tempting proposition you're offering. Tempting indeed."

"Dinna toy wi' me, man." Nerves strung taut as wire, Callum advanced, but the butler's brawny hold on his arm pulled him back. Shrugging free, he demanded, "Yeah or nay, which is it tae be?"

Gaze glittering, the earl regarded Callum over his tented hands. "I will consider all that you have said and should I elect to accept your *services,* MacDuff will contact you in a day or two."

"I'll have my answer now, I will—"

"Do you dare give an ultimatum to me, you flea-bitten whoreson." Though chair-bound, Aberdaire seemed to gain in height as, shoulders squared, he wheeled himself forward. "Why, if I were of a mind, I could have MacDuff here make *you* disappear, so I'd advise you to hold your tongue about my daughter's past liaison with Campbell and await my decision."

"But—"

"This interview is concluded, McBride. MacDuff, show him the way out. And mind this time it's through a *back* door."

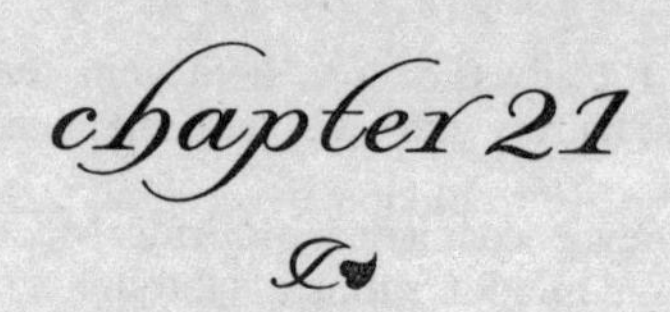

Ae fond kiss, and then we sever;
Ae fareweel, alas, for ever!
Deep in heart-wrung tears I'll pledge thee,
Warring sighs and groans I'll wage thee!

—Robert Burns, *Ae Fond Kiss*

Claudia *flattened her back to the wall and willed her body* to stop shaking. She'd been on her way to the library in the west wing, hoping a book might carry her away from her troubles if only for a while, when voices coming from Aberdaire's study had stalled her. Hearing only MacDuff and the earl, she'd started to pass on when a third voice, Callum MacBride's voice, found its way to her ear: "One thousand pounds, and ye need ne'er trouble yerself about Jack Campbell again."

Jack's earlier warning came back to her, drawing yet another shudder. *Do you really expect Aberdaire will let me live once you and Haversham tie the knot?*

Men such as Phillippe had been, as the earl was, invariably hired underlings to carry out their dirty deeds. And now it seemed that Aberdaire had found a way to turn the enmity between the two brothers to his advantage.

Turning back down the hall before she might be discovered, she avowed there was no help for it. As soon as she could, she must find a way to warn Jack.

The *smart rap outside Jack's door was as unwelcome as the* late morning sun glaring through the wavy glass panes of his chamber's window. Both reminded him that his head ached, his body ached—his *heart* ached. Barring having Claudia back in his arms and life, he wanted nothing so much as to fade into a sweet cloud of black oblivion, to succumb to the numbing forgetfulness of sleep.

Sprawled on his back on the bed, he called out, "Go away or come in if ye must. It's no locked though I dinna want for anything save clean water for washing."

The door scraped open. "It is late to be abed still, is it not?"

He whipped his head about on the pillow to see not the chambermaid but Claudia standing in the doorway. She looked very smart in a velvet riding habit of peacock blue and matching cape with epaulets trimmed in gold braid, her military-style hat set at a jaunty angle atop her blue-black curls.

Forgetting his bound ribs, he started up. "You've come." Sucking in his breath against the pain, he swung his legs over the side of the bed. "Och, but I prayed—"

"I can stay only a moment," she said and Jack felt his fledgling happiness deflate like a balloon on the receiving end of a hatpin. *"Mon Dieu,"* she exclaimed, her gaze slipping over his bare chest, still bound with Milread's makeshift bandage, "all this, it is Callum's doing?"

He dragged his hungry gaze away from the vision in blue to glance down at himself. Though by now he was accustomed to the sight of his bandaged ribs and purpled flesh, Claudia was not. Pride bade him say, "He had help, no to mention I was chained to a wall at the time." He patted the vacant edge of mattress beside him and, when she still kept by the door, said, "Bruises and cracked ribs are no catching, mind."

She sent him a look that assured him he was being a perfect idiot and then started toward the bed. Sitting beside him, she busied herself with arranging her skirts even as she said, "I am sorry you were hurt."

He wanted to tell her he'd gladly brave hellfire and brimstone for her sake, let alone men's fists, but instead he said only, "You've no come only to admire my beauty marks, I think."

Slowly she nodded. "Callum, he is in Linlithgow. He arrived at the castle not long after you left, and I . . . I overheard him speaking with the earl and MacDuff." She shifted to regard him, eyes wide and brimming with entreaty. "Oh, Jack, he means to kill you."

Jack answered with a sharp laugh. "It wouldna be the first time."

"But this time it will be at the earl's bidding. Oh, Jack, if you stay, I fear that this time he will succeed."

"I'm no going anywhere."

"But you must." She pushed at his arm then dissolved into apologies when he winced. "Go away, *chéri,* leave at once. Tonight, no better yet, leave now. And take Luicas with you."

"So Luicas is still in Linlithgow? I promised Milread I'd find him and bring him safe away." *Along with you.*

She nodded. "After what happened, he was too ashamed to face you and too afraid of Callum to return. He took a position in the stable at the Purple Mouse. It is an inn much like this one and just down from the Cross."

Curious suddenly, he asked, "How is it you managed to come here?"

"I persuaded Lord Haversham to bring me into town." Violet eyes rolled as she admitted, "He thinks I am still at the milliner's trying to decide between the dunstable straw bonnet with ostrich feathers and the scarlet velvet with the blond braiding. But at any moment he may grow impatient and discover me gone."

"You could have sent word to Luicas and had him warn me and yet you didna, you came yourself. Why, Claudia, why did you come?"

She gazed up at him, eyes moist and mouth trembling. "Perhaps because I am weak. Perhaps because I wanted to make sure for myself that you were all right, that your wounds were not serious." She drew a shaky breath. "Perhaps because after the other day, I could not bear to think that we would part forever with words of anger."

"If I have my way, we'll no part at all."

"Oh, Jack."

She started to turn away but, although it cost him, he reached out to stay her.

"Jack, do not—"

"Hush, *mo chride.* Be still." *Be mine.* He stroked the curve of her quivering bottom lip, the delicate juncture of her cheek and jaw, the pulse striking against the side of her throat. "Tell me, *mo chride,*" he said, his thumb playing in the blood-warmed hollow of her throat, "how is it that I've slept alone all my life and yet now I canna so much as close my eyes in peace without you beside me?"

She raked her teeth over her bottom lip; the gloved hand that rested on the mattress between them drew into a tight little fist. "Jack, please, *please* do not say such things. And do not call me by that . . . that name."

"Dinna call you 'my heart' even though that's what you are?" he whispered, retracing the path, this time with his lips, and reaching up to cup her breast through the layers of fabric. "And then I suppose I also may no say that battered and fevered though I am, and paining in places I canna even begin to name, all I can think of right now is how much I want to lay you down upon this bed and make love to you? Are these the things on which you'd have me hold silent?"

She turned her face to his, eyes large and luminous and beseeching. "Yes. Yes!" He took his hand from her breast and she rose. "I must leave. I dare not stay longer."

He came up beside her and started the search for his shirt. "Your Sassenach lordling must be daft to let you roam the streets without escort." Finding it, he slung it over his shoulder and started after her, already halfway to the door. "At least let me see you safely back."

On the threshold, she shook her head. "*Non,* it will be bad enough if I am seen coming from here, but if I am alone at least I may say I lost my way. *Adieu, chéri.*" Mouth trembling, she turned to go.

"Claudia?" She faced around, and it was then that he saw she was crying. "When you walk into the chapel on Thursday to take your vows before God and man and priest . . ." He took a deep breath and scarcely noticed the pain knifing through his sides for his heart's pain was so very much greater. "When you do so, I want you to mind one thing. Mind that I love you."

Tears filming her eyes, she nodded and then hurried out into the hallway before she might weaken and turn back. "I love you, too," she whispered but by then she was out the inn's main door and stepping onto the cobbled High Street. By the time the milliner's shop came into view, the tears were flooding fast and furious down her cheeks, causing the bustling street to appear awash in gray, not sunny and clear. She was halfway to her destination when she sighted Lord Haversham just ahead disembarking from his phaeton. *Zut, alors* but he was walking her way. If he sighted her coming from the opposite direction, from the inn, he was bound to wonder why, perhaps even remark upon it to the earl. Sweat filmed her forehead, dampened her underarms. *Think, Claudia, think!* Casting her gaze about, she saw that the tea shop she was coming up on had an alley running along one side. She darted a quick glance about and then ducked inside. Pulling in her skirts, she crouched behind a beer barrel just as Haversham passed, high heels clicking on the cobbles in time with the tip of his ivory-handled walking stick. She waited a moment more and then started out from her hiding place.

Behind her, a hard hand clamped over her mouth. Another caught her about the waist, pulling her against a spare, sinewy form. Struggling, her screams muffled, she caught the reek of whiskey as a hot mouth closed over the outside of her ear. "Dinna be in such a rush . . . *Lady* Claudia."

The ransom note, penned in Claudia's flawless, flourishing strokes, found its way to Lord Aberdaire that night by way of a large stone flying through the leaded glass panes of a lower-story window. The missile missed Lord Haversham's head by bare inches, not that the viscount would have noticed if it had struck. Since he'd returned hours before to give his stammering report of how his betrothed had gone missing somewhere between the millinery shop and the bookbinder, he'd downed glass after glass of brandy. He'd been unconscious for nigh on an hour, sprawled across the velvet-covered settee, unlaced belly rising and falling with each expelled snore.

MacDuff stepped forward and bent to untie the note from its wrapping of string. "May I, milord?" but Aberdaire was already nodding for him to go on. Looking up from the oily scrap of paper, he said, "It seems Lady Claudia has been kidnapped."

Aberdaire shook his fist. "Campbell, that devil. Seeking to feather his nest at my expense and with my daughter, nay less. I should have had you kill him when we had the chance."

MacDuff shook his head. "Not Campbell but McBride, milord. He demands the sum of one thousand pounds by midnight and says that none other than Campbell is to bring it to him."

Aberdaire raked a hand through his hair. "Perhaps Campbell and McBride are in league together after all. Do you suppose their show of enmity could have been contrived?"

MacDuff hesitated before answering, "I suppose it is possible, milord."

Abderdaire vented a weary sigh. Since his returning to Scotland nothing, absolutely nothing, had gone as he'd planned. "One thousand pounds. As if I have that kind of blunt setting about. Has the fool never heard of banks?" Subsiding back into his chair, he asked, "Does he say where the money's to be left?"

"The abandoned cottage on the south bank of the loch."

Aberdaire inclined his head. "Do what you must."

"N*o much longer now," Callum said and cinched the rope* binding Claudia's wrists to the post even tighter. "And I'll have Jacko and the money both. And your dear da the earl will be ruing the day he ever bade me take myself tae the tradesman's entrance, let alone await his pleasure. Och, but I'll have ye, too." Crouching down beside her, he grabbed her face in a pinching grip and yanked it up to his. "And whatever will I do wi' ye, d'ye think?"

"Och, Callum, but we hav'na time for that." Wallis, the warder from Selkirk, rose from the dust-covered bench where he'd been priming his pistol.

Claudia had just finished penning the ransom note when Callum's crony had arrived at the cottage. When she'd asked for the pen and paper back under the pretense of having left off a line, Callum had grown suspicious and snatched the writing materials away.

Coming over to them, Wallis announced, "'Tis midnight a'most."

Tears of frustration stung her eyes. In a short while, Jack would be walking into an ambush and there wasn't a blessed thing she could do to warn him.

Scowling, Callum released Claudia's face. "Is it now? Then ye'd better take position outside, hadna ye?"

Starting toward his hiding place, Wallis turned back to whisper, "Wheesht, someone's coming down the path outside."

Callum nodded. Turning back to Claudia, he replaced the gag in her mouth and then started up. Watching him slip into the shadows, she heard the click of a pistol hammer being cocked and, futile though it was, she worked her stinging wrists that much harder against the rope.

The cottage door opened to reveal a large hooded figure limned by moonlight and carrying a satchel. Tall, Claudia thought, but was he tall enough to be Jack? And the stance, slightly hunched, was not Jack's either but then perhaps he held himself thus because of his injuries? Sagging against the post, she started to pray even as the satchel thudded at her feet.

Callum sprang from his hiding place into the open. "Ye took long enough, Jacko." A flare of light streaked across the narrow room, and Claudia ducked as the bullet whizzed over her head.

The figure in the doorway leapt lithely to one side so that Callum's bullet found purchase in the plaster wall beyond his shoulder.

"Jesus, Jacko!" Callum exclaimed when the fired-upon man drew his own weapon from beneath the cape's folds. He dropped his useless pistol and backed away.

From across the room, it was MacDuff's voice that called out, "I'm afraid you've the wrong man, Master McBride, but then, 'tis the last mistake you'll ever make." A primed pistol held in one steady hand, he used his other to push back his hood. His opaque gaze flickered over Claudia for the barest instant before he shifted it back to Callum.

Hands held high, Callum cried, "Ye canna kill me, ye canna."

"Canna I? Ye'll no be the first I've offed though at least the courier took his bullet like a man, no a sniveling bairn." He cocked the flintlock and took aim. "Courage, man, we canna die but once."

Behind MacDuff, Wallis's stocky silhouette slipped from the opposite corner. Silent as a cat, he slipped behind MacDuff and brought the butt of his pistol crashing down at the back of the butler's head.

MacDuff staggered forward and then folded to the floor, the impact nearly knocking over the lantern at Claudia's feet.

Callum dropped to his knees, pawing at the satchel. "Straw! Bluidy hell, 'tis filled with straw."

Coming up beside him, Wallis bent to examine the wicked gash at the back of the butler's head. "Christ, I dinna mean tae kill him. I didna . . . did I?"

Shoving the satchel aside, Callum regarded the unconscious

man. MacDuff's pistol, loaded and ready to fire, lay on the ground beside him. Heart pounding, Claudia watched him pick it up and press the barrel to the butler's temple. She squeezed her eyes shut even as Callum squeezed back on the trigger and the pistol discharged.

Grinning up into Wallis's horrified face through a wreath of smoke, Callum chuckled. "Nay, Wallis, ye didna kill him. *I* did."

*When MacDuff still had not returned by breakfast the fol*lowing morning, Aberdaire kent he had to face the cold, hard facts. His trusted MacDuff had failed him and like as not was even now dead. Later, when he had leisure to reflect, he might find himself lamenting the loss of the man who had served as not only his legs, but also his trusted confidant and, in a way, friend for more than a decade. But for the present there simply wasn't time or energy to expend on sentiment—only action.

Accordingly, he beckoned to the white-gloved footman posted at the sideboard, who hastened to his side. "More of the herring, milord?"

Pushing away his untouched plate of food, Aberdaire shook his head. "There's a tall, redheaded Lowlander called Jack Campbell biding in town. Gather a group of our canniest lads and comb the streets. A gold guinea to the first man who finds him and bears him here to me."

"Aye, milord." The footman cast him a startled look then bowed himself out into the hall.

Chubby countenance cast with green, Lord Haversham raised his puffy eyes from the poached egg he'd been contemplating and asked, "Who is Jack Campbell?"

This time when Aberdaire turned to him, he didn't bother to conceal his contempt. "A Scot from the Border Country and, it would seem, a cannier man than I'd credited."

A slender hand descended on Jack's shoulder, jiggling him into painful wakefulness. Not that he minded, for it was Claudia—it had to be. At last she'd come to her senses. She'd come back to him.

Bruised cheek turned into the pillow, he murmured, "Claudia, lass," and reached out to capture her hand from his shoulder. "So warm, so soft . . ." he said around a sigh, then carried his prize to his lips.

"Yuck!" Abruptly the hand pulled away. "'Tis me, Master Jack."

Dragged from the depths of the dream, Jack cracked open an eye and looked up into the pale, freckled face hovering above him. "Luicas?"

"Aye," the boy said, wiping the back of his contaminated hand on his breeches. "And ye maun get up, for Lord Aberdaire's put a party o' men out tae search for ye."

Gritting his teeth against a groan, Jack lifted his head from the banked pillows. "He has, has he?"

"Aye, five of 'em, or so I counted. They came into the Purple Mouse, that's the inn where I . . . where I work, askin' had I seen ye. I didna tell 'em anything, mind, only came here straightaway tae warn ye and . . . Och, master, but ye're hurt bad."

Jack followed the boy's horrified gaze from his swollen eye and cheek down to his battered and bandaged sides and back up again. "A parting gift from Callum and his mates," he explained, shifting to slide his legs over the side of the bed. "But how is it that *you* found me?"

"There's no all that many inns in town, mind, and as ye wer'na at the Mouse and this is the only other proper house, I kent ye'd like as no come here." At Jack's questioning look, he grinned. "I was minded of how fond ye are o' your washing water and your soap."

Bracing a hand on the mattress on either side, Jack lifted himself onto his feet. "Verra resourceful, lad."

Dismissing the compliment with a shrug, Luicas reached down to stroke Elf, stretched out over the foot of the mattress. Gaze glued to the dog, he asked, "I, er, dinna suppose ye're still sore at me for bringing Mistress Claudia north instead of o'er the border tae England as ye bade me do?"

"Nay, I dinna suppose I am. Now what do you say to handing me my shirt so we can go see what Lord Aberdaire wants with us?"

"*We,* Master?" Luicas's head shot up, his whole face brightening though his hazel eyes looked almost afraid to believe.

Jack nodded and, despite all the demons he'd faced over the past week and those he'd yet to confront, he managed a small smile. "Aye, Luicas, *we.*"

Less *than an hour later, Jack stood regarding Lord Aberdaire* from across the expanse of his study floor, Luicas and Elf flanking his sides. "You wished to see me, milord, and here I am though not in a wooden box as you'd prefer, I'm sure."

Aberdaire blanched. "I've reason to believe your brother has abducted Claudia. I received a ransom demand from him, albeit penned in her hand." His silver-blue gaze narrowed and he added, "But you seem surprised, Master Campbell. Surely this is not news?"

Surprised! Jack felt as if he were back in the tollbooth cell with a half dozen fists pummeling his chest. Finding his voice in the midst of his dry, closing throat, he asked, "When?"

"We believe her to have been taken yesterday afternoon. Haversham"—for the first time the earl nodded toward the bloated dandy clipping his fingernails on the divan nearby—"took her on a shopping expedition in town and managed to mislay her somewhere along the High Street."

Thinking, Jack raked a hand through his hair, which he hadn't taken the time to tie back. Christ, but that must have been just after she'd left his room at the Hawk and Dove. He'd been a bloody fool to let her leave him at all, but then to permit her to strike out on her own was nothing short of lunacy. If Callum harmed her, he'd never forgive himself. He might just possibly lose his mind . . . *after* he killed his brother.

"What fustian!" Lord Haversham exclaimed, setting aside the little silver nail clippers he'd been wielding to glare at the room at large. "As if it's my fault the little hoyden gave me the slip."

So this Sassenach fop with the elaborate wig and puce coat was Claudia's betrothed. Barely gracing the man with a glance, Jack shifted his gaze back to the earl and said, "You said there is a ransom note. I'd like to see it."

Aberdaire reached into his coat pocket then hesitated before handing over the ragged scrap of paper. "You can read?" he asked, not bothering to conceal his surprise.

Minded that little more than two months before, a certain

French lassie had evidenced a similar degree of astonishment at that fact, Jack tamped down his rising irritation and stepped forward to accept the folded foolscap. The crumpled paper bore the faintest trace of Claudia's light rose scent, and Jack had to resist the urge to clasp it to his breast. Instead, he concentrated on the few terse, inelegant lines, clearly dictated by Callum. When he trained his gaze back on the earl, this time he let his fury take full flight.

"Jesus, man, why in God's name did you no send for me when this first came?" he demanded, anger sparking at the thought that he might have spent the night out searching instead of pacing the four corners of his narrow room.

Aberdaire hesitated, then admitted, "The possibility had occurred to me that though you and McBride pretend to hate each other, you might in fact be in league." Ignoring Jack's oath, he went on, "What better reason for him to insist that only you deliver the ransom? Another possible scenario is that Claudia is not in fact kidnapped but is in hiding. One thousand pounds would be a handsome start to setting up a household, would it not? And then, of course, she did pen the letter?"

Jaw clenched, Jack ground out, "Did it ne'er occur to you in all your grand scheming that Callum canna read nor write?"

Luicas had kept his peace up to now, but Jack had marked how his face became redder and his eyes narrower with each implied accusation until, reaching the point of combustion, he stomped up to the earl, hands fisted at his sides. "Aye, and a lot ye ken, ye wicked auld mumper. Callum burnt Jack's cottage and murdered his hawk. And 'twas Callum who fixed it so that Claudia would be hangit for trying tae escape."

Jack laid a hand on his young champion's shoulder. "Wheesht, Luicas, that will do." To the earl, he said, "Have you received a second note, anything to point to their still being in the area?"

Across the room, the earl had gone quite pale. "No, I hav'na." He swallowed and it suddenly occurred to Jack that he didn't look at all well. "What do you mean to do?"

Halfway to the door, Jack cast Aberdaire a fleeting backward glance. "I mean to find them, of course, and bring her back."

• • •

I*nside the abandoned cottage, Jack and Luicas found Mac-*Duff's stiffened body, his blood and brains caking the dusty floorboards. They also found one of the amethyst-set combs he'd given Claudia that Christmas, several glossy black strands still woven through the teeth.

Swallowing the lump that rose to block his throat, Jack called over his dog and held out the comb. "Get a good whiff, Elf. Claudia is somewhere nearby, and we've to find her and soon."

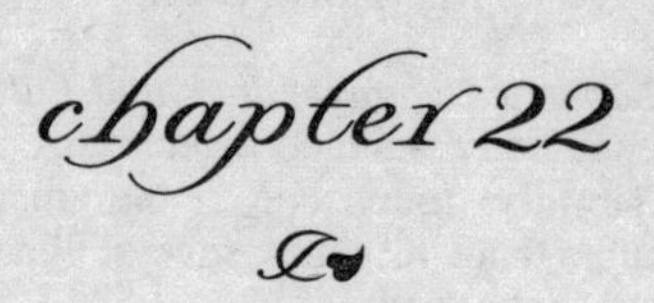

It hath often been said, that it is not death, but dying, which is terrible.

—Henry Fielding, *Amelia,* 1751

It was nearing dusk when Callum finally called for them to stop and make camp in one of the caves edging the western edge of Lord Aberdaire's property. All day Claudia had dragged her feet as much as she'd dared, leaving behind a little trail of her personal items as her hobbled hands would allow. A mile or so back, she'd even sacrificed the last of the hair combs Jack had given her; the first she'd left in the cottage not far from MacDuff's corpse. The sight of those staring opaque eyes would haunt her for some time, she knew.

But now Callum had stepped outside to relieve himself, affording Claudia her first opportunity to speak to Wallis alone. Determined to make good use of it, she looked up from the rock she sat perched upon and said in a low voice, "He is lying, you know. Whatever ransom money he gets for me, he does not plan to share it with you."

Rage washed over Wallis's face. "Shut up," he hissed, his gaze darting to the rock-hewn opening leading to the outside. "Ye're only saying that tae get me t' untie ye."

Encouraged by the warble of doubt in his voice, she pressed on. "Once your usefulness has ended, he will kill you. If you do not believe me, only think how quick he was to shoot the butler." And despite the small fire that crackled at her feet she shivered, for, like Wallis, her own usefulness would soon come to an end.

"That was different," Wallis said, though he didn't sound convinced. "That was the enemy."

Claudia opened her mouth to reply that, to Callum, everyone was the enemy when the subject of their exchange appeared at the mouth of the cave.

Scowling at Claudia, he slammed his lantern down upon the flattened bed of rain-washed rock and came forward. "If you wer'na sae slow, we would ha' made it tae Linlithgow ere now."

Hoisting her chin, she asked, "If I am so slow, why do you keep me with you? You could tie me to any tree by the roadside. By the time someone found me, you and Wallis would be long gone."

"But then I'd no have anyone tae write my wee letters for me, now would I? Aye," he said, in response to her silent question. "I mean tae send another only this time we'll see it delivered direct tae Jacko as your dear da canna be trusted tae follow orders."

He picked up the satchel that MacDuff had delivered the night before and began rooting through it. Emptied of the straw, it now contained a few items including several more sheets of foolscap and writing implements he'd lifted from a schoolhouse earlier that day.

"You will have to untie my hands then, will you not?"

He grunted to Wallis, who stepped behind her to cut through the rope. "Try anything and it'll go hard with ye," Callum warned, then laid out the inkpot and quill and paper before her.

Pain ripped forth from wrists to shoulders but, stretching her arms out in front of her, she took pleasure in the movement nonetheless. Dipping pen in ink, she balanced a sheet of the paper on her lap and waited for him to begin.

Squatting down beside her, he began to dictate. "Dear Brother Jack . . . Nay, better yet, make that Jacko."

Claudia scratched out the previous line and began anew. As she did so her mind raced to come up with what message of her own she might include, some hidden clue as to their whereabouts. If Callum could not read, then perhaps he would not notice that the note was longer than need be?

A faint but audible trilling sounding from outside the cavern had Callum breaking off in midsentence. He jerked his head to Wallis, who was busying himself with laying out his bedroll. "Go outside and see what that was."

Wallis looked up from the plaid and shrugged. "Och, it's no but a wee bird."

" 'Tis winter, idjut!" Glinting gaze alighting on Claudia, in a milder tone he said, "I'll bear the wee wench company whilst ye're gone."

Wallis hesitated and then, grumbling, picked up his lantern and stomped out.

Callum seemed to have lost interest in the letter. Reaching out, he swept the paper aside with the flat of his arm, smearing ink on his sleeve. "The writing can wait. This canna." A hard hand at the back of her head, he brought his mouth down to hers.

Claudia turned her face away and his sticky lips met her cheek instead. Lifting her freed hand, she wiped away the wetness.

Angry eyes blazed into hers. "Och, but you're a hoity-toity one, as winsome as ye are wild. But, faith, I think, like any spirited mare, ye want for breaking."

Claudia saw the bulge crowning his crotch and fear frissoned through her. Bravado had served her once before in Paris when it had been her only weapon against the angry mob bent on seeing her swing from the lamppost.

Praying that raw nerve would serve her again, she hoisted her chin and stared down her tormenter. "Do with me what you will, Monsieur McBride, only know this: Jack had me first. He has me still, if not my body then my soul. And there is nothing you can do to me, to either of us, that can sever that bond."

Callum's mouth twisted in a sneer. Gaze sliding over her, he said, "Verra touching but, truth be told, I'm no all that interested in your soul."

Behind her tormenter's shoulder, Claudia caught a flicker of movement at the cave's entrance and felt her hopes for rescue rise. A second later they plummeted, for it must only be the reflection of Wallis's lantern as he patrolled the area outside.

Shifting her gaze back to Callum, she said, "You would not be, but then, you are not fit to wipe Jack's boots let alone to call him brother. He is the better man and everyone knows it."

Glancing down, she saw that her goading had struck its mark. The bulge at Callum's crotch had flattened to nothingness; inside his trousers his penis would be as soft and limp as a water-soaked biscuit.

Following her gaze, his face flushed a vivid vermilion. "Shut up, ye wee bitch." He hauled back and landed a heavy back-handed slap across her face.

The aftershock of the blow stinging her cheeks, she blinked watery eyes. "Only a coward strikes a woman and you, *monsieur,* are a coward most pathetic."

Eyes still tearing from the blow, she glimpsed a broad silhouette shifting in the shadows. Wallis again? But no, it could not be, for blocking her view of starlit sky, he stood too tall, too straight, and too proud to be anyone other than Jack. He lifted a hand to his lips, warning her to silence and, heart swelling, she answered with an infinitesimal nod.

Voice raised to cover her rescuer's approach, she went on, "Your mother knew that Jack was worth a hundred of you; in your heart you know it, too. Yes, I think that is why you hate him so, because in your heart, you know it, too."

"Shut up, shut up I say." Callum hauled back to strike her again, this time with his fist.

Issuing forth a primal *roar,* Jack launched himself forward. He grabbed his brother about the neck and sent him careening toward the far rock wall. Callum smashed into the stones but almost at once he was on his feet again, apparently impervious to the blood streaming his brow. Eyes wild, he flew at Jack, the force carrying both of them to the ground. Jack took the brunt of the impact. His big body hit the cave floor with a heavy thud. Callum, sprawled atop, rained punishing blows on his face.

But Jack was a big man, a strong man. He quickly recovered and rolled, trapping Callum beneath him. Heart hammering, Claudia stooped and made use of her unbound hands to snatch up the dagger that had slipped from Callum's belt. The hilt clasped in her sweaty palm, she looked on, helpless, as the two brothers fought their way across the earthen floor.

"Give it up, Callum." Jack reared back and smashed a fist into the slighter man's jaw.

"Ne'er!"

They'd come perilously close to the fire. Now Callum reached out toward the stones encircling it, and his clawing fingers closed about a small but lethally sharp bit of rock.

Seeing that he meant to smash the pointed edge into Jack's skull, Claudia screamed, "Jack, his hand. Look out!"

Jack captured his opponent's wrist and torqued it, drawing

Callum's scream. "Give it up," he rasped, releasing the bone-wrenching pressure a fraction.

Sweat plastered Callum's hair to his forehead and his eyes glazed over with pain, but he shook his head. "Nay, ne'er. Ne'er, ye bluidy Sassenach bastard. I'll die before I let ye live."

"Suit yourself." Jack slammed Callum's captured arm to the ground.

"Ahhhhh . . ."

With a final bone-crunching twist, the makeshift weapon fell free from Callum's grasp and his damaged hand dangled from his wrist like a broken tree limb. A second later, Jack felt Callum's writhing body go limp beneath him. Looking down, he saw that Callum's body if not his will at last had surrendered to the pain. Eyes closed in his pale, sweating face, he appeared to have fainted.

Breathing ragged, Jack pulled himself onto his hands and knees. Claudia flew to his side and, leaning heavily on her, he gained his feet.

"Are you all right, *mo chride*?" he asked, all concern as though she and not he had been engaged in a fight to the death.

"*Oui,* yes I think so."

She scanned his face. Fresh cuts and bruises marred his high brow and there was a bloody gash cutting across one cheek but otherwise he appeared to have escaped serious injury.

"Oh, Jack," she said, and then pressed her head into the curve of his damp shoulder. Standing thus, she was just about to surrender to relief, when all at once she remembered. "Wallis," she said, pulling out of his embrace to look up into his dear bruised face. "Callum sent him outside but surely he will be back."

"Nay worries," he said, touching a finger to her lips. "He'll no be bothering us." Grinning, he explained, "He took a wee tumble, mind, and his head met with the rock in Luicas' hand. Luicas and Elf are minding him even now."

"Then I guess I'll have tae finish this myself."

They whirled to see Callum, sweat beading his pasty face, leaning heavily against the wall, his injured armed tucked against his chest. In his left hand he held the small, pearl-handled pistol—Jack's mother's pistol.

Jack moved to shield Claudia. "Dinna be a fool, Callum. Ye're right-handed, no left, and if ye fire inside and miss, the bullet may just as likely ricochet and strike you."

Callum cocked the pistol's hammer. "Only if I miss. And, *mo bràthair,* I dinna mean tae miss. The one thing I've yet tae decide is which one o' ye shall die first." After a moment's pause, he shifted the weapon to Claudia, and Jack felt his bowels turn to jelly. "Her first, I think, so I can have the pleasure of watchin' your face when she drops dead at your feet." His thumb moved to the trigger and, sending up a silent prayer, Jack prepared to lunge.

A shower of stones sprayed inside the cave. Callum started, whipping his head about. His distraction lasted only a fraction of a second, but it was enough. Jack dove, knocking Callum to the ground, and the two men fought for control of the weapon. The pistol fired, filling the narrow channel with acrid black powder smoke.

Blinded and choking, Claudia went down on her knees and crawled forward, feeling her way. Her eyes burning and feeling as though they'd been doused with lye, she could just make out a prone form on the cave floor ahead. *Please, God. Oh, please, oh, please, oh, please.* "Jack, my love . . . Oh, Jack."

Silence and then, through a fit of coughing, "C-Claudia?"

If Claudia hadn't already been on her knees, relief and thankfulness would have brought her to them. "Jack?"

Strong arms, Jack's arms, encircled her, lifting her to her feet, guiding her through the charred air and out into the bracing freshness.

"Oh, Jack. Y-you are not . . . you are not dead?"

"Och, but you'll no get rid of me that easily."

Eyes filling with grateful tears, she slid both her arms about his waist.

Luicas, with Elf, ran up to them. "Master, mistress, are ye . . . is he . . ."

"We're fine, lad. And aye, Callum's dead . . . as we would be if ye hadna thought to send those wee stones sailing inside. Callum must have thought it meant a cave in." Jack released Claudia to clap a hand to the boy's shoulder. "You did well, lad. I . . ."—he glanced at Claudia—"*we* owe you our lives."

Expression bashful, Luicas started to demur, but Claudia would have none of it. "It is true. You are a hero, Luicas."

"Aye, he is," Jack agreed, "and when he returns to Selkirk and to the village, it will be to a hero's welcome."

• • •

But first there was the matter of tending to the dead. They bore Callum from the cave and laid him to rest on the crest of the crag overlooking the peaceful pastureland below. The ground was frozen and even if it had not been they had no shovel. Luicas and Jack gathered stones and small boulders to pile atop the body while Claudia held the lantern and stroked Elf's head. Afterwards, Jack fashioned a makeshift wooden cross from two sticks and a length of Claudia's hair ribbon and then, head bowed, said a few spare words to express the hope that Callum's tormented soul might finally know the peace that had eluded him in life.

Wallis, it seemed, had disappeared altogether. Footsteps leading away from the spot where Luicas had left him suggested he must have come to and made off on foot. By collective consent, they agreed there was nothing to be gained by giving chase.

During the construction of the burial cairn, it had begun to drizzle and by the time they laid the final stone, the rain had turned to snow, the moon was riding full in the sky, and the air was raw as a fresh wound. Rather than ride into Linlithgow, they returned to the cave to shelter for the night. Almost immediately Luicas and Elf subsided into exhausted heaps but for Jack and Claudia this night, the first night of the rest of their lives, was too precious to waste on sleep. Their backs braced against the stones, they sat in each other's arms before the fire, content to say nothing at all.

Staring into the flames dancing within the circle of stones, Jack said suddenly, "What think you of America?"

Until now Claudia had not thought much about the New World at all but glancing at Jack's pensive profile, she saw that he'd been doing a great deal of thinking indeed. "America?" she said, testing the word on her tongue.

He nodded. "Aye, Virginia. 'Tis said the mountains there are as green and softly rolling as those of the Lowlands and in springtime the sky the same bonny blue. There's opportunity, too, for a man who's no afraid of hard work to make a good life for himself . . . and for his family."

Once the thought of striking out on such a voyage would have daunted her but then what were a few hundred or so leagues of sea compared to all they'd been through together these last months? Smiling to herself, she could almost swear she saw the impish faces of their future children peaking out at her from the fire's curtain. "I like the sound of it, Jack," she said at length, lacing her fingers through his and giving his big, broad palm a squeeze. "I like it very much."

U*pon returning to the castle the next day, they learned that* Lord Haversham had toddled back to England that very morning, proclaiming all Scots to be savages and himself to have made a fortunate escape from being bound in matrimony with one of them, even if she was half French. Lord Aberdaire was in his study, sitting before the fire, a rug tucked about his shrunken legs, when Jack and Claudia approached the open door.

Turning to Jack, she whispered, "This I must do alone, *chéri.*" For her to be well and truly free of the past this final battle must be hers alone.

Any other man would have insisted on coming inside to give the earl his comeuppance but this was Jack, her Jack, and as always he understood her perfectly. He bent to brush his lips over hers. "I'll be waiting for you below."

"So you came back," Aberdaire said when the door clicked closed behind her. He didn't bother to turn his chair about but then she suspected he'd been watching from the window and had seen them ride in.

She drew a step closer. "Only for the moment. I have come to bid you *adieu.*"

Still staring into the hearth, he nodded. "McBride?"

"He is dead."

"So, it's over, then?" Turning to her, he stared for a long moment and then shook his head. "Daughters are a great deal of trouble."

Once such a statement would have brought her pain but now all she could feel was pity. She had come to Scotland in search of neither a title nor lands but a father's affection, she now realized. That she would leave without it saddened her but, thinking of the rich, full life that lay ahead of her, the person she felt saddest for was the earl. With MacDuff dead, he was for all intents and purposes alone.

"I am to wed Jack Campbell. Although he does not expect it, I must insist you settle a dowry on me."

Aberdaire beetled his brows. Sounding more curious than angry he asked, "And why would I do that?"

Claudia took a deep breath, girding herself. "I was there the night MacDuff came to deliver the satchel. Before Callum shot him, he admitted to having killed the courier. I suspect he did so on your behalf."

"Perhaps but you'd have the devil of a time proving it."

Holding her voice steady even as her hands shook, she answered, "Perhaps I would. But even if the connection could not be proved, I imagine that if even a whisper of such a thing were to get out, the scandal—"

"How much? How much will it take to make *you* disappear?"

"Hmm, let me think." She tapped a finger to her cheek, pretending to consider, though in truth she had a nice round sum already tucked inside her head. "Callum seemed to think I was worth only one thousand pounds, but the sum I have in mind is rather closer to five thousand pounds sterling—*British* pounds, of course."

"Outrageous," he said but she knew he would give it to her for what choice had he?

She shrugged. "Ah well, it is less than what you were prepared to grant Lord Haversham and surely Jack and I can use the money as well as he. Better, I should hope, for Jack means to establish a carpentry business."

"A *Drummond* marrying into trade! What next?" Heaving a sigh, he sank back against his chair. Long fingers plucking at the coverlet, he conceded, "Verra well. I'll contact my solicitor and have the amount of five thousand *British* pounds deposited into an account in Campbell's name within the week."

She shook her head. "That is most generous, my lord, but I am afraid I must insist upon cash."

That got his attention. "Cash!" He stared at her.

She nodded. "Jack and I will be returning to Selkirk for the rest of this winter, but in the spring we will sail for America. Virginia."

"I see," he said, then sighed heavily. "Verra well, cash it shall be. I will make the necessary arrangements."

"*Merci.* Thank you," she said and, knowing it was time, that there was nothing more to be said or done, she turned to leave.

The earl's voice called her back. "Claudia?"

One hand on the doorknob, she turned about. "Yes, my lord?"

"Safe journey and . . . good luck to you."

"Thank you . . . Father."

Epilogue

My true love hath my heart, and I have his,
By just exchange one for the other given:
I hold his dear, and mine he cannot miss;
There never was a bargain better driven.

—Sir Philip Sidney, "Heart Exchange," from *Arcadia*

The Firth of Clyde, Saltcoats, Spring 1795

Claudia and Jack bided the rest of that winter with the MacGregors, both of whom steadfastly refused to hear tell of them taking up residence in the inn. For Jack, knowing that he would, in all likelihood, never again set eyes on his birthplace or the beloved souls that dwelt there lent a bittersweet poignancy to those final weeks. At the same time, he was gripped by a restless eagerness to begin carving out his and Claudia's future. And so even though she assured him that she would gladly call Scotland home if he changed his mind about leaving it, in his heart he knew that he was right to go. Scotland was the past. Claudia—and America—were his future.

The day of their departure dawned sunny and clear, the air balmy and pregnant with the scents of the new springtime. By collective consent, Milread and Luicas and Duncan and Dorcas all had accompanied Jack and Claudia to Saltcoats where they would meet the packet boat that would carry the couple to Cork, Ireland. From there, they would set sail on one of the larger passenger ships bound for Virginia.

But now, as they congregated on the pier, Duncan's well-rehearsed speech seemed to stick in his throat, Luicas had been stricken with the sniffles, and the women's eyes grew dewy at the prospect of bidding a final farewell to these two dear friends.

"Och, but I'm going tae miss ye, the lot o' ye," exclaimed a misty-eyed Milread, looking from Jack to Claudia. "Why, I'm even going to miss these mangy beasties." Sniffling, she patted Elf's head, then held out the wicker basket in which One Eye and Heather nestled in perfect harmony.

Taking the basket from her, Claudia said, "Come with us, then. You might like America. Alexandria, Virginia, is a port city." Grinning, she added, "There are certain to be sailors there."

Dorcas wagged a reproachful finger, but her eyes were merry. "For shame, now there's a fine thing tae say tae an affianced woman."

Claudia and Jack looked to each other and then to Milread. Jack was the first to find his voice. "Milread, lass, can this be true?"

"Aye, it is." Milread chuckled but her gaze softened as she admitted, "Alistair has decided tae make an honest woman of me and I've accepted him. Och, I ken it's by way o' being a surprise," she said, taking in their stunned faces, "but the truth is I'm a wee bit fonder of the auld devil than I let on."

"Then we wish you every happiness," Claudia said, and reached out to embrace the woman who, like so many from the little hamlet outside Selkirk, had become her dear friend.

Jack turned to Luicas and, noting that the lad's eyes looked suspiciously bright, clapped a hand to his shoulder. "If you're ever minded to journey to Virginia, you've a home with us and the chance to learn an honest trade if you want it."

Luicas made a face. "I thank ye, Master Jack, truly I do, but I dinna see myself as a carpenter's apprentice."

Duncan smiled. "Dinna be too hasty, Luicas. Carpentry's a fine trade and, as I've always said, there's no finer hand with a knife and a bit o' wood than Jack Campbell."

"And not only will he make furniture but also mantelpieces, magnificent ones suitable for the finest of the plantation houses," Claudia couldn't resist adding, her heart swelling with love and pride.

The ship's horn signaled that the time had come for final goodbyes—and new beginnings. The journey that lay ahead would be both long and arduous but, glancing up at her beloved, Claudia knew that together they could weather any storm.

Fast losing the battle not to cry, a red-faced Luicas launched himself into Jack's arms. "Thank you, Master Jack . . . for everything. I'll ne'er forget you."

Pressing a kiss to the tousled head, Jack set the boy from him. Hugs and final farewells made the rounds and then the little party turned and made their way back up the pier.

Their friends gone, Jack turned to Claudia and asked, "Och, lass, are you sure about this? I'm but a step above a pauper with naything to offer you but my name and the promise that I'll work hard to make you proud of me."

Smiling up at him, she shook her head. "You *are* my future, my life. And I have no doubt but we shall be quite comfortable." At his raised brows, she patted her cloak, well padded with her dowry money. "A wedding gift from the earl," she explained around a smile.

"I thought you looked a wee bit . . . broad." Jack shook his head, a lock of red-gold hair catching on the breeze. "So you've kept this a secret from me all these many months?"

She hesitated. "I was not certain if you would accept it otherwise. And this way you need not wait to set up your own shop." Watching his face, she added, "You are not angry with me?"

Jack shook his head. "Nay, I'm no angry, only wondering what other secrets you might have tucked up your sleeve."

Claudia swallowed hard. Could it be that he'd guessed? "It may be that I have one more," she admitted.

"You're an amazing woman, Claudia Valemont, and proud I am to call you my own. But only think, had you stayed in Scotland, you might have been a countess."

In answer, she raised up on her toes and wound her arms about his neck. "Mistress Jack Hamish Campbell is the only title I wish to claim . . . provided I may do so before we put into port at Alexandria."

A fat tear rolled down the side of his bruised face, slipping over the ledge of chin and jaw to disappear into his neck cloth. "I love you, my Claudia, with all my heart, all my mind, all my body, all that I am and may yet become. I'll marry you this verra moment if that is what you wish, though 'twas you who said you wanted to wait for a proper wedding in our new homeland."

"Well, that was before . . ."

"Before?"

She nodded and, schooling her features to innocence, answered in the Scots *brogue* she'd been mentally practicing all that morning. "Och, laddie, I maun ask ye tae make an honest woman o' me before our wee lad or lassie begins tae show."

"Claudia?" Eyes popping, he reached out and laid a light hand on her still flat belly. "Are you certain?"

Dropping the burr, she answered, "I cannot be completely so for another week or so but yes, in my heart I know it to be true." She searched his face, which appeared to be well and truly stunned. "You . . . you are pleased?"

"Pleased? *Pleased!*" His sudden joyous and utterly Scots whoop dispelled her last niggling doubt and more. Beyond relieved, her legs might have folded beneath her if, heedless of his mending ribs, Jack hadn't already swept her off her feet and into his arms. " 'Pleased' doesna begin to account for all that I feel. Humbled to be sure, but also so verra grateful, no to mention happier than I've any right to be." Looking up into her face, he promised, "I'll go and seek out the ship's captain the verra moment we take up anchor. If I have my way, and I mean to, we'll be wed before the day's end, and then never shall we be parted again, *mo chride.* Bide we in Scotland, America, or France even, while I've yet breath in my lungs you shall be at my side and I at yours."

A second call to board and Claudia's plea that she needed to breathe finally persuaded him to set her down. He brushed a kiss over her brow and then stepped back to offer her his arm. "Shall we, *mo chride?*"

Dizzy with love, heart too full for further speech, Claudia laid her hand atop his. "Lead the way, my love."

Arms linked, souls intertwined, they joined the stream of their fellow passengers starting up the gangplank, eager to put the shadows of the past behind them and embark on a new life together in the New World.

Dear Reader,

Like my hero, Jack Campbell, I was born loving animals. Underlying that love is a deep and abiding respect. Animals do more than live in the moment—they savor each and every one of them. Unlike humans, they rarely if ever sweat the small stuff. Yes, we are their guardians but oftentimes, without our knowing it, they are our teachers.

Interaction with a beloved pet has been demonstrated to positively impact human health and well-being, including lowering blood pressure and mitigating that bundle of diverse modern ills known as "stress." Caring for an animal companion is acknowledged to be one of the factors that contribute to longevity among seniors.

Many of us are familiar with the slogan, "Practice random kindness and senseless acts of beauty." As May is the host month for both Be Kind to Animals Week and National Pet Week, I'd like to humbly suggest a few ways of applying those wise words to our dealings with the furry and four-legged. Consider opening your home—and heart—to a homeless dog or cat. Several directories of shelters and other pet adoption organizations are available, notably the national database maintained by Pets911 (www.188pets911.org or 1-888-PETS-911). Offer to help out an elderly or physically challenged neighbor by walking her dog or feeding his cat. Starting September 2002, affix the nation's new "Neuter/Spay Your Pet" postage stamps to your mail and help stem the tide of accidental dog and cat births by educating others about responsible pet ownership.

Random kindness. Senseless acts of beauty. I have an inkling Jack would approve.

Thank you and happy reading,
Hope Tarr
May 2002

Turn the page for a sneak
preview of Hope Tarr's new novel,

TEMPTING

Coming in September 2002 from Jove Books!

Simon Belleville was no stranger to squalor. He'd passed his first sixteen years in Whitechapel, the worst of the London stews, among the moneylenders, whores, and grimy immigrants of Eastern Europe. The brothel's staircase was every bit as narrow, filthy, and dank as the ones he'd played on as a child. Only now he was a man of four-and-thirty. A man of property and experience. A man who'd traveled to India and back—to *hell* and back—to make his fortune. A fortune he'd doubled, no quadrupled, many times over since his return. In a country where wealth and position were bestowed at birth—or not at all—he was a self-made man. A legend. At East India Company headquarters in Leadenhall, directors and shareholders and counting house clerks all uttered his name in reverent whispers. When he walked into the Royal Exchange, a hush fell over the central court as investors strained to hear what stocks he would buy, what others he would sell. And now, owing to the past six months he'd spent in the service of Her Majesty, he was poised to add yet another jewel to *his* crown: a seat in the House of Commons.

So why, at times such as these, did he still feel like a grubby little mudlark from the docks?

His damned memory was the culprit. Even now, poised on the stairwell, he found himself fighting to hold head and shoulders above the rubble of the dark recollections crashing down on him. Struggling to remember that this descent into hell, into the *past,* was the nascence of his political career.

When Benjamin Disraeli, chancellor of the Exchequer in Lord Derby's Conservative government, had offered Simon the opportunity to head Her Majesty's Morality and Vice Commission, he'd accepted with alacrity. Not that he had anything against whores in particular. If women elected to forfeit their virtue for a few quid and a roof over their heads, what had he or anyone else to say about it? But the appointment was his chance to prove his worth to Disraeli, to the Conservatives, perhaps even to the Queen herself.

Over the past six months, Simon had applied himself to doing just that, leading raids on twenty-odd brothels. Thankfully the present establishment, Madame LeBow's, was the very last on his list. Like the others, it offered the standard fare of flagellations, deflorations, and fellatio at working-class prices. Patrons liked their sex rough, their wine cheap, and their whores young. The close air stank of spilled come and stale beer, and at least four of the eight prostitutes incarcerated in the police wagon outside were younger than sixteen.

One hand wrapped about the scarred newel post, Simon looked below to the four blue-suited police sergeants flanking the first-floor entrance. A fifth officer was posted outside to guard the women. Simon had been about to issue the order to pull out when he overheard two of the prisoners whispering about the new girl in the attic. His ears perked up. He might regret accepting this post, but he was a thorough man. A clean sweep meant just that, and he had no intention of allowing even one rabbit to escape from its warren.

Inspector Tolliver, lantern in hand, stood a few steps below him. "Shall I light the way, sir?"

Simon shook his head. "That won't be necessary. I'll go alone." He reached for the lantern, which Tolliver reluctantly handed up.

At the last whorehouse where he'd allowed Tolliver to lead an arrest, the madam had emerged with a black eye and split lip. Tolliver had claimed she'd tripped and fallen on her way down the stairs. Simon had his doubts.

Tolliver twisted one waxed end of his handlebar mustache. "Are you certain, sir? It could be a trap."

Simon wasn't accustomed to having his orders questioned. His annoyance rose. "I believe I can handle it, Inspector. By all accounts, there's only one woman up there, and if she's anything like the others, she's little more than a child."

Tolliver lifted his narrow shoulders. "Have it your way, guv. We'll be downstairs if you need us." He glanced significantly at the club swinging from his waist, then started down.

Simon felt the sudden urge to laugh. With its bicycles and billy clubs and smart blue uniforms, London's eight-man detective department fancied itself a force to be reckoned with. But then Tolliver and his men rarely ventured into the East End. Those dark, crooked lanes with their stench of urine, rotting rubbish, and spoiled dreams were a foreign land to them. To Simon, they were home.

Home. He continued up the remaining three flights to the attic, rotting floorboards groaning beneath the soles of his boots. It was nearly twenty years, and yet it might have been yesterday that he'd listened for the landlord's footfalls on a set of creaking stairs much like these . . .

"This isn't a charity house," the landlord, Mr. Plotkin, had said, after delivering what amounted to a death sentence. The three of them—Simon, his mother, and Rebecca—had twenty-four hours to gather their belongings and quit the premises; otherwise, he'd have them all hauled to debtors' prison.

It was the first time Simon had seen his mother cry since his father's death. Wringing her work-roughened hands, Lilith Belleville had looked between her two children, then back at the landlord. Then she'd done the unthinkable. She'd sunk to her knees and begged.

"Have pity, Mr. Plotkin. If you turn us out, where shall we go? How shall we live?"

"That is not my affair, Mrs. Belleville." Stepping past her, Plotkin's shoe had landed on the hem of her worn dress, leaving a muddy footprint on the clean calico.

The scene, like so many painful episodes from his past, remained branded on Simon's brain. Now someone else, some other cringing scrap of humanity, waited behind a closed attic door for him to deliver the edict that would result in her being dispatched to Newgate Gaol or, worse still, one of the prison hulks moored along the Thames.

Like grinding an insect with his heel, Simon moved to squash the pity surging inside him before it could rise any higher. "That is not my affair," he repeated, stepping off the landing and into a nest of cobwebs.

The eaves hung low, and he was obliged to remove his beaver top hat and hunker down. He lifted his lantern. The attic door was a narrow planked archway bolted on the outside and barely broader than his shoulders. He slid back the hasp and pushed. The warped wood moaned on rusted hinges, but it opened. Angling his body sideways, he ducked beneath the low-hanging lintel and stepped over the threshold.

The air inside was as foul as any draining ditch, the heat as stifling as Calcutta at midday, the darkness unrelieved by any light save the one Simon carried. Wishing he might shed his wool greatcoat, he held up the lantern and took stock. An old chest, a slop bucket—full, judging from the stench. Wedged beneath the slanted roof was a narrow rope bed, a bundle of rags piled on top. But where was the girl? Surely she didn't think to fool him by hiding under the bed?

He pulled the door closed behind him and walked inside, his footfalls on the bare floorboards sending mice scuttling. Dust motes danced like snowflakes before his eyes. The rags shifted. As his sight began to adjust, the mound assumed the shape of a small female huddled beneath a pile of castoffs.

He centered his light on the bed. "You can come out now."

She gasped. Flinging the clothes aside, she sat up and wiped hair from her damp forehead with the back of her hand. "Ye keep away from me, d'ye hear?"

"Easy now, no one's going to harm you."

He shone the light on her. She blinked owlishly, her little face puckering. This girl looked to be the youngest yet, but then those in the "maiden trade" were adept at the art of illusion. The childish night rail she wore—white cotton buttoned to the neck—made her appear innocent, almost *virginal.*

Whatever her age, she was no beauty. Her eyes were too large, her breasts too small, and her waist-length hair of undeterminable color hung in greasy strands about her pinched face. That any man would pay to lie with such a pathetic waif was almost impossible to fathom. But then London was rife with men who found it diverting to prey on the young and innocent. He thought of Rebecca, and the familiar ache lodged in his chest.

He carried the lantern to the bed. She cringed when he came up beside her, squinting as though the light hurt her eyes. There was a dark blotch on her forehead that could have been a bruise, a birthmark, or simply more of the same filth that stained the front of her night rail. But there could be no doubt that the small, red crescent on her left cheek was anything but a fresh scar.

Anger surged through him. No woman, be she a lady or a whore, deserved to be struck. Resolved that the manacles he'd brought would remain in his coat pocket, he said, "I've come to take you away."

She lifted her face, pinning him with her wide-eyed stare. "Truly?"

Before Simon could answer, she did the one thing for which he was completely unprepared. She snatched his gloved hand and pressed her lips to his palm.

"Oh sar, I've prayed and prayed that someone would come and just when I were a'most ready to give up, 'ere ye are."

Simon almost dropped the lantern. A praying prostitute? Nonplussed, he stared down at her upturned face. Was this show of gratitude some sort of scheme, a whore's trick to win his sympathy—and her freedom? Or had confinement and abuse unhinged the poor creature's mind?

He pulled his hand away and set the light atop the broken bedside table. "How long have you been here—in the attic, that is?"

"A'most a week, I think, though, 'tis terrible hard to tell night from day."

Whoever she was, she was no Londoner. The twang of the Midlands was plain in her trembling voice. Mentally adding that bit of intelligence to his mounting stockpile of observations, he followed her sad gaze to the small casement window, the glass painted over with blacking. For a country-bred girl, being shut up thus would be an earthly hell.

Leaden pity weighed anchor in his chest. Knowing he must cut himself free of it or else sink, he summoned a brisk tone and said, "Yes, well, you must dress and gather up your things. The others are waiting for us below. *Outside*," he added as an enticement.

She beamed at him. "Oh, lovely. Are ye rescuing 'em too?"

Simon stared. The poor girl must indeed be mad. Looking into her dirty face for some sign of derangement, he saw that her eyes—brown, he thought—were clear, her cheekbones high, and her mouth full. Her top and bottom lips were near mirror images, and he found himself wondering how it would feel to kiss her, to match his own lips to those soft, full ones.

It was then that he gave himself a sound mental shake. Perhaps he was the one in danger of losing his reason? This girl was no sheltered innocent but a skillful actress. Her feigned naïveté had, no doubt, coaxed many a fool to part with his coin.

Simon was no fool.

He folded his arms across his chest. "From here, you and the others will be taken to Newgate. You will pass the night there until tomorrow morning when you will be brought before the Central Criminal Court."

Her smile fled, replaced by indignation—and fear. "The Old Bailey! But I've done naught wrong."

The tension that had been building at the base of his skull since he'd discovered her cinched another notch. "On the contrary, prostitution is a serious offense." *Hypocrite!* his inner voice crowed. "But, given your youth . . . How old are you, by the way?"

"Nineteen."

Nineteen. Not a child, but young. Simon thought back to how he'd felt at that age—callow and confused and so very alone.

He cleared his throat to smooth the sudden thickening. "The judges may be prepared to show mercy . . . provided you surrender yourself quietly."

Mercy? The workhouse instead of prison? Or perhaps if she were really fortunate, she'd be set free . . . to starve?

That is not my affair. He had only to carry out this last arrest and write up his report to Parliament, then his obligation would be fulfilled. And then he, Simon Belleville, former street urchin and ship's stowaway, would be poised to seize his heart's desire: membership in Parliament. And with it power, respect, *acceptance*.

Provided he remained strong, stayed the course. Stayed strong. He focused his gaze on the girl, who was staring up at him with that curiously affecting union of terror . . . and hope.

Determined to squelch the soft sentiment rising inside him, he reached for her. "Come, they are waiting for us. Get up and get dressed."

Slippery as an eel, she wrenched free and scooted to the bottom of the bed. "I won't." A steely look replaced the raw vulnerability he'd imagined he'd seen.

But she was trapped, and they both knew it. The window, assuming it could be opened, was too small to crawl through and, even if it weren't, they were four flights above the ground.

Simon unfolded his arms and reached into the pocket with the manacles. How he'd hoped to avoid this.

"You are coming with me. Whether you do so of your own accord, clothed or unclothed, matters little to me."

"Oh please sar, I've done nothin' wrong. Can't ye set me free?"

With her steepled hands and guileless eyes, she was the very image of a supplicating saint he'd once seen in a stained glass window of St. Paul's Cathedral. His conscience, long buried, began to niggle. Why not simply go below and say he'd found the attic empty?

Don't be a fool, his damned inner voice bellowed.

Disraeli rewarded those who served him well. He was equally lavish in punishing those who betrayed his trust. Without his endorsement, Simon's dream of holding a seat in the Commons would remain just that. A dream.

"Regrettably I cannot." Leaning over, he grabbed her sharply boned wrists in one hand, pulling her up onto her knees. "Get up . . . *now!*"

"I ain't goin' "—she hesitated—"leastwise not wi'out Puss." Her regard flew over his right shoulder.

He released her and swung around, gaze searching. Puss? Could there possibly be a second woman sharing this black hole?

Then he saw it. A black and silver tabby cat curled up in a wicker basket set in a corner. Apparently unconcerned that its fate hung in the balance, the feline stretched a striped paw over the side and yawned. Rebecca had kept a cat like that once. His heart, if indeed he still possessed such an organ, lurched.

Steeling himself against the rush of painful memories, he turned back to the girl. She twisted a lock of lank hair round and round her forefinger, those damned innocent eyes of hers fixed on his face.

"Out of the question." He felt as though his darkest, ugliest secrets were emblazoned on his forehead for all to see. For her to see. Self-loathing roughened his voice. "And stop looking at me like that."

He slid his hands to her upper arms, scarcely wider than his wrist, his fingers biting into flesh-veiled bone. She cried out and somehow the sound, her pain, anchored him.

Gentling his hold, he said, "You'll do as you're told. Now get up."

No longer beseeching, she glared. "Your arse I will." She turned her head and sank her teeth into the side of his left hand.

Pain shot up his arm from fingertips to elbow. Eyes watering, he pulled back and stared down. Sticky wetness seeped through the kid leather covering his hand. He reached inside his breast pocket for a handkerchief to sop the blood. The linen wrapped about his throbbing palm, he grabbed for the iron cuffs.

But when he turned back to the girl, he saw that the restraint would not be needed after all.

She'd fainted.

Holding his bleeding hand aloft, he probed her with his right. She didn't stir. To be sure, he tickled the bottom of one calloused foot. Nothing. Collapsed in a crumpled heap, she was completely senseless. Completely vulnerable. Completely at his . . . *mercy?*

His gaze settled once more on the raw mark of violence marring her cheek. He'd spent years armoring his soul until he'd thought it had become as calloused and thick as once his hands had been. But somehow, devil take her, this slip of a girl had found the one remaining chink and slipped inside.

Hell and damnation. With the resignation of a man who'd lost not only the battle but the war, he rolled her onto her back and slipped an arm beneath her knees.

"You're a plucky little thing, I'll grant you that." He lifted her into his arms and started for the door.

Newgate Gaol would have to make due with one fewer inmate.